IRVINE WELSH

Irvine Welsh was born and raised in Edinburgh. His first novel, *Trainspotting*, has sold over one million copies in the UK and was adapted into an era-defining film. He has written twelve further novels, including *Crime* and the number one bestseller *Dead Men's Trousers*, four books of shorter fiction and numerous plays and screenplays. Irvine Welsh currently lives between London, Edinburgh and Miami.

facebook.com/irvinewelshauthor
twitter.com/IrvineWelsh

ALSO BY IRVINE WELSH

FICTION

Trainspotting

The Acid House

Marabou Stork Nightmares

Ecstasy

Filth

Glue

Porno

The Bedroom Secrets of the Master Chefs

If You Liked School, You'll Love Work . . .

Crime

Reheated Cabbage

Skagboys

The Sex Lives of Siamese Twins

A Decent Ride

The Blade Artist

Dead Men's Trousers

DRAMA

You'll Have Had Your Hole

Babylon Heights (with Dean Cavanagh)

SCREENPLAY

The Acid House

IRVINE WELSH

The Long Knives

VINTAGE

3 5 7 9 10 8 6 4 2

Vintage is part of the Penguin Random House group of companies
whose addresses can be found at global.penguinrandomhouse.com

Penguin
Random House
UK

First published in Vintage in 2023
First published in hardback by Jonathan Cape in 2022

Copyright © Irvine Welsh 2022

Irvine Welsh has asserted his right to be identified as the author of this Work
in accordance with the Copyright, Designs and Patents Act 1988

penguin.co.uk/vintage

Printed and bound in Great Britain by Clays Ltd, Elcograf S.p.A.

The authorised representative in the EEA is Penguin Random House
Ireland, Morrison Chambers, 32 Nassau Street, Dublin D02 YH68

A CIP catalogue record for this book is available from the British Library

ISBN 9781529116274

Penguin Random House is committed to a sustainable future
for our business, our readers and our planet. This book is made
from Forest Stewardship Council® certified paper.

MIX
Paper | Supporting
responsible forestry
FSC
www.fsc.org   FSC® C018179

This book is dedicated to the vivid and immortal spirit of Bradley John Welsh.

Every day missed, every moment inspiring.

An adversary is someone you want to defeat. An enemy is someone you need to destroy. With adversaries, compromise is virtuous: after all, today's adversary could be tomorrow's ally. But with enemies, compromise is an unsatisfactory appeasement.

In our modern age, we are losing the distinction between the two.

Prologue

He's stripped to his boxer shorts. Secured to the moulded plastic chair. Wrists and ankles strained white against the ties. Dimpled gooseflesh trembling. Apart from those candy-striped underpants, there's just one other item he wears: the brown leather hood we pulled over his head. But he's soundless now, as I watch him from the other end of the large, empty warehouse. I mirror his silence as I sit down in a similar chair, in order to study him from afar.

You're always a student. In this game, as in life, there is no absolute knowledge. All you have are your own experiences, what you observe and infer through your senses, nourished, hopefully, with a little imagination. And, of course, that quality that his class of people is painfully deficient in: empathy. Most of the time this deficit seems to serve them well, in their limited way, as they blunder on chasing their bottom lines and profit margins, stunningly unaware that they are also part of the world they are systematically fucking up.

How do I put myself in the shoes of this shivering figure? Well, let me give it a try: I am in a completely terrifying environment, over which I have no control. I can see nothing through the suffocating hood covering my head and face except a sliver of my own body and the timber floor of the warehouse. (This cladding oddly makes this captive look sinister, as if *he* is the oppressor. But no, he's totally in our power.)

I don't know how I'm doing here, but it's obvious he's not in a good place. Frankly, it's not even comfortable for me, as much as I'm glad to be in my circumstances, rather than his. A slight nausea is rising inside me. Will it worsen if I get closer? I stand up and walk towards him, almost tiptoeing across the floorboards to maintain silence. Speculating that every step closer might furnish me with more information as to his emotional state.

1

Yes . . . once again, he strains against the bounds. It's futile. His wrists and ankles are as if welded to the hard chair. His arms are white and flabby through indolence and decadence. Now the sinews strain demonically in them, across his oddly sculpted shoulders, under his wobbling boy tits.

Beneath his moonless amice, I'm guessing that fireworks are going off. The thin leather buckles inwards as he inhales, his tongue maybe intermittently pushing it out, as he tastes the skin of dead animal. Maybe he screws his eyes down to that vague source of light underneath his chin, yes, a chink of it, spilling through the slash in the mask, cut there to let oxygen in. Now he's obviously marshalling himself – *this is exciting* – as he tenses his body further, sucking in deeply, then bellowing, — WHAT THE FUCK . . .

Not the first shout-out since he woke, but once again he only hears his muffled voice ricochet coldly around the huge and cavernous space. He must be thinking of how he got here, what this dramatic disturbance to his existence constitutes. There's his dutiful *Samantha*, how he disappointed her. But that bitch was made for disenchantment; trained, like so many women of her class, to absorb psychic hurt and cry softly into her pillow at night, or maybe in the arms of a lover, while presenting that stoical, loyal face to the world. Their darling children *James and Matilda*; maybe it's been tougher on those kids. Well, it's soon going to get a lot thornier. That college essay to discuss, the rugby game or school play sadly missed due to *pressures of work*; those are the least of his worries now. This is the shit that the prick ought to have thought through before he embarked on his life of making others miserable. His sister, *Moira*, the barrister; what is it with them? I suspect she will feel the loss of him the most. That dull, domestic life that he never really had – his solid work of corruption and the enrichment of the already wealthy ate up all his time – how he must now crave it. What disrupted this?

My call: urging him to come back. To return to a place he was done with, apart from the visits to his sister, in order to see the kids.

2

Now he's still again. I retreat, maintaining my silence from the corner of the capacious space, sinking back into my chair. He must be so
cold: his flesh is pulsing in the raw, dank air. I know from my own
experience how you still notice those minor horrors, even as you splash
around in a sea of abject terror. I'd like to discuss this with him, but I'm
wary of slipping into the torturer's indulgence of gloating torment. This
is not the game we are playing. Above all, it would feed the lie that this
was about him. He is not, and never will be, the narrator of this tale. This
is not the final chapter. It's just the last that this particular character will
feature in.

Men like him usually tell the story.

In business.

Politics.

Media.

But not *this* time: I repeat, he is not writing *this* story. And *this*
abdication is unwittingly at his own bequest!

And she is probably the very last person he would think about. Even
less than me with my personal nemesis, whom we sadly only managed
to incapacitate: as one gets older the atrocities of childhood grow more
vivid than those in an adolescence and adulthood blunted by hormones.
But to such men, we will just be obscure pieces of collateral damage, in
a warehouse full of the souls they've ruined and impaired through the
selfish meeting of their own immediate, base needs.

He is not writing this story.

She enters, looking magnificent in checked trousers, trainers and a
short coat, which she slips off, revealing a ready-for-business tank top.
Her arms are lean and gym-toned. Her hair pinned up, under her flat
cap. In her hand, the tool bag that means this cannot end well for him.
Oh, we've learned from the last time. The slurp of the plastic draught
excluder on the door must have registered, even on the other side of
that stifling hood.

She smiles, touches my shoulder. I rise from this old chair. We walk
slowly across the floor towards him. A creak on one of the boards. His

body tenses again, as he pushes back in his seat. Now he can hear the sound of footsteps: somebody creeping closer. Is he thinking: *perhaps there's more than one of them?*

— Who's there? Who is this? His voice is softer, more tentative now.

We walk slowly around him. So close he must feel our presence shimmer. It's not the heat; it's just the aura of other human beings in his proximity. He smells something, his sinuses whine softly under the mask, as he tries to ascertain what it is. Perhaps old books. Is he in a library? It's her perfume. Unique and rare, it's called Dead Writers. It is allegedly inspired by novelists like Hemingway and Poe. The black tea, vanilla and heliotrope notes actually do make it smell like an old drawing room stuffed full of antique books. Not a lot of women would have the balls to wear such a fragrance.

But not a lot of women, or men, have her balls. If he ever did, that will very soon cease to be the case.

— What do you want? Look, I have money . . . His muffled voice trails off into a plea.

We respond with a silence so thick he must feel it clog his lungs. Drowning him.

He's brought this on himself. Again.

Samantha.

The children.

All he ever did was set self-indulgent traps for them to get through. Testing their loyalty. And he had nearly repaired his last mess, almost convinced her to join him in London, to make a go of it again, on a bigger stage, where he was reascendant.

Oh yes, we know everything about him. Neither of us are gamblers by nature. The more research you do, the surer something is. Know their vanities and weaknesses. Help them to fall on their own swords. When all is said and done, that's what they really crave, that drama of utter disgrace and humiliation. It's the most compelling chapter of the narcissist's biography. What they are always working

4

towards, in the face of whatever nonsense they choose to delude themselves with.

How he must hate himself right now. Detest the weakness that led him here. This punishment, at the hands of a force he can't understand; how much self-loathing must that induce?

He'll soon be free of it all. It's time.

Her head turns sharply to me, eyes suddenly set with a luminous ferocity. She moves at a feline speed, her arms at his boxer shorts in a sudden uncompromising tug, yanking them down. He squirms in helpless violation as his penis and balls flop helplessly between his legs. With the jerking convulsions of his body ebbing and flowing, and the nervous gurgling, I read him as scared but perhaps also hopeful. While this alludes to the darkest contravention, it also hints at a harmless if potentially humiliating rugby-club prank, one so beloved of the darker elements on the fringes of his circle.

I know this feeling.

Could this babbling yet erupt into a collusive chuckle? *The Evans. The Alasdairs. The Murdos. The Roddys. Those bloody cards . . .*

This he would take right now.

But something freezes him again. Maybe it's her scent: it says something else.

— Stop, he pleads, his high voice breaking, possibly reminding him of his schooldays. Perhaps he'd be walking home, in his uniform, running into a group of council-estate boys – or council *schemes* as they call them here – from a nearby comprehensive. Would they take delight in punching his fat arms, dancing around him in a morbid revelry at the marks they caused, knowing they would bruise? I think so.

That was a long time ago. He had made himself into a different man. The gym and sports, to his satisfaction, had sabotaged the pudgy trajectory of his youth. The victimhood had been shed with the flab. Of course there was the sloth of a complacent middle age and his career; first-class travel, lavish expenses, late nights, and he reverted to the unappetising version of himself we see now. The burgeoning corpulence exemplified by the white ball of gut, the fleshy jowls capitulating to gravity, and those moobs an infant could suckle on. But it didn't matter. Now he was a winner. He could *buy* beautiful women.

Yes, he'd *stepped on a few toes* . . . I wonder if he's trying to think: *which ones?* That terrible problem with that Graham character; a dark urge he had to satisfy. It almost ruined him.

Now her.

Now me.

Surely not: she wouldn't be on his radar after all this time.

Perhaps it was business.

And sure enough, he asks in sudden inspiration, — Is this about the Samuels contract? There's no need to – NO!

He squeals out as her hands, covered in latex gloves, touch him: he can feel the thin gossamer rubber stickiness and his penile skin retracts under their graze. — NO!

And I play my part, simply by laying my own hand on his shoulder. He recoils, and I wager he has never felt such a cold touch.

The uncompromising pulse of terror surges so keenly through his body, sparking it into a tensile spasm, that I'm briefly concerned the ties will snap under the power it fuses through him.

But there's no way: it just slashes them deeper into his wrists and ankles.

I lift my brandishing hand, leaving his body to the air that stings at his exposed floppy cock and balls. Her evaluating touch, strangely gentle, now also gone. Leaving a vacuum of even greater discomfort.

But not for long. We are not going to make the same mistake twice. Again, I touch him without touching him. Nobody has a frostier caress that me, inchoate, inhuman. His prick literally contracts a further inch under it.

She is warmer for sure, not that he will feel any benefit, as she starts wrapping the leather strap around his genitals. Applying the devastating tourniquet. Turns the wooden handle to pull it tautly.

— PLEASE!

He feels the noose tighten.

— No, please . . . he says softly this time, in response to the twisting pain. And yes, there's a brief sense of arousal; he knows these games, and the infliction of sexual pain on others, even if he was always the one in control. But not now. Now he's experiencing the air escaping from his lungs, as the sweat and tears roll down his cheeks, dripping onto his chest from under the hood as his penis engorges with the blood trapped in it . . . then . . .

. . . I open the case and she removes the six-inch knife.

. . . then the cut . . . a beautiful motion as the blood spurts out. She pulls at his cock and hacks, but it won't come away! His loud, pig-like squeals . . . we never bargained for this, the knife was razor-sharp, but we are prepared. We dispense with the ceremonial blade, as I produce a serrated one from the bag and hand it to her. Through his splattering blood and cries I feel mildly deflated – Father's knives have again proven deficient to my task of vengeance – but this does not last as under her frantic sawing, the muscles in her arms pumped, his genitals finally snap away in her hand. Eureka!

Is he, I wonder, experiencing a strange relief, a giddy lightness in brain and body, as something burdening is whipped from him . . . perhaps just before he senses it will never return?

Because she's holding it aloft, that beautifully grotesque trophy, as he ascertains that this is not an encumbrance that has been removed from him, but something close to the very essence of who he is . . .

— AAAAGGHHHEEEEE . . .

. . . An animal squeal, like nothing I have heard before; it bellows out from under the mask . . . holds its pitch in a resonant drill, as he slumps forward, perhaps hoping that unconsciousness will deliver him from the pain. Maybe he's praying for the blessed liberation of death; anything to take him into a different realm. And he surely must feel that this is happening, but only after many more screaming heartbeats in purgatory.

7

She holds the genitals at arm's length, regarding them, then him, before dropping them into the plastic box.

Does he sense the whiff of perfume? If so, it's soon overwhelmed, as he shouts out, through the burning inferno of pain that disintegrates his spirit, a familiar name: — LENNOX . . .

Day One
Tuesday

1

Ray Lennox pulls in a long breath. This fans rather than extinguishes the burning embers in his chest and calves. Fighting past the pain, he forces himself into a steady rhythm. At first it's galling, then lungs and legs start working together like seasoned lovers rather than first-time daters. The crisp air carries the fresh whip of ozone. In Edinburgh, autumn often seems the default setting, no more than a rogue isobar away. But the towering trees are yet to shed, and weak sunlight dances through a canopy of leaves above him, as he bombs on down the footpath along the river.

Trying to get into Holyrood Park through a warren of backstreets, he comes upon it: the entrance in the car park of an unremarkable housing development of flats. On seeing it, his ears ring, forcing him to stop. He can't believe it.

This isnae the tunnel . . .

It's the Innocent Railway Tunnel, completed in 1831. It lies directly beneath Edinburgh University's Pollock Halls of Residence, yet it's a secret to most of the students who reside there. He's an expert on Edinburgh's tunnels, but has never gone through this one. Stops at its entrance. Ray Lennox knows that it isn't the one in Colinton Mains, where he was attacked as a young boy, a tunnel, now bedizened in a gaudy art, that he's walked through scores of times since.

You don't scare me.

But this one does. More than their source at Colinton, this dark, narrow passageway evokes these terrible memories. He knows that despite its name, numerous deaths – including those of two children in the 1890s – have taken place in this tunnel.

Lennox can't go on. Feels his legs quivering.

It's only a fucking cycle path, he thinks, noting the bollards and mesh fencing stacked at the side of the tunnel mouth. They are about to do some work. He's read that there's maintenance planned.

Yet the grown man cannot enter the dimly lit tunnel in which the light – and liberation – at the end feel like a lifetime away. It snakes into the oblivion Lennox knows will swallow him. This one will not let him go. The eerie sensation in the thickening, gelid air, a force field that he cannot breach. His ears ring. He turns and storms back out onto the main road. Starts accelerating again, trying to outrun his shame, first to the Meadows, heading to Tolcross, astonished as to why someone who can look at dead bodies, into the eyes of killers and the haunted family members of their victims without flinching, wondering how such a man cannot run through a tunnel. He cries out, trying to banish the intrusive thoughts from his head. Circling round, not knowing where he's going, he comes upon the Union Canal, and sprints down a section of towpath, passing his local pub, run by Jake Spiers, Edinburgh's most obnoxious publican, before returning breathless to his second-floor flat in Viewforth. Here the Victorian tenements look disdainfully at the showy new-build waterfront homes and offices that will never outlast them.

Collapsing onto his built-in window seat, Lennox lets his lungs settle. He thought he had proven to be the master of his fears. The Innocent Tunnel wasn't even the guilty one. Yet he looks in trembling reassurance at the Miami Marlins baseball bat that he keeps in the corner by the door, for security purposes.

Why is this shit coming back?

He turns to survey the neat rear greens tended by the downstairs neighbours of the high-ceilinged, bay-windowed dwellings. This part of town has always seemed an independent mini state to him. He moved here from his old place in Leith several months ago. Cohabitation with his fiancée, Trudi Lowe, was mooted, but they opted against it.

Trudi had claimed to be on board with this, though after the sale of his Leith flat, she failed to see the logic of him buying rather than renting. She came around once he told her that the property market was buoyant and that it was a good investment. A couple of years at either his or her flat would allow them to rent out the other place and save more money, thus setting them up to buy somewhere bigger further down the line. She conceded to his logic. However, Lennox doesn't want to live in a house, at least not for a while. Flat life suits him. Their marriage plans were iced following a trip to Miami, which was supposed to be relaxing, but turned out traumatic though ultimately cathartic. He is a magnet for trouble of the worst kind.

It's why I was put here.

Across in his kitchen area, on the marble worktop, the mobile phone vibrates. He rises and heads for it, moving with greater urgency when he sees the display flash: TOAL. Makes it just in time. — Bob, he breathlessly gasps, settling back down into his original berth.

Nothing speaks as eloquently of disaster as Toal's silences.

This protracted one moves Lennox to explanation: — Was out for a run. Just got to you in time.

— Are you at home? Toal's voice is set in the confidential hush he knows so well.

— Aye. From the window seat, Lennox looks around the lounge-kitchen of his two-bedroom flat. The patterned wallpaper is as shit as ever. It's exactly the same as that which adorns the local pub, and Lennox suspects Jake Spiers's hand in knock-off. It's hard to live with, but stripping it is a big job, and one he has baulked at. He thinks of asking his almost perennially resting actor brother, Stuart, who fancies himself as an odd-job man, to undertake the task, though this has potential hazards.

— I'll be round in five minutes. Be ready, Toal warns.

— Right. Lennox hangs up and makes a beeline for the shower. He's concerned. Toal is a desk cop who never leaves Police HQ at Fettes if he can help it. So Lennox busies himself and is just drying his collar-length hair when his boss appears at his door.

Toal's potato-like head, decorated by thinning grey hair and deep worry lines, shakes in the negative as Lennox offers him tea or coffee. — We're heading for a warehouse down at Leith docks. Found something not very pretty.

— Aye?

Bob Toal's ulcerated pout involves a tight scrunching of his eyes and a blowing out of his lips. — A homicide.

Lennox fights back a snigger. The department has taken to using the American term for murder, as the original word in a Scottish accent was deemed to sound too close in tone to the clichéd catchphrase of the TV cop played by Mark McManus in the endlessly repeated hit show *Taggart*.

He finds seriousness easier when Toal elaborates: — A poor bastard bound and castrated.

— Fuck sake. Lennox throws on a jacket and follows his retreating boss out the door.

— Worse than that, the guy's a Tory MP, Toal adds, rubbernecking to Lennox as he charges down the tiled stair.

Lennox's response is a caustic, — Most of Scotland helping us with our inquiries then.

14

— You know him. Ritchie Gulliver. Toal's scrutinising gaze is on him.

Lennox is jarred, but fights it back with the minimal raise of a brow. — Right.

Toal coughs out the grim recap. — Gulliver came off the sleeper this morning; he uses it fairly regularly and was positived by train staff. That was around 7 a.m. He checked into the Albany, a boutique hotel he used for liaisons down the years. They're known to be discreet; he comes up by the goods entrance in the car park at the rear. The night porter was just finishing his shift and had left the key under the mat outside room 216. They brought him two breakfasts there at 7.45, but nobody saw the other party. The trays were left outside the room, the waiter chapped and headed off. Toal throws open the stair door and gulps some air.

— The second breakfast, for a lover?

— I would assume so, says Toal, opening the car door, but not getting in, looking over at Lennox.

— So you want to know where I've been this morning?

— C'mon, Ray, you know how these things work.

— I was in bed till 7 a.m., then I went for a run. No witness or corroboration, maybe some CCTV footage –

— Okay, okay. Toal raises his hands and gets in the car. They drive off, heading to Leith docks. — Everyone who was involved in the Gulliver questioning around Graham Cornell in the Britney Hamil case, Toal mutters, — Amanda Drummond, Dougie Gillman, myself; we all have to account for our movements.

Lennox remains silent. *The top brass are rattled.* He looks at the time on his phone. It's just past 10 a.m. as they head down Commercial Street. — Who tipped us off he was in the warehouse?

— There was a call, a tape sent to us at 9.17 a.m., and Toal plays a robotic voice on his phone:

15

'You will find the body of Ritchie Gulliver MP in a warehouse unit, number 623, off the Imperial Dock in Leith. Please remove before the rats take one of their own.'

— Varispeed and synthesised vocals, done on a decent recorder. We're got an IT team on it trying to remove the filters, but they say it's a proper job and it's unlikely they'll be able to clean it up.

— So . . . Lennox thinks out loud, — if he had his breakfast at around 7.45, how did he get from a city-centre hotel room to a dock warehouse, naked and dead, in not much more than an hour?

— No record of him leaving the hotel. There's CCTV at the front, but not at the back in the staff car park.

It had been assumed his exposing of Gulliver's homosexual affair with a man who was prison-bound, had this infidelity not come to light, would have ended the then MSP's career. But this didn't happen. Though they now lived five hundred miles apart, Gulliver's wife publicly stood by him, as he relaunched his career in Westminster with a safe Oxfordshire seat. It was a spectacular comeback, and his brand of racism, specialising in the baiting of travelling people, proved a locally popular platform on which to reboot.

If Lennox has little compassion for Conservatives in general and Ritchie Gulliver in particular, this changes when he sees the bound and naked body. He has witnessed some horrendous murder scenes, but this bath of blood, both shooting across the concrete floor, and bleeding out into a dark pool congealing at Gulliver's feet, puts it up there with the most flesh-creepingly awful. He has to bend down to see the parliamentarian's face.

The features are frozen in a dumb, twisted terror, as if inspecting the bloodied stumpy area where his genitals once hung, and outraged at their removal.

Did they make him bear witness? Probably not; Lennox notes the marks around his neck, not deep enough to indicate a strangulating device, but perhaps a tightened hood. The MP obviously died in excruciating agony, his blood ebbing away, possibly while he slowly choked. It's that horrific stump Lennox can't take his eyes off as he feels a spasm shiver through his own body. It takes him a while to fully register the other people in the room.

Forensics expert Ian Martin attends to the blood pools on the concrete floor. A straight-backed, bird-faced man with thinning brown-grey hair, he detachedly takes pictures. Willowy Amanda Drummond, normally pale-skinned, looks more drawn than ever, snapping on her new higher-resolution camera phone. Crew-cutted Brian Harkness gags and rubs his throat as sweat breaks from him. Watery-eyed, he waves a hand to excuse himself, running past Lennox and Toal to a toilet. It's a male one, and ironically with a set of genitals drawn onto the symbol. As he and Toal acknowledge the sound of vomiting, Lennox scrutinises the artwork. — Is this old or recent? He moves over, sniffing at it, and scents a faint aroma of the marker. — Recent. They have a dark sense of humour.

Toal pouts in distaste, looking to Ian Martin. — Get somebody to check it for dabs.

— Already have, Martin responds, on his haunches, not looking up, engrossed in the blood pattern spattering out from Gulliver's groin. — Nothing. The perp might have been playful, but they certainly weren't careless. Whether by enticement or coercion, by the consistency and temperature of the blood, he was brought here and killed around 9 a.m. They're done by 9.45, that's when they put the rat tape into us and Radio Forth. Martin looks at his watch. — We were on the scene by 10.05.

Then Lennox hears a familiar growl, — Left the perr cunt like a lassie, telling him that the hatchet-faced Dougie Gillman has just arrived at the crime scene.

This observation is followed by a high, nasal whine, — Well, sooner you thin me wi that particular lassie, Uncle Doogie, tell ye that fur nuthin – fuck sake . . . His new partner, roly-poly Norrie Erskine, is abruptly shocked into uncharacteristic silence as he sees the body.

This pair are old associates. Once known as Uncle Doogie and Uncle Norrie, Gillman and Erskine were two road-safety cops who toured the Lothian schools with a slapstick double act. Even as a dour straight man to the wisecracking west-coaster, Gillman was chronically miscast just by virtue of being cast at all, and Lennox struggles in fascination to get to grips with that incarnation of his long-standing nemesis. While Gillman got out of uniform into Serious Crimes, 'Uncle Norrie' Erskine's career took a completely different trajectory. Honing his showbiz talents in amateur dramatics before going to college and becoming a minor pantomime star, he also gathered credits as a bent cop in *Taggart* and a sex offender in *River City* on his CV.

When the acting work dried up and there was a divorce to pay for, Erskine rejoined the force. Following his transfer to Edinburgh Serious Crimes from Glasgow, his new boss Bob Toal displayed a hitherto unseen situationist humour, deciding to reunite Uncle Doogie and Uncle Norrie as a detective partnership. This move raised several eyebrows, and induced quite a few chuckles.

Lennox has heard that Erskine's modus operandi is to resume the double act, often in the most inappropriate of circumstances.

— Aye, well, somebody fucked the cunt up, Gillman muses, looking at Lennox.

— Oh no they didn't, Erskine says, obviously distressed, but forcing cartoon wild eyes at the po-faced Gillman for a response. When none is forthcoming, he turns to Lennox in half-apology. — If ye dinnae laugh, ye'll cry, he appeals, upturning his palms.

Lennox forces a tight smile. He can see that Erskine is rocked. Sheet-white, his hands shake. It's a strange reaction for a seasoned Serious Crimes officer to have, albeit that the situation is particularly gruesome. Then again, Lennox considers, being too scared to run through a railway tunnel because of something that happened nearly thirty years ago also constitutes an unusually acute display of hypersensitivity.

We are a weird bunch.

Drummond, who has put her phone away and has been conferring with Ian Martin, looks unimpressed, while Harkness returns from the bathroom, averting his eyes from Gulliver's bound body. Toal, who has studiously ignored the antics of his charges, mournfully declares, — This is going to go all over the place, with the Scottish elections next month.

Gillman suddenly decides to pitch in, putting on a Chinese accent, — Well, zis poor bastard has had rast erection by rooks of things.

As Drummond shudders and Toal pouts, Lennox sees Gillman is testing Erskine's potential to offer them even more disquiet.

On cue, a still-shaky Erskine forces out, in an oriental accent, — Drugras spreckurate crastration?

Drummond, approaching Lennox, shoots Erskine a withering glance, but Toal again pretends not to have heard. With his retirement imminent, Lennox believes his boss may now be giving up on trying to school Gillman, and by proxy Erskine, in political correctness protocol. Then his boss seems to pick up on Drummond's look, proclaiming, — Enough, as Lennox notes the old dog still has a bark.

Gillman smiles then nods, as if he's been caught cheating at a game. Lennox knows how this gallows humour operates. Underneath the forced bravado, certainly Erskine, and even the hard-nosed Gillman, are shocked at what they are witnessing

— The warehouse has been empty for years, Drummond, cradling her iPad, informs them. — Still owned by the Forth Ports Authority. The door was secured by two bolted padlocks. They were sheared off, probably with industrial bolt cutters . . . She glances at the covered body. — A security guard walks the perimeter, but didn't see anything suspicious. There's nothing in the warehouse to steal, so no CCTV cameras on this side. From the Seafield Road end there will be vehicle and foot traffic pixels, which Scott McCorkel and Gill Glover are checking out.

Lennox nods, and approaches Ian Martin, who is shining a torch at the red genital area. A couple of severed tendons hang, like strings of spaghetti. Lennox feels something shift inside him. — Strange severing wound. It's like they used two separate cutting instruments, one with a straight blade, the other serrated. Martin makes a sawing motion as he turns to Lennox. — Perhaps the first wasn't doing its job, or maybe they wanted him to feel it. To suffer, he speculates. He holds up a plastic bag for Lennox's inspection. There is a red fibre inside. — This is all the forensic evidence yielded so far.

This disturbs Lennox. Amateurs rarely get this lucky. He stops again to regard the countenance of Ritchie Gulliver, face frozen in terror, marks around his neck. Martin agrees it's likely that a hood was placed over him and secured tightly.

— Had he been drugged into unconsciousness?

— I thought so at first, and I won't be surprised if Gordon Burt finds traces of something, he holds the plastic bag up to the light, — when we get him to the path lab and the post-mortem. But do you see this indentation in his forehead? Martin points at an almost square red mark. It's like Gulliver's been smashed by something, experienced the sort of blow that would knock you unconscious. — That is puzzling.

Lennox thinks about how boxers achieve knockouts; often by a punch at speed that battered the brain against the back of the skull. This might have had a similar effect. Suddenly, he thinks of the MO of Rab Dudgeon, nicknamed the Carpenter of Lunacy. But he is safely inside Saughton Prison. Again, he looks at the waxy countenance of Gulliver, strives to remember someone who was prepared to let the innocent man he was having an affair with go to prison, in order to protect his own career. Can't see him. Despite speaking of this case so much with his psychotherapist, Sally Hart, it is just another dead face, albeit a deflated one.

One big question is hanging in the air, and Lennox asks it. — Any sign of his genitals?

— Gone, Martin sings, with a melodic aspect in his voice, — no trace at all. No blood trail, so it's probable they were bagged up almost immediately.

— So the perp took the boy's tackle away with him, Gillman shouts, then looks to Drummond, — or away with her, please excuse the sexism.

— Trophy? Maybe search the Tynecastle boardroom, Erskine laughs. Nobody else does.

— I'll be glad to get out of this circus, Lennox hears Bob Toal remark to himself, an uncharacteristically unguarded comment, which Drummond also picks up on.

She sidles up to Lennox. — What are you thinking, Ray?

Ray Lennox is thinking about an incident that took place three weeks ago in London.

2

Sitting in Bob Toal's car is always a strange experience for Lennox. His boss traditionally values silence, but the radio robustly plays 'The Lebanon' by the Human League. Lennox realises that but for the presence of his superior he would be singing along, the crawling, prohibitive Edinburgh traffic failing to dampen his spirits. Ironically, the only nagging concern he has is his own good cheer; after all, he is investigating a horrific crime. But his personal extreme antipathy for the victim, following their previous conflict, is proving hard to shake.

He regarded Gulliver as a provocative, grandstanding bigot who cynically deployed a divisive racism and sexism to gain political traction. And if their victims are finally turning on abusive men of power, then that is, perhaps, an honourable instinct for a citizen, but useless for a policeman. It confirms to him how hopelessly miscast he is. Now he is in the frame, albeit reluctantly, for the retiring Bob Toal's job. Steals a glance at his boss's jowly profile.

You can't be Toal.

You can't play politics with all those arseholes.

Reality looms in the form of Police HQ, Fettes, the featureless seventies building that takes its name from the grand private school next to it.

As if there is any doubt about whom we serve.

— Let's get on it, Ray, Toal says, glancing at his wristwatch. — Set up an incident room and we'll meet there in fifteen minutes.

He's just settled at his desk when Amanda Drummond

22

comes into the open-plan office. A furtive look in her eyes and a tightness around her thin-lipped mouth. For the first time he notes her hair has been cut shorter. Unlike most women, Lennox thinks it suits her and makes the observation, — New look.

— Yes. She matches his bland assertion with cool affirmation.

They find a room and pin an image of Gulliver, phantom smirk always threatening to break out, onto the board. Placing his movements and associates there, a skeleton of the victim's life starts to form. They then start going through videos of his speeches. The content is depressing. Gulliver has achieved a constituency among some in those socio-economic groups he wouldn't piss on if they were ablaze.

Lennox exhales sharply and rolls his eyes, turns the sound down on his computer. After all, they are looking out for undesignated people. He freezes the screen and taps it at the image of a fat guy in a brown suit, who is in the wings as Gulliver speaks. — This boy is . . . ?

Drummond has a delegate list of key conferences with portrait photos. — Chris Anstruther, an MSP who was a colleague of his before he went to Westminster . . . I think . . . She points at the chubby image and they try to reconcile the two.

This is real poliswork, Lennox thinks. *Boring, shitey poliswork.*

As the clips play on, Lennox becomes aware that Drummond is restless, manifested by changes in her breathing pattern. Senses she is working up to say something. Sure enough, as another video snippet ends, she looks at him and intones, low and measured, — You know I applied for the job? Chief Super?

— Yes, I heard.

His partner, Amanda Drummond, only recently promoted, is now cast as the ambitious outsider. Lennox knows that this will upset many long-serving officers, and Dougie Gillman springs satisfyingly to mind.

— I know I've only just been made DI so I don't expect to get it —

— You never know —

— but at least it flags me up, lets them know I'm around.

Lennox nods, smiles to himself. He remains silent as his mind flashes back to a conversation he had many years ago with a troubled mentor, Bruce Robertson. During a cocaine blitz, Lennox said pretty much the exact same words to his racist, misogynistic senior partner. He was subsequently promoted while Robertson hanged himself. He nods to Drummond as a growing cacophony of non-stop chatter in an adenoidal west coast accent foreshadows the entrance of Norrie Erskine, along with the menacingly silent square-jawed Dougie Gillman. They are followed by jittery Brian Harkness, small, squat Gillian Glover, spindly Faginesque Ally Notman, and those badly tailored veteran monuments to dubious lifestyle choices: Doug Arnott, Tom McCaig and Jim Harrower. Last are red-headed Scott McCorkel and camp metrosexual Peter Inglis, deeply locked in technical conversation.

On Lennox's signal, they settle on the challenging red plastic chairs, looking at the airbrushed portrait picture of Gulliver. Toal enters and addresses them. — First thing: we leave the schoolboy humour out of this. He lets a sweeping gaze linger a beat on Erskine and Gillman. — Second: as always, we observe confidentiality. This time we do so with extreme mindfulness. Ritchie Gulliver was a former member of our Police Committee. Ray, he turns to Lennox, — you head this up.

Lennox nods at Toal. He realises that his boss is openly putting him in pole position for the promotion, and can't look to the reaction of the others. But not for the first time, he wonders if he's the best person for his superior's job.

He points to the pinned image of the self-satisfied Gulliver. The MP, tipped for a junior Cabinet post in Health, looks like he's just advocated the mass sterilisation of working-class women or something else from his 'controversial' repertoire. — We need to investigate Ritchie Gulliver's past . . . Lennox says. — This guy's life seems to have been a monument to personal gain and self-interest, so I'm guessing we won't have any shortage of people with some sort of grievance against him; business associates, political rivals, hookers, girl-friends, boyfriends, jealous partners of either. He pauses, aware of Gillman's raised eyebrows. — Whatever you think of him, this is a heinous crime and a terrible thing to happen to anyone. You know what to do. Let's nail the fucked-up bastard who did this, he says, aware that his voice is unable to find its usual force of conviction.

More shards of relevant information from the team are placed on the board; pictures, documents, Post-it notes and scribblings. They attempt to fit them into a narrative of Gulliver's last days and hours. Gillian Glover confirms that the London- and Oxfordshire-based MP was still separated from his wife, who had stayed up in Perthshire with their children. When he came up from London to visit his offspring, Ritchie Gulliver always stayed at his sister Moira's place, which was close to the home of his estranged wife.

As the meeting ends, Lennox heads to his desk, pondering his existential crisis. He came into this game to stop sex predators preying on the vulnerable, namely children. Apprehending those who have done this admittedly unspeakably vicious and deranged thing to a corrupt man who, in service of his wealthy masters, demonised the most marginalised members of society, was never on his to-do list.

He decides to leave the office. Data sifting may now be the real police work, but he still has a strong foothold in a bygone era, and that stuff is best left to the millennial IT nerds.

Now I'm thinking like Gillman! Not so long since him, Robbo and Ginger regarded me as one of those nerds . . .

Getting into his Alfa Romeo, Lennox drives west towards the Forth Bridges, heading into Fife and journeying north. Something about leaving the city and crossing the Firth always induces a mild euphoria in him. It evokes the possibility of freedom, or at least escape from a confining life.

Taking the main road to Perth, he admires the way Scotland starts to unravel its beauty, first slowly, then with a building drama. Driving off the dual carriageway onto a largely one-track road, he passes through the small village at the foothold of a range of hills, spying the entrance to the turn-off for the cottage owned by his sister Jackie and brother-in-law Angus. Carrying on up the narrow road, crossing over a stone bridge where it satisfyingly broadens, he sees, poking through thinning silver birch and oak trees, the spires of a much more substantial dwelling. This big pile is the Gulliver family home. On arrival, he finds it locked up. He goes around the back to try and look inside, coming upon a corpulent woman with implausibly spindly legs. Putting rubbish out in a series of dump bins, she stares at him in suspicion until he flashes his police ID and she dissolves into a teary-eyed compliance. — Aye, she's at her sister's thank God, the woman who introduces herself as Hilda McTavish confirms. — It's a terrible business.

— Have you spoken to her?

— Your officer . . .

— Gillian . . .

— Aye, Gillian Glover, Hilda says, — she telt Missus Gulliver the news. I spoke to the poor woman, just for a minute, but I dinnae ken what her plans are. What is she going to tell those poor bairns?

That they're better off withoot their cunt of a faither?

Lennox asks Hilda about any suspicious dealings Ritchie had, or anybody unusual who might have been around the family house.

— No . . . he was seldom up here. He never saw those children enough, if you ask me. Hilda closes one eye. — But carrying on with other men like that, him a married man too, I dinnae approve, Mr Lennox, I dinnae approve. Hilda puckers her lips and shakes her head.

For a brief second, Lennox thinks of old British crime shows set in stately homes, *and the murderer is . . . you were so homophobic that you were disgusted by Ritchie Gulliver's actions . . . disgusted enough to remove the man's genitals . . .* then cut to a psychotic Hilda holding up a pair of bloodied bolt cutters: *Ah dinnae approve!*

Fighting down a subverting levity with the dark thought: *it's inevitable I'll be in the fucking frame myself, given my history with Gulliver*, Lennox thanks her. Returns to his car, as a phone call from Drummond comes in. She tells him that Gulliver's London flat in Notting Hill is empty. — The Met officers got access but found nothing incriminating. Even though Gulliver was a former MSP and has family and business connections, it doesn't answer why he was back home. There's no parliamentary recess in Westminster, Drummond intones in that breathless, slightly anxious way of hers. As if any intervention will make her lose the thread.

She is voicing Lennox's own thoughts. What was an MP for an Oxfordshire constituency doing back in Edinburgh in the middle of the week, other than getting tortured and murdered? Gulliver had been politically dead in the water, disgraced after his homosexual affair with a man suspected of child murder. Then he gets a safe Tory seat down south. It was an unlikely turn of affairs, even given the limp-wristed white-collar gangsterism of the old boy network. What did he have on the establishment nonces to buy such favours? One person who might shed some light upon this is Ritchie Gulliver's sister.

Moira Gulliver and her brother were close, and Lennox ironically has a tenuous connection with her through his own sister. If Ritchie's house is palatial enough, then Moira's, the traditional Gulliver homestead, a twenty-minute drive away, and where her brother was most inclined to stay when he returned to Scotland, is a bona fide castle. It encompasses a medieval tower, with Georgian and Victorian add-ons. As he rings a bell, by an impressive wooden door in a huge arch, the disconcerting bark of dogs fills the air. A woman with long dark hair and fine, sharp features answers. Lips and breasts jut out from a thin body and implausibly tiny waist, to the extent Lennox immediately suspects implants.

Moira Gulliver is a lawyer and a colleague of his sister, Jackie. There is no hostility in her voice as she greets him. — You must be DI Lennox, and her posh tones remain highly enunciated, but there's weariness in them, her eyes indicating a struggle through medication's fog. — This is terribly distressing, she says, fighting back a sob, and her grief seems real. Lennox is sabotaged by the thought that there was perhaps more to Gulliver than the opportunistic, rabble-rousing bigot he presented to the world.

— Yes. Sorry for your loss.

Moira bristles and Lennox is briefly shamed. They both know that he isn't particularly downcast. — Jackie is a very good lawyer; she swiftly changes the subject to his sibling.

— She's certainly very good at telling me that. Lennox smiles, before realising that levity is perhaps not desirable at this moment.

This is confirmed when Moira ushers him through to a large drawing room. — I wish Ritchie was here, so that I could tell my brother the same, and she stifles another whimper, pointing him in the direction of a huge armchair. Again, her pain skewers a blade of guilt into him. — Of course, she recovers her composure, — you know that Jackie and Angus have a cottage nearby. They used to come a lot when the boys were younger, and bring them over here. Do you have children?

— No, Lennox says. Trudi wants kids, but it holds little appeal for him. There are too many existing ones to be saved. — Yourself?

— Alas no. I had a hysterectomy at an early age, due to a cancerous tumour, she says, totally mater-of-fact. Lennox doesn't sense any partner. It's a big house to live in alone.

Then a giant mastiff bounds over and Lennox feels himself freeze. — Don't worry about Orlando. He really is the cliché of the big softie, she explains. On cue the dog sniffs his hand, and heads off. — Jackie still has her dog . . .

— Aye, Lennox nods, thinking about the strange mutt at his sister's. Can't even recall its name. He isn't big on domestic pets.

Moira pours herself a large glass of white wine. — Can I interest you in something, DI Lennox? . . . It seems strange calling you that when your sister is a friend and colleague –

— Ray is fine, and no thanks with the drink, Lennox says, wanting one more than he can believe. He makes a mental note to call his sponsor, fireman Keith Goodwin.

Moira Gulliver, tucking her shiny black hair behind one ear, sits down with her wine. From the bottle, Lennox can tell it's a decent Sancerre.

29

Her hurt is real, and you're sorry for that. But you don't give a fuck about her brother. In fact, you're glad somebody did the cunt.

— He wasn't a bad man, Ray, Moira states, then, — Ritchie, she confirms, in face of his inscrutable expression. — He just saw politics as a game, and a bit of a joke, really.

Lennox is far from assuaged. Politics for working people is about trying to feed their families and pay their mortgages or rents. Despite being stuffed with a constant diet of faux aspiration by the media, most would know nothing else bar a lifetime of struggle and penury. Politics shouldn't be what it has exclusively become: a pastime for bored, rich, narcissistic sociopaths, useless for any other kind of employment and hardwired only to syphon off the resources of a community into the pockets of their elite sponsors.

Moira takes him into an office. It's bright and airy, with big French windows looking out over pastures grazed on by sheep, rising to brown scrubbed hills. — Ritchie often worked from here when he came up to see us.

— Did he come up here a lot?

— Yes, to see the children. He wasn't particularly welcome at the family home. Of course, you know all this, she says bluntly, before pointing to a desk diary. — I've been through this, of course I have. Nothing jumps out.

— So no idea what he was doing in a warehouse in Leith?

— Of course not. Her eyes narrow in hostility.

— I'm sorry, Lennox offers, — that came out wrong. But he didn't tell you he was back in Scotland? Isn't that unusual, considering he generally stays with you when he's up seeing his kids?

— No, he didn't, and yes, it is highly unusual, she concedes. Takes a sip of the wine. Her face creases as if it's vinegar.

Lennox hopes that Drummond is having better luck talking to Ritchie Gulliver's political colleagues. Toffs do the poker face very well, and this lawyer is, even in her grief and rage, one of the best. — Relationships outside of marriage?

She looks at him with renewed rancour. — You would be aware of that.

— I obviously know about his homosexual affair with Graham Cornell, yes. Were there any others? Gay or straight?

Moira scoffs in a bitter irony, — He was a man . . .

Generalities of this type are always very unhelpful. Men come in all cultural shapes and sizes: habits, sex drives and moralities. And those, as he knows to his cost, can shift through time and circumstance. — Anything specific?

— Not that I know of, and she suddenly looks at him in focus. — But then men are full of secrets, aren't they?

Lennox feels the disconcerting challenge in her tone. Wonders if she and Jackie ever discuss their respective brothers. Turns away and starts to comb through the book; already sees that Ritchie Gulliver's appointments show the letter 'V' featuring regularly. Lennox wonders whether or not this is a prostitute whom he has sex with.

But he ended up bound and castrated in a deserted warehouse in Leith docks. How did he get there?

— Mind if I take this? I'll return it.

— Feel free.

Lennox sticks the book under his arm. — Thanks.

— You will find the man who did this?

— What makes you certain it's a man?

She looks at him as if he's a little crazy. — Well, I'm not certain, but I *am* a criminal lawyer, she says, with an arch of her brow insinuating: *and you are a police detective.*

Fair play, Lennox thinks. The balance of probability is overwhelming. Women just don't commit such crimes. He wonders what made him insinuate that one could have. — I'll do everything I can.

31

— Given your history with Ritchie, you can understand my concern, she says. — But I believe you. Jack tells me you're heavily invested in all your cases.

It's strange to hear someone else refer to his sister as *Jack*. Even his parents and brother never used his preferred designation in reference to successful criminal lawyer Jacqueline April Lennox. He only deployed it as it had originally annoyed his bossy, upwardly mobile sibling. But as it went from proletarian to feminist in her consciousness, Jackie embraced it. — It's not often I agree with my sister, Lennox concedes, — but on this one, Moira, yes. Your brother met his end at the hands of a very evil, committed force, and he feels the requisite conviction slide into his voice. — They've possibly done this before –

— The Savoy?

How the fuck does she know about that?

— We're obviously following up the MO for similarities to the recent London attack, but if they aren't apprehended, the chances are that they'll do it again.

— They? Why the plural? Any evidence to suggest more than one?

— I was trying to avoid the he or she, Lennox says, as unconvinced as Moira looks.

— I go back to all the cases I've worked on, she says, downcast. — Why? Why do they do this?

— Power is always relentless in its propagation and the pursuit of its own agenda. We've built an economic system designed to concentrate that power. As this happens, the opposition to it will grow more extreme. All we're doing is reaping what we've sown, he says, and he leaves her to ponder that. Wonders, as he drives away from the big house, whether she might see how her wealth, education and connections shielded her from that system's most negative outcomes. Just as they did with her brother.

Until now.

A text comes in from Gillman:

> They found the cunt's cock and baws in the Scott Monument. They were hung up and slapped a tourist in the pus.

Anyone else, he would think this was a wind-up. Gillman, though, delights in being the coarse but deadpan bearer of extremely unfortunate news.

3

Ray Lennox motors back into town, idly fantasising about having sex with Moira Gulliver. This is nothing new for him, in fact habitual with certain women he comes into contact with. But there's a disquieting element to this, and it comes from the realisation that he never allows himself the luxury of this distraction on a case that is important to him. When he thinks of her slender build, it obliterates the remains of her brother's shredded genitals from his mind.

Better sitting with an erection than a perma head fuck.

The Scott Monument . . .

Glancing at the clock on the dashboard, he opts not to head north at the Maybury roundabout in order to return to his office. Instead he goes in the opposite direction to Saughton Prison, as he recalls a meeting he had in Birmingham last week.

Frederick Goad's chin had vanished into a bullfrog neck. It was a look Lennox, perhaps unfairly he felt, had always associated with existential despair. Goad's bleak, draining tones did nothing to dispel this impression. — He was a hard-working self-starter, who travelled the country, managing different projects, providing input to various multidisciplinary teams, he said, referring to one of his employees. Lennox nodded, kept silent, even as images of dead girls, souls brutally wrenched from the cold, fish-eyed corpses left behind, burned him in conjunction with the coffee in his guts.

Still Goad continued, oblivious to his growing rancour. — He had to develop policy in a fast-paced, changing environment, influencing others at all levels as well as effectively manage numerous pieces of work . . . he was based between London, Birmingham and Leeds, Goad prattled on, regurgitating all the long-known dull irrelevances, Lennox reading him as bored as he was.

Fair enough, he had been asked about this particular employee many times. By cops, media people, his own bosses, by Lennox himself. However, this one particular Strategic Ops Manager at DfT's High Speed & Major Rail Projects Group would feature in conversations for the rest of his life. Goad's response was to sound like an HR department specification for Gareth Horsburgh's job. — In the Civil Service Horsburgh had access to a wide range of benefits; generous annual leave, attractive pension options, flexible and inclusive working environments, and much more to support a healthy work/life balance, Goad declared, evidently troubled by the idea that a man with such life advantages could go so off the rails.

This was the point Lennox lost his patience. — Unfortunately his life projects related to the kidnap, rape and murder of young girls.

— There was nothing at all that came up in his rigorous security checks, Goad suddenly gasped, almost begging.

Lennox looked the HS2 man in the eye. — What I need you to do is tell me anything about Horsburgh . . . something that I don't know.

— I know he's a monster, but he's bloody good engineer and civil servant, Goad stated, then, realising what he'd said, placed his hand repentantly on his chest and asked Lennox, — What happens to a man to make him act like that?

— As a very small child his stepfather and his mates came back from the pub and used him like a toilet. For years and years.

Goad fell into a shocked silence. Lennox left and drove north.

Now he's outside Saughton Prison, thinking of this conversation with Mr Confectioner's boss, like that with his ex-wife and his mother, considering how those stones really have yielded their last drop of blood. Yet he carries on, in his own time. The case is not finished for him. If he is to bring closure to the parents of long-missing children and young women, he has to find Confectioner's infamous yellow pages – the journals he hid in different locations, detailing his crimes. To do this, he has to re-engage with the monster himself.

The beasts' wing, the part of the prison that houses the isolated sex offenders, always depresses him. He watches them, in their maroon jerseys, looking furtively at him as he strolls through their recreation area. The former governor of the facility was a Hibernian FC fan with a keen sense of humour, and instigated this coding, designating nonces in the colours of local rivals Heart of Midlothian. Ironically, this was instituted prior to Lennox's favoured club employing a registered sex offender as team manager. He regards those snide short-eyes' lamps, fearful, yet entitled. He put many of them in here.

A flamethrower and a free pass for an hour. It would be sweet.

And the daddy of them all is Gareth Horsburgh, the man they know as Mr Confectioner. The multiple child murderer played mind games with Lennox, who tried to wring from Confectioner his elusive notebooks.

Gillman smashed a confession out of the child killer for the murder of Edinburgh girl Britney Hamil. They then tied Confectioner to the slayings of Nula Andrews and Stacey Earnshaw, in Welwyn Garden City and Manchester. The police establishment was far from happy at this outcome, as it involved freeing the media-vilified Robert Ellis, wrongly convicted for those murders. But then the killer lawyered up and refused to cooperate regarding a multitude of girls who had disappeared down the years. He hinted at his involvement, but in the absence of any physical evidence, it was impossible to proceed with those investigations. But Ray Lennox can't let it go, and in the death of Ritchie Gulliver, he scents opportunity.

This is first time in years Gareth Horsburgh has deigned to speak to him, ever since Lennox committed what the multiple child killer felt was a betrayal: setting his vicious colleague Gillman onto him. Now the detective hates himself for the surge of anticipation and excitement he feels. He meets prison social worker Jayne Melville in reception. She has helped facilitate the visit, at great risk to herself, aided by prison officers Ronnie McArthur and Neil Murray.

Jayne Melville is a short, stout woman with a pageboy haircut and big glasses. She has been obsessed with finding out what happened to her sister, Rebecca, who vanished twelve years ago. Lennox has joined her in this *idée fixe*, though he's told her the circumstances of her sister's disappearance make it unlikely Rebecca was a victim of Confectioner.

His first impression, as the turnkey Murray lets him into the cell, is that Confectioner seems to have put on some weight. There's a distinct belly and a chopsy aspect to his jowls. Prison food. How the pompous civil servant must hate it.

— DI Lennox. Confectioner smiles, leaning back on his bed, hands behind his back.

— Hello, Gareth. Lennox refuses to preamble, going straight to the missing notebooks that Confectioner has concealed. — The yellow pages . . .

— I let my fingers do the talking . . .

The second thing that Lennox notices is that Horsburgh has recovered the arrogance Gillman temporarily beat out of him. — Give me something, Gareth.

— Or you'll send in that animal, Gillman, Confectioner scoffs, sitting up. — My brief has been informed of everything. Any marks on me and –

As he pulls up the solitary chair, Lennox cuts in, speaking clearly and slowly: — I've not come here to threaten or bully. I'm just asking you, please give me something. Hazel Lloyd. He looks at the mass murderer evenly. — Her family hurt. Every day they pray to know what happened to her. They're good people, Gareth. Whatever your views on the evil of the state apparatus, they aren't part of it. Your legacy, whatever it is, isn't about torturing people like that, and he hands Confectioner a list.

The child killer takes it but doesn't look at it. — You set that thug Gillman on me. You betrayed me. Now you want to dance again?

Of course, you fucking murdering nonce!

— I want the names on this sheet. How many were down to you, the locations where they're buried. The yellow notebooks . . . give me one more. Just one. Hazel Lloyd.

— Why should I?

— I told you: it's not your legacy.

— You don't know what my legacy is, Lennox. They are all compliant. To stand aside, to live in wilful ignorance, is to take sides.

Lennox decides to play to Confectioner's ego. He's always unconvincingly claimed grander motives than satisfying his cruel and warped sexual power-tripper's desires. Perhaps he needs this belief, in order to execute such heinous crimes. Lennox sees it as a potential Achilles heel, which he's been unable to exploit. So far. — You were hunting bigger game, Gareth. Trying to get that reaction from a corrupt, moribund state and a passive public. Spreading black terror in the hearts

38

of strangers, people trying to get on with their lives, isn't the big thrill for you, I would suspect.

— And you know me, he laughs caustically.

— I don't, but I'm taking a guess that part of what you say is genuine, and he stares into Confectioner's flinty, dead eyes again. — And there's another reason.

— What's that?

Lennox shows him the pictures on his phone. They are the ones Drummond took of Gulliver. They are augmented by a more recent shot of a set of withered genitals hanging from a Gothic arch.

Confectioner studies them. There is no movement in his face muscles and his eyes stay as stony as ever.

— Taken this morning. The severed tackle this affie. If this is connected with a similar attack in London, you are old news. This new kid on the block is striking at real men of power, not dispossessed children, he declares in contrived sadness. — That is a lot more intriguing to the media and the public.

He watches Confectioner, who looks up at him and reluctantly hands the phone back. — I could do with one of these, a mobile phone, Lennox. Could you get me one?

— Possession of a mobile phone in prison is a serious offence, Lennox says, deadpan, knowing that Confectioner is serving three life sentences. — The maximum penalty on conviction for possession of one is two years' imprisonment or a fine or both.

— I'd opt for the fine, Confectioner grins.

Lennox gets back on point. — What I'm saying here is consider all your planning, all that effort to create a legacy spanning years. It could be relegated to a footnote. If you released just one yellow notebook and gave me a location, you are right back in the game. Timing is all, and he stares coldly at Confectioner. — I'm not going to be on the force forever, Gareth. I've a legacy too. I want to be the man who apprehended Britain's most dangerous serial killer, not somebody who put away a troublesome nonce who preyed on soft targets. Think about it, he pleads, rising and preparing to leave the cell, to let his captive ponder. — There's a person out there castrating powerful men. That's all the police and media are interested in right now. They don't care about the working-class girls and young women you abducted and murdered. You and I, in different ways, do.

Confectioner inhabits the silence.

Lennox glowers, then points at him. — Do not fuck this up for us.

— I'll think about it, Confectioner says with petulance. — *You* think about my phone.

And as he goes to meet his fiancée, Ray Lennox leaves the man he loathes more than any other, feeling he has just dived deeper than ever into his sewer.

4

A candle burns on a check-clothed table, bathing its occupants in the flattering light of romance. Lennox watches a suited middle-aged man adjacent to them cut into a large piece of venison that recalls Gulliver's bloodied residue. He looks across at his fiancée, Trudi Lowe, trying to shake off the morbid associations. Her hair pinned up, Trudi wears a fetching aquamarine dress. He regrets his own more casual choice of attire: a black Harrington jacket with a cornflower-blue Hugo Boss light crew-necked jumper. The shoes are comfortable tasselled loafers. Lennox feels a bit disadvantaged, knowing his Hibs-supporting brother Stuart is prone to dismissing slip-on shoes as a Jambo construct.

Trudi sits with a glass of wine in front of her. Lennox, drinking sparkling water, with a double espresso, wishes they were eating here instead of at his sister's; the food is more than acceptable in this French restaurant and wine bar they regularly favour. It prides itself on unpretentious cooking, using local ingredients. Jackie's fare will be over-fussy, and he dreads meeting his mother again.

Trudi is delighted to find her fiancé relaxed. The wine wasn't her best idea, but she rarely drinks in front of him. Only one glass of a Chardonnay that isn't too unbearably sweet. She casts a disapproving eye over his double espresso. With its slamming hit of caffeine, she has read that strong coffee is a gateway drug to cocaine. He follows her stare, knows her view, and they share a rueful exchange of pouts. The conversation settles on a discussion as to whether Lennox being promoted in the upcoming reorganisation would lead to more or less stress. — Less, Trudi declares, — because you won't have to deal so directly with all those disturbing cases, but more as you'd have to carry the can for the mistakes of others.

— So swings and roundabouts.

Trudi sweeps her hand through her blonde hair, tucks a wing of it behind her ear. Fixes a dangling earring. — What would be more stressful to *you*, though, Ray?

— Dunno, Lennox confesses, glancing again at the suited businessman next to them. Like Lennox, this man has a younger date, and flashes him a nauseously collusive smile. Lennox thinks of the London victim; he too was described as a 'businessman' and his identity was undisclosed. This incident, reportedly featuring a naked man who ran, cupping his bleeding genitals, down into the lobby of the Savoy Hotel, received scant media coverage, and would only be of interest to cops and lawyers like Moira Gulliver. This means he was someone known, maybe a senior politician, perhaps a celebrity. Certainly somebody whom real wealth and power have a stake in.

Trudi is keen to discuss Lennox's own minor interest in aspirational power, the interviews for Bob Toal's job that take place next Monday in the departmental reorganisation as the Edinburgh Serious Crimes Department undergoes a major overhaul. — They're chopping out the so-called dead wood, starting with Bob Toal.

— Isn't he due to retire anyway?

— A little earlier than planned, thanks to this reorganisation. Lennox takes a sip of water. — I reckon he'd have stayed the course if he'd had the option. But now that he doesn't, he seems invested in the idea of getting out, he says, watching the reptilian smile of the businessman as he reaches across the table for his date's hand.

— Well, that's good. Trudi takes a sip of her wine, pleased to note that her fiancé shows no signs of alcohol envy.

— So here I am, Lennox curls down his bottom lip, — reluctantly pitched into the frame for a big promotion I'm not at all sure I want.

Trudi, who has enjoyed two such elevations at Caledonian Gas, declares, — There's nothing wrong with ambition, Ray. The twinkle in her gaze indicates excitement at the idea of them as a high-flying power couple. A chance for both social advancement and removing him from the dangerous coalface of his work.

Lennox rubs the stubble on his chin. He thinks of his visit to Confectioner, how it wouldn't be the worst thing in the world if someone else managed that sort of interface. Sometimes you do get tired.

Trudi thrusts forward in her seat. Pushes a bullet-breasted cleavage out at him, as if in challenge. — What do you *really want* though, Ray?

— I want . . . Lennox says thoughtfully, casting his eye over her in her tight mermaid-skinned dress, — to take you home and bang the shit out of you.

— I would so enjoy that, his fiancée purrs, relishing the return of the old Lennox. He now seems far removed from the troubled wreckage, almost ruined by Mr Confectioner, before being strangely revitalised by his rogue adventure in Miami.

— I wish we didn't have this poxy dinner. Afterwards though. So let's not stay too long!

— Your place or mine?

— Mine, Lennox says. — I even changed the sheets.

— Way to spoil a girl. Trudi swigs back her wine and looks at her phone. — The cab is outside.

Lennox knocks back his water and stands up. The last time he saw his mother was at his father's funeral. He freaked out and created a scene. Now she has split up with her long-term lover, Jock Allardyce. Lennox's confusion is evident to Trudi in the furrowed lines of his brow.

On the cab ride through Edinburgh's dim streets as summer retreats, she urges him, — Life is too short, Ray. Be kind and don't get involved in other people's shit.

— Good advice.

Some seek out other people's shit. Others have it thrust upon them.

The traffic is sparse in the twisting, cobbled back roads the driver opts for, and although it's a shoogly fairground ride, they make good time. Trudi looks approvingly as they step onto the gravel outside the huge red sandstone villa in the Grange, greeted by Condor, the increasingly chubby golden Lab. The house belongs to Jackie and her husband, Angus. They are both lawyers, her criminal, him corporate. Lennox notes the lines of deliberation on the forehead of his fiancée. Reckons she's estimating the value of their respective flats and adding their salaries, to calculate the mortgage required to secure a residence like this.

As the dog's barks take on a more threatening pitch, Jackie opens the door. Lennox is taken aback; his sister looks about ten years younger than when he last saw her. Dropping a good few pounds in weight, she's changed her hair, touching up the roots, and has adopted a younger clothing style. — You two are bloody rail-thin, she says, looking them over.

— Looking damn fine yourself, sis, Lennox smiles.

— Yes indeed, Trudi gasps.

— New fasting regime, Jackie bubbles. — You eat anything you like but only between ten and four.

Yet, as they step over the threshold into the vestibule where they hang their coats, Lennox evidences a furrowed-browed tension in his sister. It hits him too. It *is* a special occasion;

their mother, Avril, has left Jock Allardyce. Estranged from her since the debacle of his father's funeral, Lennox enters with trepidation.

You were out of order but Confectioner had messed your head.

Apologise.

No. Don't apologise. Ever.

Acknowledging her boyfriend's shifting eyes and tight lips, Trudi's offers a hand-squeeze, as Lennox casts his mind back to the funeral, where he abused both Avril and her lover, Jock, before tearing off in a blind rage. What happened between his mother and Jock?

He was your old man's best mate and he was shagging his wife.

What a cunt.

What a hoor.

It was Trudi who insisted that he take up Jackie and Angus's offer of the family dinner and make his peace with Avril. — Remember, she whispers, as Jackie ushers them into the lounge, where Angus sits with his mother, showing her the fiercely cheerful-looking Cossack Russian dolls he brought back from a recent trip to Moscow, — life is too short.

Angus greets Trudi, and in addition to the dolls, starts showing her some framed pictures. It's evident to Lennox that her husband doesn't share the glint in his wife's eye.

She's getting her lum swept, and no by Angus.

Lennox takes the cue, nods stiffly and moves reluctantly over to cordially greet his mother, with a tight peck on the cheek. — Son, Avril acknowledges, a watery sadness in her vacant eyes.

It looks like she's doped up on the Vallies . . .

If Jackie has beaten back the years, Avril has nosedived into a brittle-looking old age since Lennox last set eyes on her.

45

Her once smooth skin is breaking down into a desiccated crêpe, evidenced most grotesquely on her bare arms. Condor's whiplashing tail slows down as he sniffs Lennox. The dog then heads to the fire, collapsing on the rug in front of it.

Angus offers them drinks, but Jackie appears, booming over him that the food is ready. They have had an outside caterer prepare the meal. Trudi is excited by some of the displayed photographs, including ones of a cottage. — Isn't that fabulous, Ray?

— Yes, Lennox agrees, thinking of Moira Gulliver and her mutilated brother.

— You guys should go there for a break, Angus says. — Pick up the keys any time. Catch the tail end of the semi-bearable weather.

Trudi squeals in excitement, — That would be brilliant! Ray?

— Sounds good, Lennox agrees.

— We're just waiting on Stuart, as per usual, Jackie says tensely, waving her phone, — but he's on his way. Let's start on the gazpacho.

— Good call, Angus agrees, waving his hand in front of his nose to repel a sudden noxious gas, and shepherding them out of the lounge, as he looks accusingly down at the dog. — It's that special Condor moment . . .

They swiftly head through to the dining room and take their places at the table. Jackie's teenage sons, Fraser and Murdo, join them. It's difficult for Lennox, and the rest of the company, not to overtly note that Fraser is wearing a dress and make-up. Only Angus seems oblivious, but Jackie and Avril are obviously edgy. Trudi steals a nervous glance at Lennox, while Murdo smiles devilishly as strained pleasantries are exchanged.

As the cold soup is served and quickly finished, Lennox

46

shares a frown with his mother, as Stuart, Ray and Jackie's younger sibling, finally arrives. The actor is smaller but broader than his brother, with startled eyes and possessed of a bustling energy. — Well, here's to you, *Mrs Allardyce*, he sings at Avril, kissing her as he hands a bottle of red wine to Jackie. — I see you despatchoed the gazpacho quick enough, he grins.

— Well, you were late. Avril stage-looks at the thin gold watch that dangles on her sun-spotted wrist.

— Did muh soup get cauld? Stuart sniggers, picking the bottle of red wine closest to him and charging his glass with claret. Lennox casts an envious eye. — Enough of that look, Raymondo! I'm celebrating! We had a cast and crew binge-screening of my new show and I think BBC Scotland might be ready to commit to a second series already!

— Which one is this, Stuart? Jackie arches a brow. — Which pearl in this never-ending chain of auditions, castings, first-day shoots, last-day shoots, wrap parties, screenings and premieres that warrant constant celebrations are we on at this particular moment in time?

— My sister's tongue doth drip with impressive scorn today, Angus . . . He turns to his brother-in-law. — Silence your fair maiden with a long and lingering kiss!

Angus rolls his eyes and looks away uncomfortably. — I'm keeping out of this.

— A wise man doth speak. Stuart raises his glass again, giving an exaggerated wink to Jackie. — It's my BBC Scotland sitcom, of course; *Typical Glasgow* – exclamation mark at the end – where I play the Edinburgh New Town snob who takes over a spit-and-sawdust pub right on the border of the East End and Merchant City, and wants to make it into a wine bar, attracting a posher clientele. Obviously the locals have other –

— We remember, Jackie cuts him off with impatience, which surprises Lennox as his sister tends to indulge Stuart as much as she criticises him. But he notes she hasn't taken her eyes off Fraser, and is building up to say something.

It's their mother who gets in first though, as Avril asks her grandson, — What's wrong with that nice jacket I bought you?

The boy glances scathingly at his grandmother. Lennox knows that look and approves. — I'll wear what I choose to wear.

— No, you won't, Jackie stridently shakes her head. She keeps her eyes on the empty soup bowl, but points at the door. — Kindly leave the table and return dressed properly.

— Jackie . . . Angus appeals.

— Just accept me, Mum, Fraser states calmly. — I'm a trans woman. Live with it.

— No. You are not. Jackie glares at him. — When you came out of me, they said: it's a boy. And you know what? They were right. Sometimes I wish they weren't, but they were.

— More reactionary TERF BS, Fraser sighs.

Jackie's teeth hammer together. — I'm a feminist, she looks challengingly around the table, her jaw thrust out, — and kids like him, acting out like this, are dangerous stooges of the patriarchy, attacking women's hard-won rights. She rounds on her son, shaking her head in loathing. — They do not understand the damage they are causing!

— I identify as a trans woman! What's wrong with that?

— You're not a woman!

Angus looks over. — Jackie, leave him be, we were the very same with Bowie.

— Silly entitled little fools with dicks creeping into women's spaces! I'm not having it!

A lit-up Stuart refills a glass Lennox never saw being emptied, and turns to Jackie. — Pray tell, mein schveet schwester, why should it be such a big deal to you how Fritzy chooses to dress?

— Because he's being duped into tacitly supporting a toxic patriarchy and making an absolute fool of himself into the bargain. A pointing spoon goes from Fraser to Stuart. — Don't you bloody well start!

Fraser abruptly rises and leaves the table.

— That's right! Go! Jackie shouts. — Walk away when things get tough. Embrace victimhood!

— Jackie, Angus groans, as they listen to Fraser's feet stomping heavily on the stairs as he makes for his room.

— He was the same wi that stuff wi other men, Avril croaks, looking to Stuart.

— Fraser's *not* with other men, Jackie snaps.

— A shining example of chastity speaks out. Stuart raises his glass in toast to his mother. — Thank you, Mrs Allardyce!

This sets off a round of bickering. Throughout it, Lennox remains silent, looking at his mother.

You saw her in the kitchen, as Jock Allardyce came down the stairs. You weren't supposed to be back so early from your long Saturday bike ride with Les Brodie. But you were. There was an incident, and your knees were skinned.

Lennox realises that he is not only staring at his mother, but she is gaping right back at him. Averts his gaze to his squabbling siblings.

— I wish Fraser was gay, then I could see the sense in it, Jackie is continuing the argument. — But he's had girlfriends, Angelica and then that kooky Leonora. It's an attention-seeking pose, that's all it is!

— Exactly, like us with Bowie, Angus says.

As he feels Trudi's squeeze on his thigh under the table, Lennox's train of thought changes. He thinks of an old police colleague, a tough, hard-drinking cop called Jim McVittie. Jim would eventually induct him into AA, which he didn't like. But through that, he found NA, which was more his style. It was in an old-school roughhouse pub where McVittie told a heavily intoxicated Lennox that he should make that his last drink. Asked him what he was hiding. Lennox reflexively replied that he was hiding nothing. McVittie said to him: 'We're all hiding something.'

We're all hiding something.

— Ray? Jackie's court voice tears him from his thoughts. — What do you think of all this nonsense?

Lennox looks around the table, all eyes hungry for his view. He settles for: — Perhaps we should all try to be more tolerant towards each other. These are difficult times and things are changing rapidly.

— Cop-out, Ray. Jackie is evidently not satisfied, but her muted tone indicates she's glad of the truce, as the main dishes are served up.

Stuart offers a pun: — What do you expect from a cop?

Lennox regards his brother. Stuart's face is bloated with drink. — Ever come across an actor called Norrie Erskine?

Stuart's eyes ignite. — The ex-fitba player! Aye, I did panto with him for a couple of seasons! *Aladdin*. Was he no one of *youse*? Stuart's voice assumes the edge it always does when talking about Lennox's occupation.

Trying not to let it get to him, Lennox says, — Aye, still is.

Stuart responds forcibly, — Disnae surprise me. Cunt was a pest; a sex case. I could tell you some tales –

— Tales we *do not* want to hear at the dinner table, thank you, Stuart, Jackie says.

Lennox is mildly interested, but that was his experience of Stuart's actor friends. The very few that weren't sluts were incels.

Stuart concedes, as Avril starts on about his language. Despite Stuart's spirited defence of the word 'cunt', the rest of the evening passes without incident. As they prepare to go, Lennox announces, — I'm going up to say goodnight to Fraser.

Jackie shrugs, but leaves him to it, contenting herself with getting the coats, as Lennox mounts the stairs. He has always liked the boy, finds him deeper and yet easier to talk to than Murdo. Has taken him to Tynecastle to see Hearts several times. He stifles a chuckle as he thinks about Fraser wearing his current attire in the Wheatfield Stand.

Taps the door. — Hi, pal.

Fraser is sat at his computer, playing some online game. The graphics announce it as Japanese or perhaps Chinese or Korean. On registering his entry, his nephew removes his headset. — I didn't mean to cause a scene, Uncle Ray. It was *her.*

— I'm her wee brother, mate, Lennox says. — She always was a bit 'my way or the highway'.

— Tell me about it, Fraser smiles. — I suppose you're going to say that I'm making a fool of myself and that I don't know my own mind. That I'm a confused youth.

— We're all confused youths, pal. We just get better at covering it up. But we remain teenagers with continually worsening skin. Lennox checks out the Hearts poster on the wall. The old pennant he bought Fraser as a small boy, which is now out of date, not including the last two Scottish Cup wins. He's touched that his nephew keeps it for sentimental value. — So no, I'm not going to tell you that. It's your business and yours alone. And if you do know your own mind, you are doing a damn sight better than most of us.

Fraser nods slowly at his uncle.

— You'll work it out, boss, this life gig, Lennox says, forcing an upbeat tone into his voice. His nephew is almost twenty and a second-year law student at Edinburgh University, yet seems much younger in so many ways. — And when you do, tell me, as I'm struggling with it all, he urges, then considers, — No, tell your uncle Stu first, he's even worse. Anyway, I'll leave you with a happy thought –

— 1902, Fraser laughs.

Lennox winks at his nephew (or his niece now?) and heads back downstairs.

In the taxi home, Trudi expresses her fascination with Fraser's attire, asking Lennox, — Did you ever dress up as a woman?

— No, Lennox lies. Once, in his mother's bedroom, when the family was out, he experimented with full drag.

Trudi seems to consider this for an inordinately long time. They opt to go back to her place, which is nearer. Frisky, she manoeuvres him onto the couch where she starts kissing him deeply. Asks in a low purr, — How would like to dress up as a woman and make love to me?

Lennox laughs, slightly nervously. — I'm not mad into the dressing up as a woman bit, though the other part is fine.

But Trudi is in no mood to let this proposition slide. — C'mon, it'll be fun, c'mon, she urges, thrusting her breasts at him, arching her back, sweeping the hair from her face.

They both know exactly the buttons she is pushing. Lennox scorns his predictability in such situations, even as he enjoys the arousing effect the prospect of this is having on them both. — Well, it's obviously floating your boat, he observes, — so . . .

She rises, grabs his hand and leads him to her bedroom. The Harrington is already discarded, the loafers and straight-legged jeans follow. Setting him down in front of her dresser mirror, Trudi makes up his face, her own intent in concentration. Then she fastens a wig to his head, before squeezing him into a floral summer dress. The garment is tight on him, and she marvels at how loose and billowing it is on her. The pair of

52

cotton panties he tries on dig into his flesh. He wants to go commando, but she insists so he grins and bears it. The shoes are even more problematic, forcing them to concede defeat and keep it barefoot, as Trudi urges him to lie down where she slides her hands up his dress and works down his underpants, to his relief, tossing them aside. — Naughty girl, she says. — No pants in this bedroom.

Lennox cannot believe how erect he is, as she crouches over him, lowering herself slowly onto him. — I'm thinking of your prick as mine, and I'm fucking your fanny with it, she gasps as she starts to work him.

Lying back and letting her do the graft has never been Lennox's thing, but soon his stupefaction increases and he feels a red mist come over his eyes. His pulsing climax travels up through his body, seemingly from the soles of his feet. He struggles to hold on but manages this until Trudi bucks herself into a demented orgasm.

— That was fucking brill, she says, as they lie fizzling in each other's arms.

— Barry, Lennox concedes, slightly annoyed that his postcoital bliss is undermined by a tug in his bladder.

He reluctantly rises and goes for a pee, watching himself with a fascinated interest in the bathroom mirror.

It's all up in the air and everything to play for.

Day Two

Wednesday

5

Lennox rises early, leaving Trudi in bed. He looks at them both through the configuration of mirrors in her en suite bathroom. Then focuses on his face, which he washed last night, unable to obliterate all the traces of make-up. So now he showers, letting a train of thought meander from recent events.

Subduing Gulliver would take a strong man, or a crafty woman. It might have needed both.

One person he and Ritchie Gulliver both have a history with springs to mind. They could offer, at the very least, some insight. Replacing the blue crew-necked jumper with a wine-coloured one he keeps at hers, along with fresh socks and briefs, Lennox retains the Harrington, jeans and shoes. Kissing his sleeping lover softly on the cheek, he exits into a cold Edinburgh morning.

When the cab reaches his home, instead of going upstairs to his flat, Lennox heads for his street-parked Alfa Romeo. As he starts up and drives off, the car heater raises the temperature satisfyingly. Halts only once at a service station on his route west to fill up the tank and pick up a black coffee.

Stirling is a 1960s-built campus university near Bridge of Allan. It resembles Lennox's old alma mater, Heriot-Watt, where he was one of the first Computer Studies graduates to be sponsored by the Edinburgh police force. It's a soulless affair of cheap utilitarian design, thrown up to accommodate the expansion of the working and lower-middle classes into higher education at that time. Nonetheless, the university is located in a beautiful setting. Built in the grounds of Airthrey Castle, it lies in the foothills of the Ochils, around a loch, and is over-looked by the Wallace Monument. It gained a reputation in the seventies and eighties of being Scotland's most radical campus. By the time Lennox arrives, the sun is rising, and to his eyes, it seems a pedestrian greenfield site with all the ambience of a business park. Students trudge wearily to lectures like factory workers putting in an early shift, and he detects scant revolutionary fervour in the air.

Lauren Fairchild, a lecturer in Gender Studies, greets him in a pleasant, plant-swathed office with large windows that overlook the campus and adjoining parkland. Its expansive, rolling and verdant nature makes the university less jaundiced in his eyes; it might be a decent place to learn and work after all. The room is full of shelved books and three tasteful Cannes Film Festival prints adorn the walls. Lennox has known Lauren, a post-operative transgender woman, many years, most of them in her previous life as DS Jim McVittie. He eyes the posters in relief, garnering some connection with the past: like Jim, Lauren is a film buff. Otherwise, there is little resemblance between the two. If to completely physically change into another person was the objective, then, posters aside, Lauren's transition is a roaring success. On the outside she seems as serene a woman as McVittie was turbulent a man. It compels Lennox to think of Fraser. To wonder if this is the journey they are on.

It appears that he's the only colleague that Lauren, now an expert in the 'criminology of gender', has stayed in touch with during her transition. And now, she explains, she's undertaken the final reassignment. — I've gone all the way, Ray, she smiles. — Would you like to see my pussy? Despite the softer voice, the blunt playfulness evokes McVittie.

— Yes, Lennox responds. Instantly he thinks: *you're still trying to prove yourself after shiteing it in that tunnel.*

Lauren rises and moves away from the window. As she pulls up her pantyless dress, Lennox is suddenly swamped with an image of Gulliver's bloodstained stump and wriggling tendons, but all that's on display is a shaved, perfect-looking vagina. — It's as tight as a fucking drum, she boasts.

— This is the point where I really do take your word, Lennox declares deadpan, as Lauren giggles. — Any regrets?

— That I didn't do it sooner. She smooths her dress and heads over to a sink to fill up a machine and make some coffee. They catch up on old times and he gets a sense of her new life. She talks about the ongoing struggle with alcohol. — It's part of Jim's inheritance that I do have to be vigilant about. No, you can't transition your genes.

For some reason Stuart's conversation springs to mind, and Lennox asks Lauren if she remembers Norrie Erskine.

— Wasn't he the panto guy? she hesitantly ventures. — Gillman's partner?

— Oh yes he was, Lennox screws up his face acknowledging the cheesy shot, and sips at the coffee. Another McVittieism Lauren has retained is a love of strong coffee. It is hitting him like a rail of cocaine.

She looks at Lennox with an arched brow and asks him, — So if I *could* do you, Ray, what could I do you for?

Lennox laughs, both disconcertingly and comfortingly. McVittie was a master of double entendres; Lauren might be a little rusty. He asks her about Ritchie Gulliver.

— Surprise, surprise. Lauren sits back in her chair. Raises the coffee mug and takes a sip. — Gulliver is a piece of shit. He is provocatively transphobic. He portrayed the odd damaged extremist as the norm, and did untold damage to our movement, with his smirking oafish act, and she's now deadly serious. — Yes, there are deluded, misogynistic narcissists who have attached themselves to our cause. These toxic men

59

are our enemies, just as much as they are the enemies of other women. The likes of them and Gulliver feed off each other. He's responsible for a lot of misery with his hate speech. I'd attribute three deaths directly to rabble-rousing sermons he made.

— Somebody carried out a far less skilled sex-change operation on him than you've undergone.

Lauren looks perplexed, her brow furrowing in spite of what Lennox judges to be advanced Botox. — That body in Leith . . . that was him?

— Aye. Stripped, bound, castrated and left to bleed out.

— Wow . . . Lauren gasps, then composes herself. — I'm not going to lie, Ray, there's part of me who thinks you reap what you sow, but it's no good for our movement to be possibly associated with that kind of violence . . .

As Lauren talks on, Lennox is confronted with the limits of his own ignorance. Terms like 'TERF' and 'cis' are meaningless to him, and hold little interest. He doesn't have any real concept of the difference between sex and gender. A cursory phone briefing from Drummond, who's up on this stuff, made it sound simpler than it probably is. Sex is biological, while gender is a cultural construct relating to our feelings and beliefs about the first. But those are in constant flux. The world is getting increasingly complex. He'll resolve to learn more.

At least wi perverts noncing bairns, you ken where you stand: on the side of good versus evil.

— Did you have any personal dealings with Gulliver?

— He scheduled a talk at the campus two weeks back. It was one of those bad faith 'free speech' events, where abuse is disguised as the right to offend, in order to provoke a reaction. I got involved in it, as I didn't want to cancel him. So, we debated, if you could call it that. It didn't end well. Factions, as they say, clashed. Our friends in blue were called. Lauren's eyes pull into sharper focus. — But then you know this, Ray. And we both know that someone who has publicly denounced Gulliver has to be at least of interest to your inquiry.

Lennox did, and is about to apologise for being disingenuous, almost ready to respect Lauren by telling her that he struggles to connect her with Jim McVittie, when there is a loud knock at the door.

What appears to be a brawny young man of around six foot four in a blue dress not so much enters as bulldozes in, a charged storm of bristling rage. He has a big hooked nose, and long, flowing brown hair, which seems to have been given the attention of crimping tongs fashionable in the eighties. On his face, a long scar bubbles thickly from under a trowelling of foundation. He has a thick neck covered by a chiffon scarf, and beefy wrists adorned with colourful bracelets. He regards Lennox, his face pinching in an aggressive distrust.

— Oh, hello, Gayle, Lauren says. — Ray, this is Gayle, who is both a student here and mainstay in our No Platform group.

Gayle maintains his hostile glare. For his transitioning to be regarded as successful, Lennox considers it would require a massive societal readjustment as to what constitutes femininity. As he looks from Lennox to Lauren, she seems to be slightly intimidated. This concerns him: Jim McVittie was never easily spooked.

— We need to talk, Gayle demands, hands on hips, the paint-stripping stare unremitting.

Lauren remains composed. Looks at her watch. — Give me half an hour, please.

Gayle nods curtly and turns in silent departure.

— Students can be a little entitled these days, Lauren observes. — I tend to overindulge, as there isn't much down for most of them, except debt and mental illness. I'm currently supervising their dissertation on trans self-determination and social justice. It's a challenging work.

— I can imagine, Lennox says, rising and thanking Lauren for her time. — Give me the usual alibi stuff in an email, he says, before remembering his breaking of Gulliver's covert relationship with Graham Cornell, then a suspect in the Britney Hamil murder committed by Confectioner, — . . . and I'll work on my own. Given my history with the deceased, I'm more likely to be under suspicion than you. Lennox smiles, leaving his new and former friend, to drive back to Edinburgh.

6

If there's one thing we both excel at, it's the gathering of information. That has been a constant thread throughout our respective working lives. We put a hell of a lot of time and effort into planning that first one.

I was positioned in the hotel bathroom's big walk-in laundry cupboard. She had picked the place for that feature, but also the renovation work they had going on in the hallway outside. With my customary awkwardness, I set my phone to record.

She's so damn good. The Venetian mask – all her idea – was a masterstroke. I confess I thought this too theatrical, then I worried that she wouldn't be able to pull it off (no pun intended), but she was so calm. Would he have recognised her without the mask? Impossible to say. But she was right not to leave this to chance.

And she was correct when she said you could remove a man's genitals easily in conditions of extreme heat.

Well, almost. He got away. Mr Ice-Blue Eyes got away. But not quite intact.

I watched him get into the hot bubble bath with her; his specs, still on, steamed up, concealing those eyes from me. He complained, wincing all the way as he lowered his pudgy body into the water. Such a contrast to her sleek, seal-like skin as she sank in, bubbles covering the nipples of her perfect breasts like a soft-porn shot. If the stakes hadn't been so damned high, and I didn't have the difficulty of filming it (everything needs to be archived), I swear I'd have jerked off in there. I reckon she was also turned on big time by what we were doing, though I might just be projecting. — I like it hot, she said to him, the sinew and musculature extending from her clavicle as she reached for his prick, — no time for the cold.

He gasped lightly, backhandedly wiping his steamed lenses, and even through the door's wooden slats I could see his blue eyes roll, the brows arching over his spec frames.

Her other hand was on the sharp eight-inch blade she'd concealed under the thick blisters of foam. The look on his face . . . like surprise and curiosity morphing into disbelief, then terror, as the water turned red . . . well, that was an absolute joy to behold.

She had done it! Or so I thought.

Then he sprang up, bent over and screaming, holding his dick and balls tightly to him as the blood poured into the bath. I realised she hadn't been able to totally detach them, and he jumped out the tub, still cupping them, running from the room!

We did not bargain for this!

It compelled her to hop out and wrap herself in a towel, heading to the room to throw her clothes on; a short dress covered by a long black coat. She quickly came back, having kicked her heels off into her bag, replacing them with pumps, as I exited the cupboard. — Give me one minute, she said, her mask still on.

I had frozen: torn between vengeance, going after him and finishing the job, and the fear that we would be apprehended. I gave her less than thirty seconds before I panicked and followed her outside, pushing aside the plastic sheeting hung in the passage by the construction people. When I got down the fire stairs to the lobby the place was in pandemonium and there was no sign of her. A trail of blood led from the lift across to the reception, where he had fallen onto the tiled floor. Horrified hotel guests and staff were bobbing about, some of them bunching around him.

They called an ambulance, but as we'd anticipated, he hesitated to get the police involved. His own people were on hand soon enough. They were professionals; the panic only evident in their shifty eyes as they secured him onto a stretcher, as who I presumed was a doctor wrapped him up down below, in order to prevent further blood loss. Of course the police came, but by then, like her, I had slipped away.

Whatever happens to us, I'll never forget our first one. Pity we didn't get his piece. Yes, Ritchie Gulliver might have been chapter one, but Christopher Piggot-Wilkins was one hell of a prologue. And it was the one I'd been waiting for.

On the empty early-morning road, it took Lennox no time at all to get to Stirling. Coming back in the rush-hour traffic, jerky with Lauren's coffee, it isn't quite so easy, especially with the high-pitched voice of Perry 'Squeak' Mortimer on the speakerphone rattling around the car.

The attack on the almost-castrated London 'businessman' by the Venetian masked hooker is of great interest to Lennox. Practically all he knows about it is that it took place at the Savoy Hotel. The stories about an anonymous naked man running into the lobby screaming, clasping his genitals, blood gushing through his fingers, hit some excited tabloids. But they were all gone the next day with no follow-up. Only real wealth and power can buy that sort of sudden disinterest. Britain operates a two-tier system of justice. Money and connections serve to keep law enforcement officers out of your life. As a cop, Lennox knows he always has to leave a softer footprint in that world.

Establishment sex offenders have always interested him. Britain is essentially a nonce state; young bodies are seen as rewards for wealthy paedophiles, who have to be protected at all costs. Trawling for information, Lennox got on the phone to Mortimer, a Metropolitan Police contact. — Who was the victim, this so-called businessman?

— We've a block on giving that info out, Ray, Mortimer predictably tells him. A cheerful man whom Lennox has met on many courses, he guesses that Squeak's unflattering nickname would not be appreciated. Therefore, he always makes the point of calling him Perry. It has been successful in eliciting cooperation.

— C'mon, Perry, give me something, buddy!

There's a silence on the tinny speaker for a couple of beats, before Mortimer's high voice intones, — You know it's a bigwig, Ray, that's a given. Don't even try to ferret politics, corporate, royalty or showbiz out of me. It's steel-ring time.

— Who's leading the investigation?

— They appointed a guy called Phil Barnard, but he went on sick leave and wasn't replaced. They've been dragging their feet about getting somebody else in, but the word is they're doing it now; obviously your case has rekindled interest . . .

— You have to be joking. Do fuck all and let the trail go cold for two weeks? That's utter nonsense!

Squeak Mortimer's silence speaks volumes.

— Okay . . . Lennox finds himself flooring the accelerator. — Any word on who they'll appoint?

— Dunno yet, Squeak trills, — will tip you off soon as I do.

— Anything else?

— Not a lot, mate, the shrill voice bores into Lennox's eardrums. — Except it was a she, though he didn't see her face as she was wearing a mask. That was the sole piece of info from the victim. The CCTV was disabled on the ground floor for a system repair. On level four, where the incident occurred, renovations were taking place, so the view of the perp is obscured by the plastic sheeting the builders had up.

— So she must have had inside info. Can I get a look at the footage?

— C'mon, Ray, I can't access that, let alone leak it. You'll have to talk to whoever is heading up the investigation. As I

67

say, I'll let you know as soon as I learn who that is. I've already given you more than my pension's worth, so for God's sake stop before it's instant dismissal!

Lennox grins into his rear mirror. — I hear you, bud. Where did the hooker come from?

— It was the playboy's birthday and he believed a friend had ordered her from an agency specialising in role play. Colleagues, they're called, based in King's Cross. But they denied all knowledge.

Lennox vaguely knows of the agency from joint ops with Vice. It's located in a backstreet that has escaped Eurostar gentrification. He thanks Mortimer, as he looks up notable birthdays around the date of the assault, before calling a press contact.

Sebastian Taylor is now known as a down-at-heel reporter on the *Standard*. But he was something of a minor hero of Lennox's back in the nineties, for his establishment noncing exposés in pieces for the *Guardian* and *Sunday Times*.

He gets through, but Taylor's voice is strange and his rambling tone makes no sense. All he can make out is, — Email . . . and Lennox gives his address.

Lennox suspects chronic alcoholic burnout. But before twenty minutes has elapsed an email pops into his inbox:

To: RLennox@policescot.co.uk
From: staylor125@gmail.com
Subject: Apologies

Dear Ray,

Delighted to hear from you. Please excuse my performance on the phone. I can assure you that I drink nothing stronger than soda water and lime these days – more's the pity.

Unfortunately the culprit is Parkinson's disease which I have had for several years, and which has adversely affected my speech. This is now by far the best way to communicate with me.

How can I be of help to you?

Best,

Sebastian

A guilty Lennox types more in hope than expectation. Taylor might have been out of the investigation loop for some time.

Just as he sends it off, a text from Toal pops into his phone:

Come and see me when
you get a minute.

It's an oddly placid missive from his boss, especially when a major investigation is under way. Where is the imperative 'now'? Ray Lennox is yet again disconcerted, as he pulls into the car park at Police HQ, happily noting that it's still short of ten o'clock.

When he reaches the office and switches on his computer, Drummond enters, heads straight over to him, pulling up a chair. She looks around and drops her voice. — Ray . . .

— What you got?

— I've been talking to some of Gulliver's political associates –

— God, I can't think of anything worse . . . how is that working out?

— Tory politicians: evasive when not blatantly lying. But the corporate associations are the ones that are more interesting. Particularly Samuels, a pharmaceutical company who are trying to land a big contract to sell a sedative to the NHS.

Lennox raises his brows to urge her to continue.

Drummond's eyes scan the office again. Then she hisses, — He was as bent as fuck. He was paving the way for them to sell their shit to the NHS. He would have been rewarded handsomely and promoted to junior health minister had he sealed the deal. Prior to entering Westminster, he was a paid consultant for Samuels. He had opposition from another senior Tory, Mark Douglas, who wanted a rival drug patented by a firm called ATF Pharmaceutical, whom he's associated with.

Castration seems excessive, even for corporate rivalries. But who else would care enough? The British public remain blithely unconcerned that the Tories shamelessly pilfer their tax pounds. Indeed, Rupert Murdoch and the BBC have done such a comprehensive job over the years that this is accepted with a resigned shrug. — So Douglas's camp might have done Gulliver to ensure their fortune?

— It's a motive, but it's a tough investigation.

— It needs a tactfulness with those establishment snobs that I don't possess, Lennox confesses. His gut is telling him that there is enough in the public purse for both Douglas and Gulliver to carry on looting, so vice is more likely than money to have led to the latter's demise, even if they were parallel tracks on the line for him. — Well, if you keep on the money angle and I keep on the sleaze, we'll uncover something.

He briefs her on his approach, and, wishing her well, is happy to leave her to the corporate and political minefield. Experience has told him such people quickly close ranks.

With any luck you'll talk yourself out of that promotion . . . or maybe into it.

8

On walking into Bob Toal's office Lennox notes his boss's uncharacteristic lack of agitation. He assumed Toal's tension would be ramped up by his impending retirement, as cops tended to want to go out on a high. However, his chief's desk is festooned with old-school print brochures of exotic locales. — So the media haven't kicked off, Lennox says.

Normally this seems to be Toal's primary concern. He's always on to the *Record*, *News*, *Sun*, *Express*, Radio Forth, BBC Scotland, STV, begging them to be judicious and sparing in the reporting of any case designated high-profile. But the Serious Crimes chief shrugs minimally. — They'll do what they do. What I need *you* to do *right now*, and Toal's voice suddenly ignites in its defining urgency, — is go down to London for a couple of days and get what you can on this Savoy attack. Find out if it's at least attempted castration. If so, we're in business. The Met aren't up for divulging anything, yet they want us to give them all our files. He brandishes a manila folder. — Fucking arrogant English bastards! I'm not pro-independence, Ray, but these are the sort of attitudes that turn people. No wonder those SNP cunts are laughing their tits off with useless fuckers like that helping them to break up Britain!

Another surprise. Toal seldom, if ever, talked politics. Besides, there is nothing new or even particularly untoward in the Met's attitude. Inter-police-force rivalry is as old as the hills. The Gulliver murder is getting big media headlines, so both forces want the glory. — So I head down there, see what info I can trade, what possible connections there are between the two cases?

— Yes. Exactly that.

— Who is the Met guy dealing with it?

Just as he asks, a text from Squeak Mortimer pops into his phone.

> The man heading the investigation
> is Mark Hollis. Good luck!

— Mark Hollis, Toal confirms, looking at his iPad. — Quite a character, by most stories.

Lennox nods, leaving his boss's office to head downstairs to Accounts. He asks them to book him onto the London City airport shuttle, knowing that if he paid himself and claimed back, it would take months for the expenses to be processed. As he waits for his e-ticket to be issued, he calls Squeak. — What's the story with Mark Hollis, Perry?

— Old school as it gets. Mr Marmite: certainly not to everyone's taste, Mortimer squeals in high fluster. — They've been trying to get rid of him or promote him for years. No success in either. Rumour has it there are some people he actually likes. You never know, he might warm to you! He won't be happy being on this, he'll feel like he's being set up to fail, or at least to rubber-stamp a charade.

— Right . . . Lennox says. — Thanks, Perry. Can you spot me his digits?

— Pinging them your way. Play nice, Squeak offers, hanging up. Almost instantly Hollis's contact details pop in.

On dialling, Lennox is met with a gravelly voice. — Mark Hollis's answerphone. I don't like voice messages, so I ain't

72

responding ta nothing ya leave here. Text me and I'll get back to ya. Otherwise, see ya around.

Just what I need, a cockney Gillman figure who will probably resent the fuck out of me being on his patch.

Lennox shoots Hollis a text, receiving a terse one back, offering an early-evening meeting in a Soho pub that's known to him. Then he calls an old friend, George Marsden, who grandly suggests afternoon tea. When he gets back up to the office, Lennox fires up his computer searching through the CCTV footage around Leith docks at the time of the murder. Most of the licence plates already seem to check out as legit.

He is aware of somebody standing over his shoulder. It's Toal. This is unusual. If his boss wants to talk, he does the summoning.

— You get booked up for London?

— Aye, just went down to Accounts. I'm getting the one o'clock –

— Get out of here right now, Toal urges, veering so close to Lennox, the strong whiff of his boss's Blue Stratos bends in his nostrils. — I've heard you're getting a visit from Internal Investigations. It's not an external IOPC affair, just officers sent in from another force. Get out of the way. But if they do pull you in, please cooperate.

Lennox's expression tells its own story.

— Pretty bizarre, Toal softly ventures, — but they have to eliminate you from the suspects list. You and Gulliver do have history.

— For fuck sake . . .

— It's just protocol, Ray. Toal looks around, drops his voice to a whisper. — So bags of tact if they see you. But as I say, go. Now. London. Remember the promotion interview is on

73

Monday. We don't want any dirt on your file before then. He pats Lennox's shoulder and takes his leave.

It doesn't take long.

As his boss departs, Lennox heads to the gents for a piss. On his way back to his desk to pick up his stuff, he finds two men standing waiting for him. The foremost, squat, bullish and about forty, asks, — Could you come with us?

Several people in the office look round. Ironically, the solidarity comes from Dougie Gillman, who moves over. He hates internal investigators and can scent them a mile away. — What's the fuckin story? You need Inglis as Fed Rep here, Lenny?

Lennox looks at the men. — I'm hoping that won't be the case. Gentlemen?

— No, it's just routine, the thinner, nervier man stumbles, and is met with a reprimanding gaze from his partner.

— I've got him on speed dial, just in case. Lennox holds up his phone to Gillman, who nods and departs. He looks at the investigators. — Lead on, gentlemen.

Follows them into one of the interview rooms. No tape is switched on. Offered a seat, Lennox declines, standing against the wall. Regards the two men. — So, I'm a suspect in the death of Ritchie Gulliver, MP.

— Why don't you take a seat, DI Lennox?

— Because I prefer to stand.

Letting out a long hiss of air, the thickset man sluggishly uncurls to his feet. — Very well. Your father was a senior union official in ASLEF, he declares. — Also a card-carrying member of the Communist Party.

Lennox, slapping his thigh, guffaws loudly. — My old man? Fuck off!

— What's so funny?

— Youse boys, playing at being 1950s FBI agents!

— We're not playing, Thickset declares, as Thin Boy visibly wilts. — His membership is on record.

— If that's the case, Lennox, in continuing amusement, shakes his head, — and I'm massively unconvinced, then I genuinely did not know that. I'd always pegged him right wing. But then for much of his life he was sexually impotent, bitter, old and tired, and he looks straight at Thickset. — Easy mistake, I suppose.

The chunky cop gazes steadily back at him. — Ritchie Gulliver. Are you really trying that hard to find his killer?

— I'm trying a lot fucking harder than you, playing at being toytown McCarthyites. Honestly, is this how you cunts spend your time? He grabs the door handle. — So on that note, the one of genuine criminal investigation, if you'll excuse me . . .

Thickset is vexed. — It would be in your interests to cooperate with us!

— Get tae fuck, Lennox scorns. — I've a plane to catch *right now*, and a load of prep to do en route. So arrest me and obstruct the fuck out of my investigation of the murder of a former member of the Police Committee. That will look good on your files, and he hold up his arms. The two investigators glance at each other. — If you've a warrant I won't resist, he shakes his wrists, — but if not, I'll consider it an assault and you might lose some teeth.

He turns and heads out, leaving Thin Boy bemused and Thickset affronted in his silent apoplexy.

Way to talk yourself out of promotion . . . bags of tact, my arse . . .

Leaving the Alfa Romeo at the Police HQ car park, Lennox grabs a cab. No time to change, he heads straight out to the airport. Toiletries will be picked up there. Checks his phone, learns from Gordon Burt's email that the toxicology report shows that Gulliver's bloodstream contained both alcohol and drugs. His frontal head wound was made by a mallet, *after* he was drugged.

Why did they want us to go down the alley of Rab Dudgeon, the Carpenter of Lunacy . . . was it to show that they know the MO of our most notorious criminals . . . ?

When caught up with his emails and texts, he occupies himself in his customary way, flicking through the names and mugshots on the 'Beasts' Regie', the Sex Offenders Register. Disembarking at his preferred airport of London City, Lennox heads across town to the Dorchester Hotel on Park Lane to meet his old friend George Marsden.

Feeling massively underdressed in his Harrington and blue jeans, he practically skates along the tiled floor in his loafers to the grand mahogany reception desk, enquiring where afternoon tea is being served. A concierge directs him to the spacious grill, where, at a corner table, he immediately discerns George, as straight-backed as ever, with his luxuriant mop of grey hair. Afternoon tea is neatly cut sandwiches, cakes, scones, jam and clotted cream stacked on an ornate silver platter stand. His friend is wearily surveying the surroundings in the plush restaurant, as if to the manner born. On seeing Lennox approaching, his face lights up. Though no longer a cop, George was invested heavily in the Mr Confectioner case. Lennox, by bringing the despised child murderer to book, also retrospectively vindicated his friend. George resigned from Hertfordshire Police, believing that they had put the wrong man away for the murder of Nula Andrews, and the Manchester girl, Stacey Earnshaw. It was Lennox who, in finding the killer of Britney Hamil, proved George Marsden's hypothesis: Confectioner killed them all. — There he is, George booms as Lennox advances. — My favourite copper!

— Great to see you, Lennox says, and it is. He always

enjoys spending time with George. Despite one man coming from a Scottish housing scheme and the other an English public school, they are strangely birds of a feather. Combatants for justice, miscast in the role of law enforcement officers.

— Swanky, Lennox says, slipping into the seat beside George.

— I love this place, George purrs, sipping at his tea. — It was one of Thatcher's choice haunts, till it all went pear-shaped and she started eating the wallpaper and pissing over the carpets, exploited by the low-paid carers she had reduced to penury. George enjoys a satisfied grin, tapping the big silver teapot with his spoon. — So . . . who has the Met got leading this case?

— A guy called Mark Hollis.

George spits out his tea. Looks around, flustered, hoping none of the busy waiting staff have observed this, as he tries to clean up the mess. — Sorry, Ray . . . but that is funny. His eyes glint with mischief. — I take it you haven't met Hollis?

— No. What's he like?

George looks thoughtfully at his Scottish friend. — He's a bit like you: a 'whatever-it-takes' sort. The book is an inconvenience. He grins widely. — I suspect he enjoys his job in a strange way, and probably hates the rest of his life.

— Thanks.

— You're welcome. George trains his gaze on Lennox. — Said it before, will say it again: jack this nonsense in and come down to Eastbourne and partner with me in security. I've a ton of work and I could do with a hand.

— You really think that type of work is me?

— Well, I do know that this Serious Crimes stuff is *not* you any more, Raymond.

Lennox displays a picture of Trudi on his phone. Passes it to George. It's one of his favourites, her soft blonde-brown hair whipping in the wind, a toothsome smile. Taken at Dunbar. — But she is, and her career is blooming.

George raises an appreciative brow. — We have gas in England too, Ray. Let me be mother . . . He adds some hot water from a smaller silver pot into the big one, stirring with the spoon as he hands the phone over to Lennox, who reaches for it. Almost inexplicably, it slips between the hands of both men and falls into the large teapot.

— FUCK, Lennox roars, occasioning the turning of heads.

A hovering waiter, solid and unflappable, picks up the silver vessel and runs to the kitchen. Ray Lennox is hot on his heels. The server pours the contents of the pot into a large Belfast sink, into which the phone drops. The waiter lifts it out, his stinging fingers spasming as he lowers it to the worktop, wrapping it in kitchen roll. The surface of the device is dry, but it's stone dead.

A flabbergasted Lennox takes the phone back to the dining room. Places it on a radiator by their table.

George has the demeanour of a cheerful man trying hard to appear crestfallen at the turn of events. — It'll probably start working again when it dries out. If not it'll mean a trip to the Apple Store, or one of those repair booths on Tottenham Court Road might be able to do something.

Lennox shrugs it off as the waiter returns with another pot of tea.

Only mildly distracted by Lennox intermittently looking to his phone on the radiator for signs of ignition, they tuck into the towering, massively expensive platter. Lennox is relieved that George insists it will be his treat, though part of him would love to see Toal's reaction at signing off on an expenses form containing afternoon tea from the Dorchester. It is highly enjoyable and he scarcely notices the elegant woman approaching the table until she is next to them. She wears an expensive-looking blue cashmere coat, which she removes and is about to put on the back of a chair when a waiter runs over and takes it from her. As she thanks him and sits down, Lennox admires her trim body in a long, tight oatmeal skirt and a fulvous ribbed polo neck. — Ah, Monica, this is Ray.

— Hi, Monica, Lennox says, already feeling like he's playing gooseberry. It's obvious that George has had a prior rendezvous here with this woman, and he reckons they've booked a room to spend the night together.

— Hello, Ray, she says in a low, throaty purr, as Lennox catches her squeezing George's thigh.

— Are you going to have a scone? Lennox invites.

She looks with amused interest at their plates and the silver platter with its adornments. — Oh no, I'll wait until dinner before I eat, she informs him, — but I shall join you both. I'll have a cup of coffee.

George points to a long silver pot, close to the chunky one he poured the tea from. — Already ordered for you, my darling, he declares, a twinkle in his eye.

— Isn't he wonderful, Ray?

— I've heard this said often, though usually by George himself. But yes, he's not bad at all, Lennox concedes.

— From anyone else, faint praise. But from a Scotsman, that's like a cascade of angels serenading me through the gates of heaven. George kisses his own fingers and bursts them into a star.

The food hits the spot and the company is good. Following Monica's lead, Lennox has switched to the coffee, which starts to alleviate his slight travel fatigue. He has to pull himself away and get on with his business. Picking up the still-dormant phone, he turns to George and Monica. — They say 'my life is in that phone' and it's true.

George looks mournfully at him. — It'll work out.

Lennox raises his brows in disbelief, says his farewells, and heads outside, taking a cab to nearby Soho.

While admiring his friend's sense of the good things in life, Lennox prefers the atmospheric old Soho pubs that are still holding on; the French House, the Blue Posts, the Nellie Dean, the Ship, the Coach and Horses, the Dog and Duck. It's the last where Mark Hollis has arranged to meet him, after that most perfunctory of texts. Phoneless, he prays Hollis hasn't revised the plans.

9

A tourist, mounting the steps of Edinburgh's famous Scott Monument, got more than he bargained for when scaling the old column. Tom Quincey, 62, of Delaware, USA, was surprised to feel something slap him in the face, as he turned the corner of a narrow passageway inside the capital's renowned Gothic structure. To his horror, when he looked up he saw the offending item was a male set of genitals, hung right in front of his face. 'I stood there for a few seconds in shock. I could not believe my eyes.'

It's been speculated that this horror may be related to the recent mutilated body found in an abandoned Leith warehouse. Edinburgh Police have refused to confirm this. Chief Superintendent Robert Toal of the Serious Crimes Division said: 'As our investigations into this matter are ongoing it would be inappropriate to comment further at this stage.'

We could have nailed Gulliver's parts to the House of Commons but then nobody would have heard a word about it. That's the way those creeps and the supine arsehole pawns of the media-owning absentee billionaires close ranks. But I don't think we've done so bad at grabbing attention!

I'm glad we picked Edinburgh, despite his initial reluctance to come here. Of course, I was aware that it had bad associations for him. It hardly has great ones for me either, though needs must. But, well, he really ought to have trusted his intuition.

The blue-eyed boy Piggot-Wilkins was the one I had really wanted. But Ritchie Gulliver is even more exciting, in that he constitutes our first unmitigated success. While I must take credit for luring him up to Edinburgh, and right into her lair, the supreme irony is that the fool initially came to me. I heard through associates that he wished to engage the services, not of a biographer, but a *ghostwriter*. Had it not been him I would have been very insulted. As it was, I was delighted to make contact through an intermediary. Our first phone conversation did nothing to dispel his reputation as someone highly susceptible to flattery. It was easy to feed him bullshit about his interesting career, and the importance of telling the *real* story of such an uncompromising straight shooter. Yet again, as with Piggot-Wilkins, it was his insistence that we keep our phone calls secret.

I told him I respected his privacy, but in London's political and journalistic circles walls did have ears. We knew of his wariness of Edinburgh, his shabby affair, which wrecked his career in that city. As with Christopher Piggot-Wilkins, she knew absolutely everything about Ritchie Gulliver. But yes, I convinced him over the phone that Edinburgh was the place for us.

So I came up on the same sleeper train as Gulliver, even observing him in the restaurant car without making myself known to him. I attempted to connect him with the depraved Alpine skier I'd heard about from her. Like I did when I tried to tally Piggot-Wilkins with the young boy I'd known in Tehran, whose father was a senior official at the British Embassy. In Gulliver's case, I did this through his gaze: the entitled and condescending way he looked at the member of staff who served him the whisky he requested.

We met face-to-face for the first time at his hotel room over breakfast. Eggs royale for him and kippers for me. I knew he only drank Macallan, and I presented him with our doctored bottle. I was briefly troubled as a spectral snigger played across his bloodless lips and sly eyes. Had he made me, perhaps through hearing of the Piggot-Wilkins attack? Had the blue-eyed boy been in touch with Gulliver, urging

82

vigilance? Did they even remain on good terms? But in spite of his perennial sneer, the MP maintained his casual demeanour. As we chatted, I saw him fixate on my hand; men like him instinctively scope out what they perceive to be weakness in others. I resolved he would soon find out how wrong he was to think of it that way.

As I switched on the recorder, I couldn't believe my luck when he immediately opened the Macallan. I thought I'd have to talk for an hour before suggesting a drink. I told him it was a little early for me, but he should carry on if it loosened him up.

It certainly did. Just at the point where he was slowly passing out, I asked him if he skied. I don't think he even registered this as he slumped back onto the chaise longue in his suite. She'd placed the laundry basket outside the room. I wheeled it in and loaded him into it. He was out of shape, but still light for a man of my size and strength. I took it downstairs in the service lift and pushed it out into the back of the van. It was still early and I never saw another soul, bar hearing some staff in the kitchen preparing breakfasts. Then I drove Ritchie Gulliver MP out to the warehouse.

She had arranged this perfect space. Another client of hers was a manager at the Forth Ports Authority, who had told of all the empty warehousing in Leith docks. People tell her everything, as they do me. That's what makes us such great partners. That's why we write this story together.

Of course, I'm more than a little in love with her. How could you not be?

10

Trudi Lowe has just come from a meeting on the promotion of a recently developed gas payment plan for pensioners. As she chats to the newest member of the management team, Dean Slattery, her phone rings. The laboured, halting breathing of her mother immediately tells Trudi that something is wrong.
— It's your dad . . . he collapsed . . . been taken to the Royal . . . I think it's his heart . . .

— I'm on my way . . . and she hangs up and looks in miserable trepidation at Dean. — It's my dad . . .

A handsome, but light-hearted man, Dean is always ready with an amusing quip. But witnessing her pain, he shows her another gear. — Come on, I'll drive you there.

In the car, Trudi, her stomach curdling, tries to call Lennox. It goes straight to voicemail. She texts, then calls Jackie.

— No, I don't know where he is, he never calls me, her fiancé's sister explains. — But you know how it is with Ray and work . . . Trudi, what's wrong?

Trudi breathlessly informs her. A sympathetic Jackie tells her she will keep trying her brother.

Dean drives swiftly through the streets, as Radio Forth announces on the car stereo:

'The police investigation into the body found in a warehouse at Leith docks yesterday is ongoing. So far the details of the victim have yet to be revealed.'

Scarcely registering this, Trudi does not connect it with Ray Lennox. All she can think of is her father, and how distraught her mother must be.

When she gets to the ward, her first impression is that he is desperately sick. Multiple tubes come from him, going into machines and drip bags. One spasm, cutting off some blood, and he's instantly rendered weaker, frailer and older. Her mother, sitting by his side, sobbing, rises and grabs her. — Our baby girl, she keeps repeating as she strokes her daughter's hair.

Dean, nervously hovering at the door of the two-person ward, swiftly takes a coffee order and heads to the cafeteria.

Trudi holds her mother, who herself seems enfeebled by the trauma, as they regard the almost formless grey figure in the bed. She looks at the sparkling ring on her finger.

Where is Ray?
This band of gold on my hand: what does it even mean?
Where is he?

11

Cutting through Soho's narrow streets, tight on the side of buildings to avoid a sudden rain shower, Lennox, devoid of a functioning phone, again prays that Mark Hollis hasn't re-arranged the time or venue. Or that the Met man would look unrecognisably different to the younger photo he's seen online. Walking into the Dog and Duck, he makes for the bar. Then looks around. Discerns Hollis straight away.

He's the man sat on a leather seat under a big mirror, wearing a Green Bay Packers sweatshirt under an open black Puffa jacket. Drinks a pint of Stella like the fizzing one thrust into Lennox's fist by the barman, which he scarcely recalls ordering. As Lennox places his drink on the table in a *snap* moment, they exchange nods and assessments.

It isn't like staring at his reflection. Though they are both around six foot, the brawny Mark Hollis carries a good thirty pounds more on his frame than Ray Lennox, much of it on an expansive gut. Bushy, untrimmed brows accentuate a receding hairline. His longer face is decorated with a too-oft-broken nose, and is pitted with acne scars. In his shabby jacket, stained flannels and scuffed shoes, the whiff of cheap after-shave competing with stale booze and baccy, Hollis looks like a refugee from a 1980s London cop drama.

A perceptive onlooker, however, might have noticed a certain similarity in the eyes of both men: shifty and evaluating, perhaps a little haunted.

Lennox opts not to mention the mishap with his phone. Reads that Hollis, gruff, though thawing in face of their small talk, might see it as incompetence or weakness. This proves not a bad call, for soon the London cop seems to feel they are enough alike to relax the tension in his big shoulders. — So, you had this geezer lose his tackle?

Lennox reckons while his colleagues were calling their bosses by the servile, eager-beaver 'guv' and ma'am', Hollis would be operating with the cynical lack of deference unlikely to enhance promotion prospects in a closed institution in England. — Well, he wasn't that negligent. Unless we're talking about the company he kept. Somebody removed them for him.

— Not been many details disclosed from your mob. Who was he, then?

It is a test. Lennox gambles. — He was an MP, and a former MSP.

Hollis looks nonplussed.

— Like an MP, but in our toytown parliament, which operates at the grace of our masters down south. Lennox smiles. Hollis doesn't respond, so he carries on. — Picture-postcard set-up; high-flyer, posh wife and kids, then he got into bother, playing away from home with another guy. His missus wasn't happy, he explains, hurtling past his own involvement in this story. — Nor were the local Tories. So he came down here and resurrected himself out in Oxfordshire. Kept up the populist baiting though; travellers, Muslims, refugees, feminists, transgenders, you know the list.

— Is it that farking ponce . . . what's it they call him?

— Gulliver, Lennox concurs. — His name will probably be all over the media tomorrow. Or not. All that's been released so far is he was found yesterday morning at ten in a Leith warehouse. But he was naked, bound and castrated, his genitals removed, probably two knives used, one of which had a serrated blade. They were taken from the body, and placed on

87

the Scott Monument where some tourist found them at lunchtime. We're checking out all the usual data lines.

Hollis nods in quiet appreciation of the information stream offered by the Scotsman.

— Interestingly, as well as indications of alcohol and perhaps drugs in his system, though we need the full toxicology report to confirm this, he'd been smashed on the head, probably with a mallet, prior to the genital removal. Not much forensic evidence so far, bar a red thread and a Magic Marker defacement of a toilet sign. Lennox looks around, slides his chair closer to the table. The pub has filled up with chattering groups, enjoying the liberation from work. He leans over. — Unless the perp knows the victims and has overpowered them through subterfuge, like alcohol spiking, then it points to more than one.

Hollis absorbs this information, brows knotting and face trenching in slow deliberation. Once he's convinced it's a decent enough vintage, he clears his throat in a rasping, jagged cough. — So they lured him up on the sleeper, got him pissed, then spiked him, but the sedative wasn't strong enough, so they knocked him out with a mallet?

— No, it was too precise and there was no sign of a struggle.

— Drug the cunt and then smash him? Don't make much sense.

— It's more like the perps wanted to mark him in that way. Lennox takes a long gulp of Stella. — There was a joiner in Edinburgh, Rab Dudgeon, nicknamed the Carpenter of Lunacy, who used to hurt boys like that, a sort of signature. He's long banged up, so it couldn't be him. It's like they tried to copy him, for some reason. Lennox shifts his seat to avoid the sunlight in his eyes. — The train staff aw ken Gulliver as a regular. He drank heavily and was often quite pished, but he didn't appear badly under the influence when he got on at Euston or off at Waverley.

— So he went on the piss early yesterday morning? Between the train getting in and his body being discovered at ten?

— It looks like it. And probably in the hotel he checked into, the Albany, a no-questions-asked place, and in his room, though nothing was missing from the minibar stock. We checked some of the early-morning boozers and hotels, where he could have had a scoop, but nothing, nor from any off-licence. Two breakfasts ordered to the room.

— So some cunt met him in the room, and gave him the drink, probably spiked, Hollis muses, taking a slug of his own poison.

— Nothing innocuous in his diaries, all business and constituency appointments. A few oblique references to a 'V' who we can't place as a family member, friend or a political or business associate.

— Regular scrubber or rent boy?

— Nothing positive, but he has form, Lennox says, sipping at his beer.

— They're officially keeping shtum about the geezer who almost lost his tackle at the Savoy, Hollis reciprocates cagily, — but he ain't no businessman.

This is no surprise. Lennox nods slowly, urging more.

Hollis hesitates for a second then cracks a grim smile. — Alright, Ray, fair exchange is no robbery. It ain't no secret that I'm being set up as silly fanny on this one. I ain't sure if they want me to ignore it, or be the sacrificial cunt who blows it all open. He shrugs. — But neither incentivises me to keep my gob zipped. Yeah, it happens, but I don't like being played by my own firm.

Lennox nods in slow and steady empathy.

— So . . . Hollis cracks that exigent smile again, — the geezer's a senior Home Office civil servant called Christopher Piggot-Wilkins. Almost Sir Christopher Piggot-Wilkins. Almost Dame Christopher Piggot-Wilkins. Hollis is evidently tickled by the thought. — Seems like a pure enticement job. Fit bird calls him up, says she's from an agency he uses, it's his birthday, and a mate has bought him a prezzy, Hollis's eyes expand, — only this agency ain't evah eard of her. Anyway, she coaxes him up to the hotel room, then into the bath, then snip, and he makes a cutting gesture with his fingers. — His wedding tackle's hanging on by a farking thread. Some Special Ops wankers were right on it; took him to a gaff in Harley Street, stitched it back on. I talked to a contact in a nearby clinic. He might eventually have as much as fifty per cent of previous erectile function, though it'll take a while.

— Bit naive of him, wasn't it? Very trusting. Didn't he whiff set-up?

— Nah, cause this bird knew this geezer's MO. Book a high-class escort girl and a suite at somewhere tasty, like the Ritz or the Savoy; in this case it was the Savoy. Drop all the right names. Geezer had no reason to suspect it wasn't kosher.

— So he'd done this before? What did he say?

Hollis's head weaves in tight rage. — Haven't a farking clue, he snarls. — They covered his arse, Ray. I was down there within half an hour but so was my boss, old misery-guts Stan George, and this is a cunt who gets a farking nosebleed if he stands up at his desk . . . *and* who should rock up five minutes later but the farking Chief Constable, Sir Cuntface Soppy Bollocks himself, and he's got some big-noise Whitehall nonces in tow. They wouldn't let us near Piggot-Wilkins. They was giving it the big one, the 'we got this' mushroom theory, feed em shit and keep em in the dark. Hollis pauses to draw breath.

— No physical evidence or CCTV? Lennox asks, knowing from Squeak Mortimer that there was.

— They was there to get rid of evidence, Ray, Hollis's brow furrows, — not to uncover it.

— So they shut you out, closing the whole thing down, and only scurrying around to desperately reactivate it after Gulliver. Lennox thinks of those trailing strands of spaghetti again. — Whoever's done this has them rattled. *They've* made the connection between your boy and mine.

— Exactly, Raymond. Tory toffs? Thick as shit in the neck of a bottle, them cahnts.

— Not a fan, then?

Hollis kills his pint in a long gulp. — I ain't no Bolshie red or poncey liberal, mate, it's all a scam of controllers. But them cahnts take the farking biscuit. An inbred mutant class who've shafted us for generations, and we still have enough forelock tuggers grateful to them for doing it.

— Agreed. Sounds like high noncery to me, mate.

— Noncery of the highest bleedin order, Hollis booms, as a nearby couple briefly turn round. — Well, I ain't gonna shut up and play foot soldier for cover-up wankers!

Lennox is starting to like Mark Hollis. — Back in Edinburgh my team are flat out on it. Any dots they join, the info is yours, and he points at the Londoner's glass. — Fancy another?

— The universe likes me. Mark Hollis breaks into a grin that strips a decade of bad consumer choices off him. — It sent me a Jock. Known a few down the years. Some very nice geezers; others not so much. But one thing they had in common: they all enjoyed a shandy. He shakes his glass. — Stella.

After the fourth pint, Hollis vanishes into the toilet and returns lit up. Collapses, with a determined resolve, back down into his seat. — I stuck a little livener on the cistern for ya. Choice is yours.

It's another test and Lennox rises immediately. In the toilet he lifts up some paper to reveal a fat line of cocaine.

It's important to bond with Hollis.

But Trudi.

The NA. Keith Goodwin. My sponsor . . .

He rubs some powder on the fringes of his nostril and sweeps the rest from its porcelain nest onto the floor. Guilt and a sense of loss, stupidity and sheer waste hit him in a crippling uppercut. As he walks back in he feels like a self-cheating mug.

Hollis is quickly in full flow again. — The farking Met, Ray, you don't need me to tell ya what a farking mess it is. Or maybe you farking do. Dunno how shit it is up there, but it's gotta be better than the useless cunts we have to deal with . . .

As Hollis rants about his employers, Lennox lets him pause for a breath before advancing the standard question he asks of all Serious Crimes men. As obvious as it is, the replies always tell him exactly who he's dealing with. — So why do you do this job?

Hollis stalls only for one second. His wired eyes focus on Lennox's. — I want to lock up scum, mate, like cunts what does despicable things to kiddies. Murdering arseholes that rip a person out of a family, or rapists that ruin women's lives. They don't have the right to do that shit and I'm farking coming for em. I don't care about some lads having a tear at the football, he shakes his big dome, — or kids stealing from supermarkets, a poor old bastard fiddling their electricity meter, some fucker who ripped off Sky Sports with a snide stick, or some stressed-out wanker double-parked.

Lennox is nodding in agreement. — You want to lock up the bad guys. Not the weak, vulnerable and compromised ones, or the duckers and divers trying to get by. Me too.

Hollis raises one of the two fresh Stellas that have appeared in Lennox's absence, compelling him to do the same. — To fucking up bad cunts!

— Fucking up bad cunts!

As Lennox toasts, Hollis abruptly lowers his glass, as if now aware of his surroundings, seeming to realise that he's more compromised by the coke than Lennox.

He suspects I didn't smash the line. Worse: thinks I'm some sort of Internal Investigations informer.

Lennox has been blitzed on coke enough times to know how to fake it. He breaks into a rant. — Gulliver was supposed to be in his Oxfordshire constituency. No record of the cunt coming back tae Scotland. He didnae tell his estranged missus or their offspring, or even his sister – this pair of tits, lips and buttocks on a stick, whom he normally stays with when he comes back up to see the kids. Then he was in that warehouse in Leith . . . the Edinburgh docks. Found fuckin starkers and bound, his wedding gear whipped off, nothing more than a couple of strands ay wriggling spaghetti left behind, once the serrated blade had done its work, and Lennox pulls out his phone, only realising as he slaps it down on the table that it's still fucked. — Dropped this bastard and can't get it working. Anyway, we got a got a call from one of those crackly robot voices, says something like: 'Gulliver scum in warehouse in Leith docks. Please remove before the other rats take one of their own.'

Hollis seems assuaged, gives another husky chuckle. — What's the word on the tape?

— Technicians still on it. It was sent at 9.47 a.m. They found the warehouse that contained the body at 10.05 a.m. Gulliver came off the sleeper at 7 a.m. The bollocks were found in the Scott Monument at 12.52.

— The perp is likely to have been a male victim of sexual abuse, Hollis suddenly contends, — probably as a kid. He's stronger now.

Lennox thinks about this, falling into silence.

That tunnel. My ongoing obsession with it; as if hanging around there would bring them back, those three men, now rendered shadowy in my consciousness. I see myself in there, fists clenched, shouting like a maniac:

C'MOAN THEN, YA CUNTS.

He is jarred out of his thoughts by Hollis's voice. It's still harsh, but now there's a fetching melody underscoring it.

— Nice dance, mate?

— What? Sorry, I . . . Lennox is startled. — What do you mean?

— With your demons. We all got em. Hollis shrugs in a sombre, gallows cheer. — It's why we're here, innit.

Lennox pulls a tight smile. It's pointless to argue. He wonders what malign spirits Hollis has to battle with. Already knows they will be extremely bad bastards.

— But don't worry; I ain't gonna tell you mine and I don't wanna know yours. Hollis's harsh laugh morphs into grim seriousness. — We gotta thank them though, Ray. That's our engine. That's wot's saved us.

Lennox feels his eyebrows rise north. — Saved us? Really? He can't keep the incredulity out of his voice. — From what?

Hollis looks around the crowded bar, his gaze falling contemptuously over its chatting occupants. — From boredom, mate. From being salaried, uniformed vegetables.

— One way of looking at it.

— We're dammed, Ray, the likes of you and me, Hollis advances, seeming buoyed by the notion. — What we get ta do is take as many bad cahnts down with us as possible, and he shakes his empty glass. — Now get em in, you tight Jock cahnt!

— Your words are truly inspirational, Hollis. Lennox rises and winks. — See how quickly I get to that bar.

When he does arrive there, he feels buzzed by osmosis.

Hollis's company is like passive drug taking. He looks at the chunky figure, now laughing to himself in soft convulsions at his own exploding thoughts. This man draws from booze and cocaine the energy he needs to take on the world. A universe with too many Hollises would descend into chaos. One without any would be dead. Returning with the drinks, Lennox asks where Piggot-Wilkins is.

— Probably holed up in his Surrey mansion. Can't get near the cunt. Saying zilch on record. Seems he don't want to be known as the geezer who lost half of his wedding tackle. So, wanna check out the crime scene? Obviously it's been long put to bed now. Never seen the cahnts tidy one up as quick.

As they glug back their pints, the lights in the bar go dim. This adjustment made by the barman mirrors the peppering dark of autumn London. The weight of the Stella in his guts and its fuddling of his head makes a heavy-limbed Lennox further regret not smashing that line. *That was a fucking waste.* They step outside and grab a black cab, Lennox considering that Hollis is so old school he just can't see his new colleague travelling any other way.

They disembark at the Strand and the ornate entrance to the luxurious building where the bronze soldier stands above the iconic glinting green neon letters announcing the Savoy. Hollis explains they are meeting Colin Neville, one of the doormen. — Tasty welterweight back in the day. Had the best and worst possible ability in boxing: he could take a punch. Maybe not as sharp with the gob, but the ears and eyes work and nothing gets past Nev. I'm treating ya both ta the card at York Hall in Bethnal Green. You like the fight game, sahn? he asks. — Course ya do, he decides without waiting for a reply.

A stout, blue-coated doorman, white hair just visible under his top hat, greets them. — Tom, Hollis nods, and exchanges pleasantries. Then he asks, — Nev inside then, mate? The doorman's response is affirmative and as they pass the reception area, Hollis asks Lennox, — Ere, whatcha reckon ta old Squeak?

— Don't really know him well. Lennox takes in the lobby with its black-and-white granite chessboard flooring, beautiful ceilings and cornices, and wood-panelled walls decorated with classical art. — A few tech and forensic courses. He's generally been a helpful contact.

— Watch the cunt. Hollis taps his nose. — They should be calling him *Squeal*, if ya get my drift.

Lennox nods, as a smiling, vacant-eyed man sitting in a big upholstered chair rises to greet them. — Alright, Marky!

— Nev . . . this is Ray. We're all off to York Hall in a bit, mate. Sorted us aht.

— Nice one.

— Can you show us the gaff?

— Follow me.

Lennox can see that this amiable man is punch-drunk, having been the recipient of too many shots from hot prospects on the way up. Boxers often have to be protected from themselves: it's evident Colin Neville wasn't.

— Bad management, Hollis confirms in a whisper as Nev gets a set of keys from reception and hands them to him. He waits as Lennox and Hollis go up to the room via the lift. — Piggot-Wilkins came down in this one; starkers, holding his bollocks to him, blood everywhere. Of course, not a bit of farking footage from here, he points up at a camera, — or the lobby. No record it ever happened bar some eyewitnesses who were strong-armed into opening their phones and erasing their images by some special unit cahnts.

— Fuck sake, they started the cover-up quickly.

— It's known they got a contingency unit to protect high rollers, Hollis says. — Up till then I hadn't seen them in action.

But we was pushed aside and made ta feel like farking cleaners. Hollis grinds his teeth as the lift stops and the doors fly open. — Thought the cahnts was gonna ask us to grab a farking mop and have a go at taking care of the farking claret all over the marble floor. They step out into the corridor, where Hollis points at another CCTV camera, waving his phone. — But we've got some shit from up here. I've called a couple of lads from our investigations team. They're on their way.

Down the corridor they observe the painters' plastic sheeting, still up, but no longer covering room 461. As they enter, feet sinking into the lush carpet, Lennox regards the four-poster bed, as he walks through to the large bathroom with more marble black-and-white chessboard tiles.

Hollis maintains the coke-fuelled running commentary. — I reckon your theory is bang on, Ray: two of them cunts. Piggot-Wilkins goes up to the suite, boner visible from space. She's wearing a mask, like Venetian, all that *Eyes Wide Shut* shit. Cahnt's probably ready to cream as soon as he walks in. Bird probably ain't saying who this mate was wot sent her. Hooray Henry's cool with that; reckons he'll find out soon enough, toffs scratching each other's backs for favours ain't exactly unknown.

— So the perp, or perps, knew his MO and who booked him, and set this up.

Hollis nods in affirmation. — The bird keeps the mask on, giving it all that 'let's take a bath' palaver, knowing that a germ-obsessed ponce will be all over that. The taps are already running and soapy bubbles are frothing away. The water's hot and the blades already in there, concealed by the foam. Then he gets in and relaxes, and bingo . . .

— Sex-change territory . . . almost.

— Thing is, after he scarpers, holding his tackle to him, freaking out in reception, screaming for a driver to take him to

Harley Street, not an ambulance and A&E, she ain't far behind. Hollis is highly animated, his breathing laboured. — But, and check this out, if there was two of em, Hollis points to a slatted door, pulls it open to reveal a big walk-in cupboard with hung bathrobes and shelves full of towels, — the other one was hiding in here, I reckon, watching the action. Course, they wouldn't let us dust it. Their private little force, at the taxpayer's expense, took care of all that.

— What do you reckon to the cunt in here, Lennox swings the doors, — getting off on it, and/or there to offer assistance if it went wrong . . . ?

— Yeah . . . but they ain't the only ones who had assistance. As I say, our big noises cleaned up the crime scene sharpish, and the mug who is retrospectively designated investigating officer, Hollis points to himself, — don't even get ta sling a decent butcher's. Ever get the feeling you're being set up to fail?

Lennox nods grimly at him.

Hollis looks at the suite front door opening. — Ah . . . here's my boys . . . Lennox glances up to see two men standing in the doorway. The one tapping on the door frame is a tall black man with shorn scalp, smartly suited and in his early thirties. The other is white, with a sandy mop of hair, and in his twenties, sporting a badly fitting jacket. — David, Soppy Bollocks. Hollis nods them in. — Thanks for coming along. Ray here has come down from Scotland to civilise us all, right, Ray?

— Far too big a job for one man. I'll stick to pinching sex cases if it's all the same with you.

Soppy Bollocks gives a light chuckle, but David remains impassive as he pulls out an iPad from a leather wallet and fires it up.

— Was just going to ask about the CCTV, Lennox says.

— This floor was being renovated, David responds in a clipped Oxbridge accent that causes Hollis's face to fall in a crease. — They obviously knew that when they booked it, and he points to the screen. — Dust sheets cover the egress by the back staircase. This happened at 12.45. We have no footage from the lobby. It was switched off for legit maintenance.

— A perfect storm of maintenance in the lobby and renovation up here, Lennox says. — Way too much of a coincidence.

— We've been all over the maintenance company and the painting firm. Both legit. We've leaned on the management here, Hollis explains. — There's nothing so far. This job had been planned for a while.

— Somebody knew the story, but anyone with access to the computer would be able to obtain the schedule of work without arousing overt suspicions. David hands Lennox a printed list of around two hundred names. — And a semi-decent hacker could sort it easily, he says slightly ruefully.

— Play it, Lennox requests.

— Is this really . . . ? David asks, looking from Lennox to Hollis.

— Yeah. Carry on, sahn, Hollis barks.

The naked Piggot-Wilkins, eyes glazed through his gold-rimmed glasses, thrashes the plastic sheeting aside, dramatic-ally splattering it with blood as he charges down the hallway. As the makeshift curtains spring back, a figure emerges be-hind him. But rather than follow Piggot-Wilkins through the curtain, they head towards a stair fire door. It's a brief image, like that of someone in a shower, but Lennox can pick out a long black coat, blonde hair and a dark Venetian mask. Then, some thirty seconds later, a second blurred backlit silhouetted figure is following, heading towards the same fire exit. It's impossible to discern much more than the shape, but Lennox can see that Hollis's probable voyeur in the cupboard is bigger and bulkier than the masked woman.

David freezes the action and points to a section of the screen. — As you can see, the plastic sheet was taped to this section of the hallway . . . they step outside the room at his urging, — . . . it obscures the view of the two figures leaving the scene by the stairs, he points to the fire-escape steps, — . . . after Piggot-Wilkins leaves in a hurry . . .

Lennox considers the two figures. — These are both women? The second figure is bigger but they're wearing billowing clothes, maybe a dress?

— Perhaps, David says.

Hollis nods to Lennox, and takes him aside. — I thought so too. But in this era, positive discrimination and all that bollocks, they ain't particularly desperate to show that skirt can be as nutty as us. You think they'd be all for equality, he chortles, looking around. Soppy Bollocks laughs, both Lennox and David stay neutral.

— You never know, Lennox offers, — the times they are a-changin.

David and Soppy Bollocks look blankly at him.

— Anyway, let's have a chat with Nev, in more informal surroundings, Hollis says, heaving out a sigh, then nods at the two men. — Thanks, chaps, as he and Lennox head to the lift.

— What's the story there? Lennox asks.

— A high-flyer and his sidekick; corporate wankers, Ray. They didn't like me sharing that shit with you. Wouldn't put it past the cunts to grass me up. He bares his teeth. — That's the kind of spunkers wot's replacing the likes of us. And they'll have a higher clean-up rate. Course by then . . . A ping of the lift arriving as the doors fly open and they step inside. — . . . everybody who's been nonced up will be microchipped and we'll just wait for them to commit a crime. Be like fish in a barrel.

As the lift descends, Lennox asks, — You think that every single nonced-up kid grows up to be a nonce themselves?

— We know most do. That's how them viruses transmit, Ray. Chip them all and if they do no wrong, all to the good. Yeah, double punishment for a kid who has been abused to then be stigmatised on a potential short-eyes list, but civil liberties won't be much of a thing in the near future.

Nev has gone ahead to York Hall and they get outside to find a taxi to take them to Bethnal Green. Then Hollis, suddenly inspired, says, — Let's make a little detour first, to King's Cross. Check out this agency; see if they can verify Piggot-Wilkins's regular custom. The geezer that runs it is well known to Vice. One of yours, he says. — Scotch, he explains, before shouting to the driver, — King's Cross!

Lennox feels like telling Hollis that Scotch is a drink, but from the Londoner's lips it sounds oddly comforting, like an aural sip of a twenty-year-old malt. — Right . . .

Then, the sudden roaring surge of an angry engine snarls at them. They look round to see a van hurtling towards them. — FUCK SAKE, Hollis yells, pushing them into the taxi, spreadeagling Lennox on the floor of the vehicle. He slams the door behind them, but the retreating van clips it.

— CAHHNNT! the cabbie shouts. — Did you see that?!

— FOLLOW THE FARKING CAHNNNT!! Hollis barks, pulling out his ID.

The cabbie needs no second invite, accelerating after the van. But it turns and moves out of sight before they can even catch the plates. — That might be on camera, Hollis says, rattling with cocaine, adrenaline and nerves, — I'm putting in a call, and gets his phone and rants into it. — Wankers, he says, hanging up. — All they farking do is moan about what they can't bleeding well do . . . He hunches forward in his seat, before laying out what his intuition is. — Piggot-Wilkins or his boys wouldn't do direct business in King's Cross. I reckon the third party wot books the hookers for him is a geezer called Toby Wallingham. He's a failed toff, a typical trust-fund blow-out merchant. Well known in cop circles.

— So you reckon he set Piggot-Wilkins up with the masked hooker?

— Dunno, that's why I'd like to talk to the cunt. But if he did, the perps was probably using the soft cunt; nobody wants to see one of their regular shaggers lose his old fella. You're farking up your own business. But we gotta tread careful, Hollis raises his bushy brows. — The cunt is like the rest of them, lawyered up to the max.

— London toffs. It's like you need an appointment to investigate the cunts.

— Don't like this, Ray, none of it, but first let's check out the lowlife, Hollis says, and as they step from the cab into a dingy backstreet that has escaped the gentrification of the area, he shakily crams some notes into the hand of the driver. Lennox looks around, and recalls this as more like the King's Cross of his youth, before the attentions of Eurostar, bursting with a sleaze and repressed menace. Hollis, eyes ablaze, at odds with the cold threat of his voice, tells him, — As is the way of these things, I find myself wanting to take it out on some cunt.

Lennox locks his gaze on Hollis. It was a close call, and somebody means them harm. — I know that feeling, he agrees, feeling the dampness of the still-tea-discharging phone in his pocket.

12

It's possible that the Colleagues agency is still manned. Sure enough, as the taxi trundles off, a woman in a business suit is leaving the shabby Victorian building. — KEEP THAT DOOR OPEN, Hollis roars, as he runs towards her, waving his police ID in her face. — What's your name?

— Greta . . . she says, in an East European accent. — But I have done nothing wrong!

— Nah, you ain't, Hollis says, putting his foot in the door to prevent it from closing, Lennox reading him as rattled, but by the renegade driver as well as the coke. — And you don't wanna start now. So tell me who's up there, in that Colleagues office?

— Just the boss. His name is Simon.

— Right, now scarper. Hollis spits out some gob that splatters on the cold concrete step.

Greta heads off, passing Lennox without making eye contact. They watch her retreat, at what in high heels is an impressive speed. Then they go inside, mounting the narrow stairs to the top floor, both anticipating the surprise they are about to spring on *Simon the boss*.

Simon David Williamson is just finishing up at the grubby offices of Colleagues Professional Consultancy and Administrative Support Services, and is shutting down his Apple Mac. He tenses as the two men enter his premises. He doesn't make them out as cops straight away: it's just as plausible they are villains. As he enjoys some protection by association, he half

prays for the latter. He meets the men with a bug-eyed stare.
— I'm just closing, and I only do appointments online.

Lennox recognises not the man but the accent. — What's your name? he asks, flashing an ID.

Williamson screws up his eyes to study it, then looks at Lennox. — Edinburgh Polis . . . what the fuck?

Hollis follows suit, with his Met card. — We all want ya, mate. How lovely to be so popular!

— Whatever you're after, you've come to the wrong place, Williamson declares, launching into what the two cops read as a well-worn pitch. — We provide a service matching respectable businessmen with associates who act as their administrative assistants in meetings and at dinners. It's all about show and power. There is no sexual contact tolerated, and if I ever hear of this, the party responsible is struck off our register and rep—

— Fuck off with the bullshit, Hollis snaps. — We don't give a toss about your scrubbers and johns. Wot's your name?

— Simon David Williamson.

— Do you know Christopher Piggot-Wilkins?

Williamson remains poker-faced. — I keep my client list confidential. Your officers came a couple of weeks ago and I furnished them with it. If you'd like another copy from me, bring a warrant or a court order. Or perhaps ask your boss if you can have a look at his.

His comment wounds Hollis, mainly, Lennox thinks, because of the truth in it: he's being used by his bosses to give a veneer of legitimacy to an investigation they've had closed for their own reasons. — A geezer used your agency name to set up Piggot-Wilkins with a scrubber. He was badly assaulted, Hollis barks. — You could do serious time.

— I see. Williamson doubles down on his terse pomposity, slapping his own head with an open palm. — You come into

104

my place of work and threaten me. Is this policing? Is this law enforcement? and he briefly pleads to an invisible jury, as well as the cops he's addressing. — I've already spoken to your people *extensively*. I've said it till I'm *blue. In. The. Face*: this man may have used the Colleagues name, but the woman who assaulted Piggot-Wilkins was not on our books. I have repeated this *extensively. To. Your. Colleagues*. Williamson reprises the self-slapping motion. — What else can I do?

His name and face have finally registered in Lennox's villain Rolodex. — You're an associate of Frank Begbie.

Williamson looks at him, literally batting his eyes in incredulity as he exhales deeply. — Because I had the misfortune to grow up with a psychopath, whom I haven't seen in *years*, I'm somehow an *associate*? He shakes his head. — They send some snide Jambo fuck down here from West Edinburgh Gumleyland at the taxpayer's expense to furnish the Met with *this* startling revelation? He turns in outrage to Hollis.

But the London cop is making similar connections. — Greek Andreas . . . Lawrence Croft, he says. — These might be more *recent associations*.

Williamson noisily lets out air again, but this time more slowly. Defeat moulds his features. — I told you, Piggot-Wilkins doesn't book here.

— No, Hollis says. — But I expect ya know who regularly books on his behalf. A Toby Wallingham by any chance?

— Your people have been through my files and phone records. You know that Wallingham has booked here.

Lennox looks to Hollis, knows, in spite of his ashen bearing, that this is the first time he's heard this confirmed. Hollis glares at Williamson. — Has he ever booked for Piggot-Wilkins?

Williamson shrugs. — Wallingham is known to have . . . more manly tastes. It's safe to say that any female associates he's booking are on behalf of somebody else. But I certainly never had one from the Savoy. I would have remembered that, and he points to his desk computer.

— Good chap, Hollis smiles. — A bit of willing cooperation goes a long way.

— I'm no grass, Williamson declares, his gaze suddenly burnishing, — but those entitled cunts are no friends of mine. They have disrespected this organisation in the past, and he twists his head around the grubby office with its eighties job-lot furniture, surveying it as if it's an Egyptian palace. — For that arrogance, you must always expect payback.

— Was any of them rough with the girls? Wallingham's bookings? Hollis asks, as Lennox looks in distaste at a Hibernian FC calendar on the wall.

— Speak to Ursula Lettinger. Williamson passes him a card. — You get used to not believing women in this game. But I know terror when I witness it. If there's nothing else? He looks to the door.

Lennox looks to Hollis. Then he nods at Williamson. — Good to see a local boy doing well in the big city. He casts his eye around the shabby office as they depart.

— Nice shoes, Williamson says, looking at the loafers on the feet of the departing Edinburgh detective. — Not outrageously fashionable, but *sensible*.

13

Hollis has been furiously tapping his phone, cursing loudly at the ineptitude of his big, stumpy fingers. His persistence bears what Lennox perceives as unlikely fruit. — Right, he says. — Tracked Wallingham down to one of those nonce clubs up west he uses.

Lennox is excited, though slightly disappointed. He was looking forward to an evening's boxing.

Hollis reads his thoughts. — We get a hold of this dozy cunt and ask him some questions, and we'll still make the fights over at York Hall . . . That cunt in the van that tried to do us, I saw nuffink, Ray. Did you get anything on him?

— He tore off sharpish. Seemed a big frame, shades on, cap. He could have done us, or come even closer. Maybe he was just trying to scare us off.

— Thinking the same, Hollis grimaces. — As likely to be our own fuckers as anyone, but that don't bear thinking about. I keep telling myself not to be paranoid . . .

— Your self doesnae want to listen to that, bud.

— Ain't that the truth, Hollis penitently concedes.

The arts club they walk into has never become an international brand like Soho House, or even a revered local institution like the Groucho. But in its faded grandeur it retains an exclusivity that enables it to attract a certain clientele. These are people who generally like being seen, but opt to come here on the odd occasion when that isn't a viable option. If you were a disgraced celebrity who just couldn't stay indoors, the chances are that this would be your refuge of choice. Therefore, a whiff of scandal always seems to permeate its walls.

At the desk, Lennox envisages that entry is going to be a struggle. The receptionist is young and beautiful, casting flinty, unimpressed eyes over him and Hollis. His colleague cracks a big smile. — Alright, darlin?

Her features fuse in haughty disapproval, but just then a flummoxed-looking man with slicked-back grey-black locks spies them. Lennox takes him to be the duty manager. Dispensing a withering stare at the penitent young woman, he waves the detectives in. Immediately he says to Hollis in a scandalised French-accented whisper, — Mark . . . he is on the third floor . . . but please do not cause a scene in here!

— Oi! Discretion is my middle name, Hervé. He pats the man on the back, mounting the stairs, urging Lennox to follow. As they depart, Hollis whiplashes, announcing to the Frenchman with a lavish wink: — Slate wiped clean, bruv.

The stairs are steep, and Hollis wheezily explains to Lennox, — Silly fanny got caught in the honey trap with a couple of scrubbers wot tried to squeeze him. They don't like that shit here. That's for guests, not staff. I made it go away, Hollis pants, his face reddening in the climb. — With toff noncery, you need all the help you can get. A working-class community will generally expel its filth . . . Hollis settles at a bend in the stairs to get his breath, — . . . a toff network will protect them at all cost, usually cause they know too much about other toffs.

As they take their seats at the down-lit third-floor bar, Hollis looks across to where three men are seated close together at a low table. — There he is, Hollis nods, — ponce in the waistcoat.

Toby Wallingham indeed wears an ochre-coloured satin

waistcoat. Flowing locks, black with grey streaks, cascade from his head, over his shoulders and down his back.

They observe the London dandy over pints of a microbrew lager neither man has ever heard of. There is no Stella. — Paedo's pish, Lennox offers, and Hollis nods first in agreement, then over at Wallingham, who rises, excusing himself from his company.

— Here we go. Hollis springs up, Lennox following suit.

They pursue their prey to the gents, entering just as Wallingham finishes up at the urinal. — Tobes! Worra surprise! Racking them out then, sahn?

Wallingham looks at Hollis in distaste, then at Lennox in mild curiosity. — DI Hollis. He shrugs in weary concession. — Anything for our city's finest.

The three men move into a tight toilet cubicle. It's so uncomfortable that Lennox realises they are literally putting the squeeze on Wallingham. Hollis's laugh is like the outboard motor of a launch. — Get em chopped out, sahn.

— It's a little crowded in here . . . perhaps your friend –

— I'm Raymond. Lennox grins. He's already thinking about the damage that Hollis's heavy hands might do to Wallingham's fine features.

— Well, Raymond, if you –

— LESS SLOPPING, MORE CHOPPING! Hollis roars in his face.

— Okay, okay . . . Wallingham, alarmed, turns to the cistern and starts cutting out lines. He then stands back to allow Hollis first go.

— Piggot-Wilkins said it was you who set him up with the prostitute, one that tried to detach his old fella, Hollis says, smashing a line.

— Rubbish, Wallingham scoffs. — What is this?

Lennox looks at the line and Hollis's urging expression. This time there's no hiding place. — Do you know Ritchie Gulliver? he asks as he snorts the line back.

That old surge, it feels so good. This gear is more than decent . . .

— No. Wallingham is petulant, pushed uncomfortably against Hollis's protruding gut. — I now wish to leave this cubicle. You've abused my hospitality and I'm going to call my lawyer, and he works the phone out of his cramped inside pocket.

— What about your line? Hollis asks, head twisting towards the cistern.

— You have it, Wallingham snaps.

Hollis rips the device out of his hand. — Farking lawyer, is it?

— You can't –

Hollis drops the phone in the toilet. — Clumsy me!

Lennox, moved to touch the damp and disabled phone in his pocket, ruefully observes, — Accidents will happen. Cramped conditions, class A's . . .

— You bloody . . . As Wallingham crouches down to cagily retrieve his digital life, Hollis grabs those vibrant locks in his fist . . .

— AGHH . . . LET ME GO!

. . . and ducks his head into the water.

— FUCKING –

All this does is force Hollis to silence him by pushing his face more firmly down into the bowl. Lennox looks to see the gurgling bubbles rise to the surface. — There's a big piece of shit stuck in the toilet, Ray. See if you can flush it away, will ya, mate?

— Of course. Lennox tugs the chain. Water cascades out, reducing Wallingham's locks to rat-tail-like tendrils.

Hollis pulls Wallingham's head up.

— NO . . . YOU . . . AGHH . . . Wallingham shrieks.

Hollis keeps his grip firm. — Shut it. His voice drops to an ominous whisper. — Don't try and mug me off, you farking wanker or I'll have every farking tooth in your head smashed. We want two things from you! I want to know about Piggot-Wilkins, and my buddy wants to know about that ponce Ritchie Gulliver. So talk!

— I . . . I don't know any . . . Ritchie Gulliver . . . he gasps.

— Piggot-Wilkins then! Tell me about that cunt, and Hollis pushes his head down again.

Wallingham holds his hands up, and Hollis eases the pressure, while keeping his grip vice-like. — I got no call . . . to sort out any whore . . . for Piggot-Wilkins . . . I was a little put out as he usually comes to me . . . I've set him and some of his friends up at various hotels before but this time I didn't send anybody . . . Who said I did? Was it fucking Williamson at Colleagues?

— So you sent no cunt?

— No. I swear! I heard about the Savoy attack . . . that some iffy security detail took over the investigation . . .

— Have you talked to Piggot-Wilkins since his assault?

— No!

— Who do you think did make the call?

— I told you I don't fucking know!

— Oh, but you *do* know, mate. Even if you didn't speak to them you'll know the MO. Who else does Piggot-Wilkins's mob use?

— I don't bloody know! I'm not his social sec—

— WHO THE FUCK ELSE DOES HE USE? Hollis yanks on Wallingham's locks, then nods to Lennox, who tugs the flush again.

— LAKE! Wallingham shouts out, gurgling. — Billy Lake . . .

111

Hollis's fingers loosen on the mane. — What the fuck . . . he says, then a knock on the toilet door is followed by a booming voice. — Who is in there? There's more than one person in there!

Hollis throws the door open. — It's DI Hollis from the Met. Ask your boss about me while you can, before I step out there and rip your farking lungs out. Capeesh?

The steward nods curtly and heads out. Nonetheless, Hollis nods at Lennox, and they decide to beat a quick retreat.

— You have not heard the last of this, the wretched, soaked Wallingham screeches.

As they get onto the stairs, Lennox asks, — Will he call his lawyer?

— Nah . . . he was in the toilet with two other geezers. Don't look so good, does it? Hollis ponders. — But I'm more concerned about the name he gave.

— Billy Lake? Can't say I've heard of him.

— Often these days the most successful villains is those you ain't heard of. This is very worrying, Ray.

— What now? Lennox asks as they walk out into Soho's failing light.

— We go to the fights at York Hall and we get another flaming drink. That's where the inspiration comes from.

They jump into another cab, heading for the East End.

14

At York Hall, Hollis and Lennox jostle through a robust, good-natured crowd. As they gratefully seize some Stella, Lennox regards the generic fight-fan faces; the club boxers and officials, the sport's aficionados, the small businessmen sponsors, the gangsters, and the packs of young hooligans hoping that the scrap spills outside of the ring, perhaps with a mob that has attached itself to another fighter. And then those who can never quite make up their minds which category they belong to.

Hollis introduces his brothers, Danny and Steve, who are with Nev. They look like younger, smaller versions of their brother. Lennox immediately thinks of the grinning Russian Cossacks on his sister's mantelpiece. They inform them they missed a very tasty first fight. But rather than take overt interest in the ring proceedings, the brothers' necks seemed craned towards the audience.

— Old-school Bushwackers, Hollis confirms, chuckling. — Never at ease in West Ham territory.

Lennox notes that Hollis exudes far more serenity here than any cop should. His pulped nose signals an ex-boxer. This is confirmed as he looks Lennox over. — You seem in decent shape. Ever get between the ropes yourself?

— I do a bit of kickboxing. Mainly bags, pads and sparring, but I've done the odd inter-force bout and a couple of charity tear-ups with the fire brigade.

— Pansy's game, Hollis says absent-mindedly, then qualifies, — No offence, Ray, nice white-collar pastime. Keep you in shape more than the boozer, and he grabs a handful of his own gut.

— So, you were a boxer?

— Yeah, decent enough record in the amateurs. Hollis eyes the fighters who step into the ring. — My mistake was turning pro: different farking game altogether. You really got to want it, and he looks in some envy at the fighter in the blue shorts. — That geezer's well tasty, could go far. Then, maybe not, he thinks, suddenly cheered, — you never can tell. This, he waves his glass of Stella, — this ain't no good. Booze, chasing skirt, they don't lead you to fitness and focus, mate. He slaps his belly again. — Was never great at making the weight.

The second bout is over in inside a minute. A crashing right from the rated fighter in blue catches his deer-in-the-headlights opponent cold. The third is a scrap between two game but technically limited welterweights. It makes for an absorbing encounter and gets the bay-for-blood thug element much more aroused than it does the connoisseurs of the sweet science. If Hollis seems as uncomfortable as Lennox here, it's the next fight that is the real painful watch. They both can't help glancing at Nev as they witness an old pro being slowly dismantled by a gifted, showboating prospect he might have been a good match for a decade ago. — Not pretty, says Hollis, — but let the young un enjoy his place in the sun. He's more likely to end up like the other geezer than the hero with the belts.

But Colin Neville looks physically sick as the old fighter eats a head–body combo of hooks, uppercuts and crosses, sinking to the deck. Hollis turns to Lennox. — Poor cunt looks as lost as Wallingham with his noggin down the toilet.

Lennox hopes the veteran isn't going to make the bell. He doesn't. He feels his pulse race and his mouth dry. Hollis excites the *folie à deux* of vengeful adrenaline that old partners like Bruce Robertson and Ginger Rogers sparked in him. It wasn't great for his personal life, but this is what he sees the job as being about.

Hollis is furiously texting on his phone as the bewildered veteran in the ring is administered smelling salts by his corner. Colin Neville seems to have had enough, departing, shaking his head and mumbling as he heads to the exit.

— Maybe the gadge being pummelled was a bit triggering for him? Lennox ventures.

— Yeah, possible, always was a bit one-skin-too-few for this game. Hollis gets back on his phone.

Lennox watches the vet being helped to his feet, too dazed to fully acknowledge the dancing, performative young man who dispenses him a perfunctory embrace. He feels his own disabled phone in his pocket, can sense the calls and texts racking up. Wonders about Trudi and case breakthroughs, as a roar goes up advising a local favourite is about to hit the ring.

In profile, he regards Hollis, who is grimacing tensely. It takes Lennox a few seconds to realise that his new friend is in some kind of distress. The colour has drained from his chalky-white face as he looks furtively at his two brothers. They are both now focused on the contest. Lennox asks Hollis about the combatants, but the London cop's teeth are clenching as he holds his arms tightly into his chest. — I have to go, Hollis declares, and as he stands up, blood soaks the back of his jeans.

Lennox is stunned, looking at the Hollis brothers who are oblivious to this, in their ring concentration. His first bizarre thought: *has somebody stabbed him?* — Jesus fuck, Mark, I'll get an ambulance —

— Leave it, Ray. Hollis ties his Puffa jacket round his waist, covering his arse. Then he stumbles forward, scattering some unoccupied seats in front, his eyes rolling into his head.

The people around him are on their feet, Lennox rising first. Hollis is lying in a pool of blood, wedged between two rows of seats. His brother Steve whistles for the paramedics, who are quickly to hand.

Hollis is ranting deliriously as they hoist him onto a stretcher and take him away. Red blood stains the seats and the wooden floor. This looks bad. Lennox and the Hollis brothers follow the paramedics who lead the blacked-out Mark Hollis from the hall. At the rear of the car park, they help them load him into the ambulance, then the brothers promptly exit the vehicle, leaving Lennox to travel with Hollis to the hospital. — Don't mind, do ya, Jock? This fight could be tasty, and they shut the doors on Lennox and their semiconscious big brother.

As Hollis groans, the ambulance tears off.

The ambulance, siren blaring, tears through traffic towards the thankfully nearby Royal London Hospital, vehicles making way for it. Looking out the back windows, Lennox is just thinking *this is fucking serious*, when the stricken Hollis appears to focus a little on him. — Sorry, Ray, he groans, — this is the worst they've been.

— What is it? What's going on, Mark?

Hollis averts his gaze from Lennox, looking at the roof of the vehicle. Sweat drips from him. — The Harry Styles, mate. I was due to go into hospital next week to have them done under general. I was dreading it . . . hopefully they'll move it forward now . . . do it straight away . . .

Lennox can scarcely believe his ears. Looks into the front of the vehicle where the paramedics sit, one tense at the wheel, the other one mimicking his edginess. — I've never known piles that severe. Fuck sake, I've got them myself . . .

— Nah, mate . . . these ain't your normal Rockfords, Hollis gasps, his eyes bulging as he swivels his head to

116

Lennox, — they're potential killers. You can bleed out like a haemophiliac from them. The consultant warned this could happen any time . . . should have been done years ago . . .

They reach the hospital and Lennox sits with Hollis for a bit after they administer sedatives and stem the bleeding. The specialist confirms that Hollis is suffering from chronic ruptured haemorrhoids. Far from being trivial, this is the worst case the doctors have seen and he needs to be operated on straight away.

Compelled to return north of the border, Lennox asks Hollis if there's anybody he should call.

— Nah, you're alright, Ray. I just wanna get this done and get the fuck out, as quietly as possible. Some cunts in the Met will see this as . . . Hollis shakes his head, deadpan, — well, you know how that goes . . .

— Your secret is safe with me and no doubt a few thousand Millwall. Lennox smiles as Hollis's face creases in grim recognition. — Good luck, and I'll check in when I get back home.

— Thanks, Ray, Hollis says. — You're a diamond.

Lennox squeezes his big shoulder and exits the ward, picking up a cab in the hospital car park.

He heads for the Premier Inn at Euston, fuddled with alcohol, cocaine and a maddening disorientation as he tries to piece events together, placing the still-malfunctioning phone on the radiator in his room. It's only then he sees the note on his bedside table, or rather a series of them, advising him Toal has called and that it's urgent.

He groans, and sucks in a breath, steeling himself, dialling on the hotel phone.

Toal immediately snaps, — Where the fuck have you been?!

— My phone packed in, Lennox half lies. — The first attempted victim here is Christopher Piggot-Wilkins, a Home

Office luminary. They've closed ranks and the case obviously isn't being handled through normal investigative channels. We've been staking out people Hollis believes might be able to shed some light on things.

Toal has seen through Lennox's 'daft laddie' defence, the recovered bite of his reaction telling the detective his boss has received instructions from on high. It's evident that the Chief Super knows all about Christopher Piggot-Wilkins. — Leave it! Don't be getting involved in Hollis's extra-curricular bull-shit, he was told to pull back on that case! I need you back here in Edinburgh right now.

— But, boss . . . Lennox is stunned to hear his own voice, that of a petulant teenager told he can't stay out past ten o'clock — . . . I thought I might give it another day. A few developments here that have –

— Return immediately, Ray. The first flight tomorrow morning.

— Okay, Lennox says. — What's happening?

— Gulliver's funeral is tomorrow afternoon.

— Jesus, that was quick.

— Wasn't it just! I want you there.

— Right, and Lennox sighs, hangs up, pulls off his clothes, and sinks into the black hole offered by the Hypnos mattress.

Day Three
Thursday

15

Morning drifts in. A cold, slate London sky, as Ray Lennox wakes up in the Euston Premier Inn with the worst hangover he's had in a long time. Only the contemplation of his unstable guts and badly cauterised sinuses afford him minor respite from the attentions of his banging head.

With a shaking hand, he forces down some of the hotel's bottled water. He avoided the blizzard of cocaine, but that solitary line in the club was still enough to wreck his cavities and add an hour on to normal excessive drinking, before Hollis's incident called time. From the radiator a light blinks through the darkness: divine hope and sickening fear are in instant stand-off for control of his senses. His phone is back and his wrung-out body springs into animation.

As well as the texts from Toal, there are many from Trudi, Jackie, Drummond and some others. But it's his fiancée's that grip him. Skimming her road map of mounting despair and deadened resignation, he tremblingly dials her. It goes straight to voicemail. Fires off a guilty text:

> Honey, I'm so sorry to hear about your dad. My phone has just come back on. I had a bizarre accident with it. Call me. Love you x

Jumping in a cab to City airport, he buzzes Drummond, once more compelled to explain the plight of his phone. Then he asks, — So what's new?

— Not much . . . Drummond wearily concedes, and he wonders if, given the hour, she's still in bed, — banks, phones, bills, bookings . . . working through the usual data, trying to piece together Gulliver's movements, associations and rivalries. No shortage of people who don't like him, but someone who'd take him out like that is more difficult to manifest . . . How's London?

Lennox shudders, thinking of the van hurtling at him and Hollis. One or both of them could have been seriously injured. *Assassination attempt, or random nutter? Related to the Piggot-Wilkins case or long-standing enemy of Hollis?* — The top brass is protecting the guy who was the victim of the attack . . . Lennox can't say the name. Not yet. — Hollis, the investigating detective, is on it; has plenty ideas and we're following up some leads. We have to tread carefully though.

Drummond is silent for a bit. Lennox guesses she's trying to decide whether or not to ask him who the London attack victim is. She opts for, — So the two cases *are* related?

Lennox blows through pursed lips, stopping when he realises that it will sound like electrical static to Drummond. — It's obvious, but until they're candid about the identity of the Savoy victim, we can't tie him in with Gulliver.

— Well, the post-mortem has confirmed that Gulliver was smashed on the front of his head by a mallet. They found some wooden microfibres there. It is the Rab Dudgeon MO.

— Interesting, Lennox says, meaning 'old news'. — Anything else?

— Toxicology positived him for alcohol and Rohypnol.

— So he was definitely unconscious before this blow?

— Yes, though it cracked his skull and they discovered that brain fluid was pushing down on the front membrane.

— What does that mean?

— Without treatment he'd have probably died within a few hours.

— Difficult to see castration and bleeding out as a mercy killing.

— Not how I'd choose to describe it, Ray.

— Of course not, Lennox mumbles. *Drummond has changed. She now sees you as a rival for Toal's job. Nothing more, nothing less. Perhaps you have too. The matey collusiveness of ex-partners is gone.* — We're checking out the London victim's movements, associations and, of course, any possible connections with Gulliver, he explains. — Nothing obvious so far to suggest they even know each other.

— No overt old school tie connections?

— Not yet. He thinks of Hollis in the hospital bed. Wonders how much investigating David and Soppy Bollocks will be doing on his behalf.

An acerbic bite she rarely shows on investigations tinges Drummond's voice: — These people are only one degree of separation from each other.

Lennox decides to take advantage. — So, what's your gut on this?

— Gulliver was a piece of shit, so some person or persons, whom he'd probably wronged in a heinous way, decided to take grim retribution. Going into some of his past incidents . . . there's been three alleged rape and sexual assault victims. And you remember Graham Cornell, from the Confectioner case . . .

— Right . . .

— All settled out of court, one a Judy Barless, several years back, the other two designated Ms X by the media. I've spoken to Barless, she was paid fifty grand to be quiet. I absolutely believe her account of the rape at a Tory Party conference weekend.

— So, we're trying to identify the two Ms Xs?

— No luck so far. What do *you* think about all this?

— Not a lot, apart from the obvious, that Rab Dudgeon's inside. Thanks to the tabloids, the world knows his MO, but I'm not sure why anybody would rip it off to get revenge on Gulliver.

— Like a lot of things to do with this, it makes very little sense, she observes. Then she changes tack. — Are you okay?

With the Drummond of old, Lennox would have taken this as genuine concern. Now he's not so sure. — Think I might have picked up a bit of a bug, he contends, — but nothing incapacitating, so far.

— Take care.

— Thanks. He hangs up, a little confused.

Is Drummond fishing? Looking for weakness? Perhaps of the sort that cocaine brought to the party? Or are you just being paranoid? Coke paranoid?

He laughs to himself. Thinks of her trying to 'cop him oot' or 'polis him tae fuck' as his old senior partner Bruce Robertson was prone to saying.

We're off duty, so dinnae cop ays oot.

The City airport check-in has minimal fuss. Lennox, in his jeans, loafers, scarf and Harrington jacket, surrounded by suits that cast disapproving eyes over him, is relieved to be airborne and heading home.

You're protecting the wealth and power of cunts that think you're a fucking jakey.

Arriving back in Edinburgh, feeling like he's been away for a week instead of just one night, he checks his phone: still nothing from Trudi. Curses himself for not having her mum's number. Texts her again, jumping in a cab to her place. En route he checks his emails: an interesting one from Sebastian Taylor.

To: RLennox@policescot.co.uk
From: staylor125@gmail.com
Subject: Ms X

Dear Ray,

You might want to look at this case from 15 years ago:

Ms X was repeatedly raped by two men, in a cable car in the exclusive resort of Val d'Isère in the French Alps. She was working as a barmaid. The men were described as from good homes and of good character. Justice Aubrey Humphries QC said: 'I'm afraid this seems to be a case of young people in high spirits enjoying too much alcohol and getting carried away. This young woman went skiing with these two young men. I suppose it must have been an exhilarating experience for her.'

It's been an open secret in Whitehall for years that Chris Piggot-Wilkins is one of the two men. His family pulled strings to keep the names out the paper in case it wrecked his Civil Service career. Ms X's identity was concealed too. I've no intel on who they could be, unfortunately.

You can quote me if you like. Not much they can do to me now!

The second Ms X case I've no information on, other than that it took place in a Brighton hotel eight years ago.

Best,

Sebastian

*If this cunt Piggot-Wilkins was one of the ski gondola men,
then Ms X might have the motivation to do that to him. Who was
the other man? Could it be Gulliver?*

In the spirit of cooperation, he forwards everything to Mark
Hollis.

Just as he gets to Marchmont, pushing some money into
the cabbie's mitts and stepping out the taxi, he sees Trudi
coming out the stair door. She's with somebody; a suited guy
her age, around thirty, who offers an escorting arm, ushering
her into a brown BMW. Instead of going to her, the detective
in him makes Lennox pull back as he steps behind the bus
shelter on the main road. The BMW takes off at the same
time as his taxi, leaving him standing in the street, contemplating his losses.

Fuck sake . . .

A brutal thump of despair hits. All adrenaline leaves him.
He's aware of a keen hangover pulse. It throbs in his head,
erupts in sweat from his pores.

*It was your fucking phone . . . an accident . . . you were
almost fucking killed by some cunt in that van . . . and she's
hanging out with – probably riding – some slimy fucker in a
BMW . . .*

Lennox cannot think of what to do. Does he go to the hospital? Falls into a trance, letting his subconscious do the
decision-making, dispirited as a cab pulls him into the driveway of Police HQ at Fettes.

He heads to the office of a strangely dishevelled Bob Toal.
His boss now looks as if he's been sleeping in his clothes,
sparse but normally well-tailored grey hair sticking up in tufts.
This uncharacteristic shabbiness hints at a man who has
recently taken to advanced binge drinking. With the barrier
of the large desk and a force field of Blue Stratos between
them, Lennox cannot get close enough to detect alcohol

126

fumes. He's ready to ask how he is doing, but Toal nips in first. — Glad you're in, Ray, I need you to brief the team . . . Any developments? No, I'll hear it all in the briefing . . . Look, I didn't want to tell you this on the phone, Toal stumbles, — but Jim McVittie . . . Lauren . . . well, you know she turned . . . Toal's mouth puckers as he slides a file over the table. — It's a bad one, Ray.

Lennox reads the top sheet in disbelief:

Trans activist Lauren Fairchild was found badly beaten in a Glasgow street. After visiting several bars with friends, she was attacked in the alley by Queen Street station, when preparing to get on the late Stirling train.

Seemingly unrelated events scramble together; Lennox tries to form connective tissue between Lauren's plight, Gulliver's murder, Piggot-Wilkins's attack, the speeding van outside the Savoy, and the shadowy web of posh sex fiends around Wallingham that Hollis is on to. On one level it's ludicrous to imagine another conspiracy or cult, but the notion of a protective network in operation is far from fanciful. All criminality is to some extent social; a web of friends and family either positively enable or, more usually, are in mass denial of the sex fiend in their midst. An old boy network is simply a well-established extension of that.

— Jim . . . Lauren is in a coma and not expected to survive, Toal tells him.

Gayle. Lauren was wary of that big lump. It didn't sit right. You need to find him, or her. Surely he wasn't driving the van at the Savoy . . .

— I have to go and check some stuff out.

— *After* the briefing, Toal insists. — And, Ray, stick to Gulliver; keep the London case and Hollis out of this for now.

The top brass have definitely got to Toal.

— Is that wise? They're obviously related.

— Do you *want* to be promoted, Raymond?

— We should tell the team, boss. They'll find out through the grapevine soon enough, and it would be undermining and unfair to let them ferret around blind when every cunt in the Met knows. We need to tie Piggot-Wilkins to Gulliver, and to the perp . . . I got sent this . . . and he produces the article from Sebastian having printed off a hard copy for his boss.

Toal puts on his specs and reads. A strange sound between a mumble and a growl escapes from him, then he shuts one eye, fixing Lennox in his Cyclops stare. — So this fucked-up old journo, who probably has a ton of grievances against Piggot-Wilkins, is claiming he was one of the rape assailants in these cases. Of course, no evidence at all provided. And you're saying the second Alpine gondola rapist is Gulliver, and the victim, Ms X, is his killer and Piggot-Wilkins's assailant?

— Well, I'm *not saying it is*, just that it's a worthwhile line of inquiry.

— Okay. Toal lets out a long breath. His face crinkles in pain. — Pursue it. No, he snaps his fingers. — Drummond and Glover will pursue it. They'll operate with discretion.

— Yes. Lennox forces a taut grin. As he regards his boss, he reminds himself that ulcers are caused by a certain viral infection or bacteria in the gut, and have nothing to do with stress. However, it's hard to escape the impression that Toal's stomach is an acid-manufacturing plant, which will corrode its lining, and sharpen the potency of any blemish caused by infection. Lennox's mind spins with nervous humour about Toal and Hollis in an ulcer-vesus-piles suffering stand-off.

128

Looking at his watch, Toal indicates it's time. Lennox resolves that he will tear through the briefing at speed, then go and see Lauren. As they get to the conference room, a low-ceiling head-wreck of fluorescent lighting, Toal wisely swerves the canteen-issued industrial-strength coffee, settling on a custard cream. Lennox, succumbing, knows he will pay.

A high, nasal accent tells them that Norrie Erskine is in full flow, — . . . so the wee Glesca lad says, 'Aye, miss, but muh da's been in the jile fur ten years!' Haw haw haw . . . yuv goat tae laugh!

A trademark scowl indicates Dougie Gillman is growing tired of his Glasgow sidekick and the constant stream of jokes mythologising his home city.

Erskine doesn't notice. — Did ah tell yis the wahn aboot the boy in the pub? Nah? Boy walks intae a pub *in Glesca*, he says, implying a laugh.

Billy Connolly has a lot to answer for, Lennox considers. In his wake, every Glaswegian seems to think they are brilliant comedians. To be fair, many are.

But not all of them.

As they prepare to commence, Gillman confides to Lennox in a low whisper. — I'll fucking swing for that fat Weedgie phantom. If ah git the promo, first thing ah'll dae is send that spastic tae traffic!

Sipping at his coffee, stronger than many lines of ching Lennox has had, he keeps his counsel.

— Right, says Toal, as the group assemble, Harkness and McCorkel being the last of the stragglers, — Ray . . .

Stepping forward, Lennox opts to play it cagey. — Thanks, Bob. Okay, then. He nods at the gathered officers. — They targeted Gulliver, planning this meticulously. We still don't know why he was here in the first place. Neither does his sister, Moira, nor his wife, Samantha, nor his business or political associates up here. So what's going on?

The first to comment is Gillman. — Revenge attack. Cunt's obviously been at the Mick Ronson. Find out every fucker Gulliver Cadbury'd and the killer is maist likely on that list. Two Ms Xs, or one ay them or her felly, must be prime suspects. And Graham Cornell, he panelled that cunt once, and he looks at Lennox in satisfaction, recalling an incident from when Lennox outed the relationship Gulliver was having with the civil servant.

Drummond comes forward, looks to Glover. — We checked him out. He has an alibi. He was working at a birds of prey sanctuary. Judy Barless couldn't have been directly involved either, she was at a conference in Belgium, though that's not to say either of them couldn't have gotten associates involved.

— Need tae find they Ms Xs, Gillman snorts, looking at Drummond.

— It has all the makings of a revenge attack, Lennox agrees. A very vicious assault, but that's what bugs me.

— How so, Ray? Peter Inglis asks.

Lennox avoids looking at Toal. Decides to drop a bomb. — The brutality of the assaults seems out of sync with the meticulous planning of the entrapments. The first one suggested that they were no strangers to cold, analytical planning, but perhaps not so experienced in the messy theatre of violence.

— Served the apprenticeship wi that London boy, then made nae mistake wi Gulliver, Gillman says, looking pleased with himself.

— Use of the plural, Ray, Drummond says excitedly, as if happy to drop Lennox in it. — Anything more from London to tie Gulliver to the Savoy case?

Toal's rancorous stare tells Lennox that he has already fed

130

too much of the Savoy assault into the mix, and this has not impressed his boss. — Can't say for certain yet. Let's stay focused on this case.

— What are you saying here, Ray? Drummond pushes.

— We can't discount the possibility of more than one perp, Lennox contends. — Perhaps at least two people, working as a team.

Gillman looks snidely at him. — Obviously the London case backs this up.

Lennox thinks of the two shabby CCTV figures through those plastic sheets, the first masked one obviously female, the other an indeterminate mass. — I wouldn't have gone down there had there not been some similarity in the MO, but there's no hard evidence to link them so far.

— As I said, we shouldn't be ruling anything out, Drummond says.

— Ruling fuck all out, Gillman snaps, then smiles. — Just hypothesising.

— Well, Dougie, Drummond pumps herself up, — as always, your tone suggests otherwise!

A round of bitter asides follows as Lennox looks to a wearisome Toal. The unspoken thought hangs between them: *Monday's interviews for the job have just started.*

— Right. Lennox raises his voice, silencing the room. — You know what to do. Keep up the door-knocking and poring over the footage and the data. Good luck!

As Lennox hurries off, Gillman, breaking rank with Erskine, pursues him down the corridor. — Lenny! Hud oan!

Lennox stalls. Turns around.

— Brains and brawn combo, this one, Gillman states. — You're on the right track here, then lowering his voice, he quickly amends the subject. — Watch Drummond. Ah ken you two have form, but she's no your pal. In it for herself, that yin: just made DI and now wants tae queue-jump over us for Chief Super? She's right up Toal's erse!

Lennox allows himself brief amusement at the thought of Drummond in a strap-on ramming Toal's anus, before he thinks of Hollis in the hospital.

Then Lauren. Gayle . . . maybe Gayle was in London, driving the van at Hollis and you . . . No, behave. You're a mass of anti-tranny prejudice like everyone else . . .

— What? Gillman is confused with his posture.

— I can't be bothered with this.

— My advice, Lenny, Gillman declares, — be bothered. She's gaunny fuck you like you fucked Robbo. And we aw ken what happened tae that poor cunt. He draws a finger across his throat. Then seems to reconsider. — That was in bad taste. He cocks his head to one side, yanking it up with a hand on an invisible noose as his tongue darts out and eyes bulge.

— You, me, Drummond, Lennox says, maintaining a cool facade, — we all bring something different to the table. Reckon they'll go ootside anyway.

— Mibbe, Gillman says.

Lennox shrugs and drives off to Glasgow, full of perturbation, to check in on his old friend. En route he opts to detour via Lauren's home base of Stirling, taking the Kincardine Bridge, feeling fortunate to have avoided much of the oft-nightmarish traffic.

Professor Rex Pearlman, the Dean of Lauren's university faculty, is a reluctant cooperator. Lennox quickly susses out that his priority is to avoid any scandal attaching itself to his department. A thin, athletic man with a mop of salt-and-pepper hair, he speaks in an accent Lennox judges as Canadian rather than American. The ice-hockey memorabilia, some decorated with maple leaves, confirm this. Lennox asks him for a list of students in Lauren's classes. — What was she working on?

— She was concerned that the movement of genuine trans people was being hijacked by a coalition of toxic, mentally unstable, needy and highly sexist men, Pearlman discourses, his tone loosening up, clearly in admiration of Lauren's work, — attention-seeking young narcissists and, even worse, serial harassers and sex offenders. She was preparing a paper to be delivered in support of the genuine transgender and women's movements against those noxious interlopers, and he looks at Lennox as if for a reaction.

You don't know, and you don't really care. — This is fascinating stuff. All a bit of a mystery to me, I must confess.

— Things are changing so rapidly, Pearlman confirms, — I even worry that my ice-hockey stuff sends some sort of trans-exclusionary message.

For fuck sake . . .

Lennox leaves the Dean with gratitude. Heads to the campus coffee bar to quickly fire up his laptop, looking through social media accounts. The big unit called Gayle seems active on Facebook and Twitter. He switches to look at Trudi's profiles.

Nothing new. Facebook still has her in a relationship. But with who?

Then he sees a smiling, denture-flashing picture of the new man. Traces it through her friends to the profile of: Dean Slattery, Dunedin Power. 'You'll find me all over the place, except between three o'clock and five o'clock on a Saturday, when I'll be at Easter Road, cheering on the mighty Hibees!'

A Hibs bastard too . . . fuck sake . . . all bland shit: he sounds a right boring cunt.

Calls up the profile on LinkedIn. Slattery, after being head-hunted from Shell, has recently joined Dunedin Power as a Senior Account Executive.

Young, handsome, ambitious, not fucked up; what does she see in him? Lennox finds himself sniggering in a nervous, manic dissatisfaction, jumping back in the Alfa Romeo to carry on west to Glasgow.

It could be perfectly innocent. Her dad might be seriously ill. Keep the desperation out your tones.

He types:

> Baby, you have to let me
> know how you are and how
> your dad is doing. Please
> call me. xx

The hospital is in an area of the city he doesn't know well, up a steep hill, close to Strathclyde University and the Merchant City, but also bordering the poorer East End.

An eerie stillness pervades as Lennox walks across the car park, coming to a fire door held open by what looks like gym weights. He walks in, following temporary handwritten signs for the designated ward. As he enters, the building inside maintains the spooky *Mary Celeste* feel. At one stage he thinks he can hear footsteps behind him. Stops. Turns. It seems to be his imagination.

Then he comes to the ward. The doors are shut. He presses a switch and a voice on the intercom asks him to identify himself. He does, and is instructed to push a green button. He complies and the doors give way. Lennox thinks of Confectioner, and how hospitals and prisons seem to get more like each other. A morbidly obese nurse sits at a desk, jowls up-lit

by a table lamp. She seems not to see him. — I'm looking for
Lauren Fairchild, he says.

— Room B10, she offers, jabbing a pencil to his left.

He walks down the empty corridor, looking through the
windows into the rooms of sick, wizened and battered people.
Sees a note taped to B10:

LAUREN FAIRCHILD

Pushes the door.

16

Ray Lennox has seen many assault victims. Humans rendered less so, by the brutalising force of violent, unremarkable men. After a while, the battered become just repellent, unsavoury things to look at, like a full ashtray to a non-smoker. But something about the state of Lauren induces a deep dread in him. Smashed up, she looks as if she's reverted to a shabby version of Jim McVittie. And that's because she's been so badly pulped that now gender really is irrelevant.

All that *work*, rendered obsolete.

Jim . . . Lauren . . . just wanted to get on with it . . .

A tug on his bladder compels him to head into the toilet in the small room. Through the relief of his jet gushing into the water, he can vaguely hear a nurse administering care to his friend. He washes and dries his hands. Opens the door to see the screens pulled round the bed. Something makes him look in; he sees what he takes to be a large female nurse with powerful forearms, colourful bangles at the wrists, holding a pillow over his stricken friend.

Pressing it down over Lauren's battered face.

There's a gelid heartbeat where both parties regard each other. Some long strands of hair poke out from a surgical mask and cap the intruder wears. Through a space between them, two eyes blaze at Lennox, who shakes out his inertia and leaps forward. The intruder grabs a metal stand and hurls it at him. The bag splits and Lennox feels a tepid chemical coat his shoulder and the side of his face: the aroma instantly tells him that it's piss . . .

Taking advantage of his confusion, the intruder smashes him with a powerful right hook, rattling his jaw. Its force and weight suggest a knuckleduster in the hand of the assailant. Lennox manages to stay on his feet, grabbing the screens, which snap from their rail. He boots out a leg, catching the retreating invader as they turn to exit. His opponent is briefly forced off balance, but with impressive agility for their size, they manage to correct themselves, careening through the door. All Lennox sees in departure is a hulking body, powerful calves, in a nurse's dress.

Gayle . . .

Attempting to follow, he slides on the piss, ending up on his arse, the screen falling around him, as his coccyx makes disabling contact with the tiled floor. Forcing himself to his feet, he staggers to the door, screaming in frustration and burning humiliation for the staff to attend to Lauren, as the intruder whips round the corner. His slow stumbled pursuit is futile; by the time he gets to the fire escape that they have pushed ajar, all he can hear is the receding sound of feet slapping on stairs. This is followed by a further set of doors crashing open.

He goes to phone it in: no signal. Follows down the stairs and out the fire door, his tailbone still throbbing. A young couple are on the ground; the boy frantically pulls up his trousers, the girl straightens her skirt. — We were just . . . she gasps, pointing up the street, — they came tearing out the door, they went that way!

— Aye, fuckin pure mental, by the way, the boy observes.

As Lennox turns the corner, he hears the roar of a car engine, and a Toyota tears towards him. Over the mask: a pair of crazed eyes. He throws himself on the embankment as the car hurtles past him.

Again! For fuck sake!

Lennox pulls out his phone, trying to get a snap of the plates, but the vehicle has gone. Instantly thinking of the Savoy incident, he looks around for CCTV cameras. Can't see any. *There must be some.* All he is aware of, in the still, cold car park, is the racing heartbeat in his chest and the smell of piss in his nostrils and an almost jaw-broken throb in the side of his face. It's deserted bar the young couple, who are leaving, and he hears the girl observe, — That boy wis mingin.

He calls Chic Gallagher in Glasgow Serious Crimes. Heads back onto the ward, getting cleaned up as best he can, checking that Lauren has been stabilised. Fortunately, there seems no further adverse change in her condition, which the doctor explains remains perilous. Gallagher swiftly arrives. — I'll get a uniformed spastic tae keep a lookoot, he confirms.

Almost too shaken to register that Glasgow Serious Crimes have appropriated their Edinburgh colleagues' designation for uniformed officers, Lennox thanks Gallagher and the staff, then heads off.

Those bangles . . . it had to be Gayle; that powerful, manly build with the accessorising of a woman. Whatever pronoun you adopt, the antagonism to Lauren is palpable. But why you? Does Gayle think you're getting closer to this than you are?

It must have been a shit mark in the essay . . .

Along the M8 motorway tension gnaws at his guts. Images burn through his head; the most persistent being Trudi, and he fires off a text to her:

> Please call me! Where are you?

Then he scrolls his contact list. Under 'G', Keith Goodwin, the piously cheerful fireman who is still, nominally, his NA sponsor. Hesitating only briefly to feel the extent of his vexation, he gratefully pushes on to 'H' and his psychotherapist, Sally Hart.

Sally's voice is reassuring; neutral, calming, Edinburgh bourgeois tones tailored with detached professionalism. — Ray . . . the last time I saw you, you had just come back from Miami.

— I really need to talk to somebody.

— Of course, but this is not a quick fix, or crisis management stuff. Sally's voice takes on an authoritative charge. — If I'm to help you, you have to commit to a proper counselling relationship again. Can you do that?

— Yes, Lennox says, seeing an open stretch of road and opting to switch lanes. A BMW cuts him up.

Fucking spazwit cunt.

The idea of sticking his police siren on the roof and pulling the occupant over grips him tightly. Instead he draws a long breath.

— Then I can fit you in tomorrow, he hears Sally say.

He then phone-checks the CCTV footage sent by Chic Gallagher: the retreating back of a powerful man, bangles evident on the wrists. It has to be Gayle. Shouldn't be too difficult to find. He calls Scott McCorkel, the ginger-headed Serious Crimes IT whizz kid. — I want you to find out all you can about a Stirling University Gender Studies student called Gayle. A well-known figure, around six foot four of solid muscle in a dress and highly visible custom-made heels, bracelets, bangles, belts and bag.

— Right . . . Male or female? McCorkel asks cagily.

— If you can find a satisfactory answer to that question, Scott, you should be a world leader instead of a polisman.

On his return to Edinburgh, Lennox heads to his flat and gets cleaned up. Even the rat-trap local of mercurial landlord Jake Spiers tempts him. He fights alcohol's nag. Trudi has still

139

not responded to his texts. Drives back to hers: once again empty, so heads on to her mother's place. Also deserted. Looks through the letter box. An ominous feeling of abject despair seizes him as he returns home.

Mr BMW has moved her in . . . probably the old girl's in the spare room . . . fuck . . . what the fuck . . .

> Please! Just call me! I'm at
> my wits end here!

It looks pathetic, but he presses send. At the flat he checks the time. Tears off his clothes, pulls on a white shirt, black tie and navy-blue dress jacket. He has to be somewhere. Gets back in the car and drives north to Perthshire.

The burial takes place in a small graveyard within the family estate. Mourners are sheltered from a blustery wind by huge stone walls and an assortment of fir, pine and silver birch trees, which look like skinny-legged giants half dived into the soft soil. The funeral, turned around in great haste, seems designed to wrong-foot media attention. The post-mortem was completed with strings obviously pulled to issue the death certificate the next day. The plank-faced, John Lennon-spectacled minister is evidently a family friend. Nonetheless, this is far removed from Warriston Crematorium, the proceedings' affluence illustrated by the formality of the mourners, who line up in expensive dark suits and black ties, dresses and hats. If Lennox's instinct regarding attire to err on the formal is vindicated, he still manages to be an effortless pariah. Glances of outright disbelief and naked hostility are all trained his way.

Goth Ascot . . .

Lennox eyes several politicians, a TV presenter and a man

140

habitually described as a comedian by the media, but who has never managed to wring so much as a chuckle out of him. Yet it's important to be here. Statistically, there is a good chance that the murderer will be in attendance. They often find it hard to keep away from the victim, even in their death.

Inside the box: Ritchie Gulliver.

Lennox thinks about this man, who worked so relentlessly hard to forge himself as a totally abject, worthless piece of shit. Watching the mourners around the coffin, as John Lennon dispenses pieties, he wonders if Gulliver would perversely regard his demise as a fitting one.

A timely text from Gillman:

> Ask them if the undertakers put
> a false cock and baws on the cunt.

As soon as the service is over, the mourners begin to make their way up to the stately home. Lennox scans them, but his eyes invariably go back to Moira Gulliver, who seems to linger close by. She's talking to a man he recognises as James Thorpe, a disgraced property developer, just recently released from a cushy open prison after a major mortgage fraud.

Lennox tries to work out how a criminal lawyer can be close friends with a recently released felon. But he knows enough about the wealthy to realise that they seldom consider their own behaviour as actually or even potentially criminal. They've been compartmentalised all their lives; boarding school and university, home, trips during holidays. They are conditioned into thinking of themselves as operating in, and inhabiting, closed, secret institutions, where what they do is private and not the concern of society at large.

Suddenly his sister Jackie is marching towards him. She

bristles with the vivacious intimidating power he recalls from his adolescence. — You've got a bloody nerve coming here, and she glances apologetically at Moira. — And why aren't you answering your phone? Trudi's been in bits, she –

— I know about her dad.

— Have you talked to her?

— Been trying to. Lennox shakes his mobile. — She won't pick up. I had an accident with my phone and it was broken. I reckon she thinks I was up to something or didn't care about her dad. Anyway, it's all just a misunderstanding. It's back on now.

At that declaration, his device springs into action, announcing Hollis. It seems to vibrate with more urgency when his name burns on the screen. Lennox nods to Jackie, stepping towards a robust oak tree close to the stone perimeter wall of the graveyard. He watches his sister follow Moira and some other guests up a cut-grass bank to a huge glass conservatory, which stands out against the grey-stone building with its turrets and spires.

Before he can mention he's at Gulliver's funeral, Hollis shrieks in panic mode, — They're on to me, Ray. They got goons, those posh cahnts, hired scum who'll top any cahnt for a few grand. I reckon it was them wot tried to do us in the Strand. They're here in the hozzy. We're out of our depth, son. We ain't bringing them down!

Lennox instantly suspects cocaine psychosis, and asks Hollis what is going on.

In a long, rambling spiel, Lennox gets that Hollis believes he's being spied on in the ward. He thinks of Lauren's attack. Dismisses the thought.

In the departure of the mourners, he catches Moira, literally two eyes, staring at him from the distance before she

142

moves up the steps that split the bank. He turns away, into the cemetery wall. — Mark, listen to me.

— You don't get it, Ray, those cahnts –

— Shut the fuck up a second, Lennox barks, as a loitering couple, admiring some plants, turn round. He smiles in tight apology, waving the phone.

— Okay! Okay! I'm farking listening!

— Now start consciously breathing, Lennox commands, walking away from the grave, his feet sinking into the turf as he moves by the family plots towards the conservatory, — in through the nose and out through the mouth.

— Right . . .

A long silence down the line, bar something that sounds like traffic speeding past, cars passing intermittently. He realises it's Hollis's jagged cocaine sinuses creaking with every breath. — Now, listen . . .

— I'm listening . . . Hollis says, his tones stroppy, but more composed.

— I've had this said to me a million times, so it's not moral-high-ground bullshit. It's just the point we sometimes hit: you need to sack the fuckin ching for a bit. At least while you're in a hospital bed, for fuck sakes.

— Yeah, I am, Hollis concedes. — It's fucking up my arsehole. That wound pulses like a cahnt when I smash one.

As Hollis is deadly serious, Lennox is engaged in a battle to stifle laughter. But again, the lamps of Moira Gulliver burn him; she's loitering in the patio area in front of the conservatory with Jackie and another woman, and he finds his solemn demeanour. — Are they giving you anything to help you get to sleep?

— Yeah, I got them pills. But I'm worried about some cahnt trying to get onto the ward when I'm out of it.

143

It happens . . .

— Mark, nobody would be crazy enough to attempt that. Just try and settle down, Lennox urges, looking over towards Moira Gulliver, who is now stepping inside.

— Yeah, I know . . . a bit of a panic attack, Hollis acknowledges in calmer realisation.

— But listen, wot did happen is that I got ole Soppy Bollocks to check out that Ursula Lettinger bird your Jock mate Williamson name-dropped. He thought she was being shifty. Then he gets hauled over the farking coals, told by our guvnor that she was off-limits. That cahnt David wasn't even gonna tell me. How can you investigate an assault and murder if the people pertinent to the inquiry are off-limits?

— It's not easy. But the ching and booze won't help us.

— Yeah, gotcha, sorry, mate, lost it a bit there . . .

— No worries, bud; just take it easy. And take care. Just because we're paranoid et cetera . . . Call you later.

His own nerves jangling, he phones Trudi again. Once again: voicemail. He looks up to the huge conservatory, its tables laden with food and beverages. Despondency hits him like a train. Lennox has seldom felt more like an outsider. He opts not to go in. Doubts he'd be welcome, even by, or especially by, Jackie.

Instead he goes round the side of the house to the driveway, where the Alfa Romeo is easily the shabbiest vehicle present. Drives straight back to Edinburgh. Ditching the car, he finds himself wandering the streets, trying to piece together what's been happening with the case. But Trudi buzzes in his head.

Aye, her dad's sick, but you've nearly been run over twice! Where the fuck is she? She's with the BMW bastard . . .

It's getting dark and cold and his treacherous feet have carried him to within a stone's throw of the dive bar known as the

Repair Shop. He goes inside, craving its poisoned warmth. Some faces are already present. The hardened Serious Crimes guys seem less like cops, more a confessional support group for useless fuck-ups. Gillman looks on as Erskine holds court with Ally Notman, Brian Harkness and younger officers like Scott 'PC' McCorkel. He wants to deter this decent young man, and for that matter himself, from this company. Yet here they are. — Of course, Erskine roars, — ah goes onstage and the audience just starts laughing. Didnae realise that Rikki Fulton wis behind me, pulling faces.

Gillman turns to Harkness and in Lennox's earshot snaps, — Does that bloated ratshagger ever shut the fuck up?

A call comes in on Lennox's phone, but it's not Trudi, it's Amanda Drummond. — How was the funeral?

— Awful. I shouldn't have gone. I'm in the fucking Repair Shop now, and he watches Erskine, oblivious to Gillman scowling murderously at him. — I really wish I was somewhere else.

— If Marcello's fits your definition of somewhere else, feel free to join me here.

— Are you in company?

— No. My friend cancelled as she has a date. I didn't feel like staying in.

— Then you've just rescued me from the same pish I've heard every single day of my working life. Leaving now.

And he heads to the toilet before sneaking off and out the side door.

Situated no more than a fifteen-minute walk from the Repair Shop, through a warren of Southside tenement streets, just past the National Museum, Marcello's Wine Bar is culturally light years away. Its cushioned seats and soft, up-lit aspect, artworks on the walls, make it more palatial to those from a certain social niche, but it too contains an element of desperation obvious to Lennox as he enters and looks around. It seems full of couples that are forlornly avoiding the people they are married too. Drummond is settled into a corner table, partly obscured by a huge yucca plant on a stand. Always on stakeout, Lennox thinks. He orders a bottle of Malbec from the bar, with two glasses, and also asks for a double espresso.

Fuck Keith Goodwin. And fuck Trudi Lowe.

Lennox settles down and pours himself a glass. — What's that you're drinking? he asks, looking at her almost-empty glass.

— Rioja, she says, finishing it up.

— Is Malbec alright for you?

— Great. So how was the Repair Shop?

— I'm redesignating it the Despair Shop, he says, then, noting she seems more relaxed and lit up than of late, implores, — I need re-educating, Amanda.

— We all need that, Ray, she smiles.

— I'm still trying to learn as much as I can about all this trans stuff.

— How long have you got?

— As long as you can spare.

The waiter comes across with his double espresso. Drummond takes this in, then asks, — Have you noticed anything strange about Bob lately?

Lennox has, but plays dumb to get her take. — Such as? Don't tell me he's transitioning . . . into a cop?

Drummond does not join in his levity. — Well, for one thing, he's never around.

— I think he's moving into retirement mode.

— It's very unprofessional, she snaps, sounding genuinely vexed. — I would never have thought that of him.

He wishes to steer the conversation back to the trans issue, but Drummond reminds him that the Chief Super interviews take place on Monday and is obviously keen to discuss this. Lennox reluctantly acquiesces. They agree that whoever wins the promotion, it won't affect the respect they have for each other. — I've learned so much from you, Ray.

— It's a two-way street, Amanda. I've learned a ton of new things from you.

Drummond shoots an evaluating look at Lennox, trying to determine whether or not he's taking the piss. Apparently unable to decide one way or another, she moves on. — I'm not looking forward to the interview.

— I'm not going to take it too seriously. Lennox stretches and yawns, recharges their glasses. — They'll pick who they want. I don't know if I see myself in that job, he contends. He looks at the coffee.

Drummond's eyes expand. — But it's an important post! You could get so much done! We need more resources to tackle serious crime! Our clean-up rate needs to be higher!

— I agree. Lennox looks over at the paintings. It seems to be all local artists on display, none of them very good. — But I doubt if arguing for them is where my strengths lie, he whips back to her. — Maybe Bob started off as an idealist and got ground down by the system: all that tabloid-led hysteria, the opportunistic politicians, the arse-covering careerists.

A silence hangs in the air, as Drummond seems to think deeply about this.

— I have to thank you for hooking me up with Sally. Lennox shifts to another theme. It's time to let the double espresso blitz his oesophagus. He needs a boost, and preferably not one of the cocaine variety, though he'll pay with the heartburn tax. — She's become a bit of a lifebelt when things get . . . choppy. He touches his nose, a reflexive gesture when nervy.

Why are you exposing your vulnerabilities to Drummond?

She's a rival, but is she a rival for a job you really want? Is she, then, not more of a potential saviour?

Drummond getting the post would smash plenty of egos, and while his own would most certainly be dented, it might be worth that collateral damage to see Dougie Gillman's face every single day he showed up for work.

— Sally's great, Drummond confirms. — So good at what she does.

— Do you know her well?

— Not as well as you think.

Lennox smiles and raises his hands in surrender, but his tones are pointed. — Come on, Amanda; some disclosure appreciated here please, pal; after all, I'm seeing her as a client at your recommendation.

— The point is confidentiality.

He remains silent, shrugs and takes another sip of his coffee. Though cool, it still nips his tongue.

Drummond looks at him as if she's contemplating being evasive, before suddenly settling for candour. — I was seeing her as a client too, she confesses, — but you knew that.

— Well, you did tell me about the obsession thing with your ex, but it's your business, and I'm not prying any further –

— Of course you are, Ray. She laughs loudly. It ruptures the tension between them. — This is who we are and what we do!

— It's just . . .

— What?

— It's hard to imagine you in that sort of scenario. You always seem so . . . in control.

She doesn't even permit herself an ironic smile. Lennox suspects that, since her last promotion, something fundamental about Amanda Drummond has changed. Maybe grown. Perhaps hardened. — I stopped at half a dozen sessions. It was enough, she says, now reassuringly coy again, like his old partner, a confidante, as she discloses, — You know I got a little too fixated on Carl, my ex. Sally was terrific.

— This was the guy in Dundee?

— Aye . . . I told everyone he didn't handle the break-up well, which was true . . . She looks at him.

Lennox waits it out.

— . . . but the truth was that *I* handled it even worse. We actually broke up back in Dundee, before I moved here. He wouldn't see me. To forget him, I transferred here. But I couldn't let it go. As I said, I was *inappropriate*.

From within Drummond's lexicon, this is the most self-damning word ever. Perhaps, he considers, with the exception of *unprofessional*. Under the dipping lights behind them, Lennox measures the weight of it on her.

— The experience with Sally was helpful and clarifying, she states. — It allowed me to put that relationship in its proper place.

— Where was that?

— The past.

Lennox immediately thinks of Trudi, how they seem to be putting each other in that exact same place. He watches Drummond sit up straight in her chair, becoming even more brittle. She locks her assessing gaze on him. The silence between them has taken on a charge. — What are you thinking? she asks.

— I'm thinking that you're always asking me what I'm thinking these days. This reminds him of Trudi again, and indeed, every woman he has ever gone out with.

— C'mon, Ray. Drummond giggles a little.

— Honestly?

— Of course. Her gaze has a ferocious luminosity.

In the face of Trudi's probable infidelity, Lennox can see

149

no reason not to reference the previously undefined chemistry between them. Even more so, since her last promotion: they are no longer senior and junior partner, but peers. — I'm thinking that I ought to have kissed you properly that time in the pub at Ginger's do, when I had the chance, he says, recalling that night. They eventually left the bar at a time close to each other. They didn't sleep together, though, as is the way of office politics, many assume they did.

— That, Drummond looks around, — is still on the table.

When Lennox goes to speak, he is silenced as Drummond locks her lips on his. He feels her tongue in his head, and they are dancing together in the caverns and crevices of each other's mouths, a wild, trippy performance, part physical but mostly psychic. He feels his penis thicken, and as he thinks of her vagina, imagines it dampening in concert.

When they break off, her hand rises to stroke his face. She looks deeply into his eyes. — You seem so strong and so fragile at the same time.

Once again, Lennox has heard this from practically every woman, all his adult life. In a way that few men are able to, they can all scent that scared wee boy in the tunnel, just as he shows them the tough, stoical cop. He has a defensive line for such occasions. — You just described every human being in the world.

She seems not to hear him. Looks right into his eyes with a force and intimacy that causes them to moisten. — Are we going to my place, or yours?

A brief fabrication of the disarrayed flat plays in Lennox's head; the sink full of dirty dishes, surfaces covered in takeaway cartons, and, most of all, a bed that, though seeming normal to him, would register as a sweaty, fusty swamp to a stranger. So they go back to her place, before it dawns on him that actually his flat is currently tidy in preparation for Trudi's return, and his concerns are unfounded.

Lennox is surprised at how functional Drummond's apartment is; none of the accessorising prints, plants, rugs and soft furnishings that women in particular deploy with such taste and skill to make a house a home. This is a spotlessly clean version of his place: devoid of any style or sense of aesthetic. She picks up on his reaction. — I haven't done anything to it. I'm renting and had planned to move by now, but two places I went for fell through.

— Right.

— We're going to bed now, she says.

All Lennox can do is manage a minimal nod. He's aware that Drummond has been making the running. Maybe this has always been the case with him and women. They seem to like him, yet he's always more predisposed to chasing sex offenders than sex partners. It's a terrible thought, and one that dominates over any considerations of Trudi, who already seems a figure from a distant past.

In stark contrast to the basic utilitarianism of the rest of the flat, Drummond's bed is a lavish king-sized affair with a luxuriant, firm mattress. As he removes his clothes and slides into it, Lennox is shocked at its sheer magnificent comfort. It is like that of a luxury hotel. — Great bed.

— It's something I never scrimp on, she says as she gets into it with him. She is rail-thin with small breasts that seem barely more than nipples. The fluid confidence of her movement arouses him, at odds with the gawky awkwardness she often displays in clothes. — You spend around a third of your life here. Imagine that, being able to sort out thirty-three per cent of your whole life for just a few grand? What a bargain! If only the other sixty-seven was as easy!

— Never thought of it that way, he says.

Drummond slides closer to him under the duvet and they kiss again, before locking each other in an embrace that seems as much an acknowledgement of the cold as motivated by any erotic charge. As they grow warm, Lennox focuses on kissing her deeply. Drummond is responding, perhaps also aware this is the key to making the first time more than just perfunctory. He starts to touch her lightly, letting her body do the work. The intensity builds slowly but inexorably. At first he fancies they might both come that way, but suddenly it seems too intimate for Drummond, and she demands, — Fuck me . . .

He pushes into her, watching her quickly turn red under his thrusts. She makes no noises but seems to be coming as her breathing changes and her eyes water. Then the tension spills from his own frame as he climaxes, as demented rage suddenly flows through him, coming from nowhere, something he has never experienced with Trudi or any other woman.

As they lie in each other's arms, he can feel the unease mounting in her body. It reaches critical mass as she twists away from him. Hopes she experienced his bizarre anger purely as passion. The darkness of night takes hold, swamping the room, and he feels her falling into a slumber. He lies awake, not knowing whether to stay or go. Watches her stick-thin figure, as if miles away from him in the king-size. It barely makes any impression on the contours of it. She seems already asleep, and although she's turned from him, he senses belligerence in her expression. Succumbing to tiredness, he allows himself to fall into a pit of sleep.

The mound in the bed next to you . . . who is it . . . does it even matter? You tether yourself to one person, to one city, like the dock of a port. But it could be any dock, any port. And you see them all slide past, the faces of women you've made love to and men you've put away to be locked up forever . . . and you realise that it all has nothing to do with them, it's all about yourself . . .

... the light is thin ... you can see her face ... it's big, chunky, manly, unshaven ... it turns to you with a brutal sweetness and rasps in a West Midlands accent: Noice boike!

Panic: the thrashing heart in his chest as he furiously blinks awake into a strange room and bed. A diffuse life shoots back into his head from all over the world, reassembling in his brain in two seconds. *Drummond*. Lying next to him. Turned away from him. Dread creeping through his veins. She's slept in the very same position, as if she hasn't moved at all.

Registers an intermittent bleeping sound: his phone on the floor. Struggling with the thin light spilling in through the shutters, he swings his legs out the bed. The word 'Trudi' on the screen now appears so macabrely unreal that it already seems to be a signal from beyond the grave. A vain thought: *maybe her phone has been broken too ...*

He rises and moves through the murky room towards the door. — Trudi ... he croaks, as he looks at the thin figure in the bed, a vague disturbance in the duvet now rendered a seismic force.

— I've just come from the Royal Infirmary, she flatly tells him. — It's my dad. He's dead.

17

Where did all this madness start? For her, in the French Alps. For me, even earlier. My very last happy memory of my home city of Tehran took place during Muharram, the celebration of Imam Hussain, the grandson of the Prophet. He was killed by Yazid, the Islamic ruler of that time. Occurring in the first month of the lunar Islamic calendar, Muharram is a serene celebration. As Shias, we Iranians tend to be more contemplative in our enjoyment of this festival than the majority of the Arab and Muslim world. Black-cloth-clad mourners walk, often for kilometres, to mosques outside of their locale. They pray, lighting candles for Hussain's memorial, asking God for their wishes.

Nowadays Tehran is too often engulfed in haze. The peril of pollution permeates many city districts, with the stench of chemicals and putrid decay destroying the scents of saffron, sage and blossoming trees. Every year when the air grows cold, on those windless days the fumes disgorged by cars and factories are trapped between the peaks of the spectacular Alborz mountain range which embrace the city like a crescent moon. This thick blanket of smog reduces the setting sun to a yellowish coin. Now on some days, from the burned-out site where our old home sat, you can see only the blurred outlines of high-rise buildings and the Milad Tower in the distance.

This was not the case when I was a twelve-year-old boy. As I child I always loved Muharram, due to the sense of togetherness; rich and poor, old and young. Families who had the means, like our own, would cook large pots of food, offering it to the poor of the neighbourhood. At my last observed Muharram, I was known as Arash Lankarani. My sister, Roya, fourteen, and I were part of a group of young people in our street who did our customary thing at that time of year, offering our sholeh zard, sweet saffron rice pudding, a traditional Persian dessert on which the names of our Prophet and leaders are written in cinnamon, to passing mourners and old ladies.

Our house was not quite the biggest but certainly one of the most beautiful in our district, which at this time of the year was full of street vendors. At the front of our home, a huge, bushy Persian ironwood tree, which seemed to dance sensually in the slow breeze. A magical and spiritual atmosphere permeated the air. We were largely removed from the stink of death that choked many adjoining streets: a bubble of joy in what often seemed a sea of anguish. I was always big for my age and at twelve already had stubble on my chin. Even though the war was over, and I could not be put on one of the buses and taken to the killing fields as a human sacrifice, my size troubled my mother, Fariba, a college teacher of English, and my father, Mazdak, a journalist who worked for an Arabic news agency. They still feared I'd be conscripted into the guards, and insisted I always carried a photocopy of my birth certificate.

My parents were liberal intellectuals, and Father's reports were critical of the fundamentalist clerical regime. On one occasion, police and green-baseball-capped Revolutionary Guards came to our home, taking away several Iranian and Western books and video films. They looked at Father's ornate, wine-coloured laminated cocktail cabinet, but opening it revealed none of the whisky and gin he would illicitly bring back from his travels. Those were secreted under the floorboards. It seems he had been made aware that he was on the list for a potential visit. All that was stored inside the cabinet was his collection of five bone-handled Arabian knives, sitting in their display case, picked up from a bazaar in Khartoum. They had the distinctive, classically medieval Middle Eastern scimitar look, curved-bladed daggers broadening towards the tip, varying in size from four to twelve inches.

I recall voices being raised, and my mother taking Roya and me out into the back garden at my father's request. We were scared, but the guards and police left shortly afterwards, and Father, his face strained but smiling, beckoned us back into our home.

Thankfully such incidents were rare. My mother kept a beautiful, fragrant house, constantly patrolling the hallway and living room, polishing the delightful wood inlays and of course Father's pride and joy, the cocktail cabinet. But the most regular recipients of her shining and waxing efforts were the grand mahogany table where we would sit and eat, a contented family quartet, and the shelves in the drawing room, where sat the real treasures of the house. Those gateways to other worlds we prosaically referred to as *books*. I read prodigiously from an early age, as did Roya. My sister and I were always encouraged to discuss matters beyond what I sensed were the normal parameters for our years. I loved nothing more than to sit in that glorious room and read. At the time, I had just started Balzac's *Cousin Bette*, having been encouraged to learn English by my parents. Father preferred books in that language. — Those clowns, he said, pointing outside, obviously referring to the green-shirted Revolutionary Guard, — barely understand Farsi, never mind English.

As the sun fell on this Muharram, we dutifully packed up our stalls, preparing to follow the mourners headed towards the mosques, where we would listen to noha, our quotes of mourning, and eat the Nazri food. It was the part of the day I loved best. Nothing is more truly divine than when the mosque lights are turned off, and people start praying and saying the dua. I did what I had done the last few years and sat contentedly, thinking about my life and what I might achieve. Perhaps write great works of literature, like the ones in Father's library. I was transfixed at the time by Cousin Bette, the vengeful spinster who destroys all around her, and the dishonest Valerie. On that day, sitting in the mosque with my sister, I never thought I would know anything other than peace.

Of course, I was wrong.

On our road home, we heard the distant but ominous rustle of a crowd. We looked up to see smoke billowing into the air. It seemed, at the same time, both inevitable and inconceivable that we would be affected. But it was true. We pushed through the crowds in mounting dread to find our house was burned to the ground with our parents

dead. I felt physically sick, as though I might wilt in the chaos of neighbours dancing in horror in the street around us, shouted at by sneering
guards. This, in a place that only a few hours earlier had been so full of
joy. I looked up to the star-filled sky. It had once brimmed me with rapture. Now, in its gleam, I detected only treachery. My sister grabbed my
hand tightly and screamed: — NO! THIS CANNOT BE . . . so loudly
and resonantly that everyone in our vicinity briefly fell silent. Then her
grasp eased and she fell heavily to the asphalt pavement.

Day Four
Friday

18

He can't take her hand. It's the path. It's too narrow for anything other than single file.

Would she let me?

The weather changes quickly as they traverse the long, curved trail ascending up a steep brae. The pathway rises and collapses dramatically, so that you might not see something coming until it's upon you. Perhaps that blinds Ray Lennox and Trudi Lowe to the hazard from above. Perilous black clouds swooping in, blocking the light, now empty their guts on then. Nothing forecast: the couple caught without waterproof garments. Both are soaked through by the time they get to the village. Trudi doesn't seem to care, almost catatonic as she trudges up the muddy path, rain plastering her hair to her scalp.

So fraught has been the walk that the onslaught of the elements strikes Lennox as inevitable. The words 'Dean' and 'Amanda' have burned on his lips for hours. The need to know about one is cancelled by the imperative of concealing the other.

Drum— Amanda . . . what the fuck . . .

Lennox tries to convince himself that his restraint is at least partly about being mindful of Trudi's overwhelming upset. When she does talk, it's all rambling, incoherent stuff about her father, followed by abjectly miserable tears.

Ahead: Jackie and Angus's cottage, long and white, with its refurbished slate roof. They immediately decanted here, on the strange whim of two hurting, confused people. His desperate suggestion was that they go to a place where they can talk about her father's death, perhaps get the relationship back on track. Broach those big silences. The ones like the brooding clouds above, which fill the vacancy when love is leaving town. However, it became something else; on this rambling walk, Lennox suddenly realised they were passing by the pile of Ritchie Gulliver's family, and he excitedly mentioned this to her. At his insistence they stalled and got closer to look around, until they heard dogs barking, forcing them to beat a retreat. Trudi didn't even appeared dismayed, and he took her resignation as acquiescence.

She has said little since, as the creeping awareness of just how spectacularly he has come up short thickens between them like gel.

She needs you and all you're doing is letting her down.

You can't fix this.

You can't fix you.

They get back inside the drizzled dwelling intent on drying and warming themselves by the fire. But when Lennox goes out the back into a yard decorated mainly by a large wooden kennel with CONDOR painted above the entrance, the wood he finds, stored in a plastic bin with the unsecured lid blown off, is sodden. Sure enough, the firelighters burn out, failing to ignite it. Exasperation finally bubbles up through Trudi's sullen depression. Arms wrapped around herself, snot trickling from her, she looks around the cold cottage. — Let's go back, Ray. This isn't working out.

Lennox doesn't know whether she means the break or their relationship. Can't bring himself to probe. A kind of stunned idiocy, sullen, belligerent, takes over. — But we were . . . eh, are you sure?

— Yes, she says in brutal coldness. Her eyes are like slits.

Suddenly, her finger hammers at her own breastbone. — *I want to go. Now.*

— Okay, we'll go back into town and get some lunch, Lennox concedes, noting that she has already started packing, throwing her things into a holdall.

Her father, Donald Lowe, was always a fit, strong man. He doted on her, his only child. Trudi, Lennox reasons, must be thinking about how he will never see her marry. Never know any children she might have. *No wonder her heart is shattered.*

And you . . . you dragged your feet so much. There was always something. Now it's too late.

Watches her stuff into her bag garments she previously neatly folded up. He has felt her love for him, her *Ray of sunshine*, as she has called him. Though a tender, affectionate man when removed from the shackling imperatives of his investigations, she has learned such respite is fleeting. Forcing shut the zip on her bag, Trudi moves over to the kitchen area. Her eyes swivel to Lennox, now sitting in a chair looking out the window. Picks a tangerine from a bag of groceries they bought from the village shop earlier. It's sour and she screws up her face and spits it out into the bin-lined bucket. Their eyes briefly meet at that point, then quickly avert.

When the love dims, it is replaced by a sense of duty and a nagging vexation. Lately, her most abundant emotion has seemed a saccharine pity, which galls him. But now a new one has surfaced: contempt. With Lennox continually exposing himself as a time-wasting emotional retard, one who will never get past his demons, Trudi has realised she is squandering her life waiting for him to shape up.

The drive to Edinburgh is undertaken in complete silence. Trudi, her hair drying in a frizz, stares out the window most of the way. They are driving south, the noon sun tepid. The fields bare and dark on both sides of the road. Frost still caps the furrowed ridges. Forlorn, dingy clouds streak towards the horizon. Around them grey seeps in. They can see the dulled city lights while still a long way off, tickling the low sky. Willing themselves to be there. To be out of his car. Aware of the mess of it, Lennox knows she's registering this acutely too.

Does she look like she's shagging some other cunt? How can you tell when she's so bereaved? Surely not. Why the fuck did you – who the fuck is this guy who is comforting her when you ought tae have been daein that?

Some cunt fannying aboot wi the gas supply when you're oot getting run doon by a fucking maniac while trying tae find oot who cut a racist prick's baws off . . .

Dean Slattery, some inbred papish bastard two or three generations from a Connemara bog, waltzing aroond in an Armani Exchange off-the-peg, ehs shiny erse in the driving seat ay a BMW, working fir the fucking gas board and thinking he's the shit . . .

. . . nah . . . stoap this . . . stoap this caveman pish, you're better than that. Leave the racism and the jokes tae near-extinct losers like Gillman, who think we laugh with them but really laugh at them. Sitting with a wry smile, all the time thinking: you're actually quite a sad, thick cunt, aren't you?

Distracted by solving a murder and a papish cunt steams muh bird . . . cut that fucking gasman's filthy livestock-shagging dick off . . . ha ha ha . . . this is mad . . . ah'm fucking losing my marbles . . . AH NEED A CUNTING PEEVE AND A FAT LINE AY FUCKING CHING.

As the city manifests in the form of one of the drab satellite shopping centres on its periphery, he asks, — Where do you want to go?

It's all Trudi can do to shrug in response.

She's depressed. She was close to her dad. The BMW papist took advantage. She'll see that when the mist clears from her eyes. Then you pay that fucking Fenian bastard a visit. That smug fucking hobo Lochend Hibs cunt . . . stick one of those airm-scratching twats in a tin flute and call him an executive . . . executive director of spoon burning and choring . . .

Opening an app on his phone, he picks a restaurant in Victoria Street that they both like and books a table. When they arrive at the establishment, situated on two floors, a fawning waiter escorts them to a window seat on the ground level. His smile is literally sucked from his face by their brusque, rigid tones and body language.

The food arrives. It's good but they eat in a desultory manner. Both want to leave as soon as possible, and it's evident the waiter regrets seating them where they are on exhibition, advertising the vibe of the establishment. The silence between them is as dense as a black hole in space. Lennox asks her about her dad.

It's important to let her to talk about him.

— I'm heartbroken, Ray, she says, engaging with him for the first time. — He was the kindest man I've ever known and he gave Mum and me so much love. It feels so painful inside. It'll never repair.

This makes him think about the Repair Shop. He wishes he were there now. He considers his troubled relationship with his own mother. How it fell apart completely following his father's death and her affair with his best mate, Jock Allardyce.

Fucking relatives. The good ones die young. The shite ones go on forever.

Trudi. She's fucking somebody else. And she's doing this because you're never there.

165

All Lennox can do is squeeze her hand. But looking at her and thinking of her being with BMW Dean is too much to bear. So, he glances outside the window to the wet flagstones. But then, at the edge of his vision: a familiar figure in an unaccustomed setting. Rubbernecking to look intently, he sees Dougie Gillman across the street, going to his car.

That cunt is in pure stakeout mode!

— . . . Dad loved Mum with all his heart. He told me once: when I first saw your mum in the ballroom with her friends, I had never seen anything so beautiful in my life . . . they were devoted to each other . . . I'm so worried about Mum, thank God she's staying at Aunt Cathie's . . . I should go there soon . . .

But who is he spying on?

Then Amanda Drummond leaves the bar opposite, wearing a long coat and woollen hat. She walks across the street with a squat, dark-haired woman, whom Lennox at first thinks is Gill Glover but maybe isn't. Gillman waits for them to pass, and then follows them. Lennox can't believe what he is seeing: *Is Gillman fucking stalking Drummond? No! Who is the other woman?*

— . . . but why am I telling you this? You obviously don't care.

He has the vague sense that Trudi is still talking. — What –

— You're not even listening to me, are you? and she pulls her hand away from his grasp.

— I'm sorry . . . I just saw something.

— What, Ray? What was it? Whatever it was, it certainly wasn't *me*.

— It's . . . He looks at her. — Nothing.

— We should go, she says, waving her hand tersely at the waiter, indicating the bill. — In fact, she slips off her

166

engagement ring, placing it on the table, — I'm going. I'll let you pay for it. Goodbye, Ray, and she rises, walking out.

— What did *you* see? Did it come in a BMW?!

Trudi stalls fractionally, but recovers, moving on. Doesn't turn around and heads out through the door.

The other diners, mainly office workers, and the staff now have their eyes locked on Lennox, convinced that he's bad news.

— Trudi . . . Lennox springs up, signalling to the waiter, who needs no encouragement, to hurry with the bill. Then he looks outside again. Gillman and Drummond have gone. — Fuck . . . He turns to pursue Trudi, but the buzz of his phone tells him he's left it on the table.

FUCK . . .

He turns back and grabs it, with the engagement ring, as the caller ID stipulates: HOLLIS.

Something makes Ray Lennox pick up. Maybe it's to do with the waiter scrambling to get the bill printed off and onto a silver tray with the card payment machine, or perhaps more about the programmed stupidity of men, that extreme narcissistic belief that, godlike, they can sort everything out, that they have infinite capacity to repair a situation that seems damaged beyond all reasonable hope. — Mark . . . Lennox lamely gasps as he watches Trudi charge past outside.

But he can't move.

Hollis's voice rasps thunderously down the phone. — Discharged myself, but ain't never known pain like this, Ray. Me arse is fucking wrecked worse than with the actual Duke of Argyll's. They told me what they had to do: farking pulled those varicose veins out and grafted skin from my thigh right up my farking coalhole . . .

— Fuck sake . . . The waiter heads towards him.

— I'm on the painkillers. It's bleedin agony and I just wanted aht!

— Are you being looked after? Lennox asks, as the advancing waiter proffers the card payment device with the bill.

— I'm fine on me own, mate, Hollis declares. — Got a sister who loves ta fuss but I ain't letting her near me cause she'll do my farking nut in. The ex . . . well, best left unsaid. As for my bruvs, well, you saw them. Handy lads to have alongside ya when you run into a bunch of West Ham in Rotherhithe Tunnel and great if I want an endless stream of jokes about my condition, but not that good with the old emotional or practical support.

— Work colleagues in the Met? Lennox asks as he pushes his card into the machine, trying to steady it to key in his pin, as he tucks the phone into the nook of his neck and shoulder.

— Don't even go there, mate. Hollis's voice is muffled.

— How long are you housebound for? He punches in the first digit: 1 . . . as he senses the eyes of the other diners on him, willing him to leave. He gives the waiter, now stony-faced, a tight smile.

— They reckon anuvah two weeks in dock before I start to feel a bit more normal.

— Okay, bud, the phone seems about to slip as he keys in number 8 . . . — I'll keep plugging away on the dickless toff trail and let you know what I come up with . . . He taps in 7 . . . — As yet, nothing more, and he punches in 4.

As Lennox manipulates the phone back to his ear, the card payment machine announcing CONNECTING TO SERVER, he hears Hollis say, — I've put in some calls, but I've obviously been preoccupied. And, Ray?

— Yes, Lennox says, almost surprised when APPROVED comes up on the card machine screen.

Hollis's voice is in the low growl of a wounded animal. — Watch those Internal Investigations cahnts. Wankers have been sniffing abaht here. Fuckers are on the toff payroll. Nuffink surer.

— Will do . . . later, Mark. Ray Lennox grabs his card from the machine and hangs up, bounding out of the restaurant. The waiter and the other diners look on in relief as this disturbance to their atmosphere vanishes through glazed doors.

19

In pursuit of Trudi, Lennox rushes out into feeble afternoon light. The street's pervading stillness is broken only by an arm-in-arm couple. Then it's breached spectacularly by a loud, swaggering group of lads huddled together, making sure the world knows the pavement is theirs. They scowl warily as they pass Lennox, unsure of his potential victim or predator status. Craning his neck up and down the street, he has another target and is oblivious to them. There is no sign of Trudi.

He calls her. It goes straight to voicemail again.

Uphill to George IV Bridge, or downhill to the Grassmarket?
The Grassmarket.

He runs down the hill, turning onto the old cobbled street. Students and tourists bunch hopefully outside its pubs, smoking, drinking and chatting, as if willing the sun to appear.

But there's no Trudi.

Flagging down a taxi, he heads to her flat in Marchmont. His stupidity dawns on him: *obviously she'd have gone up George IV Bridge and across the Meadows.* But his gut proves correct; when he arrives at her home, there's no sign of her. He phones again: still nothing.

BMW Dean . . . no . . . her mother's . . .

But she said her mother was staying at her aunt's. Where the fuck does her aunt live?

Texts her:

> Honey, I'm so sorry. This case has kicked off big time.

To his surprise, a message comes back almost immediately:

> Fuck off. All you do is gape into space and phone that woman in London.

He's perversely heartened by this response. At least she's talking to him. *Perhaps we can make this right again.*

> It's not a woman, it's Mark Hollis. He's a colleague on the Met. Where are you?

> What the fuck ever. Do not call me. Ever. I can't be arsed with you. I do not want to marry you. I do not want to see you. It's not your business where I am. Fuck off.

What a fucking . . .
Rage strangles him.
She started this pish!
His fingers pummel the keys:

> **MARRY YOUR FUCKING
> BMW CUNT THEN**

He heads back to his flat, his body stiff as an ironing board yet possessed of an almost spectral resonant vibration. In a kitchen cupboard his shaky fingers locate a bottle of vodka, then call a number he's deleted many times. While easy to remove from the contacts list, it invariably resolves to stick in his mind.

His cocaine dealer, Alex, arrives around twenty minutes later. Scanning for the activity of neighbours in the stair, Ray Lennox affords him entry. It's immediately obvious that Alex has gone up in the world. Clear-eyed, he's evidently no longer high on his own supply. The traditional grubby hooded top has been shed in favour of a dandyish plaid three-piece suit with a button-down shirt. His hair, cut shorter and slicked back, gives way to groomed stubble on his chin. Yet this substantial rebranding is only given cursory attention by Lennox. All he really cares about are the five grams of cocaine in Alex's possession.

— All good, aye? Alex asks, warily observing him.

— Yes.

— You look a wee bit edgy . . . you sure about this?

— I've got a psychotherapist, Lennox says, remembering the appointment with Sally he mentally cancelled due to going away with Trudi. — Funny, but she never tries to sell me ching.

Alex pulls out five small plastic bags and lays them on the coffee table. — Point taken, Ray, but if you ever need to talk, you know where I am.

— Fuck sake, are you trying to do yourself out of a job? You're here tae cater for misery and confusion, no tae try and repair it!

— I only do this for a few people now, namely, those who can be discreet. Alex nods grimly, then hopefully adds, — That includes you. I took a university access course last year. Now I'm at Edinburgh Uni studying Medieval History.

— Delighted for you, A, Lennox says, — really . . . but if you'll excuse me.

— I'm kind of sorry about this, and Alex regards the bags on the table. — I mean it, man, we've all got to be there for each other. But the fees are expensive, and if you don't get it from me, and this is top-line gear by the by, you will from someone else . . .

— Quite, Lennox barks, as Alex raises his hands in surrender, slipping out the door, leaving the host to contemplate his purchases on the glass coffee table.

He cuts out one line. His appointment with Sally Hart is soon, *but just one* . . . he craves the buzz, needs the illusion of power that will surge through him. He rolls up a crisp twenty. Then he puts it down. He realises he would have missed Sally's appointment if it wasn't for Trudi's desertion.

Trudi . . . what the fuck . . .

Jumping into his mind's eye: the face of his fireman sponsor at NA, Keith Goodwin. Keith was quite useless really. That big, round smiling face, dispensing platitudes like 'Work the programme, go through the steps . . .' It's still over an hour until his late-afternoon appointment. He calls Drummond. But she isn't picking up. He thinks of Gillman: *why is he stalking her? What is happening to this fucking world?*

He calls Glover, on the pretext of a detail on the case, but really to see if she is with Drummond. — Gill, are you at the office?

— Ray . . . I thought you had taken a day's leave. Yes, still working on the link with Gulliver and these NHS contracts. He's much more careful about covering his tracks than most of them.

— Great, let me know if anything comes up.

— Of course. How's bonnie Perthshire?

— Wet, he says, hanging up and sluicing back some vodka and ice.

It wasn't her . . . but it doesn't mean Gillman wasn't stalking Drummond . . . Amanda . . . fuck sake . . .

Trudi . . .

Tears are coming. He feels the dampness liberate under his blazing lids.

You fuckin left us . . . we could have sorted it . . . your dad . . . Amanda . . . fuck sake . . .

He looks at the note, pushing it into his nostril, smashing the line. The ducts in his eyes seem to suck the tears back into them. Fires up the Sex Offenders Register on his laptop, looking at the mugshots of the beasts, hoping upon hope that one of the three tunnel assailants, all these years ago, will suddenly jump out from the grim catalogue of faces flashing through his overheated brain. A choking exasperation mounting inside him. Clicks on some porn, scrolling for someone who looks like Drummond, then Moira Gulliver, both women so thin; he wishes to see what Moira, even skinnier than Drummond, save the breasts, would look like naked . . . but is distracted by a girl who reminds him of someone he can't quite place. He is mid-stroke when he stops in horror, realising that this someone is his nephew, Fraser.

Jesus fuck . . .

174

He switches to a transgender porn site ... one performer looks a bit like Trudi ... then Drummond ... a harsh-faced boy-girl viciously being fucked in the arse by an outsize dildo ... wearing it, a woman who resembles Sally Hart, his psychotherapist ... It's only when a thunderous orgasm explodes from him, followed by a stream of dank jiz, that his conscious brain fully permits he's been masturbating, as a numb cock crumbles in his hand.

Scrolls Sally's number on his phone. Studies her picture above it. A tight and minimal smile, but still radiant. He has to leave now. Stops for a moment to enlarge the picture.

Women fill your life with beauty, so casually.
I wonder if they know that they do this.
They know so much.

20

I tried to fight my way into the blazing building to save Mama and Papa, but was restrained by the Sartur family from across the street. They delivered Roya and me to my Aunt Liana. She had arrived on the scene, almost as expressionless as the guards.

Two of the Sartur women, friends of my mother, had helped Roya to her feet. She was still crying, but more quietly, beset with halting, choking sobs. My aunt, her eyes closed, muttered prayers.

Many neighbours stood in groups, some of them in tears. A cluster of Revolutionary Guards looked dispassionately on. None of them tried to help and the emergency fire services only arrived when the rapacious blaze threatened to spread to nearby homes. Then the wind changed direction, the crowd dispersing in flight from acrid smoke that stung eyes and scorched lungs. I did not move, regarding this discomfort as a penance that was due me.

I thought of my beloved parents and contemplated all those beautiful books. I began to cry the stinging smoke out of my eyes. Another whip of the wind and Roya returned to take my hand. Although I was almost thirteen, and already much taller than her, I couldn't resist the tears and sobs that broke from me. We went back to my aunt's house, a small apartment in a drab compound in District 11.

The speculation of who had burned our home down and murdered our parents dominated our talk, and those of the neighbours who visited us in District 11. Most of the fingers were pointed at a renegade zealot faction within the Revolutionary Guard. My father had grown bolder in his writings for foreign newspapers, encouraged by the election of President Khatami, who was determined to establish a civil society based on the rule of law.

Aunt Liana was my mother's older sister by eighteen months, but a less fortunate version of her. Thin as one of Father's scimitars, rather than blessed with the bountiful curves of her sibling, she had lost her lover in the war and never married. Instead she devoted herself to a life based around her employment at the British Embassy, where she worked as an interpreter. Like Mother, she was an English Language graduate.

Following the 'terrible incident' as she called it, Aunt Liana would not let us out of her sight. She was fearful that the people who destroyed our home and murdered our parents might come for us. While this was unlikely, the point of fear is that it is seldom rational and serves as an effective control mechanism. Tyrants throughout time, and the lackeys who do their bidding, understand this very well.

First guards briefly visited my aunt, asking only for perfunctory details. Then a police officer called. He initially questioned her, then briefly Roya and myself, asking us if we were aware of any strange people coming to the house. I was not, nor was my sister. He then enquired whether either of our parents were prone to leaving home at unsocial hours.

I watched my aunt's eyes bulge anxiously as Roya defiantly told him, — My father was a journalist, he flew to places all over the world.

— Do you know why?

— To work, of course!

The policeman looked at her, then me, as if we were dirt. Even then I knew that his enquiries were not centred on trying to find the murderers of my parents but attempting in some perverse way to justify this horrendous, cowardly and inhuman act. I hated them all and I swore I would attain vengeance. I thought of how, one day, I would bring the havoc visited upon us back to those miscreants. We would destroy them all, Roya and I.

The police officer left. We never saw him again.

We buried my parents in the local cemetery. A tenet of Islamic faith is that burial takes place as soon after death as possible. However, our parents' bodies were so badly burned, it took several days to excavate them from the rubble. They had been in the basement when the house collapsed around them. Why? They were obviously locked in there, or killed first, before accelerants were then used to make the fire as prolific as possible. We were not permitted to wash their bodies and cover them in sheets to transit them to the mosque.

I was numb throughout the funeral and recall very little of it. The bodies were turned towards Mecca, and the imam led the funeral prayers. I was in the front with the other men, neighbours and work colleagues of my father's, while Roya, wearing a veil that could not conceal her blood-red eyes, was behind me with the line of women. Aunt Liana was comforting her. Through my stupefaction, I nursed a blazing wrath. The words of the Koran, once so inspirational to me, now seemed only nugatory and platitudinous.

We went back to Aunt Liana's small apartment, sitting there day after day, playing endless games of cards. My aunt cooked, but was not as accomplished as my mother. There was very little light in the dwelling, which had small windows and was towered over by a larger building, blocking out the sun. Worst of all, there were no books here. No escape. Not even a copy of the Koran, or any language books. My aunt explained that she kept all those at the office in her workplace. In the stultifying boredom Roya and I grew more anxious.

I felt I was going crazy in such confines. One day, when Aunt Liana was on an errand, Roya and I left her apartment building with our backpacks, and walked several miles to our old home. Even though we had buried their charred remains, I fantasised that my mother and father would be there waiting for us, unharmed. I wondered if a single book might have escaped the ravages of the blaze, perhaps Balzac's *Cousin Bette*, which grim circumstance had decreed me unable to finish.

When we got there, I was despondent. I smiled thinly at Roya, and could sense her dismay. The lot that our house had stood on was now nothing more than scorched rubble. Even the beautiful ironwood tree was reduced to resembling a dark and spindly old beggar. It seemed that nothing had survived as I rummaged with the desperation of a starving scavenger. Then I saw a piece of burned wood with the maroon laminate surface still visible. The remains of Father's cocktail cabinet. That symbol of Western decadence, it would have been as hated by the regime as all the books and films he'd collected. As I pulled it aside the sunlight above gleamed on tarnished surfaces. They were my father's set of Arabian knives. The case was burned away but the blades and their bone handles, though discoloured, remained intact, and would scrub up. I placed them carefully in my backpack. Even then I knew that these blades would serve as my instruments of retribution.

After a few days Aunt Liana explained that she had to resume her duties, and took us to her place of employ at the British Embassy on Bobby Sands Street. Originally called Winston Churchill Street, the Iranian government redesignated it in 1981, in honour of the Irish hunger striker, a man who martyred himself against the British state. These antics were indicative of the antipathy between the two countries, and the embassy was more often than not closed. Now my aunt was part of a skeleton staff who would sometimes have to brave angry crowds of protesters to enter their place of work.

Few buildings are more beautiful and tranquil than the British Embassy in Tehran. A temple-like structure with a dome, spire and arches, it boasts sumptuous landscaped grounds comprised of mature hanging trees, manicured hedges and lawns with a huge decorative pond at the front. But from the street, apart from the mounted lions and unicorns, it looks like a bleak, militarised compound. Its blue metal gates, set in brick walls topped with big spikes and rolls of barbed wire, offer little comfort to the passer-by. This is further enhanced by the presence of armed uniformed men situated on both sides. Inside the gates, the embassy detail; on the outside, the Revolutionary Guard.

How I hated it every morning when we walked through those gates past those scowling sentries. My aunt instructed us that under no circumstances were we to make eye contact with any of them, unless directly addressed, in which case she would do the talking. This nerve-racking experience was even worse at night, when we left the embassy to head back to her apartment, which I could never think of as home. Mostly my gaze was fixed on the pavement, but sometimes curiosity would gain dominion over my senses and I'd glance up to be met by hostile eyes.

One guard in particular possessed the cold but burning glare of the fanatical zealot. He looked right through me; a dim, dark soul, programmed to hate. I would witness his look again, on subsequent travels as a journalist. It was present in the gaze of tyrants everywhere. I called him Cousin Bette, after the manipulative character in the Balzac novel, referring to his sidekick as Valerie.

At my aunt's I cleaned and polished Father's knives with great care, steeping them in vinegar to remove the stains of the fire. They were all that survived of my parents. I often wonder what might have happened had I been able to take my beloved books instead of Father's knives to District 11 with me. I polished them until they gleamed, sharpened them compulsively, taking great pride in my restoration work.

The knives gave me confidence. I soon took to carrying the shortest of them on my daily journey to the embassy, concealed in the inside pocket of my coat. This afforded me a swagger that offered some kind of a psychic shield against Cousin Bette's hateful stare.

If going in and coming out of the embassy was a twice-daily ordeal, it was a surprisingly worthwhile one. I loved being inside that building. Apart from the beautiful gardens and grounds, which were always tended, even when the embassy was closed for diplomatic operations, there was the library. It reminded me of home and what I'd lost. But there was no *Cousin Bette*, just the guard to whom I had given that designation.

The election of Khatami had precipitated the restoration of diplomatic relations, following the Mykonos restaurant assassinations in Berlin. In response to a German court ruling that our intelligence services were responsible for the murder of four Iranian Kurds, the UK and the other EU countries withdrew their heads of mission. Although full ambassadorial status was not re-established, some of the staff had returned. They included Aunt Liana, for the first time in four years sitting in her office working on papers.

For Roya and me, having the run of this great building was an amazing experience. I was just turning thirteen years old and was spending my days in a colonial mansion. Sometimes I could almost forget what had happened, then the terror and the burning acrid aroma would lodge in my throat and I would choke with sadness. I tried to hide my grief from Roya and be strong for her, as I sensed she was doing the same on my behalf.

The key member of staff was Abdul Samat, a tall, angular man with a permanently haunted look. My aunt described him as the Ambassador's assistant. Abdul never spoke directly to us, rarely looked us in the eye. But we would see him whisper an instruction to Aunt Liana, who would then approach Roya and me with his command.

Then one day the Ambassador, a straight-backed man with a shock of dark hair, took up residence. His willowy blonde wife and their son accompanied him. The boy seemed not much older than me, and possessed the same hair as his mother. They looked so exotic, like magnesium-flame-haired gods. This family had little to do with us at first, even the boy, with his piercing blue eyes like sapphires and the same imperious air as his father. Abdul warned us, via my aunt, to keep away from their quarters. This was not difficult to do, as there was plenty of room, and if not walking in the garden, I would be reading in the library. The books were limited, with the shelves mainly empty. But there was a *Complete Works of Shakespeare*, which I enjoyed.

It was when we were making our way there, heading down the corridor, that the boy suddenly introduced himself to us, shaking my hand. — Hello, I'm Christopher, he announced.

At sixteen, he was older than I first thought. He was friendly to us, offering us delicious British chocolate bars and inviting us to walk with him in the grounds. As we set off, I noticed that his eyes kept going to

Roya, looking her up and down, as he chatted to us in English and Farsi. She did not seem to notice. Christopher told jokes and made up stories about the staff, especially Abdul, which made me laugh, but only drew polite smiles from her, which I sensed exasperated him. Unlike me, driven by obsessive fantasies of revenge, a crippling sadness had beset Roya, who turned her rage in on herself.

As my aunt started work early, we often had breakfast at the embassy in the large oak-panelled dining hall. I looked forward to this, especially now that the proper cook had returned, along with more staff, as the embassy prepared for the restoration of full diplomatic relations. I loved the British dishes. While we were forbidden to eat the marvellous-smelling bacon, the omelettes were wonderful and the porridge thick and creamy, so unlike the gruel I had sadly gotten used to at Aunt Liana's.

One morning Roya wasn't around for breakfast. This was not unusual; often she had no appetite and took an early-morning walk through the gardens. After some fried eggs and toasted bread, I headed out in search of her. Walking around the perimeter of the grounds, I suddenly heard muffled screams emanating from behind some rhodo-dendron bushes.

I saw him, the Ambassador's son; he was lying on top of Roya, his hand over her mouth, with her blouse ripped, cruelly exposing her small breasts. I had no experience of sex or this sort of violence but I knew exactly what he was doing. I ran over and pulled him off her. His zip was down and his cock exposed. He looked at me in a strange violation, and put away his penis. Then he punched me. I struck back, and we fought. He was older, but I was a freakishly big, strong boy for my age, and driven by a righteous anger, I got the better of him. Full of rage, I pounded his face with my fists, kicking at him and roaring demented curses, and soon he was cowering. Roya, screaming through her tears, got up and tore her nails down his cheek.

Enraged, he struck her across the face, and she fell to the ground, while he came towards me. I pulled out the gleaming four-inch knife and slashed at the air in front of him to deter his advance. It didn't to any significant degree, and I twice made contact with his stomach. The second one halted him in his tracks; I watched blood come out from between his fingers. He looked at me with a sour pout, as if I had cheated at some sort of game. — You don't know how much trouble you're in, you stupid wog, he shouted, then turned away, lurching towards the embassy buildings. We didn't hear his theatrical screaming until he was some distance from us. I kept telling a crying Roya that we had done nothing wrong. But we couldn't move; couldn't go back to the embassy, could do little except wait by the big willow trees for them to find us.

— He tried to kiss me, Roya said, her mouth shivering and fraught. — I told him I didn't like it and he grabbed my hair and pulled me onto the ground and started ripping my clothes off. He was forcing his *thing* into me . . .

Her voice was metallic and distant; unlike I had ever heard it.

They came for us soon after. The two security men employed by the embassy ordered me to surrender the knife, which I did, then they seized us both roughly by the hair. This violence, particularly against my almost-catatonic sister, was shocking to me. I frantically tried to explain what had happened, but struggled to find the words. They remained silent as they marched us into the stateroom with insect determination.

The Ambassador was waiting for us with Aunt Liana, who was begging him for mercy. I could see his son sitting in a corner, red-faced with his angry crying, as a medic tended to his wounds. There were only two slashes, just one deep enough to draw blood. I thought of Roya's screams and I resented my own cowardice: I should have stabbed with force to injure, rather than slashed to discourage his attack. Yet I witnessed and drank the humiliation wrought all over his face. After all, he was sixteen and had been bested by a thirteen-year-old native.

My aunt kept pleading to the Ambassador and his assistant, Abdul, that we had a suffered a great tragedy through being orphaned in a blaze.

The Ambassador held up the short Arabian scimitar. It shook uncontrollably in his hand as he scowled to the extent that I thought he would use the weapon on me. — So this is the damn instrument! This is what you stabbed my son with! You could have taken his life with this dastardly act of cowardice!

I tried to tell them I was saving my sister, and Roya's expression, the bruises on her face and arms, and her torn garments must have spoken for themselves, as he shot a brief, spiteful look to his son. Then he said, turning to Abdul, — Get them out of here! Let their own kind deal with them!

My aunt fell to her knees in front of the Ambassador, grabbing his hand and pulling it to her chest. He brushed off her grip and stepped back, his face aghast in horror. Despite her protests, the security men marched us down the corridor, their boots thumping violently on the wooden floors, as Aunt Liana sobbed, and had evidently now turned to God, rather than the Ambassador, in her plaintiff appeals.

We left the building and were forcibly ushered towards the gates, outside of which a mob had inevitably gathered. It was habitual for people, often led on by the Revolutionary Guard, particularly Cousin Bette, to protest in this way. They were visibly excited by the obvious commotion coming from our side of the barriers, and chants started up.

Abdul stepped forward to the bars, megaphone in one hand and holding up a gold Rolex watch in the other. He pointed at me, addressing the crowd in Farsi. — This watch belongs to the Ambassador. It was stolen by this . . . boy . . . this little *street thief*, whom we helped out of pity! You must decide his punishment under your laws!

In fury, the zealots in the crowd roared, as if they were about to storm the building. After some weird chant I couldn't decipher, another round of the standard 'God is great' started up. Then a small gate was opened and the security staff pushed Roya and me outside. As I looked back, I saw him, the Ambassador's son, grinning malevolently at me through those tight lips and ice-blue eyes. The Revolutionary Guard immediately seized me, thankfully ignoring Roya, who managed to get away.

I looked up into a hate-filled glare, as bleak and soulless as any unbelieving Shaitan. Felt myself wilt under the rancid excrement-eater's breath. So repulsive was this vile monster, existing in the borderline of light and darkness, that I glanced to his feet to see if they were cloven, as in folklore.

I was in the grasp of Cousin Bette.

21

The basement flat in Albany Street in the New Town has its courtyard festooned with the obligatory potted plants, which give this area of Edinburgh much of its charm. Lennox rings the bell and is afforded entry by a woman with shoulder-length blonde hair, who wears a red jersey and a black-and-white-checked skirt.

When he first went to see her, on Drummond's recommendation, after being broken up by the Mr Confectioner case, Lennox's impression of Sally Hart was that she was strikingly good-looking. In possession of high cheekbones and expressive blue eyes, hair tinted various layers of blonde, she wore her clothes well, neither highlighting nor attempting to conceal her evident curves. Most people would open up with such a woman taking an interest, albeit professional, in them. It was a sub-conscious desire to please. Yet whenever they sit down opposite each other in two chairs, he invariably finds such anticipated dynamics irrelevant; Sally is just very good at her job. Open-ended questions, followed by probing ones, and an intuitive sense of what's going on with him, make Lennox feel at ease but also that he's being led somewhere in a strange dance.

This room normally relaxes him, with its big floor-to-ceiling windows leading onto a basement patio garden, the two plush chairs, and the lounger that he thinks of as a traditional psychiatrist's couch. There's a toilet and a fitted kitchen space off the lounge area. It's replete with soft furnishings and stylish prints.

But he really wants more cocaine. That wrap in his pocket. He can feel it dance.

One line is too much.

Hollis.

These veteran cops and their dinosaur-like ways. That uncanny excitement ignited by working with them. How easily they lead him into darkness.

I wonder if they know they do this.

Alex's 'top-line gear' is still Edinburgh cocaine, cut with its Vim, brick shavings and talc, scrunching at his sinuses. He must try to conceal this from Sally. — Dreich weather, he offers, sitting down in one of the chairs. — Been soaked to the skin a few times this week. Nasty cold, so don't get too close!

Sally makes vaguely affirmative noises, pouring two glasses of water from a bottle procured from a small fridge, setting one in front of him, taking the other to the chair opposite, and settling down. — How has work been?

— Okay . . .

— Any more disturbing cases?

— They're all disturbing.

— Hopefully not like the Confectioner one? That really did get under your skin.

He thinks of the images of Gulliver. That angry red wound. But he does not want to talk about this. And he can't yet talk about Trudi.

What do you want to talk about?

Lennox is normally candid with Sally Hart in a way he hasn't been with previous counsellors. But no, he just can't talk about the mess with Trudi, not yet. Instead he starts to disclose more about that old disused railway tunnel that defines him. — I'm thinking about it less, definitely, he says, wondering, if that's the case, why he is so moved to mention it now.

Trudi. To avoid talking about her. To hide the fact that she's gone for good.

No, she'll be back. She's just hurting about her dad. Head turned by the smarmy Hibs cunt with the BMW . . . no . . . stop this pish . . .

As his brow sweats and furrows, Sally remains silent.

Lennox carries on. — It's not been looming so large. Which is good. I just wonder why.

— Can you still recall the details of the assault? I mean, you've found it, understandably, very difficult to talk about.

Lennox feels something rising in him. It always burns, but down the years he's gained a measure of control. How much more of this jurisdiction might he be able to exert if he could talk about it in its excruciating detail? Reduce it to just another mundane story?

Sally seems to read his train of thought. — Might this be the time that you can talk about what they actually did to you in that tunnel?

— I obviously find that difficult, and he hears his own voice inverting into a whispery croak.

Sally nods slowly. — It's a natural PTSD reaction. It's physical.

— I don't want it around any more.

Then Lennox notes she's adjusting her hands, folding them on her lap. They are quite big hands for a woman her size. — What if I were to induce mild hypnosis in you? It would relax you, perhaps make it easier to talk?

— Eh . . . what does that involve?

— Well, I'm a qualified hypnotherapist. It would only be a very mild state of relaxation.

— Okay. I'm game.

Sally asks him to watch the hands on a pendulum device she places on a stand in front of him. — One . . .

Lennox feels his itchy, jerky limbs grow heavy. His eyelids start to accumulate mass, so he lets them fall. Otherwise, his face does not change.

— . . . two . . .

His ragged breathing evens out. No more sweat escapes from his ducts. No familiar thunderbolt to his gut. Just a tranquil and abstracted feeling, almost as if he's been drugged.

— . . . three . . .

The jagged glass, pushed flush against your cheek. Him toying with exerting the force or applying the sleight of hand that would break the skin. His flies opening, the faint stench of sweat and stale urine . . . they've been drinking.

Hears himself saying: — He made me perform fellatio on him, by holding a broken glass bottle against my cheek.

. . . his rancid cock popping out like a jack-in-the-box, a slithering eel used to bottom feeding in sewage-ridden waters . . . stiffening . . .

He senses Sally Hart remaining still and quiet. She seems to suck in a breath. Lennox suddenly feels a struggle take place inside him. It's not that he cannot continue; part of him really wants to, he just cannot stop.

He opens his eyes a little to see Sally's widen, urging him on. Lets them shut again. There's something so blissful in this counter-intuitive surrender. The physical burden falling from his tired shoulders. — The man who assaulted me, the older one, he left me with the younger guy, and went to help his friend.

Nonce number three . . .

— This would be the third man in the tunnel? Sally's voice seems to be coming not from her any more, but an unspecific part of the room. Perhaps even from inside his own head.

189

— Yes, Lennox confirms, sensing his speech as slow and muffled, — he'd got my mate Les down on the ground. But Les was struggling, fighting . . .

Sally's voice; it now really does seem internal to him. Coming from within. — The younger man was holding you while the other two brutalised your friend?

— Yes . . . I couldn't look, Lennox recounts in slow recall, — I just heard the screams as I turned away . . .

Sally seems to move a little closer in her chair, as if to better hear him. His eyes remain closed, but he senses this. The disturbance of the air. The distinctive whiff of her perfume.

He was fucking scared . . . when you're being restrained by some cunt that is themselves terrified, it's the very worst . . . because they know what's going to happen to you . . . you were just a young laddie . . . your ma, your dad, in the house, only a mile or so away, him maybe washing the car, her making lunch . . . how did you get here? How is this happening to Les, who is caught between snarling defiance and pleading for mercy? They are on him like fucking hyenas . . . your bike, your new bike, on its side . . .

— . . . I could smell the man holding me, that burning tin odour of fear. He was just a young guy, maybe little more than a boy himself. I can see that now.

He feels Sally holding the silence like the cape of a matador in front of a bull.

— I begged him to let me go . . . Lennox starts, then briefly hesitates, biting softly on his bottom lip, — and I can't remember if he did . . . or if I just tore away from his grip . . . but I ran to my bike, jumped on it, and pedalled away . . . my calves were tearing as I pumped as hard as I could . . . terror driving me on . . . waiting for the hand on my shoulder to wrench me off the bike onto the hard ground . . .

And Ray Lennox feels a heavy weight in his chest. He

senses his voice going soft and high, perhaps childlike, all the while retaining full awareness that she'll experience this too. But he has moved into a realm beyond social embarrassment, and he carries on. — I left poor Les . . . to be abused by the three of them. By the time I got help he was coming out the tunnel, and they were gone.

Pedalling . . . away from them all . . . away from Les . . . his muffled screams in the tunnel dying as they probably gagged him in some way . . .

— They all raped him?

Lennox feels his teeth slam together as he transports jarringly from the riverside track by the tunnel back into the room. Senses himself coming out of the spell. It was only there to get him into the zone. Now it's left behind and the adrenaline starts to flow through his body. His calf muscles tingle in the memory, as his eyes open fully. His voice is harsher, more adult. More cop-like. — He never confirmed the details, but from his reaction I could tell it was as horrible as it could be, he says, feeling ice in his veins. — He went a bit off the rails after that.

Sally is as still and cool as the darkest of autumn nights. — What did you do?

— I became a hunter of those people.

— Interesting.

— How so?

— In that you don't describe yourself as a cop.

Lennox thinks of Hollis, then casts his mind back to warmer climes. It was after the Confectioner case. When he and Trudi went to Florida, supposedly to relax and plan their wedding. — It hit me when I was on holiday in Miami Beach.

Sally arches her back slightly, perhaps inches a little forward in her chair. She's interested in this. He hasn't talked much about it. He wonders what he *has* discussed with her.

Perhaps all those old cases that messed him up? Or did they? They were all just symptoms, not the root cause, although they obviously picked open psychic scars. — I got involved with a young girl who was a victim of a paedophile ring. It had nothing to do with me, he stares at her, — but I had to help her. That's when I realised I wasn't a cop, never had been . . . There's this guy in London, working on a current case with me; he's cut from the same cloth. I'm drawn to him, to his energy. Most of us in Serious Crimes are damaged cases in some way. I'm just driven to hunt those people down. Those sex offenders.

Sally Hart draws in a long breath. — And the motivation for this hunt is that you want some kind of vengeance?

— Yes, Lennox's reedy voice confirms. — Justice through the system isn't enough. I know they're like weeds, you cut them down, and more come back. But somebody needs to do the chopping, and he looks coldly at Sally. — I find that work satisfying.

Sally Hart keeps her eye contact steady. Lennox thinks he detects a slight flush on her cheeks. — You've put away many sex criminals.

— Yes, but nowhere near enough.

— How does that make you feel? I mean, apprehending them?

— It's always good to jail them, but there's an inherent anticlimax there too.

— How?

— I feel like hurting them.

Sally Hart remains focused on him. No noise in the room apart from the ticking of the clock. — I'm going to ask you something. Please do not take offence. And I stress that I'm only talking about feelings here, not actions. I only ask because it is important.

Lennox feels his neck move in a slight nod.

— Do you ever feel like hurting children?

Ray Lennox breathes in through his nostrils, fighting down an anger rising in him. He looks at her open expression, suddenly feels the rage slide.

She's just doing her job. She has to ask.

— No. Never. He shakes his head in grim finality. — I feel like hurting adults. They're the ones who soil and spoil our humanity.

This seems to give Sally Hart no comfort. Not a muscle in her face twitches. To Lennox, the way the light hits her, she looks like a porcelain goddess.

22

Cousin Bette roared, so deep-throated that I could see nothing of his face but a black cavern under the green baseball cap's visor. Then he seized me, twisting my arm up my back, grabbing my hair with his other hand. — Now we show this thief the justice of Allah!

Following the revolutionary fervour, a barbarous practice had reasserted itself, but only in isolated events, and rarely here in Tehran. Now, as a reaction against the move towards further liberalisation, it seemed the tyrants wanted their say. The guards were intoxicated by their own anger and madness. Yet I could not believe what was happening, even as they fetched a length of rope and a knife. — Our laws allow us to take the hand that steals, Cousin Bette shouted to cheers, as he wrenched my arm so hard I thought I might black out with the surge of pain.

Then they secured my right forearm by a tourniquet to a heavy block of wood as I heard someone saying something about the courts. He was shouted down. I actually laughed through this terrifying process; the grim, collusive cackle of the class clown who knows he's the stooge, but gains an aberrant status through being part of the prank.

It had to be a joke!

I looked back to the embassy gates, but through the surrounding bodies could no longer see the Ambassador's son. My mind's eye, however, could not erase the notion that he was watching: willing them on to do what it seemed inconceivable that they would do.

It was no joke.

Cousin Bette, in his green uniform, kept his thuggish grasp on me. I kicked out, eliciting a curse, wishing I had my knife, now of course in the possession of the embassy. I turned in appeal to his sidekick, Valerie, who did not look at me. My screams and pleas couldn't invoke his pity or provoke his conscience. Part of me thought they would never do this, not to a young boy, never so publicly. They only meant to scare me, surely. I swept my gaze around the mob; transfixed, wanting, *needing*, to witness this spectacle.

It all happened instantly. I had read about it taking two blows of an axe. I only saw the gleam before I looked away; it was an Arabian scimitar, a long one. I don't remember the pain I suffered or how much I screamed out. Stuck in a state of disbelief, where everything froze, I saw my arm pull away from my hand, after just one blow at the joint, and watched the cord of blood splash from me under the impact of the blade. In my stark terror and the rising sickness that swept through my whole body, all I registered were those eyes. It was uncanny because although I know them to be those of Cousin Bette, in the distortion of memory's recall they always manifest as a different set, the evil intelligence of that ice-blue stare of the Ambassador's son, Christopher Piggot-Wilkins. I do not know who physically carried out the mutilation Cousin Bette engineered, but had the sense that it was not him. Then came the voices, muffled at first, as I felt somebody wrapping me up in a blanket. I shook in a shivering fit, leaving my body, bearing witness to myself being held high before being hurried into a car. Again I heard the cry, — God is great, this time spoken in a fearful defiance.

Cousin Bette.

First I could feel the mob as a tidal wave, engulfing me, now I sensed it ebbing away as the extent of the damage it had perpetuated became clear. So anxious to join in an atrocity, then when it stared them in the face, they reverted to frightened individuals, terrified to own it.

I was taken to the Torfeh Hospital, a large, new public facility, and operated on straight away under general anaesthetic. I was recovering in the ward when Roya came to me. She was silent and grave, looking fearfully at my bandaged residue as I began to talk, to rant really, stopping as my aunt appeared at her shoulder. She almost had a smile on her face as she said, in serenity, — A great wrong has been done to you, but those responsible have been apprehended and punished.

I looked at my bandaged stump. I could not believe my hand had gone despite the evidence of my eyes. There was now no pain, just a strange itch. — Who? I asked urgently. — Who has been punished?

It wasn't Christopher Piggot-Wilkins. It may have been Cousin Bette and his associates. I never received a reply.

I was in hospital for two days. When I was discharged, my aunt told Roya and me that we would never go back to the embassy. This more than suited us. That place of beauty had become a house of terror in my eyes. When I returned to District 11, I looked at my handless append-age, utterly despondent. I cried only once in pain, but many times in frustration as I struggled to open doors, brush my teeth, wipe my arse, dress myself, and tying my shoelaces was a daily humiliation.

Then, a few days after the discharge, there was a change of heart. We were informed that the Ambassador wished to receive us for tea. I was terrified to go back to the embassy, Roya even more so, but Aunt Liana now insisted. She stressed that it would be to our benefit.

To walk through those gates again induced great fear. But now things were different; this time there were no chanting crowds, just spare clusters of onlookers. Even the Revolutionary Guards, Cousin Bette conspicuous by his absence, had, if not benign, then studiedly neutral expressions on their faces. The full embassy functions had now been restored, in preparation for the next fallout.

We were taken to the library, and served tea and scones. Abdul the assistant could not look at Roya and me. The treachery with the Rolex — had he been punished for that? What knowledge did the Ambassador have of this stunt, or his son's rape of my sister? Other than Abdul, and the Ambassador himself, the staff seemed largely new. In contrast to our last encounter, he was polite. He asked me about my hand, the hos-pital, and declared that I was a very brave young man. — You have a terrible disability, but you are to be well compensated.

Even as a thirteen-year-old, I felt the whiff of performance in his clunky overtures.

A payment was made to my family, to be administered by Aunt

Liana. The amount was never disclosed; not to Roya and me at any rate. It was described, even at that meeting, as 'provision for you both to go to England for schooling'. My aunt nodded, looking smug and vindicated. It was obviously our mother's sister who had negotiated this package. She was subsequently promoted to head of interpreting services.

— This business is highly regrettable . . . let me be mother . . . The Ambassador himself deigned to pour the tea, served in bone-china cups. He sipped at his, pinkie literally in the air. — Of course, the incident did not take place on embassy property, nor under our jurisdiction, and your nephew is not in the employ of Her Majesty's government, he addressed my aunt. — Nonetheless, we take a dim view of this . . . well . . . *atrocity* and will make provision for the boy . . . and his sister. You do understand this is all unofficial, and your discretion is *strongly* advised.

A wide-eyed Aunt Liana praised the Ambassador as a good and virtuous man. I evidenced neither his Rolex nor his son. When I looked around the room for those sapphire eyes, I noticed that the library had been restocked; its empty shelves were filled. My heart leapt as the spine of a paperback, *Cousin Bette*, by Balzac, jumped out at me. Then I heard the voice of the Ambassador. — Do you have anything to say, young man?

— I have one request.

He raised his brows cagily. In stark contrast to his toilet-brush hair, they were thin, feminine strips. Then he nodded slowly.

I rose and withdrew the paperback from the shelf. — Might I take this book?

— Of course, he sang cheerfully, obviously relieved at the modest nature of my plea. — Heard you were a reader. Love old Balzac. Good show!

They sent me to live with my uncle and attend public school in England. I thus received an education among the ruling classes of the country who had precipitated my butchering.

197

Uncle Jahangir was a scientist who had fled Iran following the revolution. He had a badly scarred face after being attacked and mutilated as a young boy by a rabid Great Dane. Since then he had devoted his life to the cosmetic industry and specifically to product testing on animals. He hated dogs and cats especially, and would fix a predatory gaze when the neighbour's spaniel barked or their sleek black tom climbed over the wall into his garden in Islington. Jahangir was an intellectual, who had many Western bourgeois friends keen to show how cosmopolitan they were by accepting a dark-skinned man into their midst, even as they bussed their own children long distances in order to avoid them being schooled alongside blacks from inner-London housing estates.

I was a 'one-handed wog', described as such by a sniggering prefect on my very first day at school. But one-handed or not, I was big and angry and I could hit hard with my solitary hand. I was crazy about sports. My disability meant that I couldn't play rugby or row, but I spent as much time in the gym as I could. That is not to say that the handicap did not still, on occasion, flummox and frustrate me. I went through a series of prosthetic hands with various degrees of dissatisfaction.

My intense physical training was undertaken solely in preparation for my revenge. While I was disciplined, Roya too seemed to thrive. Our life in Islington was comfortable. Jahangir was jovial company, very much my father's brother, with little interest in exercising any parental control. He treated us like adults, allowing Roya and me to come and go as we pleased. The freedoms of Western life appealed greatly. I quickly discovered alcohol and girls, but was never inclined to let either intoxication or romance blur the focus of my mission. Attending university at Cambridge, Roya specialised in virology and infectious diseases. She went on to become an expert in this field, teaching and researching at Edinburgh University. But this was all on the surface. Roya struggled with depression and anxiety. I once received a call from a housemate telling me that she had overdosed on sleeping pills. I immediately headed north to Scotland. I told her she couldn't do this to herself, and to think of her brilliant career as a virologist.

— Abusers of children are the real spreaders of virus, she told me weakly from her bed.

She survived this incident, and seemed to get on with her life.

I had also gone to university, at Oxford, then into journalism. I changed my name from Arash Lankarani to Vikram Rawat. Iran and the West kept falling out; it was more fashionable to be Indian. I passed myself off as one. Worked for various newspapers. I wrote my book, *A Privileged Wog: My Life in the English Public School System*. Moved to Paris, then back to London. Authored my follow-up: *A Token Wog: My Life in the Last Days of Fleet Street*.

My planned career specialisation was to follow in my father's footsteps. I would investigate atrocities in corrupt regimes, and thus hold oppressive power elites to account. Then I realised two things. Firstly, the masses were beaten down, stupefied and frightened by the pace of change. Thus, driven to servile drooling by the tabloid-led power-and-status culture of reality TV, they tolerated, or even worshipped, the abuses of the elites. They had the rage of victims, but they turned this on each other, or any other group they perceived as being better treated than them. And this perception was almost wholly controlled by the ruling establishment through their media. The second thing was that, in any case, I got no direct satisfaction from this attempt to expose power's abuses. I wanted to make them squirm. To feel the fear and helplessness they wantonly dispensed to others. I decided that I would befriend these men of power and entitlement, who felt they had a God-given right to destroy lives willy-nilly. Then I would bring terror to them.

Building on my skills as a writer of my own memoirs, I started to take an interest in writing about the lives of others.

I became *the biographer*.

All my emotional and physical training was geared towards winning the confidence of such vainglorious men. When the time was right, I would wrench the diseased souls from their weak flesh.

I had several prosthetic hands over the years, before eventually finding one that really suited me. It was forged from a brass alloy, a heavy instrument for sure, and thus worthy of the power my biceps, shoulders, core and legs could generate.

Then I was called back up to Edinburgh on a heartbreaking mission. Roya was dead: this time her overdose had been successful. I was devastated, but far from surprised. At the funeral I gave a eulogy, and asked everyone to pray that she found the peace in death that the beasts had taken from her in her life. Revenge scorched me stronger than ever. I had dossiers on all my intended targets. Yes, it was a dish best served cold, but I had nursed it for too long. Now I was ablaze. But how could I get started?

Then fate struck.

Afterwards, at the muted memorial reception for my sister, a beautiful, blonde-haired woman approached me, looking me in the eye. — I worked with Roya, she said, extending her left hand to reach for my solitary one. Generally people tried to grab my right hand, shuffling in embarrassment as I pulled it away, compelled to explain my disability.

I said something to the effect that I didn't know her, or recognise her from among Roya's circle of friends. I would certainly have remembered someone so strikingly attractive.

— But I know everything about you, she whispered in a quiet, urgent confidence. — Specifically your interest in vengeance.

23

A cold east wind has asserted itself again, the sun having retreated behind the clouds. On his way back to the car, Lennox switches on his phone, reviewing a series of missed calls, the most disconcerting of which are three from his prison social work contact, Jayne Melville. No message left. He gets back to her, hearing words that fill him with sickening, exhilarating dread: — Gareth Horsburgh wants to speak to you.

More cat and mouse games. Fine. As long as there are missing children and young women, and parents consigned to the living hell of not knowing what has happened to them, Lennox stoically remains at the notorious multiple murderer's beck and call. As long as other yellow pages exist, those concealed notebooks where, in spidery longhand script, Horsburgh recorded the meticulous planning and details of his crimes, Ray Lennox, the one part of the state apparatus that the child killer will see without his lawyer present, will keep participating.

Driving through Sighthill, he sees Moobo, an overweight young man with curly hair. One of Alex's associates, he'd further cut the drugs Lennox's dealer issued to him, knocking out bad coke and useless pills. Lennox, suddenly inspired, pulls up alongside the furtive young man. It would be good to have something to trade with Confectioner. — Get in the car, he commands.

Moobo looks around, and complies. — Get us the fuck oot ay here, I cannae be seen with a bizzie!

Lennox floors it and drives to the industrial estate, parking in an empty space behind a printworks. Moobo turns out his pockets, displaying several wraps of coke. — It's for percy, gen up.

— I don't want your shit coke, Lennox says. Quickly changes his mind. — Fuck it, gies a bump.

Moobo, open mouth hanging underneath bemused eyes, consents.

Arriving at Saughton Prison thirty minutes later, Lennox finds Horsburgh lying on the bed in his small cell in the sex offenders unit. Yes, he's definitely bulkier, that maroon sweatshirt straining at the gut. And Mr Confectioner seems distracted. Normally voraciously engaged when Lennox appears, this time he barely registers the detective's presence. It's all he can do to sit up on his bunk.

— Gareth.

Confectioner's eyes are circled and his shoulders slump.

Lennox pulls out Moobo's old Nokia phone, on a no-questions-asked snide account. He's informed Moobo he'll be headed for prison if he stops the payments before Lennox clears this case. It gives him pleasure to think of the drug dealer paying for Confectioner's calls.

Seeing the device, Confectioner becomes animated. He stretches out his hand.

Lennox pulls the Nokia away. — Earn it.

Confectioner licks his lips, regarding the phone like a cat looks at a wounded bird. — There's a well in Perthshire, near Killiecrankie; close to the River Garry, and his own words seem to energise him. He meets Lennox's eyes with the trademark glare. — Its waters were believed to have healing properties, and in pre-Reformation days, they would take sick children there . . . Confectioner's lip-tightening smile makes Lennox's stomach flip.

Don't react . . .

— You know what you'll find there. And maybe two birds with one stone, so to speak.

Lennox looks into those strange eyes: one of a sly pig, the other a deranged goat. The soul they were the vantage into now long dead. — It seems inappropriate, but thank you.

The abyss stares back at him. — I never wanted thanked, Lennox. I just want the phone.

He senses Confectioner's underlying anxiety. The cell is routinely searched; both know the screws will find a concealed phone quickly. But he wants to contact someone urgently. Lennox knows that this is all sorts of wrong but he's way past caring. — Good. He chucks the Nokia into his lap and goes to leave.

Confectioner smiles. — Norrie Erskine. Now there's a cop who knows how to play slapstick pantomime.

— What? Lennox is gobsmacked. — What do you know about Erskine . . . are you saying that he's mixed up in these cases? How could he be?

— I'm suggesting you should check that well.

Lennox looks at Confectioner in threat, goes to say something, but stops himself. — Later, he says, exiting, thanking Neil Murray, the turnkey, and Jayne Melville. He is aware that their collusion in the bending of procedure has put both at risk.

As he hurries across the car park, he calls Mitch Casey, a veteran Perthshire-based cop, arranging to meet him at the well. Then he sets off and as he reaches the outskirts of the city, activates the speakerphone and calls his brother.

Stuart answers immediately. — El Mondo! How goes?

— Good, Lennox lies. — Listen . . . he drops his voice, — . . . mind you were saying that Norrie Erskine was a bit of a sex case? What did you mean?

— Oh, known for it, Stuart booms. — But we all are in the

203

acting game! Our vice is shagging rather than the one indulged in by you bastards in blue, namely fascism.

— Right . . . Lennox feels a familiar weariness seep into his bones. *Gie it a rest, ya cunt* . . . — Nothing specific?

— Oh, I'm sure . . . let me have a wee think, make a couple of calls . . .

Lennox knows Stuart will neglect to do this. — Great, thanks, forcing grace into his voice. — So how are things otherwise?

— Excellent! Word is that my BBC Scotland sitcom *Typical Glasgow* – exclamation mark – will be nominated for a Scottish BAFTA! They reckon it's either us or season eighty-four of *Still Game*. It airs on Friday.

— Good on you, Lennox cuts in.

— Off everything; ching, booze, et cetera . . .

— Sex? he asks, recalling Stuart's elastic and evolving sexuality. Was it men or women that were in vogue right now?

— No way. I've hooked up with this *amazzzing woman*; posh, super-sexy and game as fuck. The relationship is *primarily* a spiritual one though; tons of meditation, yoga and all that stuff.

— Fabulous news, Stu, catch you later. He hangs up.

He meets Mitch Casey at the Killiecrankie well. The seasoned lawman sports an old-school Bobby Charlton or Arthur Scargill comb-over, and wears no hat, so the whipping winds mean he fights a constant rearguard action, flattening the mad display of wild strands of hair back over his scalp. As they walk through a lush glade to the well, he explains to Lennox that it has been emptied and dried out for decades, when the river was diverted, probably due to some agricultural activity. The recovery team is present, setting up their equipment. A tall man, who looks more like a Scoutmaster, with flowing red locks and beard, comes forward and identifies himself. — Sandy Gilbert, Scene Evidence Recovery Manager.

As Gilbert starts to talk technical business, Lennox says urgently to him, — Where's my rig?

— This is a specialist activity.

— I'm the ranking officer on this case. I've been on it for fifteen years, and Lennox's eyes blaze. — I'm going down.

— I can't advise that –

— I've done full abseiling training with retrieval teams at the Outward Bound.

— From a health-and-safety point of view I would urge you to think again. You're not at Benmore with instructors, easing down a smooth cliff face in broad daylight. You're going into a narrow hole and total darkness. We don't know the integrity of the sides of the well. It's possible that this has been compromised and could subside at any time.

This strikes terror into Lennox's heart, and he flinches, but not the way Gilbert reads it. *The yellow pages could be buried. I could lose everything . . .* — I've reason to believe that in addition to at least two bodies, there's crucial evidence pertinent to ongoing cases in the bottom of that well. I'm going down, end of discussion. I appreciate your health-and-safety advice though.

Gilbert lets out a long expulsion of breath, and nods to the team members. They fit Lennox up in his harness, connecting the vest to an electrically operated pulley device. Sandy Gilbert fits a head microphone to him, sticking a small black transmitter into a pocket of his garment, as Lennox bounces on the balls of his feet. — This radio signal will probably cut out when you get past thirty feet, and it's around fifty to the bottom, Gilbert explains, hooking a torch onto his rig.

He swings his legs over the stone circle.

Look up, not down . . .

Begins the descent. Darkness closes in around him almost immediately. He feels his pulse race. Looks up at the faces above receding in a tightening circle. The rope so taut, as he can hear the faint creak of the pulley, as the purr of the engine fades. It's clammy and claustrophobic. The harness is not comfortable; he can feel its crush on his groin and armpits. Sweat pours from him; he feels it at his collar and down his back. His jaw starts to tremble; he is literally descending into a black abyss, his Adidas-soled feet bouncing off the sides of the well, as he slowly threads his rope out. Gilbert is right, the whole experience is nothing like anything he's done before.

The tunnel . . .

. . . they had Les held down; your friend's terrible screams as they penetrated him, the big guy looking at you as he pumped Les, saying you were next . . . you looking in fear at the young guy's face, breaking his grip? Or being released? Fuck knows what . . . but running for the bike . . .

Above him, the light vanishing into a blue disc as Lennox feels his head spin. Blood pulses in his temples. He struggles to breathe; the air seems so thin, yet it thickens like syrup in his lungs. Regrets every line he snorted, as his sinuses slam shut, compelling him to snatch-inhale the dank air through his mouth.

They'd leave sick children here overnight believing the waters of the well had healing properties to cure sickness of the eyes and joints as well as whooping cough . . .

Suddenly, under a touch of his foot on the stone wall, a section crumbles, like the action of a tongue on a slack tooth. Lennox swings away from falling debris, banging his dome on the other side, feeling the wall behind it collapse under the impact as he sees stars; it's almost as if they are coming from the opening above him. Another cascade of debris spills into the black hole. Fighting to clear his head, he hauls in thinning, dusty air, as he hears the stones hit the bottom of the well. He's about to signal to get out of there, when the rumbling subsidence settles down. Nonetheless he operates the walkie-talkie. The signal is already weak. — Don't send any-body else down: the walls are crumbling, he barks.

— I'm getting you the fuck out of there, Lennox; we're winding you in –

— NO! Lennox roars. — That is an order! If you start to pull me in, I'll remove those fucking harness clips and jump down!

— On your own head, Lennox, you fucking idiot, Gilbert snaps. — Fucking Serious Crimes cowboys are going to cost me my –

As he falls further, the signal cuts out, ending Gilbert's tirade. Lennox shines his torch over the damaged walls. The borehole doesn't have a lot of time. He hopes he does.

Why the fuck did Confectioner come out with Norrie Erskine's name? Two options. One: he's always known there was something dodgy about Erskine. But Norrie was either working in theatre or in Glasgow when Confectioner was undertaking his killing spree. Erskine never investigated Confectioner in any capacity. Unless . . . option two: somebody is feeding Confectioner information about Norrie Erskine . . . the phone . . . Erskine would know the MO of Rab Dudgeon . . .

Then a scrunching sound as the soles of his feet slap on solid mass. He puts one foot forward in a tentative step. Firm ground. Takes another. Fumbles for the torch. The light slices through the pitch-dark. The beam confirms he's at the bottom of the well. The ground is surprisingly smooth under his train-ers, bar some of the rubble he dislodged. He shines it up, can see nothing but darkness above, perhaps a hint of a pallid blue at the top, though it could just be tracers in his eyes. Looks around the darkness. Unclips his harness. Feels the bolt of fear like a fist in his chest as the rope dangles in front of his face.

Could you meet them here, the occupants of that tunnel? No. Stay calm. They are human monsters, not the ghosts you are making them into. They have nothing to do with a disused well.

It's all okay – no it's not . . . the missing girls . . .

. . . Francesca Allen, 14, Selly Oak, Birmingham – 18 months ago . . .

. . . Madeline Parish, 17, Pontefract, West Yorkshire – 3 years ago . . .

. . . Alison Sturbridge, 15, Preston – 4 years ago . . .

. . . Juliet Roe, 12, Luton – 6 years ago . . .

. . . Fiona Martin, 14, Sheffield – 7 years ago . . .

. . . Angela Harrison, 15, Wolverhampton – 7 years ago . . .

. . . Hazel Lloyd, 14, Portobello, Edinburgh – 8 years ago . . .

. . . Valentina Rossi, 14, Dunfermline – 11 years ago . . .

. . . Caroline Holmes, 16, Finchley, north London – 14 years ago . . .

. . . it's not okay . . .

— FUCK –

In the pitch-dark blackout, Lennox stumbles over something. Sticks his hand out, feels it crunch through a delicate structure. A frozen second, as he wonders about where he's put his palm, as a primal terror shoots through him, telling him what it has to be. Then Ray Lennox raises himself to his feet, and feels the rough residue on his hand. Almost drops the torch. He presses harder, but it's like his grasp still feels numb and insipid on the device. As if he's gripping an open blade, and the tighter he squeezes, the more he will only lacerate his fingers.

They are –

Two bodies, revealed by his light; one a small skull, still with some straggly straw- hair on it, the eyeballs shocked caverns of blackness. But the skull is partly pulped; he put his hand right through it. — Aw for fuck sake . . . naw . . .

That blue gingham dress he has seen in pictures a thousand times: it is too horrible, a child reduced to what lies at his feet.

Hazel.

It was once Hazel Lloyd. His misty eyes go up, looking for the source of light, the escape route for that most unfortunate of girls . . .

NAW . . . NAW . . . I'm sorry . . . I'm sorry . . .

The second body lies a little apart from Hazel's wrecked remains. Like her, it is badly decomposed. Smashed, the bones broken, in this case one arm detached as the flesh and connective tissue has dissolved or been eaten away. They've been thrown down here. Would Confectioner have killed them first? The question that should be academic gnaws invasively at him. Lennox now feels complicit with Confectioner in desecrating them. He punches his own head, bends his knees, and breathes.

A gold chain sparkles under his torch. He lifts it through the slight mound that remains of what was once Hazel's neck. He looks back at the other body, can't ID her by the clothes.

Who? Which one is this?

He flips through the missing persons Rolodex in his brain; suspects Alison McIntyre . . .

How did I forget her on that list . . . ?

Lennox knows what will confirm this, before the science people do their DNA sampling. He shines a torch around, the beam skimming the big stone walls. Sees it almost immediately, the glow of the tatty yellow notebook, crammed in between two jagged rocks. This will confirm who the second girl is. The book contains the story of the terrible fate of those two: and maybe some more.

He sticks it in his pocket, looks up to see the dangling lifeline and attaches it to his harness. He tugs and feels the tight, slow pull upwards, as he begins a leaden ascent. It will be a long way back, out of this well and its suffocating darkness. But he is lucky, he thinks, as he glances at the bones, quickly fading into black. He will make it out.

24

Each of us has our talents. We must all strive to make the best, in my case literally, of the hand we are dealt. Not many men, for example, can punch a hole through plasterboard. I find it almost effortless.

She has more aptitudes than most.

Whether as accomplice or subject, she's by the far the most formidable person I've worked with. A truly gifted woman is such a breath of fresh air. Those vainglorious serial killers and gangsters on my roster – all driven by the same narcissistic ego, replete with that sense of entitlement that the dimmest specimens now embrace so freely. Utter bores, spewing the same turgid, self-satisfying drivel for the consumption of the hopelessly lost and the pathetically impressionable. That terrible disease of our age; humans remoulded as the crass, reductive embodiments of neoliberal and technological stupefaction. Then there are ones born into privilege, yet who adopt a ludicrous rags-to-riches posturing to legitimise themselves. The stupid poor and the stupid rich: playing their bizarre, pathetic game of faux equality, but always to the extreme benefit of the stupid rich. Just don't get ever the bank accounts and assets mixed up.

My own accounts are fine. Such degradation pays the bills. He called me, that mass killer and rapist of young girls. I will make a ludicrous sum of money telling the story of this hollow, depraved monster. The money will be reinvested in destroying other beasts. How fitting.

With her it's also about more than revenge. That's why she's my perfect partner. She's driven to understand everything. Wants to look outside as well as inside. I want to help her. And help myself. All I need to do is sit her down in the chair, pour her a glass of water, activate the record function on my device and let her speak. And that's exactly what

I do . . . despite the muffled screams of the bound, bug-eyed man on the floor between us. I wish he'd cease his struggle and listen. After all, this is for his benefit too.

— The blonde hair is the beacon that draws them in, she declares, giving hers an illustrative flick with the back of her hand. — This is backed up by empirical research: blondes blind men. I get away with a lot professionally, distracted as they slaver on, opening up their secrets to me, all the things they can never tell their lovers, and she looks at him on the floor, his face red and swollen. — He was easy. She slips off her shoes, looking at him to see if there's any recognition, as his eyes go from her to me.

A strange whimpering from beneath his mask. It shouldn't come from such a man: it makes me feel a little bilious.

Then she pulls off the big, bushy wig she uses to augment her hair and enable her disguise. — I put on a bra that pushes my breasts up. The short, tight dress shows my legs. For eighty per cent of men, *this* is the Rohypnol. You basically have them in your power . . .

I'm tempted to gloat again. Perhaps ask him if he likes this room, in this rented house. Wondering if he can discern it's a detached dwelling, in quite a sought-after suburb. She scoped it out. After the near-disastrous bath incident at the Savoy, we decided that nothing in our future endeavours would be left to chance.

So it was with Gulliver. So it will be with this one.

— The male ego always fascinates me, the delusional power of it, she contends, glancing sadly at him. — He's out of shape, overweight, badly dressed, hair thinning, yet he really believes that he just got lucky. In his line of work, and he wasn't even suspicious.

He's still whining through the gag.

— When his bemused eyes finally got that something wasn't right, he did attempt to fight the mounting drowsiness.

— Yes, I agree, thinking of Gulliver succumbing in the same way in that hotel room.

— Then his head slumped against the back of the couch, and she

211

points, signalling for me to switch on the camera, positioned on a tripod, angled down at him. As he's in perfect position, I concur, then remove the long-handled wooden mallet from my bag.

I grip it in my *good* hand, then position it in my *evil* hand, like a croquet mallet and I smash him in the forehead as hard as I can. I swear I hear bone crack this time.

Now his big, scandalous eyes are fully closed.

The killer the police called the Carpenter of Lunacy would befriend and drug lonely young men, then assault them in this way, before sexually abusing them by performing anal rape. Only two of his seven victims died. The others were too ashamed to come forward, until one broke ranks. There are probably many more. Appropriating this modus operandi means nothing to us. It's just a red herring to throw in.

I look at our man. I've obviously hurt him badly. While I've come to see the inevitability of violence, I gain little pleasure from it. We put on our plastic robes and sheet him up, getting him out through the attached garage, dragging him into the boot of the car. It's a short drive to our private place where we will work on him, before taking him to the dumping ground. I feel the ten-inch knife in my inside coat pocket. This side of it I find it much harder than she seems to.

For all her brilliance she isn't infallible. Of course she would never admit it, but she has the tendency to pick up lost causes. It was her mistake in getting that big fool involved, first as a driver, then as a pair of extra hands. He was besotted with her, but such infatuations can easily change. A loose cannon with no discipline, he could ruin everything. So I resolved to remove him.

We had discovered that Ritchie Gulliver, despite mocking trans people, was very much into sex with them. But she furnished this information to the big idiot Gayle, who planned to seduce Gulliver and fuck him up before his visit to Stirling. Then Lauren Fairchild, a trans lecturer at the university, a tutor and confidante of our fool, learned of this and went to blow the whistle. I instantly thought: *if this trans academic met with a mishap, then a certain jailbait idiot would be in frame.*

I was roughly the same height and build as Gayle. I reasoned that if I could stand the ignominy of disguising myself like that with those stupid dangling bangles and belts, the public would only see another ridiculous freak making an unedifying exhibition of themselves. Then Gayle, of course, would be ID'd as the killer of Lauren Fairchild.

Two pretend birds with one stone.

I messed that one up due to the intervention of a man whom I knew to be DI Ray Lennox. I almost didn't get away. He's a reasonably robust specimen, though no problem physically for someone of my power. However, I've been made aware of his doggedness in his desire to figure out our enterprise. I witnessed this at close hand as I prepared to finish the job and snuff the life out of that other unfortunate specimen. Thankfully, Lennox is *so far* blissfully clueless to the fact that he himself he is very much an integral part of all of this. Now I have to convince her that he is a problem.

Like the others.

It's no good to just castrate them. They need to be held accountable for their crimes, and made aware of the repressive machinery they are part of. Repentance, while welcome, isn't really what we're after, as it does them no good. We just want them to understand why we're doing what we're doing. It's not like we're negotiating or anything.

We do not negotiate.

25

The house is neat and cosy. Her picture, in a simple black frame, still sits on the shrine-like mantelpiece. She is smiling. That blue gingham dress, degraded to the rag wrapped around the pile of bones in the bottom of that Stygian, desolate well, left for the team to retrieve and bring to the surface. The long blonde hair, dishonoured to scarecrow straw, framing once-beautiful eyes hollowed out to a deathly gape. The skull . . .

Oh my God, Hazel, I am so sorry . . .

The other girl was quickly confirmed as Alison McIntyre, who disappeared after walking home from a night at Calton Studios ten years ago. She was intoxicated and had an argument with her boyfriend. She went to get a taxi, and had been on the missing persons list ever since. There had been bogus 'sightings' in London and Leeds.

Hazel . . . Alison . . . he has to pay . . . the cunt has to pay and you're indulging him instead of making him pay . . .

As the invasive thoughts hammer him like coffin nails, Lennox almost falls onto the couch. Then, suddenly aware where he is, he tries not to show how much he is hurting. Glances at the beguiling picture again . . .

. . . he has to pay more than he has . . .

— Sit down, son, the man says. Alan Lloyd is probably a few years older than him, but looks and acts at least two decades his senior. Lloyd's shoulders hunch and stoop, his eyes seeming like they've been removed from his head and pickled in a jar of aspic, before being scooped out and stuffed back in.

Oh God, Hazel . . . no . . . no . . . no . . .

Confectioner did that. He did that to all of them.

Lennox feels his fingertips tingle. Imagines fragments of Hazel's brittle, powdery skull underneath his nails. When they hauled him to the surface of that well, he went and scrubbed his hands until they were raw. It didn't help.

Joyce Lloyd, Hazel's mother, sits in a chair across the room from him, bloated and pumped up by grief, as steadily and implacably as it has reduced her husband. Yet, even after all these years, the tension and misery is wrought all over her fleshy face. The McIntyre family, he doesn't know them. Alison's disappearance took place when he was on a temporary switch from Serious Crimes to Vice. Who is left to mourn her? What hell did those girls go through, here on Earth?

Who has the right to do that to another human being? They have to be hunted down. They have to be dismantled.

— We've found her body, in the well near Killiecrankie, I'm sorry, Lennox says in flat tones, aware of a mounting force burning him. — The killer was Gareth Horsburgh, known as Mr Confectioner.

— I want to see her, Alan Lloyd declares.

You crushed her skull like it was a packet of crisps.

— I wouldn't recommend that, Mr Lloyd, the voice of the professional struggles to take over. But all Lennox wants to do is wrap his arms around this man and his wife. Swallowing hard, he feels like the movement of his Adam's apple would be visible from space. — Her body is decomposed . . . and Ray Lennox is fighting now. He craves drink, drugs, any stepping stones to oblivion. — Everything, all that made her Hazel . . . it's now gone. Except for one thing. He pulls out the locket

215

and hands it to Joyce Lloyd. It contains the picture of her parents as they were.

The couple look at it, then painfully embrace, Alan's thin arms around his meaty wife's frame, as they break down in synchronised, halting sobs. How often have they played this scene, as their bodies changed under an ageing grief?

Would they have been altered anyway, by time, genetics or lifestyle choices?

No. Confectioner ruined them. Joyce took comfort in a packet of biscuits. Alan just wasted away as his beautiful memories battled his terrible thoughts.

— She's at peace now, Joyce . . . but us . . . she needs us tae be at peace too, Alan coos hopefully. He looks at Lennox. — This man cares, Joyce, he really wanted to find her. He caught that animal Horsburgh . . .

— I'm so sorry that I couldnae find her alive. Lennox feels the whining child voice slip subversively from him, with his own tears trying to follow. He slams his eyes shut. All those years of trying to be a professional policeman, all gone, trickling away, like the rivulets squidging out from under his lids, forcing him to raise the back of his hand across his face. — I tried so hard. I really did.

Distilled to a reedy croak, Alan Lloyd's voice still possesses a weird power and conviction. — We know that, son. Right from the start you were different to the rest of them. We knew you cared.

Lennox fights down a convulsive sob, and stands up and nods. — Yes, I care, he suddenly intones in the pained voice of an unjustly wronged kid. — I hate those people! I hate them, and he's shaking with fear and rage, and then he's in a Lloyd sandwich. The two of them, the mother and father, holding him tight.

This is what you wanted from your mum and dad when you came in from that tunnel . . .

He takes in the scent of the Lloyds; Alan's faint aftershave, Joyce's powdery fragrance. This is all so *inappropriate*, as Drummond would say.

— Yes, son, but we'll be able to say goodbye to Hazel now, thanks to you. You've given us peace, Alan coos thinly, — now you need to find some for yourself.

— Peace, Lennox says, pulling away from them. A thought grips him, as he looks to the picture. Sees it as Trudi, a young version of her on her mother's mantelpiece. The Lowes, their one child, daughter of Joanne and Donald, who was now also gone. — Was Hazel your only one?

Alan nods blankly.

Then Ray Lennox takes his leave of the Lloyds. It's a long set of steps to the front door of the council house. With every one he takes, he thinks of Confectioner.

You hate the cunt. You want to rip him apart with your bare hands. If you could just visit that pain on him: teach him about hurt and fear. Dismantle him. Change him.

Turning his back on the Lloyd household, he heads down the cold street, into the murky night. Hunches along a submerged section of the old Edinburgh suburban railway, those arterial walking paths under the skin of the city. Lennox opts not to return to Police HQ at Fettes, but still craves the company of the most damaged cops.

Along those subterranean routes that few tourists and visitors know about, he winds into town, bound for the Repair Shop. He moves into the bar like a dark spectre, disturbing what passes for peace. But the man he wants to talk to is the only one not present.

There is no sign of Norrie Erskine.

Workaholic Scott McCorkel, perched at the bar, looks up from his computer. Inglis glances across from the dartboard, where he's just thrown a decent one hundred and forty. Only Gillman, eating a fish supper brought in from the chippy across the road, seems oblivious to his entry.

Standing next to him is a nervy Guinness-quaffing Harkness. — So the gang's all here, Lennox sings breezily.

— Hi, Ray . . . except Erskine, Harkness says, taking the bait. It is instructive for Lennox to have confirmed that the other two absent Serious Crimes officers, Drummond and Glover, are exempt from 'the gang' by virtue of being female.

Gillman looks up from his fish supper. — Aye, there's nae sign ay the Weedgie cunt. He was oot oan the lash last night, heading up tae the Pubic Triangle tae fill up the tank. Then probably off tae the sauna tae empty the lot! Cunt's probably goat a brutal hangover so aw he's good fir the day is chugging ehsel blind tae porn.

What the fuck is going on with Erskine, and are you stalking Drummond?

Not acknowledging what he's heard, and resisting the urge to intervene – Gillman would smell cop mode – Lennox, ordering a Stella, hears McCorkel chip in, — Pornography has been proven to desensitise men, making it harder for them to achieve and sustain erections.

Gillman looks around the bar incredulously. — So the big expert on hard-ons, he points at McCorkel, — is the one cunt present who's never had ehs hole? The fuckin incel king? Get tae fuck, PC, he laughs.

McCorkel's face matches his hair, as Lennox sits down next to him.

— Check this. Doug Arnott, whom Lennox thinks of as a typical veteran Serious Crimes cop – divorced, alcoholic and nursing an unspecific wrath against the world – holds up a picture of a naked young woman on his screensaver.

— Too auld for unshaven fannies, Gillman roars, knocking back a drink. Lennox averts eye contact, the word 'Thailand' hanging between them. — The missus came in wi it done the other week there. Ah jist goes: geez a fuckin brek, for fuck's sake.

At this point, two hipsters enter the bar, sporting emotional beards.

Gillman and Erskine . . .

— Some fucking fannies should be shaved, Gillman spits. — It ought tae be compulsory.

The good guys . . .

Suddenly, almost in one unhinged gesture, Lennox glugs back his pint and orders another. — We're winning, he cheerfully declares, looking manically round at his colleagues. — Winning the war.

In the face of his wild-eyed, demented energy, they exchange nervous glances. Even Gillman seems reticent. McCorkel, face wrought with gun-shy concern, asks him, — What war are we winning, Ray?

— The war against life, Lennox grins, and toasts them. His eyes bore into the sign on the gents' toilets, as he feels his sweaty forefinger and thumb on the plastic bag of cocaine in his trouser pocket.

Day Five

Saturday

26

Morning's wrecking light creeps in, flooding Ray Lennox with initial relief. He's woken up in his own bed. This is the only bit of good news his senses afford him; he's also wired, disorientated and leaden-limbed. He drank too much last night. Maybe one really is too much for him. In his mind's eye, he sees Keith Goodwin's smug face. Hears the sweetie-wife 'recovering addict' platitudes. But his nose, simultaneously bunged up and running like a fountain, informs him that cocaine does the real damage: it makes you stay up past your bedtime. Sometimes several days past it.

He picks up his phone to a message from Trudi:

> Where the fuck are you, Ray? It's against all my instincts, but we should talk rather than leave it like this.

Rage wells up in him like a geyser. He types:

> Talk to that fucking BMW nonce, hoor-drawers. I'll keep trying to avoid getting murdered.

223

But he doesn't send it. Instead he looks at the text. Laughs loudly, his gooseflesh shaking as he pulls on his dressing gown. Deletes it from his phone.

Glad I typed it, but delighted I didn't send it.

Just as he heads to the bathroom, a text drops into his phone that cuts him to the quick. It's not from Trudi, but Moira Gulliver. He has to read it three times to believe what it is saying:

> Lennox: you are so damn sexy.
> Confession time: all I do is think
> of us being together. I was up all
> night masturbating about you.
> I want you so badly. Can we get
> together in a hotel room asap and
> just fuck all our problems away?

Lennox blinks in a rapid spasm as he feels his heart pound in his chest.

Game on! So your instincts were right. Despite her grief, she was up for it! Maybe even turned on by the thought of shagging her dead brother's nemesis. That's posh birds for ye! Well, if she wants it, she'll get it . . .

Fuck you, Trudi, and your Hibee BMW wanker.

And you, Drummond, ya uptight Jutland hoor . . . and that stalking weirdo Gillman . . .

Then:

> I'm so sorry, Ray. That last text, it
> was sent to you in error. How very
> embarrassing. I sincerely apologise.

224

What the fuck . . .

Hangover lust keening his brain, Lennox immediately gets on the phone. — Moira . . . those texts . . . there's no need for games or embarrassment. We're both adults. I've been feeling something too, so please don't think that –

— As I said, I apologise, she abruptly cuts in. — It must have seemed strange, but that text genuinely wasn't meant for you.

— 'Lennox, I want you so badly'? Seems explicit enough! No need to be disingenuous here . . .

— I'm not. God . . . look, Ray, I'm genuinely sorry for the embarrassment, but the text really wasn't meant for you. We are indeed, as you say, adults, so please accept both my error and my apology. Goodbye.

And she hangs up.

What the fuck . . . 'Lennox, I want you so badly' . . . who the fuck is that for, if not for me?!

Then: a missing beat in his heart as his chest tightens.

Stuart! The little cunt is nailing her! This is his posh bird!

He texts Moira again:

Well, all the best with my wee brother.

He waits for a response but none is forthcoming. He texts Stuart:

Nice one with Moira, you creepy wee
cock-blocking fucker. Typical Glasgow!
Sounds TYPICAL Weedgie pish, btw.

Lennox showers and gets dressed. Deciding to walk in order to clear his head, he emerges into a squalid morning.

Gulls shriek overhead. A car zooms past, almost mounting the pavement, causing him to brace in terror. But although it's as if its occupants are intoxicated from last night, it's not close enough to be about him. Jake Spiers stands at the bottom of the street, supervising a beer-delivery lorry. As he passes, the two men make surly eye contact. Lennox heads down Gilmore Place to Tollcross.

By the time he turns onto Lothian Road, the hangover is still severe, but bearable. Suddenly he sees what looks from the back to be a familiar figure, as a slender woman in a business suit and heels cuts across Festival Square, making for the Sheraton. His heart races and he turns away in a teen-like embarrassment. A second glance across at the woman, simultaneously painfully thin and voluptuously provocative, confirms her as Moira Gulliver, Stuart's unlikely lover. As she disappears into the hotel, Lennox wonders why she is heading there.

Possibly going to the spa or gym, but she has no sports bag, or perhaps more likely a business meeting with a client. Or . . .

. . . she'll be meeting that wee cunt Stuart . . .

Lennox decides to follow her into the hotel. As he goes to the reception, there's no sign of Stuart in the lobby, and he glances over to watch Moira head into the lift. The indicator tells him she's meeting his brother on the third floor.

Snidey wee cunt . . . well, another prospect bites the dust. Fuck all you can do about it.

The hotel is busy doing breakfasts; there is obviously some corporate event going on. Crestfallen, Lennox opts to stand at the bar. It's open, but it doesn't have an early licence for non-residents, so he forfeits the Stella he craves for a strong coffee.

Then a firm hand on his shoulder, as he turns round to see Jackie. — What are you doing here?

— I, uh . . . Lennox hesitates, touching his nose, regressing, in the time-honoured dynamic between those siblings, to

226

his customary role of prepubescent boy confronting a bossy teen. He assumes she's here for this corporate event.

Jackie's face tightens in sour evaluation. — Are you spying, Ray? Are you spying on *Moira*?

— No, I – what the fuck, what's this got to do with Moira? . . . Some crazy awareness crashes like a set of cymbals in his head. — *You* . . . you and Moira Gulliver . . .

Jackie exhales a long breath, and raises her eyebrows skywards. — Yes. We're lovers. What of it?

— Well . . . uh . . . Lennox says lamely, then tries to fuse some levity and dynamism into his tones, — you always liked guys! I never thought, you know? It's just a bit of a surprise!

Jackie looks pointedly at him. Then lets her head swivel around to check out nobody else is in earshot. — So it should be, she says, turning back to him. — I'm not a lesbian, Ray. Well, maybe I am, because Moira utterly excites me, and she briefly shuts her eyes and tightens her lips to savour what is evidently to come. — But it's the first time I've ever had an affair . . . of this kind.

Lennox fights to maintain composure. — You've cheated on Angus before?

— Only with other men, Jackie says, screwing her face up at his shocked expression. — Oh for God's sake, don't look so bloody prudish, Ray. You're not twenty. Angus has had a string of affairs himself.

— Angus?! For fuck sake . . . *Am I the only cunt in this fucking city no getting his hole?*

— We lost interest in each other sexually a decade ago, and Jackie sees a suited couple move briefly into the vicinity, and flashes a light-bulb smile. — I mean, we get on perfectly well otherwise. He's my best friend, and the father of my children, so it's the most sensible arrangement, she declares, then snaps, — Don't look at me like that! You've gone from thinking

Mum to *Stuart*, haven't you? Well, maybe not unreasonably, as Moira wants me to leave Angus and move in with her.

Lennox remains flabbergasted. Realises he knows nothing. His sister has always seemed quite a mysterious force. But he put that down to her being a girl, swotty, and a bit older. Now, as he glances at them in the bar mirror, she looks a decade younger than him. — I never thought that I was the most conventional of the three of us.

— *This is* conventional now. What kind of world are you still living in with those Serious Crimes dinosaurs?

His phone rings with Trudi's caller ID. He lets it ring out on mute.

Get tae fuck. See how you fucking like it!

Jackie's brow furrows as she regards Lennox's phone. She is about to say something, so he heads her off at the pass. — How's it going with Mum, now that she's left Jock Allardyce? What happened there?

— We don't talk about it. You should come and see her.

— No way.

— For God's sake, whatever you fell out over, put it the fuck behind you. You know how you were with Dad. Life's too short.

— Maybe I should. Lennox keeps his tone conciliatory. Then looks at her sadly. — Mind that time I came back on my bike and I went upstairs to see you in your room and you were getting made up? I was shaking . . . you told me to fuck off?

She looks blankly at him. Then something sparks. — Oh . . . right . . . a guy I was getting ready to go out on a date with, Roddy McLeod-Stuart . . . I really fancied him and I was so nervous . . . What did you want to talk about?

— A guy in the old railway tunnel made me suck his cock while my mate was being anally raped.

Jackie looks around, agitated. Is relieved nobody proximate seems to have heard her brother. — I know you see some disturbing things and it's a coping mechanism, but your Serious Crimes humour is very inappropriate.

Then Hollis calls. This time he picks up.

Lennox half expects another cocaine-fuelled rant, but Hollis's voice is softer than he imagined it could ever be. He no longer seems scared, more broken and resigned as he makes a soft plea. — I need help, Ray. Can't ask nobody down here. Shit has hit the fan big time.

Ray Lennox doubts he could be more anxious; feels as if his insides are liquidised and his organs will spill out of his arsehole as he drains away. — What's happened, Mark?

— Can't really explain, can't leave me flat. Can't call anyone here. Something fucking big went down last night, and fuck me, do I need help.

Lennox can see Jackie looking at him in some anxiety. He barely hesitates. — I'm heading to the airport to get a standby shuttle to London City right now. Sit tight.

— Right. Thank you, Ray.

It's Lennox who is relieved. Glad to get away from Trudi, Drummond, Police HQ, Stuart, Jackie, Moira Gulliver, Edinburgh; everyone and everything, in a life he feels closing in around him. *Hollis will know. Hollis will understand.* And London provides that wonderful service Edinburgh cannot offer a drowning man: it does not even pretend to care. It has too many souls to be bothered paying lip service to the plight of one.

— Is everything okay? Jackie asks in concern.

— No, Lennox says, suddenly emboldened, jumping forward and embracing his sister, — but hopefully it will be. He pulls away, leaving her looking at him in confusion. — Have fun!

Jackie watches him turn to retreat. Recovers enough equipoise to say through a tight mouth and half-shut eyes, — Oh, I will.

27

At the airport bar Lennox, brain a fracas of confusion, sinks two medicinal Stellas. When he arrives at City airport he jumps into another cab, looking at his texts, now willing one to be from Trudi, or even Drummond . . .

Fuck . . . You've had sex with her and you still think of her as Drummond rather than Amanda. No wonder she's avoiding you . . . hope she's avoiding Gillman . . .

You need to be away.

That's what you do, isn't it? You run away from them all.

Les Brodie. Your old mate. Ran away and left the poor wee cunt to be rammed by three beasts in a tunnel.

You were a boy; what else could you do?

Then a text comes in from Jackie. Moira has evidently told her about the mix-up:

> Moira and I have been having a
> bloody good laugh at you, Ray!
> God, the male ego! But what is
> going on with you and Trudi? If
> you are having issues, you can
> talk to me, you know! I love you,
> you silly wee brother man! xxx

Nice of them to take a bit of time off from the fanny-licking, in order to have a fucking good laugh at cunty baws here . . .

> Appreciated, Jack. Apologies to M
> for the mix up! I love you too.
> Hook up soon. xx

Alighting from the cab at Elephant and Castle, he walks down Walworth Road. Turns down a grey, semi-razed backstreet. Guilt and humiliation seem to be running alongside him, mockingly whispering songs of his inadequacy into his ear.

Hollis's flat is above a minicab office with a flashing amber light. It reminds Lennox of a bottle of Irn-Bru on its side. Almost beyond cliché, it's exactly the sort of place he envisaged the divorced, troubled maverick cop living in.

Why are you doing this? Why have you run from Trudi? You went fucking nuts when your dad died! You should be there for her! Why here? You barely know Hollis!

But that is pure pish. You know Mark Hollis better than you've known almost anyone in your life. Hollis is everything you wanted Les Brodie to be: a genuine partner, by your side, taking the war to the nonces! And they are trying to kill us both . . .

It's not enough to clean up the mess they make. We have to eradicate them. Hollis gets that. Hollis understands.

He hesitates before pushing the top-flat button. It's the stair door; the Yale lock has been freshly broken. Splintered wood is evident on the badly stained carpet. He steps inside. Ascends a narrow stair. As he grips the banister, a sticky sensation makes him reflexively pull his hand away. Blood. It is streaked with it.

At a bend in the stair he sees a door boarded up. This flat looks long unoccupied. From above: a low resonant growl, which morphs into a squeal, before cutting to silence.

Feels his own blood chill in his veins.

Now would be the time to call Squeak Mortimer at the Met for backup. But Hollis wouldn't thank you for that . . .

He presses on. More blood on the banister: *what the fuck happened here?*

As he gets to the top floor, the blood has thickened into sticky pools on the carpet. In some trepidation, Lennox knocks heavily on the door of the flat. It swings slowly open under the impact of his blow.

He steps inside, into total darkness. Senses he is in a narrow passage. Is taken back to the well and the meagre remains of those girls. Then a shallow breathing sound, like a wounded animal might make. Something tells him not to shout out.

A table light clicks on to the side of him. Lennox almost jumps out of his skin as he sees Hollis standing close by him, a knuckleduster in his hand. Feral-eyed, the Met cop pants heavily, his light blue T-shirt stained with blood. His non-weaponised hand holds a glass of whisky. The fumes of booze, old and new, waft from Mark Hollis, who looks at Ray Lennox for a primal second or two of naked hostility, forcing his visitor to confirm, — Mark, it's Ray.

Hollis screws his eyes and gasps in recognition. Lennox has suspected he wears contacts, which are now obviously not in. But it's evident that the alcohol and lack of sleep have fuddled his brain. He looks exhausted. Flesh hangs ruddy and slack on his big face, eyes so dark and sunken it's like he's gone to town on mascara. — Ray . . . thank you, thank you, thank you . . . Mark Hollis turns down the hallway, still walking uncomfortably, almost mincing like a catwalk model.

Lennox follows him into the mess of a flat. Its walls are red-streaked. Bloodied handprints indicate somebody was gripping the door frame under pressure.

— I had visitors, Hollis confirms, as they enter a kitchen-lounge.

Handcuffed to a radiator is a man shaking like a shitting dog in a public park. His pulped face is covered in blood and he holds a cushion tight to his stomach, behind which most of the bloody leakage seems to have come from, spilling onto the hardwood floor like dark treacle.

— What the fuck happened here?

— Two of them burst in on me, Hollis recounts in rasping breathlessness. — I battered one, who scarpered, then stabbed this cunt. He points at the radiator man, reading Lennox's incredulous look. — I can't call it in, Ray. I don't trust my bosses. Not with toff involvement and noncery. They sweep that shit under the carpet, every time. They drove a car at us, Ray.

Twice. Lennox thinks of the hospital in Glasgow. Then his thoughts turn to Miami. How the rogue cop he encountered there turned out to be the leader of a paedophile syndicate. He nods slowly at Hollis.

— I took this playboy prisoner, Hollis confirms, nodding at the bust-up captive, as he pulls Lennox into the hallway and drops his voice. — I want to know who's paying him. I need this cunt to squeal.

Lennox bends his head back to look at the man on the radiator: stocky, square build, crew cut, flinty eyes blazing through a cowl of blood. But as Lennox peruses him, his target's gaze quickly averts.

They step back into the lounge, as Lennox regards the prisoner. — Who is he?

— Fuck knows, no ID. He's obviously been around, takes a fair old slap and still keeps shtum, but his mate was an amateur. Coming round here . . . Hollis looks at the man, igniting into rage, — . . . a farking monkey.

The scene confirms Lennox's earlier mental note: *don't fuck with Hollis*. The boxer's punch is the last thing to go and Hollis becomes more emboldened, explaining how he probably broke the first intruder's jaw. The second one, his captive, came at him with the knife and cut him in the chest. Hollis pulls up his shirt to show only a minor scrape; very little of the blood on him is his own. — I took it off him and plunged the cahnt. He points at the shivering man and then the bloodstained knife on the kitchen worktop. — He tried to get out but I wasn't having it. Went after him, caught him on the stairs and dragged him back in here. Don't think I chived him anywhere too naughty cause he's just been bleeding out slowly. He moves over to the man. — Been waiting to hear what laughing boy here gotta say for himself, and Hollis makes a fist, backhanding the man in a casual brutality that makes Lennox feel both queasy and excited. There's a tang of metal in his mouth, as he thinks of the men in the tunnel.

Take that, you noncing cunt.

Sucking in a breath to compose himself, Lennox waves Hollis off, crouching beside the man. — You really should speak up. You're not getting paid enough to remain silent in the face of what we'll do to you.

The man stares ahead, but his eyes are taking on a glassy aspect and Lennox can tell that he's scared. It would be hard not to be in such circumstances, as he looks up at Hollis. The renegade Met man, in his bloodstained shirt, looks every inch a plump, psychotic butcher.

— Brought my mate along, Hollis says cheerfully. — We got different moves, ya see!

— Indeed, Lennox says, as Hollis goes into his pocket, producing the knuckleduster and slipping his hand through the holes.

— Wait! The man finds his voice. — You're cops! You can't do this!

— Legal stuff I ain't too much up on, mate, Hollis makes a fist, holding it appreciatively up to the light, — and from your behaviour I'm guessing it ain't your area of expertise either.

Lennox laughs in the man's face. — So you think I'm a cop. That really is a new one, he says with utter conviction. Standing up, he pulls a towel from a rail in the kitchen area. — I'm going to choke you with this, and he starts to wind it tight. — My friend here, well, he'll be punching you in the stomach. Opening up that wound in your gut. Lennox pushes a fist into the cushion, hard and resolute. The man squeals out and his eyes pop. Then Lennox snaps a left jab into his face. The man raises his free hand to try and protect himself. — Head body, head body. It'll be hell, he explains. — But we won't stop.

Are you Gillman? You've watched him do that.

The towel, as used by Gillman on Confectioner, is snapped in front of the man's face before Lennox quickly places it around his neck. As he twists, it starts to do its work. Mark Hollis looks on, deeply impressed. Not to be left out, he dispenses two cutting jabs, before a wretched tangle of truth starts to spill from the lips of the man. — My name's Des . . . I'm from Dagenham . . . I was sent on a job, with Tommy, to put the frighteners on you. I didn't know you was filth!

— WHO SENT YA? Hollis roars.

— My boss provides muscle for hire . . . this geezer's been a reliable client . . . so it's no questions asked. He wouldn't know you was filth either . . .

— Who is your boss?

— If I told ya we're all finished . . .

Hollis smashes him in the face with a clenched fist that looks like a bag of rocks, as Lennox tightens the towel. Des from Dagenham's eyes bulge so wildly, Lennox is concerned they will pop out of their sockets.

— It's . . . and as Lennox loosens, Des forces in air, wheezing out, — . . . I dunno . . . the geezer's name . . . he had a

235

plummy voice . . . my boss has worked with him before, he's always been kosher . . .

Lennox and Hollis look at each other, both thinking: *Wallingham*.

Hollis again holds his knuckleduster hand up to the light. — This is where I ask you once more. Sadly, although I've had fun, it's the final time. Then, after we're done, your poor old mum won't recognise you afterwards. Any skirt you been nailing are suddenly washing their hair rather than stepping out with you. Cause I will find out one way or another. Hollis smiles, reasonable tones incongruent with the comical malevolence of his expression. — Who you working for? he demands.

Dagenham Des shudders, before fusing into a defiant sneer. — Billy Lake.

Lennox can see this name once again elicits a strong reaction from Hollis, who nods slowly and rises. He gestures to Lennox and they step back into the hallway. — As I suspected, but didn't want to hear. We've some fences to mend, Ray, and he picks up his phone. — I'm gambling that Billy Lake has been fed some dodgy information.

— This mystery villain of yours? Who would set him up? Lennox says doubtfully. — What if you're wrong and he was paid to take you out the game if you knew too much about him and became expendable?

— It's a possibility, Hollis glumly concedes. — Suffice to say that I have to go into the lion's den, or worse for my postcode, the Hammer's den, and talk to him. If I don't see you again, my hunch was wrong and it's been nice knowing you.

— I must be one crazy fucker, and Lennox points to the protruding bloodstained T-shirt, — but I'm backing your substantial gut. I'm coming with you.

Hollis looks at Lennox in a pitying gratitude. — You really are farking crazy. But I appreciate it.

236

28

A battered and sorry-looking Des McCready, hands cuffed behind his back, sits forlornly on black bin liners in the rear of Mark Hollis's Ford Capri. By his side, the London cop. Up front, Ray Lennox drives them to Southend. — I'm bleeding to death, the Dagenham man wretchedly moans. — Billy will have you for this . . .

Hollis sits with a navy-blue dress jacket on top of his bloodied shirt, which makes him look beyond seedy. He shoots Des a mean, snide look. — Well, that's one way of looking at it, he grins. — Another is that Billy and I have got a bit of form. If he don't know it was me them Hoorays wanted done, he might just get a little narky with a certain mug wot didn't do his farking homework properly!

— Yeah, well, we'll see, won't we? Des asserts, but his confidence is waning. — If I make it there, he suddenly shrieks, looking down at his wound in horror.

— Going as quickly as the law permits, Lennox observes, poker-faced, slightly cheered after a text from Chic Gallagher tells him that there has been some improvement in Lauren Fairchild's condition. — Don't want stopped by some uniformed spastic.

— Correct, Hollis says, appreciatively musing on the Edinburgh detective slang for uniformed officers. — Uniformed spastic. I like than one, he wistfully declares, before snapping into the present and pulling a bin liner tighter across the seat. — Watch your farking mess! You farking two-bob dirtbox slag, he scowls at Des.

— You plunged *me*, Des protests in misery.

— Yeah? Well, it was your blade and you made a farking miserable attempt to chiv me! Had to take it off ya and show ya how it was done, didn't I?

Lennox feels his phone vibrate in his pocket. It announces Jackie. She very rarely calls him, but circumstances are far from normal.

This fucking embarrassment with Moira . . . or maybe Trudi got in touch with her . . .

He hesitates; can't put it on speaker with Hollis and McCready in the back. Looks at the road ahead and behind. It's quiet. He peels off into the slow lane and tears some headphones from his pocket, stuffing them into his ears. — Jack . . . it's not a great time –

— It's Fraser, she gasps urgently. — He's gone, Ray! He hasn't come home . . .

Thank fuck . . . — Maybe just teens being teens, have you –

— . . . he never came home last night and none of his friends know where he is!

Fuck . . .

Finally, it's personal. There's no guilt that accompanies his surge of adrenaline. Because Lennox is racked with an intuitive shuddering despair that his nephew is somehow linked to this mess.

— I need details, Jack. Where was he last seen? Who by? Who are his associates? Which ones haven't you been able to contact? Lennox barks, fighting to get Jackie's trained barrister mind working, short-circuited as it is by maternal concern and guilt. *Fuck motherhood,* he thinks, feeling unclehood to be a burden devastating enough in the circumstances.

Jackie coughs out as much as Lennox can absorb.

— I'm going to look for him. A colleague will be round to

talk to you in more detail, see if there are more things you recall.

— Yes! I will! There was a girlfriend, or an ex-girlfriend. Leonora Slade, Jackie says breathlessly, — I have a contact, because a package once came for Fraser. I know it was wrong but I took a snap of the sender's address on the packet. Why did I do that? she moans in self-recrimination as it pops into Lennox's phone. — Had a blazing row with Angus, who practically accused me of driving Fraser away . . . he's out searching now . . . told me to wait here in case he comes back . . . So what are you doing, you said you would talk to a colleague?

— Yes, I'm just going to call her now.

— A colleague . . . it's *Fraser*, your *nephew* . . . where are *you*?

He has always wanted his cool, analytical sister, as she dispensed her cold legal platitudes, to be more human. Now her distress seems too much to bear witness to. — I think I told you at the Sheraton, I'm down in London, but I'm right on it, Jack. My colleague has specialist skills in missing teenagers, Lennox lies, thinking of Drummond. — Either I or she will be in touch.

— Please, Ray, find him. Find my baby, she sobs.

— All over it, Jack, he says.

As Hollis and his sparring partner are silent in the back, Lennox calls Drummond. This time, to his great relief and eternal gratitude, she picks up. — I need a big favour . . . his urgently charged voice begs.

It has the desired impact of derailing any expressions of buyer's regret and that 'we need to be more professional' speech he anticipated she was loading up. — Of course. What's up?

He fills her in on the details of Fraser's disappearance, and passes on Jackie's contact number.

— Right, she says with what sounds to him like a tepid level of enthusiasm.

— Thanks . . . and, Amanda . . .

The silence hangs.

— Watch Gillman. He's a bit unhinged these days.

— Since the mid-1980s would be my guess.

— Seriously. He's been acting strange –

— I have to go, and she hangs up.

Fuck you. Get stalked by a bam then.

Erskine's name and his conversation with Confectioner pops into his head.

Why would Confectioner reference Erskine like that? Were you maybe too quick to get down here?

They are just past the halfway stage of their journey when a call comes in from McCorkel, whose tones are etched in concern. — Ray, Amanda's got me looking for your nephew . . .

She delegated that one sharpish . . .

— Aye, Fraser Ross, Lennox says, pressing the buds into his ears as the squabbling cockney Punch and Judy show behind him starts up again. Lennox grimly acknowledges that a man bleeding out from a hole in his stomach and his assailant who was initially attacked by him in his own home while convalescing from an operation for chronic piles would hardly be the best of travelling companions. — Anything for me?

— Tracking his movements, Ray, Scott says. — Seen at the university at 3.20 p.m. yesterday, stopped off for a vegan pie in Eatz at South Bridge, then walked down the Bridges, picked up by CCTV cameras in St James Quarter at 5.07, then in John Lewis at 5.38 p.m. Comes out the bottom exit and crosses the roundabout at Picardy Place. No indication so far that he jumped into any of the vehicles around . . . been tracing all the ones that passed the roundabout through the DVLA at Swansea. Roadworks have made it single lane and slowed them down. It looks more likely he's gone on foot to a local address, somewhere in the East New Town or Pilrig areas. We're cross-referencing the address of his associates with EH1, EH3 and EH6 postcodes. Will have a list soon. Will text it to you asap –

— So . . . he vanishes between the roadworks and traffic?

— Aye . . . but he stopped just before that to talk to a girl, about five three, short dark hair, slender build . . . She disappeared too . . .

Leonora Slade?

— Thanks, Scott, good work.

— Meantime, there's something else that will be of interest. I found some CCTV footage of Gulliver's talk at Stirling University, just where it all kicked off.

— Go on. Lennox tries to force enthusiasm into his voice.

— Well, it's just that Fraser is one of the most prominent demonstrators. McCorkel pauses, and Lennox feels his attention ramping up. — And I'll bet you can guess who another is, whom Fraser's alongside . . .

Fuck me . . .

— Gayle . . .

— Yes – formerly Gary Nicolson. A registered sex offender under his original name. Did a stretch for rape three years ago.

You thought there was something familiar about that big cunt: his mugshot. Fuck . . . Fraser . . . Gayle . . . they're mixed up in this Gulliver stuff? Lauren? What the fuck . . .

— Great work, Scott, send me the footage asap.

— It's on its way to you. The Fettes internet has gotten crap again and the download's taking forever.

As Lennox thanks McCorkel, the screech of brakes and the smell of burning rubber accompany a long roar of a horn, as an articulated truck moves onto the hard shoulder to avoid them. Lennox focuses, correcting the car. He whiplashes behind him, — Sorry, lads, but his passengers are oblivious as the mounting argument between them gathers pace. Des McCready seems to have decided that his wound is not going to kill him, and has gotten over his chronic squeamishness at his own claret; in the process recovering some bravado. — You think that Billy Lake is going to side with a slab of washed-up old south London Met pork against one of his own lads –

Hollis silences him with a heavy backhander. — Funny how them cunts that don't know when it's time to start talking are also the very same ones that don't know when it's best to shut the fuck up, the Met detective cheerfully sings.

McCorkel has picked up the commotion. — Everything okay, Ray?

— Aye, Scott, thanks again, and good work. Lennox hangs up, focusing with intent on the road as they roll into Southend. As they follow the signs for the marina, the contretemps between the indistinguishable cop and villain has abated, as both seem to contemplate their likely reception.

— I texted ahead, Hollis says, his features tightening. — We're expected.

The doubtful expression on Ray Lennox tells its own story. If the cards were to fall badly an element of surprise has been forfeited.

Hollis reads his disquiet. — It's all about manners, he says, looking to the silent McCready, willing him to say something.

Parking up, they quickly locate the boat. It's not difficult; Billy Lake's vessel, the *Boleyn*, is one of the biggest in the marina. As they walk down the gangway towards the impressive gleaming structure, Lennox feels his unease grow. Such environments always smell of high-end noncing to him. The seafaring vessel is the wealthy sex offender's vehicle of choice. He thinks of the former highly senior

British politician who was a keen sailor and was rumoured to make the orphans he entertained on his yacht disappear once he tired of them.

They haven't even started the climb onto the vessel when two burly men appear, coming down the gangway at no-nonsense speed to intercept them. As Des protests to the silent men, — These cunts, they farking tortured me, I'm bleeding to death here . . . they are given a quick search, which reveals Hollis's key-ring duster. This is confiscated.

They are ushered up the wobbling gangway, mounting it precariously, especially the still-cuffed Des McCready, as Hollis pulls a heavy-faced expression that Lennox registers, for the first time, as dread.

Des shouts out, — This fucking –

— SHUT IT! A roar from overhead and he falls silent, as a huge man emerges onto the steps at the bridge. He heads down to meet them on the deck, crackling with a violent energy.

Billy Lake, well tanned, wearing beige flannels, a white shirt and gold chain, has, apart from a slightly distended lower gut, muscles in his spit. Most top villains that Lennox has encountered down the years have been ruthless men, possessing a dark expertise at climbing into heads. But very rarely have they been they as physically imposing as Lake. They would generally stick to their specialism of psychological violence, hiring muscle, like the two men escorting them. Then a fourth giant, a darker-skinned man wearing sunglasses and a well-cut black suit, his hands in leather driving gloves, walks down the steps. His hair is slicked back.

Lake turns impatiently to him. — Sorry, Vic, summit came up. I'm just about done for the day anyway. Let's go for the same time on Wednesday.

The man smiles in the affirmative, dispensing a conceited,

minimal nod at Lennox and Hollis. Then he displays a slightly pitying grin, as he disembarks the craft on the gangway. Lennox tracks his departure.

I'm sure I know that cunt from somewhere . . .

A database of sex offenders rolls through his head. Nothing is sticking.

Hollis holds his hands up, like a villain done bang to rights by a copper. — As I texted, Bill, I fucked up your boys. Sorry about that, but it was me or them.

Lake looks at him, then Lennox, then the silent Des, before letting his gaze settle back on Hollis. — Ya did, did ya?

— They broke into my gaff, Bill. Meant to do me serious damage. I know you wouldn't have sent them for that. Had I known they were your geezers, I'd have put them straight. But I didn't.

Lake contemptuously regards Des, cuffs behind his back. — Where's that other muppet, that Tommy?

— I dunno, he took off when it got heavy.

The glower of raw rage dispensed by Lake makes Lennox feel sorry for Des. The crime boss then turns to one of the henchmen. — Find him, Lonnie, once we get this cahnt sorted out. He looks at a trembling Des, then turns to Hollis. — You got the keys to them cuffs?

— Yeah, Hollis says, moving over to uncuff Des.

— Take this planet-distorting cunt out of my line of vision, he says to the muscle, waving Des away. — Get him cleaned up and take him to Pete Jackson to sort out his injuries.

— Sorry, Bill, Des says. — I took the job and –

— SHUT YOUR FARKING MOUTH! Check out who you put farking heat on! Hollis does not get touched. Ever, and he looks at the detective, and qualifies, — Not without my direct say-so, then he turns back to Des. — Got that?

— Yeah, I'm sorry . . . I just . . .

— Due farking diligence! Do it! Lake taps his head.

— But –

— GET OUTTA MY FARKING SIGHT!

As a broken Des is led away by Lonnie, Lake turns to Hollis. — They didn't say it was you. I was just told some narky cahnt needed squeezing. Said fuck all about Old Bill, or I'd obviously have asked questions. So you fucked them up?

— Yeah, Hollis says. — One of them scarpered after a good right-hander. He shakes his head. — He's no good to you, Bill. That Des geezer was quite tasty but I plunged the cunt . . . he watches Lake's eyes widen, — sorry, mate, and then we did him over, to find out who he was working for. He told me he was on your payroll but wouldn't divulge who you'd subbed him out to.

— Well, the cahnt did one thing right, and Billy Lake looks to Lennox, then Hollis. — Who's this cahnt?

— Ray Lennox –

— Dint farking ask *you*. Lake points at Lennox without taking his gaze off Hollis.

— He's Old Bill, from Scotland, but he's alright, Hollis says, in a way that makes Lennox wonder just who he's working for.

Billy Lake is far from pacified, regarding Hollis in smouldering fury. — You do over my boys and now you bring some Jock bacon down here? On my fucking boat? You really are pushing your luck, Hollis!

— Ain't like that, Bill. The arrangement we got, the way we bring each other them undesirable sorts that gets taken care of, one way or another –

— I know what our arrangement is, Lake snaps.

— Well, thing is, Ray here, he got a similar set-up norf of the border, Hollis states, and Lennox is intrigued at what this arrangement is, and wishes it were so. With previous partners like Bruce Robertson and Ginger Rogers, it was almost the case. — So we need to know: who put the call into you?

— No. You do not get to come ere and dictate!

— It's a request, Bill, Hollis backpedals, — that's all. They did get a little personal with me, but yeah, fair play: it's me who owes you the explanation.

As Lake bristles in a stagy vindication, Hollis starts to tell the gangster the story. He informs the increasingly volcanic Lake that Piggot-Wilkins was set up for an anonymous date at the Savoy through what he assumed was a friend. But it wasn't his usual contact, Wallingham, or any of the agencies he used. He met the woman there.

As Hollis falls silent, Lennox sees something that might be hesitancy in Lake's eyes: the idea – the fear – that he might be being played.

— We wanted to find out who did him, but the toffs closed ranks. Then I got a visit from your lads, Hollis explains. — Well, with our form, I thought you'd be the last person to try and scare me off from bringing such nonces to book.

Lake listens with strained patience, turning his thousand-yard stare on first one cop, then the other. — Them cunts that use my boys, I had them down as rich ponces, not nonces. Consenting adults. There was no suggestion of short-eyes activity, and on my mother's life I did not know it was you they wanted to put the frighteners on.

— I know that, Hollis says with utter conviction.

Billy Lake's brow furrows, and pointing to the stateroom of the boat, he beckons them inside. Pulls some beers from an ice bucket as they sit down at a table. — Now somebody whips the wedding tackle off one of them soppy cunts, it don't mean nuffink to me on a personal level, but that's filthy and I don't like that sort of dirt around, he declares. — It ain't right, and it ain't like a geezer's thing, we don't behave like that.

246

— Yeah, some cahnt's decidedly lowering the tone, Bill, Hollis agrees.

— But what drives somebody to that extreme behaviour, that Mexican cartel shit? Lake speculates. — Either they've been nonced up or a kid of theirs has.

— That's what I'm feeling in my gut, Bill, Hollis contends. — Ray is too. We've been hunting this scum forever. Yeah, the murder and the assault was proper smutty, but as you say, they smell like revenge attacks.

Billy Lake nods slowly. Raises his San Miguel. Takes a sip. — If this cahnt Piggot-Wilkins's been kiddie fiddling, he deserves everything he got and more. This has got me curious. I don't work with nonces. I get rid of nonces.

— I know that, Bill, Hollis repeats. — That's why I need a name.

Lake looks darkly at Hollis, who remains, Lennox thinks, impressively impassive. — I think you know who it is, he finally growls.

— Wallingham, Hollis says. — He didn't book the scrubber, but he did set you up to fuck me up. I had to be sure though, Bill. I don't go against any cunt like that without clearing it with you first.

Bill nods tersely. — If it's rape or kiddie stuff, feel free to take the poncey cunt apart. And keep some back for me. He looks out to sea. — I'll make sure there's a nice little barrel full of holes for him. Big enough for the fishes to get into and feed. But . . . he looks at them both in a mesmerising stare, — make sure it ain't just scrubbering those geezers are up to. Capeesh?

— If I thought it was just that, Hollis says, — I wouldn't be here. And if it was, he wouldn't be sending your boys to visit with nasty intentions.

Lennox bristles a little, thinking this is a poor play from

247

Hollis, directly insinuating that Wallingham has taken Billy Lake for a mug.

Lake stares at them. A murderous rage appears to sweep over him like a shadow, before it's gone. — Just make sure, he says softly.

On the way back to London in the car, Lennox says, — You sailed close.

— Had to gamble. I wanted Lakey to think Wallingham played him for a cahnt. He won't like that.

— What if he hasn't?

— That, Hollis rolls his eyes, — just don't bear thinking about. But we should find Wallingham. If he's any sense he'll have gone to ground, because the geezer that used his name to employ Lake has to be the killer.

But all Ray Lennox can think about, as he compulsively fiddles with his phone, is getting back to Edinburgh and finding his nephew.

29

He's aware that something is being pushed into his mouth. Small and waxy-tasting, perhaps it feels familiar . . . Opens his eyes, and under a blindfold, feels the constraints on his limbs, but probably sees the second blue diamond-shaped pill at the end of a finger and thumb. The pellet clashes with her long red nails and pink flesh. He bristles, as if feeling this might be the time to deploy some kind of resistance, to bite on those fingers, but my second mallet blow smashes across his fore-head . . . I can feel its weighty impasse by the way his face snaps back, though what we've given him means there is little pain. She wrenches his mouth open and shines the torch inside . . . there is little fight in his slack jaw as he swallows the second pill . . .

— All gone down the hatch . . . good boy, she says.

Then his head falls to the side, as sleep takes him again, and this is the part I find most unsatisfactory. What, I both wonder and crave to learn, is going through his head? He's aware that his body is some-where uncomfortable, only made bearable by his anaesthetic. The dreams that follow I fancy to be a mixture of the blissful and the erotic. I have grounds for such speculation: his erection pokes out, into his consciousness . . . he can hear sex noises in his head . . . as he . . .

. . . once again wakes up strapped to a bed, his head forced up by a very firm series of cushions, not pillows, which I picked up from John Lewis. This is compelling him to look at a TV set positioned by means of a telescopic leg in front of his face. On the couch, a man and two women are performing a series of sex acts on each other. But . . .

. . . just below this, his erect penis, already bearing the now merely ceremonial slash mark administered by the edge of my four-inch knife, is protruding through the blades of a heavy-duty industrial bolt cutter.

Or it was.

He looks up at her lipstick-smeared face, with the blonde wig slightly askew. Her fingers with the painted nails are wrapped round the handle of the cutting device. My good hand switches on the music, the incongruously cheerful Northern Soul song 'Skiing in the Snow', and we see it, that spark of recognition through the fog. Now he knows for sure.

Then her teeth are barred, and in one violent joining of her hands, his cock is guillotined off close to its base.

Falling from the bed, it's already contracted to half its size by the time it hits the floor. A dark hole above his hanging balls discharges a deluge of red blood.

We haven't finished yet: a new touch. Though a blur he must feel us working on his eyes, doing something to them. He must wonder: *are they taking my sight too?*

No.

We have not taken the gift of his sight. It's quite the reverse.

Blood runs over eyeballs he cannot close. He is forced to bear witness. He is condemned to see.

He is at once there and detached: a distant observer of his own mutilation.

The blaring track, singing about being *warm in the cabin below* . . . he hears a voice, chilling, familiar. — We're the toughest skiers in town . . .

A deadpan intelligence comes into those big, goofball eyes. Of course: it's her. How could he have not realised?

The law enforcement officer has done his last case. He watches the blood spill from his eunuch body, spreading between his legs, across the TV screen, and onto the sheets . . . He knows that life never ends well.

He just did not think that his would end quite so badly. Quite so soon.

He's the third man. The last one we wanted. But the killing won't stop here. There are too many people invested in this game. I wonder how it will end for Toby Wallingham.

And I wonder how it will end for Ray Lennox.

30

Ray Lennox sits with Mark Hollis at the bar in City airport, waiting for the last flight to Edinburgh. They are wired from the events of the day and the lines blasted in the toilet. Or rather, the solitary one for the Met man, as it has indeed reactivated his pulsing piles operation wound. Lennox, however, partook with an enthusiasm that occasioned both awe and jealousy in his English counterpart. Hollis, not relishing the short drive home, distracts himself with his phone by trying to track down Wallingham. — Either he's been tipped off and vanished or he might be doing the Jacques Cousteau act – minus the oxygen tank – in the Norf Sea.

The flight is called, and as he bids Mark Hollis goodbye and makes his way through the gate towards the plane, what Lennox has been waiting for comes in courtesy of McCorkel: some blurry CCTV footage of Gulliver at Stirling University.

But prominent, and drawn to his attention by the IT expert, is a young woman wielding a placard, which declares that TRANS RIGHTS ARE HUMAN RIGHTS. In fact, it's his nephew, Fraser. Just as crucially, the large figure in the dress standing in close proximity to him, who subsequently decks a security guard with one solid punch, trademark bangles in evidence, is unmistakably Gayle.

Beside them, a tiny-looking woman, who resembles Leonora Slade from the photograph McCorkel has sent, along with the addresses of the friends of Fraser that Jackie couldn't get in touch with. The footage, glaring, awry pixels aggregating less than their parts, stings his eyes, but he can make out

Lauren, shouting into a megaphone. She's caught between deriding Gulliver and appealing for calm among the demonstrators. Despite the foggy images, Lennox evidences the rolling eyes and protruding jaw, indicating that his showboating old nemesis is thoroughly enjoying himself.

It would have been great to ride that cunt's sister tae fuck.

Although exhaustion depletes him, he opts to bypass home and bed after studying McCorkel's list of addresses:

Charlie Hamilton – Montgomery Street

Anthony Walker – Scotland Street

Linsey Cunningham – Barony Street

His first port of call: the South Clerk Street address of Leonora Slade.

When he gets to Fraser's ex-girlfriend's, he hits a button and mumbles something that sounds like 'delivery'. Even though it's almost 1 a.m. the door buzzes open. Curses a nippy tear in his ankle tendon as he mounts the tenement stairs.

Fuck . . . need to get back in the gym . . .

How many of these dark Victorian structures has he wound his way up over the years, through work or just going home? It now seems way too many. When Ray Lennox was a young man from a council estate, these buildings were, in his imagination, steeped in stories of the ages. He was excited to live in them. Now the issues of either those ghosts or the current incumbents are not nourishing him, just distractions, clamouring for attention in his crowded mind.

His fist thumps on the substantial door of a top-floor flat.

Within half a minute, a small but large-eyed, kinetic young woman, buzzing with anxiety, stares out at him from behind owl-like spectacles. When he explains who he is, Leonora Slade gasps, — Oh gosh, Fraser, and ushers him in.

As Lennox enters, a white cat saunters over to him. When

252

he leans against the worktop of a well-furnished lounge-kitchen, it jumps up, rubbing its head against him. Leonora grabs the animal and drops it on the floor, as Lennox surveys his surroundings. She is a second-year student and her place is much more salubrious than his. Obviously bought by wealthy Home Counties parents as an investment. — I was hoping you could help me find him, he says, tentatively bending to pet the mewing cat. He is allergic to some, but not all felines.

— I really can't think where. Have you tried the university?

— We're on it, he says, relieved that McCorkel was going through CCTV footage, and probably Glover too, once she's talked to Jackie. Both are exceptionally thorough, the virgin nerd and the taciturn gay woman. He trusts the younger staff in his department, more than his peers and elders, to get things done. Digital technology has changed the world, this no more manifest than in both crime and its policing.

— But where was she last? Leonora asks. Now she is running the investigation.

— He got out of university and was seen heading down Nicolson Street, towards the East End. Then he was in St James Quarter. After coming out of there, via the John Lewis department store exit, he vanished at Picardy Place after running into someone who fits your description on CCTV. So . . . I need to ask you some questions.

— Of course! Yes! Leonora's eyes are wide in enthusiasm. — I met her for a coffee in Human Beans at the top of Leith Walk. We were there for about half an hour, just chatting about university work and life.

— And protests around trans rights?

— No. We're both activists, but we don't discuss that *all the time*.

— So where did he go after he was with you?

— I don't know, she didn't tell me. She said it was best . . . That was when the mood changed.

Lennox lets his brows rise. — How so?

— She said it was best for me that I didn't know anything as to her whereabouts. But I heard she was at Danny's, then Linsey's.

— Linsey is Linsey Cunningham, right? Barony Street. Who is Danny?

— Danny Hopkirk. Not sure where he lives but he's at the university. He's an old friend of Fraser's from school, and the chess club. They go hillwalking a lot, Leonora explains. As she does Lennox is furiously texting Scott McCorkel, to check out these leads.

— Has he been hanging out with anybody new lately . . . ?

Leonora hesitates. Then she averts her gaze before looking at him and venturing, — Gayle . . .

Suddenly re-energised, but fighting to retain composure, Lennox asks, — Tell me about this Gayle.

— We're all involved in a No Platform organisation. Leonora fires up her computer, directing Lennox to the group's site and social media. From their Twitter and Facebook pages he notes that some trans activists of a certain type seem to look up to Gayle. Leonora points out a user called Five-One. — That's Fraser, she says. — She normally posts all the time, but hasn't in a few days. But this was the last exchange. She taps the screen:

@killergayle
I don't think we should put anyone on a pedestal.

@five-one
I don't think anybody is doing that.

254

@killergayle
There should be no hierarchies in our community. Everyone has a story to tell. Lauren is no more or less important than anyone else.

@five-one
You're arguing with yourself here, Gayle.

@killergayle
Don't presume to tell what I'm doing and what I'm not doing, you arrogant little shit.

@five-one
Very good.

@killergayle
Very good indeed. It'll be very good when we continue this conversation face-to-face.

Looking at Leonora, he scents her fear. And he knows who is inducing it. — Where can I find Gayle?

— I really don't know. I wish I did, she says miserably.

Then a yawn he is unable to stifle threatens to tear Lennox's jaw from his face. He needs more cocaine or his bed. Decides that the second is the best option. Leonora gives him a look, acknowledging the lateness of the hour. This waiflike figure was supposedly once his nephew's girlfriend. — Did you split up with Fraser because he came out as trans?

— No, of course not, that was very brave, Leonora declares. — And anyway, I identify as pansexual.

It's another term he hasn't heard of. — When did you split?

— Last month.

— How long were you together?

255

— Two months.

Lennox tries not to react adversely, remembering the age of them. Thinks of girlfriends past, from Murrayfield Ice Rink, Clouds disco, school, college. Two months was a lifetime then.

Exhausted, he leaves her at 2 a.m. and heads home, hoping McCorkel's nerdish insomnia will once again reap rewards.

As he gets into his flat at Viewforth, he sees a light is on in the hallway. Immediately senses another presence inside. His fists ball as his heartbeat thickens to a thump in his chest. The blood pounds in his temples.

He moves into the lounge. Again, a small lamp is on. Looks to the coffee table, sees some jewellery, bangles . . .

Gayle . . . here . . . Gayle's tracked me down . . .

Reaches for the Miami Marlins baseball bat resting in the corner. Then he looks back to the coffee table. A set of jewellery. Placed there.

Then Trudi heads out of the spare bedroom carrying the stuff she left at his, some clothes, make-up and toiletries, in a bag. — Oh . . . I . . . I couldn't sleep. Went for a drive and found myself passing here. There was no light on, so I thought you'd be working. I came up to get my stuff.

— Right, Lennox says, as an almost eldritch charge sweeps through him.

— I'm done, Ray. It's over, she says calmly, as if the anger and bitterness have gone. She slips the jewellery from the coffee table into her bag. — I've tried as hard as I can, but you're interested in nothing but your job. You think it can be the salvation of how fucked you are. It never can. She shakes her head sadly. — All it can do is show the world the mess of you.

— You're correct, Lennox coldly concedes. — For what it's worth, I think you've made the right move. Now from my point

256

of view, I really do need to be left the fuck alone to do what I have to do.

Trudi looks at him. A precipitous, devastating sadness hangs between them. It is as if he's confessed that he really is doomed and that her love cannot save him. And that both must now acknowledge this fact. She speaks in a clear but trembling voice. — I was stupid enough to think you loved me.

— I do love you, Lennox says, then adds with a surge of contempt, — But love is a bit like the fucking job, Trudi: it won't save you.

— Yes, it will, Ray, Trudi says evenly. — I dodged a bullet not tying myself to the purgatory of being with someone who believes that. Love will save me from a life devoid of it. You might realise that one day. When you're a big enough man to let it in, instead of a scared wee boy cowering in an old railway tunnel. She recovers her emotional ballast. — Grow a set, Ray, and she slaps the spare key onto the coffee table.

It cuts him to the quick, and all the more so for the truth in it. — I wish you well, he manages to cough out in a reedy voice. Then, with more spiteful conviction, — You and BMW man.

Trudi smiles thinly at him. Lennox can see that she has no tears left, just a rancorous acceptance that this pointless phase in her life is now over and she can move on. She turns and walks away.

— Nothing to say then, and he hears pettiness score his voice. It's a special sound. That break-up voice; deployed on all his previous girlfriends. *Emotionally vengeful. Ultimately pathetic.*

Trudi stops, pivots. Looks at Lennox as if he's a piece of shit on her shoe. Whatever spell of love bound her to him, it's now truly broken. — In Miami, while you were messing around with those two women, I fucked this estate agent.

— Well, for the record, Lennox retorts, the blood icing in his veins, — I never fucked either of those women.

— I sincerely hope you don't regret that now, Trudi says, and heads off.

Lennox has read somewhere that a woman never seems as beautiful as when she is walking away from you, and never more devastatingly so than when she is walking away for good. Certainly, the air seems to thicken and ionise around him, his innards buckling and warping as his future strides gracefully from him in Reebok trainers.

The radiance of her is beyond ethereal. Loss smashes him, deep in his core. He realises that he will never touch or kiss or hold her or make love to her again. Never see her mouth and eyes crinkle as the laughter spills from her in response to something he's said. The scent of her will be purged from his imagination. All the joy and rapture they've shared, all those small social kindnesses that are the cement of lovers: it has all gone.

But that loss is also already battling against another emergent force he feels will triumph over it: a euphoric surge of freedom. *Now I can do whatever the fuck I like* . . . a host of opportunities, presented mainly in the form of women and travel, cascade through his mind. He knows however bleak he feels in this moment, it is the right thing to do. They were simply done.

It leaves Ray Lennox stuck in his grim present of chasing a killer he likes. He goes to the fridge and places two ice cubes in a glass, pouring cold vodka over them, enjoying the delicious bone-cracking sounds, then chops himself out a poddle's leg of a line.

Sleep can wait a while longer.

Day Six

Sunday

31

An exhausted sun comes up. It has no fight for an Indian summer. The runner, a man named Andy Moston, feels the chill of the buffeting winds that slam him as he moves steadily through the Gyle Park. An English teacher at nearby Craigmount High School, even though it's Sunday and he doesn't need it to set him up for a long day at the chalkface, he still habitually rises early to go for his run.

Up ahead of him is what he perceives as a pinky-blue heap, dumped on one of the football pitches, right in the centre of the large conglomeration of playing fields. With every step he takes closer to this cold and formless mass, with each hot breath he expels, an ominous sense builds. Even as he decelerates in front of what he ascertains is the naked body of a middle-aged man, Andy feels his heartbeat soaring. The man has no genitals. Or rather, he has no penis: it's like it's been snapped off above his testicles. Also: he is missing eyelids.

Andy freezes. He is crushed. His sprightly legs are leaden as an overwhelming sadness grips him. There is badness in the world, this he knows largely from news reports. Now it's here, in his life and in his city. How can this be? He is only out for his morning run. Thinks of the kids he teaches. What is their future to be?

He averts his eyes from the sight because he knows he will lose the light breakfast in his stomach if he looks again. Hopes its vivid ferocity will, in time, fade from his memory. His trembling hand pulls the phone from his tracksuit pocket.

32

A persistent tapping seeps into his consciousness. At first its source seems far away, as if from another world. Then, as he wrestles awake, it grows in volume and menace into the dread sound of banging on his front door. It's still dark as Ray Lennox rises, grabbing his phone from the bedside locker which tells him it's only 6.12 a.m. A deluge of messages. Doesn't have to read any to know that something is seriously amiss.

Trudi Trudi Trudi, ah ha, ah ha, ah ha . . .

But his texts and missed calls show none from Trudi. Most are from Jackie in a state beyond agitation:

> He's still missing! Please call me,
> Ray! I'm at my wits end! Please
> give me some news!

Fraser . . . oh fuck, the wee man . . . the wee whatever . . .

On a hook on the back of the bedroom door hangs his dressing gown. Wraps it round him in face of another sequence of peppering bangs. Fighting down the debilitating bolts of panic that besiege him, Lennox counter-intuitively stomps down the hallway. Building anger at this early violation, still feeling the alcohol and drugs, he hurls open the front door with an indignant ferocity.

Amanda Drummond stands blinking before him. Her distasteful expression overrides her brief shock, then, remembering why she is here, lets it fall into gravity.

262

The something that has happened is bad.

Lennox rolls his palm over his head to ascertain his hair is spiked up, then his chin to find his face rough and unshaven, as he regards her through bleary eyes.

This is more than just purchaser's contrition.

Drummond's voice is the high, officious way it gets when she aims for consequence, but it's also tinged with an upset that alarms him. — They found a third, similarly mutilated body, Ray. Less than forty minutes ago. She regards the Fitbit watch on her wrist. — Here, in Edinburgh.

— Fuck, Lennox gasps. *Fraser. She wouldn't be here unless I knew who . . . No, for fuck sakes . . .* — Who?

— It looks like the murder victim is Norrie Erskine.

— Oh . . . Lennox muses, knowing he should be horrified that this has happened to one of their team. But it's not his nephew, so he can't help but experience a massive unburdening of his keening senses. He turns and heads down the hallway into the lounge.

Drummond follows him cautiously, Lennox suddenly realising she'll be eyeballing the drug paraphernalia and detritus on his coffee table. He swivels back to see this confirmed. — Do you want some coffee?

— No time, Ray, she snaps impatiently. — We need to be at the park in South Gyle, and she swallows hard. — I'll wait downstairs in the car while you get ready, her discomfort in the shabby surroundings and fusty air, much of this coming from his own ripe form, palpable.

As Drummond turns in departure, Lennox augments the atmosphere by unleashing a burp of tainted carbon dioxide. Feels his ringpiece struggle with the noxious Stella-and-ching gases bubbling in his gut. Lets go a vaporous chemical onslaught – *much better here than in the car* – as he heads to the shower, and despite soaping himself all over, feels his body remain stale as he throws fresh clothes over it, reaching for his favourite maroon leather Hugo Boss jacket.

Confectioner: what does he know about Erskine?

Emerging from the stair door and climbing into the car, he tries to seize some authority from the situation by urging an obviously antsy Drummond, — Let's go.

She keys the ignition and pulls off, the mild rise of her thinly plucked brows indicating she's not dignifying his lame bid for credibility. All the talk is centred on work. The tacit agreement is that whatever happened between them is not to be mentioned. Both know this cannot be broached right now, let alone processed. Ray Lennox has never regretted having sex with anyone. From the odd one-night stand to serious long-term relationships, he's always regarded any romantic encounter as a beautiful positive; a gift of being able to enjoy the ultimate intimacy with another human being. For the first time ever, as he steals a glimpse at Drummond in profile, he thinks: *that was probably a bad idea*. Then a surge of tenderness as the words 'I think Gillman is stalking you' freeze in his mouth.

Lennox checks his phone. A message from McCorkel tells him that Fraser didn't contact Charlie or Anthony, but stayed a night at Linsey's before heading off. She doesn't know where.

The Gyle Park is a series of football pitches, with changing rooms to their north, at the Glasgow Road end, and a housing scheme opposite. On its west side there's a leisure centre. Across from this, a playground, then several retail units and some more housing border the park. Lennox recalls his Sunday-league-playing days on that vast open space where a constant battering by gale-force winds made any attempts at skilful football impossible. Back then he remembers how it used to be classified as on the edge of the city, before the relentless spread of Edinburgh westwards towards Glasgow continued apace.

But the park remains almost reassuringly expansive and windswept, replete with squawking seagulls having some strange mass roost on one pitch. But it's the playing field occupied by humans that gathers the attention of Lennox and Drummond, as they walk from their Glasgow Road parking spot across the marshy turf.

Uniformed police have shut down the park, sealing it off at its entrances. One lone vehicle, a big police transit van, almost in the middle of this collection of pitches, flashes a blue warning light. Figures surround it, in a zone further sectioned off with more yellow-and-black hazard tape. It looks like some kind of game is in progress, with a small crowd of spectators and the stationary vehicle blocking the oncoming Lennox and Drummond's view of the performance. Norrie Erskine was one of them, and Ray Lennox has never seen as many police officers at a crime scene, gathered in the open around the body. — Where's the fuckin tent? he asks.

— They can't find it, Drummond reports, in a mixture of embarrassment and disgust.

— You're joking, Lennox says, incredulous, yet knowing from her tone that this is far from the case.

It's police procedure to immediately surround any body found in a public place with a large canvas tent, in order to shield it from the view of local citizens.

As he and Drummond swerve through the huddle, Dougie Gillman spies them. He shoots a look of condemnation so violent that Lennox is almost ready to confront him about what he's been up to, before the squared-jawed lawman averts his gaze.

It's his partner that's deid. And some cunt has lost the tent. Stay cool.

Stepping forward to view the body, it's immediately evident to Lennox that this third murder bears all the hallmarks of the first two, and more. It's not the horrific genital mutilation he observes first, but Erskine's grotesque bulging eyes. — The eyelids have been cut off with surgical scissors, Ian Martin, registering his reaction, contends, as he hears Drummond gasp by his side. Lennox feels shamed but he can't help thinking of Erskine as the Master in the American cult series *Kung Fu*. — Perhaps they wanted him to see what they were doing, Martin muses. — Industrial bolt cutters probably used, the penis again missing. This time, though, the testicles were left intact, and he looks from the dead, hanging plums at Lennox and Drummond with a slightly challenging make-of-that-what-you-will expression. — Interestingly, there is a deep incision just above the severing wound, closer to the body. It's as if they tried to use the ceremonial knife again, then gave up. From the angle of the wound, the subject . . . he looks guiltily around at the assembled officers, particularly the seething Gillman, — . . . I believe he was erect at the time.

A collective gasp can't be stifled, which Bob Toal, emerging from the lone police transit vehicle, misinterprets as he furtively edges up to Lennox and Drummond. Bristling in distaste at the former's appearance, he nods in a dark plea, — This time it's one of our own.

One of our own.

Lennox already expects this cliché to be aired many times, and perhaps most often from the agitated Toal. His brother once told him that it's common for a director to suggest that an actor play a scene as if they were bursting for a piss. That's Toal, who constantly shifts his weight and cranes his neck around. He wants out of this park, out of this job, as soon as possible. He is past viewing Erskine's fate as a personal inconvenience; now that he has decided he is leaving, Toal really has just had enough of all the horror and sleaze. Lennox has long thought that his boss spends his days hiding in his office

266

because he is lazy. Now he sees that it is because the job fundamentally disgusts him. He's done with it. — You two need to sort this one out, Toal declares. — Erskine was drinking at the Pubic Triangle before he vanished, and he glances at Gillman, Harrower and Notman, all silently bunched together. They are staring not at Erskine's body, but at two vehicles, one an ambulance, which are making their way across the football pitches towards them. — Be discreet, but find out who Erskine was with and what they got up to.

— What's the story wi the fuckin tent? Lennox asks.

Lennox has never seen his boss so angry, as Toal shoots him a look of sheer loathing. — Fuck knows! Spastics had one fucking job . . .

Drummond blushes red at her Chief Super's uncharacteristic use of this term. — Should this not be an issue for Internal Investigations?

Toal looks at her for second, as if trying to ascertain whether Drummond means the missing tent or Norrie Erskine's recent associates. Decides on the latter, and is unimpressed by her playing by the book. — I don't want those fuckers anywhere near this! Sort it out, he snaps. — Don't knock yourselves off the promotion list. Fuck this up, he stares at Drummond, then Lennox, — and they'll bring in somebody from outside, for sure, mark my words! Toal's eyes narrow. — I know that this has come at the wrong time, but the both of you, and Dougie, he glances over at Gillman, who sucks on a cigarette, — need to perform tomorrow morning at these interviews. Show them we aren't all a bunch of losers at Edinburgh Serious Crimes, for fuck sake, he pleads. Toal might be done with his cases, but having a successor from within is the legacy parting shot he has evidently settled on. He turns to a uniformed officer, and Lennox can't hear what he says, but you don't need to be an expert lip-reader to fancy 'find that fucking tent' is a strong candidate.

Red marks score Drummond's cheeks like welts from a whip. Lennox feels his hand touch his nose. He shivers. Edinburgh is so much colder than London. But Drummond is trembling too. They go back over to examine the body again. There's now a sheet over it, but it seems makeshift and doesn't cover his head. Erskine is blue in the face, a darker shade of it coating his lips. His mad lidless eyes seem to be going off in different directions, and his thinning wispy hair blows in the wind. Lennox pulls the sheet over his face, and it comes up to Erskine's knees, but thankfully avoids exposing the wound. Then the wind whips it up, briefly doing just that, before Lennox pulls it back down.

— Oh . . . they cut that man's willie oaf!

Lennox turns round. Two young boys, aged around ten, on their bikes, have somehow got into the park, sneaking right up on them, unnoticed.

He shouts at a red-faced uniformed officer, — Get them oot ay here and seal this fucking place properly!

Fucking typical incompetent uniformed spastics! They bairns shouldnae have tae witness this kind of thing . . . the fucking tent . . . fuck sake . . .

As the kids are ushered away, Lennox's thoughts snap to him and Les Brodie, around the same age, on their bikes.

In the tunnel . . . those stone walls, closing in, those men, surrounding us . . . kids shouldn't have to deal with this shit . . . they need looked after . . .

— Definitely a bolt cutter, Ian Martin confirms, snapping Lennox from enclosed tunnel to open park. — And yes, by the wound angle and the blood pattern, he was erect at the time.

— Having a bolt cutter round your cock would derail your passion . . .

268

— Unless he was full of certain drugs or stimulated in some other way. I've taken some samples, but we'll get him down to the path lab for a session with Burt, Martin offers. His coldness makes Ian Martin a hard guy to like, but equally, his thoroughness ensures he's a difficult one not to respect. — He struggled against bonds. Martin indicates the marks on first the wrists then the ankles. — I'd hazard it was done a few hours before, but the body was dumped here, and he looks over the park, — in the centre circle of the pitch nearest the pavilion.

It's a good spot by Martin, and to Lennox's mind it does hint at ritual.

Erect at the time. The eyelids cut off. Was he made to watch something, like his genitals being removed? Child porn, or perhaps some of his own recorded sex acts?

Dumped in the centre circle of a football pitch.

Who the fuck was Norrie Erskine, anyway?

Lennox peels away from the others, and turns from the slapping gale to view more texts from Jackie, before he calls Hollis. — Third body, roughly the same MO, with some modifications. One of ours, a cop called Norrie Erskine.

— Fuck sake . . . Hollis barks, obviously not yet fully awake. — Did he have a sleazy rep?

— Serious Crimes, Lennox says, looking over at his colleagues. Watching Gillman's square jaw protrude, he recalls the Thailand beano, where his rival broke his nose with a headbutt. — How's things your end?

— Can't thank you enough for yesterday, Ray . . . Yeah, I'm ferreting around, trying to be discreet . . . but you know how it is.

It's Hollis is how it is.

— Yes, bud, no worries. Stay cool and let me know what's happening. I'll keep you posted.

— Done, Hollis says.

Lennox hits the silencing red and heads over to his comrades. It's evident that even the most hard-bitten Serious Crimes vets are shocked. Especially Dougie Gillman, who cannot believe his partner's demise. His gaze is glazed and unfocused. — The soapy cunt got on my nerves, he manages, — but . . . fuck sake . . .

Through the crowd, taking notes on her iPad, the reassuring presence of Glover. — Gill, can you speak to everyone who was with Norrie last night? Let's get a picture of his last movements.

Glover nods, as some of the male cops in the vicinity look uneasy.

It's best to get them onside. Especially Gillman. Fuck knows what's going on with him these days. Was it definitely Drummond he was stalking? Who was the other woman with her?

He strides across to him. — What are you thinking here, Dougie?

The response from the normally overemotive veteran cop is eerily mechanical. — I want tae check through Erskine's associates, and the previous crimes he investigated in Glesgae, he says. — If Soap Dodge City is as brilliant as he always claims . . . claimed, why did he transfer here?

— Good thinking, Lennox agrees. He witnesses the pain in Gillman's face and eyes, and they share a moment of what might be empathy.

It only lasts a second before Gillman, as if in awareness of being emotionally compromised, roars, — Fuckin oan it, and tears off.

Drummond nods at Lennox and they traverse across the park to her car. He watches the wind blow her hair back off her forehead. Feels a charge pitched somewhere between eroticism and anaemic poignancy. They drive off, but stop at a coffee shop in Corstorphine and order a skinny latte for her and a double espresso for him.

She calmly lowers herself into the seat, pulling out her iPad and phone, prompting him to do the same. Both of them can see that Glover has wasted no time in talking to the male officers, as her emails fire into their boxes. Then an unnamed call comes into Lennox's phone. Stands up, moves to the door, visually tracked by Drummond. — Uncle Ray, it's me.

— Fraser . . . are you okay? Where are you, pal?

— I'm fine.

— You have to tell me where you are. Your mother –

— If I tell you, you'll just tell her. So, I can't really do that. All I need you to do is let her know I'm okay.

— Fraser, please, pal, we're all worried sick! I know you've got mixed up with some dodgy people through trying to do the right thing –

— If you know who they are, you know why I can't tell you, and why I'm ending this call. Tell Mum and Dad I'm fine. Goodbye, Uncle Ray, he says calmly.

— Fraser . . . please . . . but Lennox is talking to a dead line. He calls back but the phone is switched off. Tries to take stock. Looks round to see Drummond's eyes burn in enquiry from across the room.

Tell her fuck all.

And now Jackie is back on. He heads outside the cafe and Drummond's earshot, into the grey, rainswept St John's Road, before picking up.

— RAY! HAVE YOU –

— He's okay, Jack. I just spoke to him. He's fine.

— Oh my God . . . my wee boy . . . my beautiful wee boy . . . thank you . . . Where is he? Bring him home!

— He won't tell me where he is. He hung up with the phone he's using and that's now off. I don't think he's in any danger or being held or controlled by anybody. I think he's trying to protect somebody.

— What? Fraser?

— He's got involved in some bad stuff with some dodgy people. But it really isn't his fault. He's a good kid and he's been trying to do the right thing and help people out.

— Who . . . who are they?

— That's what I'm trying to find out. I'm tracking them down and I'm bringing him home.

— What . . . when? Where are you?

— I have to go. I'll call you later, I promise.

— Don't you fucking dare hang up on me, Ray!

— I'm sorry, Jack, but he's okay, I'm trying to find him but I'm working on solving a multiple homicide, including your girlfriend's brother. I'll call you.

— RAY!

Lennox kills the call and heads back inside to Drummond, his brain in overheated upheaval.

They sip their coffee in silence, punctuated only by shocked platitudes about Erskine. Lennox starts to read out the emails, then worries briefly about mansplaining, but it's clear that Drummond welcomes the intervention. — It seems that Erskine left a few of them, Gillman, Harkness, McCaig, drinking in the Repair Shop, then hit the Pubic Triangle, he watches a brief flicker of disdain in Drummond's eyes at his use of this term, — then decided to have a nightcap in CC Blooms. It's nominally a gay bar, but in reality it's favoured by late-night drinkers of all and no sexual orientation, Lennox says, and there's a certain edge between them as he catches Drummond's eye. — It seems he talked briefly with a woman, who then left. Gill's asked them for the CCTV footage. Let's follow his route.

Drummond nods in hearty agreement while they finish

their refreshments. They drive to the Pubic Triangle, as the collection of exotic dancer pubs at Tolcross is magniloquently known. At the first two establishments, both male proprietors look through photographs and hand over their books. They have saggy, enervated faces, like life has stuck them in a withering limbo, yet sucked from them the motivation to change their circumstances. There is no recognition of Erskine in the glassy stares.

They strike gold at the third bar. The manager, Mary Manderson, a tall, angular woman, more like a Morningside cake shop proprietor than publican of a strippers' bar in Tolcross, nods in immediate recognition at the image of Erskine. — He comes in here a lot. He's mostly with other cops, but sometimes alone.

— Was he here last night?

— No.

— What were they like, the other cops? Drummond asks.

Mary Manderson raises an acerbic brow. — Male, obviously.

— But sometimes he was alone?

— Yes, he hung out here. Made a big fuss of the girls. They called him Uncle Norrie. I think he got quite close to some of them.

— Can you give me the names and contact details?

— Sure, and Mary heads to the office and prints out a professional-looking personnel file with the details of eight dancers, and hands it to Drummond.

— Thanks. Can you also email me a digital copy?

Mary obliges, and under Lennox's urging, Drummond immediately redirects it Glover's way. They depart, and by the time they get down to the car park, both Drummond and Lennox have the strippers' bars' CCTV files on their iPads. — Glover is good, he observes, as he starts to study the images.

Straight away, one person stands out. A tall, bulky individual with long brown hair, wearing a dress, leans defiantly at the bar drinking a pint of Guinness. Gives off such an edge that even the hardened drinkers not only refrain from making harassing comments but avoid eye contact.

It's Gayle.

Lennox freezes the frame. Shows it to Drummond. They follow Gayle's devastating gaze to a fat, red-faced man. He stands with a big smile, at the side of the stage, watching a dancer.

— Erskine, Drummond whispers.

Lennox's mind is ablaze with what the Serious Crimes crew sometimes refer to as *polis join the dots. Fraser. Lauren. Gayle. Erskine . . . Confectioner.* Checks the time code on the hospital's CCTV. It certainly makes it hard for Gayle to have attacked Lauren the second time – before his timely intervention – though not impossible. Can't ascertain if that burly figure he caught trying to finish Lauren off was Gayle, but who else could it be?

Surely the bangles gave it away.

More on point, the Erskine and Gulliver murders and the Piggot-Wilkins assault . . . why? What ties Norrie Erskine to them? What the fuck was Confectioner on about?

— Let's get up to the office and brief the team, he says, and Drummond nods.

A call comes in on her phone. — Right . . . thanks for letting me know. She hangs up, looks at Lennox. — It seems that Tom McCaig borrowed the crime scene tent to go camping. Didn't secure it right and it blew from the clifftop in Helmsdale into the sea. He was in the process of replacing it. He's been suspended immediately pending an investigation.

33

They pull into Fettes car park in a drizzle. As they exit the vehicle, Lennox, flicking up the collar of his maroon Hugo Boss, turns to Drummond. — The other night . . .

Amanda Drummond lowers her head and raises her hand. — It was a mistake, Ray, you and I both know it. I compromised myself with alcohol, sadly not for the first time, she says ruefully, — and you did too. You have a girlfriend. Let's just leave it at that.

— No, it's over between Trudi and me –

— Your business. I'm not in the market for a boyfriend, nor have I any desire to be one of your break-up trysts.

Another angry text from Jackie buzzes in:

> Where the fuck are you, Ray?

— It's not like that, he pleads to Drummond, as he punches into his phone:

> I'm out looking for your son!

Drummond is looking over his shoulder. She taps him on the elbow.

— LIAR! Lennox turns round to see Jackie emerging from a black Range Rover. Slamming the door behind her, she storms towards them. — YOU FUCKING LIAR!

275

Drummond raises her eyebrows, heads across the car park towards the Police HQ entrance.

Lennox can only move forward and embrace his sister. — I'm sorry . . . I have to look at every aspect . . . I'm going to find him, but the important thing is he's okay. He looks over at Drummond, who shrugs and heads inside. — I know it's tough, but he's alive and well. Here's where you need to trust me to do my job.

Jackie emphatically pulls away from him. — Why would I do that? Why? I can't even trust you to tell me where the fuck you are!

Lennox reaches out and grabs her shoulders. Jackie permits this but keeps her blazing eyes trained on her brother. — I have to do a quick briefing on these killings. A cop, *one of our own* in Serious Crimes, has been murdered. He omits Erskine's castration and eyelid removal in case Jackie connects it to Fraser, as he himself can't help but do. — Then I'm right back out, chasing up leads. In the meantime, who else knows about him? Then he ventures, — Moira?

Jackie violently brushes his grip off her. She leans towards him, teeth bared, but her voice is pure courtroom. — Oh no, because you hated Ritchie Gulliver, *you do not get* to implicate Moira in the disappearance of my son!

— It's nothing to with that, I have to –

— What is it to do with then, Ray? Jackie's eyes grow bigger. — Because Moira wouldn't give you your fucking hole you try to pull her into this? How pathetic you little men are!

Close to them, behind her, a pigeon, chest implausibly puffed up, chases a skinny, wild-eyed would-be mate across the tarmac, as if in illustration of her point. They look at it, then at each other. Fight back a laugh; settle for a shared grin. — I *will* bring him home, Lennox insists, rubbing her forearm.

— I need to see him, Jackie explodes in exasperation. — I

don't care how he dresses, he needs to know how much I just love him and want him back!

— He does know that, and he says he wants you to know he's okay, and not to worry. I spoke to him, Lennox looks at his watch, — literally half an hour ago. I've not told anyone in the office about him calling me. As far as they're concerned, he's still missing. I don't want them letting up on finding him. So please keep quiet about him being in touch with me, or I'll be in really big trouble. Coming down here and making a scene doesn't help. Got that? He scans the empty car park. Two uniforms leave the building and get into a patrol car. One of them, a roly-poly officer, struggling with weight issues, applied to get out of uniform and into Serious Crimes. Lennox scowls at them, as if to inform them not to get closer.

If you get the promo no way will a uniformed spastic bloater get into Serious Crimes.

— Yes, but –

He steps forward and grabs Jackie by the shoulders again. — I said: *got that?!*

— Yes . . . but you have to keep me posted, Ray: as soon as you hear anything –

— Of course . . . and Lennox feels a slight shaming buzz at being in a position of power over his bossy sister. — Stay at home so you are there when he gets back, which he will do. I love him, and I love you. I swear to God he'll be home soon.

— And I love you too, she wrinkles her nose, — even if you are in need of a shower, and both declarations genuinely sound to his ears like more than just good manners. Then her eyes take on a harsher focus. — If anybody lays a finger on that boy, I will fucking kill them.

— You'll be behind me in the queue, Jack. Lennox kisses his sister, squeezing her hand. Turns, leaving her in the car park with a strangely hopeful but desolate look, heads into Police HQ.

34

The incident room seems smaller than ever, packed with detectives. Lennox screws up his nose as the wafting scent of smelly trainers and BO hits him, trying to locate its source. Realises, to his horror, it's him. Self-consciously lets his hand go to a stubbled cheek. The overhead fluorescent lights are unforgiving, but he's far from the only wreckage present. He looks around the assembled faces; Gillman, Arnott, Harkness, Notman, Harrower, McCorkel, Inglis, Glover and Drummond. Absent: the suspended McCaig. The murder of Norman Erskine pulls into focus how dishevelled most of the male Serious Crimes officers have become. Erskine, whose incongruously cheesy, smiling panto-star image is pinned onto the board alongside Piggot-Wilkins and Gulliver by Amanda Drummond. Lennox watches as Gillman, touching the mole on his chin, looks at her in something akin to hate.

But then, they've always disliked each other. And Gillman's further unhinged by Norrie's death. Doesn't mean he's stalking her with intent to harm.

Doesn't mean he isn't, though.

Ray Lennox thinks back to the time that he and Les Brodie were in the tunnel with their bikes. When they were set upon by the three drifters. Men who had obviously behaved in this way before, and would be expected to do so again. But nothing has presented itself. All those years compulsively going through the Sex Offenders Register, which he knows like a priest does the Bible; it has yielded zero. It was like the three men – all of them – literally vanished into thin air.

He still hasn't told any colleagues that his nephew called him, and Fraser is technically no longer missing. This is a policeman wasting police time. *Not for the first time.*

But Fraser has a connection with Gulliver, and Gayle . . . and now Jackie and Gulliver's sister . . . this all has to be coincidence . . . surely tae fuck?

With the unique, ostentatious throat-clearing sound of Toal conspicuous by its absence, the only thing telling Lennox to focus are the confused, urging expressions on the faces of his colleagues.

Therefore, Ray Lennox dutifully explores the links between the three male victims; two murdered, one brutally assaulted. — The first two were privately educated in what only Orwellian, class-ridden Britain could describe as *public* schools: Piggot-Wilkins, Charterhouse in Surrey; Gulliver, Fettes, which he glances out the window to see looming across the way. — Piggot-Wilkins was an alumnus of Balliol College, Oxford, and Gulliver, St Andrew's. Norrie Erskine is the out-lier here, he says to the group, but mainly Drummond, — not an establishment figure, a council-scheme boy from the Wedge. He turns to Gillman. — Drumchapel, wasn't it, Dougie?

Lantern-jawed Dougie Gillman snaps back, — Garthamlock.

Lennox forces a nod of gratitude. — Briefly a professional footballer, played for Hamilton Accies. That career faltered as the pounds piled on, so he joined the cops. But he remained a flamboyant stage-Weedgie at heart, who OD'd on Billy Connolly, Lennox half smiles, some affection creeping into his tones, as Gillman stares ahead, — and the lure of greasepaint proved too much. So why did he stop acting to rejoin the police? Lennox asks, thinking of Stuart, wishing he'd listened more to what he was saying.

Another fucking fence to mend . . . but if Norrie was a sex case, he's just one more pervy Serious Crimes cop. Another sad addict in a broken collection of men, like Drummond now believes you to be. And she's far from wrong.

The assembled cops remain silent.

— A revenge attack for previous sex offences seems the probable motive. But with Norrie . . . there's nothing. He taps the folder. — I know this is emotional, and nobody wants to grass anybody up, but Norrie's behaviour might lead us to this killer. So . . . if you have anything at all . . . visits to hookers, escorts, saunas . . . he keeps his eyes from Gillman's, — do not keep this information to yourself. Everything here is in confidence.

There is a studied silence all round. Then Harkness, a slight twitch in his eye, says, — Look . . . we've all –

Gillman shoots him a hundred-yard stare.

Harkness falters under its searing beam, but continues, — What I'm saying is, we've all . . . he looks to Drummond and Glover, — . . . most of us have been in strip clubs and bars. Sometimes in the line of duty, sometimes just to . . . well, you know . . .

— Let's be clear again, Lennox asserts, — nobody is being judged by how they choose to spend their leisure time –

— Aw, is that right? Gillman snaps. — Because that's no the feeling ah'm getting, and he trains an eviscerating stare on Drummond, then Glover, which both women react to in different ways. Drummond's face flushes, while Glover just looks coolly back at him, although her eyes are glassy.

Lennox pitches in. — Arguing about how cops are, how they should be, what they should do, it isnae gaunny help us find Norrie's killer, so let's not waste any time on it. I'm asking about Norrie, his particular habits, not cop sociology in general.

Drummond quickly regains her composure. — Why did he

leave the force back in the day? she asks. — Anything more than the desire to tread the boards?

An obtrusive thought jolts Lennox: Drummond's flush is like the pre-orgasmic one he experienced during their shag. Her body, how lithe and athletic it was in bed, as compared to how thin and brittle it now seems, in clothes, on duty. Thinks again of Gillman stalking her. Focuses on his colleague's slitty predator eyes, that heavy jaw, the outsized facial mole. Feels the blood leaving his head.

You want to fuck her and kill him . . . you have to tell her what he's up to . . .

Aware of chattering and arguments flaring up around him, but the pornographic hypnosis of these violent, sexual thoughts is hard to shake off . . .

— Means fuck all, a growling slur from Gillman. Directed at Drummond, it pulls Lennox back into the room.

— Look here! Drummond urges, talking over Gillman, as she pins the picture of a woman to the board. Lennox senses her as his boss. Running the show. — This is a case in which a claim of sexual harassment was made. It was dropped, nothing proven. It was the nineties, and her mouth and eyes pinch antagonistically. — Might not mean nothing though: Norrie Erskine left the force a year after that.

— Who is that? Lennox finds himself asking, looking at the photograph.

— Andrea Covington, Drummond declares to the gathering, sinew in her neck straining. Lennox is briefly entertained with the notion of him being househusband to a promoted Drummond, dutifully eating out her tense pussy every night when she comes home from a hard day's work. It's ludicrous, and he's forced to stifle a giggle, as she carries on. — She was briefly a WPC. Wasn't forthcoming then. Might be more so now, she says, watching Gillman shake his head. — I'll talk to her, she declares, then ponders, addressing Lennox, — Might the fact that his body was dumped on a football pitch mean the killer is making a statement?

Lennox flounders under the direct questioning, shrugs minimally, raising his brows to invite contributions.

— Edinburgh Sunday leagues, Harkness says, — what sort of a statement is that?

Drummond shrugs. — Maybe one that someone who doesn't really understand football that well might make?

Another paint-stripping glare from Gillman, as Lennox considers this. Then Erskine's blue, castrated, naked figure jumps into his thoughts . . . *Trudi, walking away . . . Fraser, unbowed in his dress* . . . all the anguish of the world seems to flood his veins. — Norrie was one of our own. He mouths the hackneyed banality without any irony. — Let's find this evil bastard, and now he's emoting, — you know what to do.

The team members return to their respective stations. Lennox sits alongside Drummond, who is at her computer. Catches a whiff of her perfume.

— The connection might not be each victim to the other, but another person all have been involved with, she contends, looking through Erskine's personnel file.

Lennox forces himself to focus. — I'm not sure. I'm still pursuing the Lauren angle, with this Gayle character. They might be involved in Gulliver's death, possibly Norrie's, though Piggot-Wilkins seems a stretch. But they're an elusive and mysterious individual. Sexual identity is a murky enough business but in the trans world . . .

Drummond does not react in any way to this.

Lennox wants to pull her aside, tell her he needs to talk to her. Or hold her. But he doesn't know what to say, and it would be ridiculous. So he rises and heads back to his own desk. Then, unable to settle, is up by the board, looking at the pictures, notes, connections. Wants to place Fraser Ross, his own nephew, right at the centre of this.

Then loyal Scott McCorkel, at his shoulder, asks him if he's okay. Lennox nods, winks and heads off in departure. Leaves the young man energised by the acknowledgement of the intimacy, yet a little troubled and short-changed. Lennox needs to see Toal, to tell him that he has to find his nephew. Now he knows that Fraser is alive but scared and in hiding, it seems even more crucial to find him before whoever is looking for him does. Lennox suspects that someone to be Gayle. It's pathetic in a grown man, but he's also aware of how wary he is of incurring his sister's disapproval. How Jackie evokes the childhood passivity he's constantly railed against all his life.

Swings by Toal's office, but he isn't around. Calls him but he's not answering his phone. His boss seems to communicate mainly by text these days. Lennox wonders if he's still at the Gyle Park, or down at the morgue.

> Boss, I really need to talk.
> Where are you?

> Meet in Inverleith Park.
> At the pond.

Robert Toal's transition is more mysterious to Lennox than any gender reassignment. The Serious Crimes boss is usually never far from his desk. The windswept park is a short walk from police headquarters. Arriving there, he finds Toal with a boy of around five. They're sailing a boat in the pond. Toal looks up as Lennox approaches. — Ray. How goes?

— Good, boss, Lennox lies. — Yourself?

— Not bad. Just taking a bit of time out to look after my grandson, Bertie here. He nods at the kid, who contemplates the yacht slowing sailing over the still pond. — My daughter is at the dentist, emergency root canal.

Toal . . . babysitting on duty . . . the world is going fucking nuts . . .

As Bertie continues his intense supervision, walking round the edge of the pond, Toal confides: — Fannying about, Ray, like most of us on the force do for years. Spent all morning talking to McCaig and the coastguard, trying to find that fucking tent. What a joke.

— I never thought you'd be so cynical about the job.

Rolling his eyes, Toal produces a pantomime shrug Erskine would have been proud of. — At first I wanted to go out like the old cop cliché, on a high, closing a big case, he grins in cheerful defeat, looking around at the browning trees surrounding the pond. — But now that I know I'm done, I really couldn't give a fuck. So I'm sorry for Norrie Erskine, but I've tapped out. I'm finished with murderers, rapists, paedos, sadists and weirdos. And, no offence here, Ray, or to poor Norrie, God rest his soul, but I'm also done with the fuck-ups who lock them up.

Lennox feels violated. Forces a shrug as if to say, *none taken*.

— Thank God they exist, Toal slaps his back, — but fuck them, and grinding his teeth, he rewarms to his theme, — and fuck the department and its bureaucracy. Fuck the opportunist media, politicians and the elites they play office boy and girl for. Most of all, fuck the dumb citizens of these islands who are too sheepish and dim to deserve to be anything other than patronised prey for those bastards.

— Fair enough, boss. Lennox blows compressed air out of his tight chest.

Fuck sake . . . has that cunt Hollis taken demonic possession of Toal's body? When you start getting affirmation from fuckers who used to keep their heads down, then you know it's game over . . .

— That's not to say I don't want you to get the job, Ray. Toal looks at him in baw-faced serenity. — Have you prepared for tomorrow morning?

— I have, Lennox says.

You haven't given it a fucking second's thought!

Toal nods in slow approval as they watch the boat skim the pond. When it gets into the middle, the wind cuts out as if a fan has been clicked off at a switch. It loiters in its own doldrums. Lennox thinks of Billy Lake, on his vessel, literally rolling out a barrel, full of holes, replete with the screams of a rival or former associate, as the roid-munching villain and one of his brick shithouse henchmen gleefully trundle it overboard into the North Sea. Perhaps accompanied by Sid James cackling, as celebratory beers are popped open on deck.

Then a snappy gust of wind manifests and Bertie's boat starts to wobble. It blows over, capsizing and sinking to the bottom of the pond. The kid cries out, — Grandad!

Bob Toal punches Lennox lightly on the arm. — I exempt the bairns from this. They don't deserve this shit.

— I know, that's why I needed to talk to you – my nephew, he –

— I heard, Toal cuts in, saving Lennox from the burden of deciding whether or not to tell him Fraser phoned. — Find him, Ray. Fuck Erskine and the rest of the shit for now. Find the kid, and he moves across to his upset grandchild. — It happens, pal, he says soberly. — C'mon, we'll go and get a new one and pick up your mum. He ruffles the boy's hair and turns back to Lennox. — Later, Ray.

Lennox watches his gaffer depart, holding the hand of the unhappy boy. Recalls taking Fraser to Tynecastle, when he wouldn't have been much older than Bertie. How he had to ask the drunk sitting in front of them to stop his loud cursing. The man turned round with an angry leer, as if ready for aggro, till he saw the sad kid. He instantly apologised, offering Fraser two fingers from his KitKat bar. They then struck up an easy conversation. It was a nice moment.

You need to find him.

But now Lennox has another appointment.

35

Opting to walk to Sally Hart's office to try and clear his head, Lennox cuts along Stockbridge to Canonmills. Heading through King George V Park he traverses up Scotland Street and Dublin Street.

Calls Confectioner on the mobile he issued. Nothing; the line seems dead. Whoever the serial child rapist and murderer needed or wanted to get in touch with, it wasn't him, and the phone has probably been confiscated by now.

Makes a call to Melville. — Jayne, it's Ray. I need to see him. Confectioner. Is everything okay?

You're checking on the welfare of that cunt! What a mess! But if he dies, the books die with him. The peace for the families dies with him.

— Yes, as far as know. I'll speak to him, see if he's amenable. But, Ray . . .

— Yes?

— There's a new governor starting at the prison. He's reorganising staffing and Ronnie McArthur is retiring. The new man will tighten things up. This is the last time I'll be able to help you out here.

— I understand. I appreciate everything you've done. Then he clears his throat before saying, — I'm sorry I wasn't able to find Rebecca, but I guarantee I'll never stop trying.

— Thank you, Ray, Jayne says softly.

On his arrival at Sally's, as he settles down in the chair, the first thing she contends is that he seems under stress again.

You can't mention Trudi . . . or Drummond – Amanda, for fuck sake . . . Fraser . . .

— Yes . . . he acknowledges. — This case I'm on . . . some person or people . . . they're castrating men. These are powerful men who are possibly, in fact, probably, highly abusive individuals. Sex offenders, but protected by the establishment. I'm investigating this but I'm . . .

As he hesitates, Sally finishes the sentence for him. — . . . Conflicted?

— No, Lennox says, fused with a sudden certainty. — Not at all.

Sally Hart looks at him, her eyes expanding in a penetrating revelation. — You're on the side of the assail— whoever is doing this.

Lennox feels his head nod slowing in recognition. It's good to be with someone who gets him. — It's never been like cops and robbers to me, all that cut-and-dried good-versus-evil bollocks we con ourselves into believing. He hears the scorn infiltrate his tone. — A lot of coppers depress me, he states, and he suddenly spits out, — I hate Dougie Gillman, and wish death upon the cunt . . . Thailand, I told you before about . . . when I saw him with a lassie who was obviously underage and I reminded him of what we did for living . . . and the cunt nutted me. Are the likes of him any better than some of the people we lock up?

A thin smile plays across Sally Hart's lips. Then she blows it out with a steely gaze. — Obviously, it's not my place to pass judgement. But you have told me in these sessions that you yourself have been compelled to do things that you would normally find morally reprehensible, for the greater good.

— Yes . . . he says, — the job has it's ugly diktats. But . . . and there's a sincerity and pomposity in his tone that shocks him, — you can't take it into your own life. I've no time for people who do that.

Lennox is shaken by his own hypocrisy. *Trudi, for fuck sake! Was that not a salutary lesson? It was a matter of degree . . .*

Sally looks as if she's going to challenge him, but lets him ramble about various cases he has a feeling he's dumped on her before. He also hears himself go on about transgender people, how he empathises with the plight of someone who feels constrained by the designation given to them by the world, but finds it too complex an issue to reduce to basic premises, and cites Lauren and Gayle as examples. But she lets him go on until she glances at her wrist and informs him that their time is up.

He emerges from the session with his head mangled by his own verbal torrent.

Find Fraser . . .

Talk to Trudi . . .

Talk to Amanda . . .

Find the cunt that killed Norrie . . . Confectioner has to fucking know . . .

Then he checks his texts. One is from a nameless number:

> I hear you need to see me. It's feeding time at the reptile house! Do come! I think we've loads to talk about!

It seems Confectioner has held on to Moobo the dealer's Nokia. Sure enough, within a few minutes, Jayne Melville calls. Gives Lennox a time for his last visit.

Toal's voice resonating in his head, Lennox opts to go via the Southside, in search of his own missing person. At

Leonora's flat there's nobody home, though he can hear the cat mewing. Peeks through the letter box, to see two slitty eyes look up at him in judgement. Wants to kick the door in. Instead knocks on the neighbour's across the way.

A hatchet-faced woman, cigarette stuck to her bottom lip, answers. — She's been in, saw her yesterday.

— Does she have regular visitors, like these two? and he shows her pictures on his phone of both Fraser and Gayle.

— She has aw sorts roond there . . . The woman holds the phone implausibly close to her face. — I recognise those two awright, and she hands the phone back to Lennox. — A bit weird, but live and let live, ay.

— A decent philosophy, Lennox concedes, thanking her and leaving. In the stair, an email pops into his phone:

To: RLennox@policescot.co.uk
From: ADrummond@policescot.co.uk
Subject: Erskine Homicide

I spoke to Andrea Covington about the sexual harassment case with Norrie Erskine. It was the usual stuff, they had a fling, she broke it off after finding out he was married. He kept harassing her, and she filed a case against him. The department took his side. No charges were brought. Andrea left the force, and Erskine did shortly after that, to pursue a career in theatre. While she's obviously aggrieved at her treatment, the focus of Andrea's anger is the department, or the force in general, rather than Erskine. She claims to have no knowledge of either Piggot-Wilkins or Gulliver, has never met them. I don't think she's lying.

Best,

Amanda

He types back:

To: ADrummond@policescot.co.uk
From: RLennox@policescot.co.uk
Subject: Erskine Homicide

Great. Thanks.

When he gets to the prison, Lennox finds Confectioner in a buoyant mood, despite Moobo's Nokia having been confiscated. — The phone proved incredibly useful, Lennox. Not for texting you, but for having conversations with the journalist who is writing my biography!

— Delighted for you, Lennox says, experiencing a sinking sensation. It was inevitable this would happen.

— I'm sure he'll want to talk to you in due course, Lennox. This is our big chance to shine!

He bites his tongue, thinking of the two bodies in the well. *What the fuck have you done, colluding with this cunt?*

— You look somewhat beleaguered, Confectioner smiles. — How was the well?

Lennox remains silent.

— You went down yourself, didn't you? Sooner you than me these days, Lennox. Confectioner pats his paunch. — Did you find my presents?

— What do you want, Gareth?

— I hear your fellow officer Erskine met a sticky end! Toal will not be happy, and how will this sit with our friend Gillman?

Both of youse two creepy cunts that stalk women . . . and Erskine . . . what the fuck? — How do you think? What's the

291

story with Erskine? How do you know him? Your biographer . . . who are they?

— I'm a transactional sort by nature, Lennox. I don't see another phone here. Or anything else that might pique my interest.

— You and I, he advances, it's important to make Confectioner feel that they are in the same game, invested, albeit for different reasons, in the slaughter and torture of innocents,

— Erskine was never involved in *our* case!

— My lips are sealed, and he pulls an imaginary zip across his mouth.

— Do you know who killed him? What was he involved in . . . ? Lennox's mind, violated by the bodies of the girls in the well, by his hand going through that powdery skull . . . he grabs Confectioner by the throat. — TELL ME ABOUT ERSKINE! WHO THE FUCK IS THIS BIOGRAPHER?!

Confectioner, even as his face reddens and his eyes water, settles back, not raising an arm in resistance; it's almost like he is playing an auto-asphyxiation game as he wheezes out, — If you want to see any more of those books . . . you should let go.

Lennox complies, looks at Confectioner, then his own hands, as his tormentor hauls in breath, then rubs his throat. Puts his fists together, placing them under his chin, as if in preparation for prayer. When he speaks, his tones are soft and eerie, as if he's trying to lure a child into the woods with a bag of sweets. — The Gillmans of this world will always defeat the likes of you, Raymond Lennox, because he understands darkness. He'll go to places that you can't, because, fundamentally, you're a coward. You do not have the will to power that he and I possess.

The cunt uses that voice when he wants to infantilise you, wants you the wee laddie back in that tunnel.

A sneer moulds Ray Lennox's face, as he disdains the

paedophile murderer with a hearty laugh. — You want me to be an arrogant, soul-dead abuser like you, and possibly even him. I'm no apologising for no wanting tae go there. For being human, and Lennox's sudden ignition into a smile perplexes Confectioner.

— How is this virtue rewarded in your life? How's the engagement working out . . . or perhaps it isn't? No! I don't think so, he grins, savouring the burn on his adversary's face. — She'll already be in the bed of another man. He'll be running his hands over her naked body, fucking her, and she'll be groaning with pleasure, in the way you obviously couldn't make her. How does that feel, Lennox?

But Lennox only emits another cruel laugh in response. — If only I had encountered a murdering child rapist for sex advice earlier, I may have enjoyed a more successful romantic life. He shrugs. — I suppose it's all about timing.

— Something is different about you, Lennox. Confectioner's eyes narrow. — You seem rather carefree, unburdened . . . An expansive glare follows. — You're leaving the force!

— No. Lennox maintains his grin. — I could never do that. I would miss our little talks. Anything else for me?

— I thought you'd be enthralled by the news I had a biographer. This, as you said, is both our legacy.

— Just tell me who they are.

— Or is it you who really is now feeling usurped?

— Give me another notebook, he urges with a collusive smile. — Another case to open.

— As I said, I have someone else to tell my story now.

All he can do is repeat, — Who are they?

— That would be telling. You'll learn soon enough.

Lennox knows that in negotiations, the control of the other party's level of uncertainty is crucial. — Ever thought that this biographer might just be playing you? Think about it. If you ever feel like giving me a name, I'll check them out. See it as all part of the service. Something to think about, he winks and departs, without looking at Confectioner's reaction.

As he's heading outside, a text pops in:

> A bunch of us are down the Repair Shop.
> A piss up for Norrie.

Dougie Gillman. The rarity of a Gillman text, particularly a social one, makes him laugh manically and loudly.

Maybe you were a bit harsh in therapy, wishing death on the cunt. You didn't mean that . . . ish. Actually, Douglas, I was just with a fellow stalker friend of yours. He spoke highly of you, as always.

36

We prepare for another one of our sessions. Nowadays everything must be recorded in order that everyone other than the person doing the recording can subsequently ignore it. But our *deeds* create the relevance. We *make* them care.

Sally Hart, my partner, is keen to tell the story of DS Norman Erskine, but first I need her to talk of somebody else. Our unstable ally whom we hired for these adventures. Once serving some kind of a purpose: now an increasing liability. — Tell me about Gayle.

Taking a sip of her water, she sits back in the chair and begins. — Gayle was a troubled young man named Gary Nicolson. When he first came to me, like most people who do, Gary was a little lost, confused and struggling to find his place in this world. He wanted acceptance. Sally smiles. — That's pretty much all of us, I know. Most people who come to me self-describing as trans are genuine. Others, like Gayle, or Gary, are just forlorn, damaged souls looking for a hook to hang their neuroses on. To find something, one *thing*, that explains it all; something that they can designate the source of all their problems. Of course, he was as toxic as any of the abusers I regularly met, but he was malleable. Like so many people today, he basically just needed to be told what to do.

I consider this truism: all those meaty, mouthy proponents of *freedom*, battling to death for their right to be enslaved by corporate algorithms.

— It was obvious that he wanted to have sex with me. But since the French Alps incident, I've never found this to have much appeal. I had learned the tactics of dissociation, of being able to mentally remove yourself from the horrendous event. It involves deploying a very similar tactic to what people do naturally in the realm of dreams, to move from first-person participant to third-person observer during the attack. It wasn't successful back then.

She stops.

I let the silence hang.

She eventually steps in. — One of them in that gondola knew what to say: the threatening whisper, the laugh; worse, the subversive caress that your body responded to, pulling you back into that horrific present.

She has moved the subject matter away from the troublesome Gayle and back to them, the people we had to deal with.

— The smart ones are the most dangerous. They know exactly how much elitism the white, middle-class patriarchy, specifically, has sponsored: imperialism, the division of labour. How they fuck us all. Then there's the imbecile apologists, genuinely blind as to their role in maintaining this on behalf of their masters. Those are the ones who look on in bemused confusion when you take your revenge; those who have *why* etched on their stupid faces, even as you remove their pride, she explains, building up momentum.

We're going back over old ground, but it's a tale she needs to tell. We both know that it sometimes takes more than one visit to the toilet to get rid of all the shit.

— Erskine was once an upstaging pantomime star. Not in the league of Rikki Fulton or Alan Cumming, either of whom could deploy a rubber-faced gesture that would send the crowd into hysterics, while the bemused actor in the foreground performed a sober piece, looking concerned that the audience was not taking their big moment *seriously* enough. Then they would look round . . .

DS Erskine. Far from the worst, but an associate of evil and not just on a summer job when the theatre work had dried up. Any accomplice of Piggot-Wilkins is an adversary of mine. And, most certainly, they are an enemy of hers.

— I saw many of his shows, following his career even as I developed my own, once we returned home from that cold place. The police force, the stage, back to the police force again. I thought he might have been the innocent party in that desperate trio. That he was coerced into setting it up. There was a time I emotionally separated him from the other two. I even laughed, retrospectively, thinking about some of his stage jokes. But then I heard about his antics from Freda Miras. She was a Hungarian prostitute he went with, who was a pro bono case of mine. Behind his jovial facade, there was a blemishing darkness, subsequently alluded to by his colleagues Amanda Drummond and Ray Lennox.

Ray Lennox. That troublesome cop. Without even being fully aware that I exist, he seems to be getting closer to me, sensing my presence. He's Sally's client, her *patient*, yet he crops up first with Gareth Horsburgh, and then, completely out of place, on Billy Lake's boat in Essex. And, in his most potentially hazardous intervention of all, that Glasgow hospital ward with Lauren Fairchild.

And this is the man whose name was the last word that Gulliver spoke.

Lennox.

I do not believe in coincidences. I believe in energy fields. Lennox is at the centre of all this and so far hasn't been able to join up the dots. But he will. He's certainly far more troublesome than Wallingham, whose modus operandi I found out from Lake, whom I expect to unwittingly do the dirty work there. The idiot, Lake, sack-of-rocks dumb, deluded enough to see himself as some kind of criminal mastermind, yet wondering in confused aggression at our last session *who grassed him up*. The answer was: he did it to himself, by spilling all to me, the fool. Of course, neither he nor Wallingham will ever know this but at least one of them will pay.

— Freda showed me the marks, Sally is now focused on me, — told me his specialism was burning parts of her with a cigarette. That would get him off. But it was never enough. On each visit, the cigarette butt had to blaze longer on the skin. Erskine was as damaged as the others, she says, ice in her gaze.

I let her meander, as she loves to do this, particularly as she has to be so structured with her clients. But there are a few facts that I need to know in order to write our story. It's all in the details. — How would you compare Erskine to the other two?

— I suppose that after Gulliver and Piggot-Wilkins, he was something of a soft target. But taking out a brutal henchman of the patriarchal state is a valid response, is it not?

I nod in agreement. Thinking of Roya. Letting my hate smoulder. I ought to have finished off Piggot-Wilkins while I had the chance. Taken the cock he put into my sister, like the hand he took from me. That would have been justice. That's what Sally must be made to fully understand, to paraphrase herself: Lennox, no matter how benign or well intentioned he seems, is the servant of a corrupt state that exists to prevent that justice.

She hesitates for a full minute, before reciprocating to the nod. She knows my thoughts. In that beat, I can see the stern glint in her eye that perhaps says: *you were once part of that same state apparatus.* And of course, this is correct. In the media, my job, just as much as that of the police, was to protect the wealthy and their property. I was just in the propaganda wing of the elite supremacist movement. Past tense. — Then Ray Lennox came in and told me about Gillman, she continues, — and specifically, a little trip to Thailand. Not as bad as Erskine, but his partner and an easy touch. Our next target.

— Thanks, I tell her, trying to press the stop switch, nimble despite my heavy hand. I'm pleased to manage to execute so deft an operation. When I think of the number of phones I've wrecked, great strides have been made . . .

I unscrew my hand.

She looks at the stump for only a few seconds, before lifting up her skirt, and pulling down her panties. — Make me care, she asks, as I apply the gel to my wrist. When they removed the hand, they stitched the skin over the protrusion. Many women like this; a big boner which never loses its power.

298

I'm slow, as I work it in, but relentless, as I build up the rhythm. Soon I hear her breathing change, then soft groans spill from her. Watching her shine, I sniff her hair. How I long to kiss her mouth. But this I cannot do. That is not allowed. I rub up against her leg as I pump her with my love wrist. A scarlet mist in front of my eyes as my cock explodes my jiz against her, always before she achieves her own brutal ecstasy. Though spent, I must pump on. I feel her grip me with her pelvic muscles. All I can do is listen to her moans, as she begs me for more force, her face already screwed up as my forearm smashes in and out of her cunt. — Don't stop, she pleads.

— We will never stop, I whisper in her ear.

When she does fold in ecstasy, my arm is sore at the elbow. I pull it gently from her aching hole.

We lie still, next to each other. She says to me, — I'm not sure I'm capable of love, but what I feel for you is as close as I'm likely to get, and I feel her grab my hand in hers as my stump, reddened, hangs on my other side.

Gillman is getting closer. I saw him follow the policewoman Drummond. But Ray Lennox is also. Of course, I can't tell her that. She's become attached to him. A bit like another mutual friend, of sorts, the one the detective and I share. But we'll take care of them.

All of them.

No, we do not intend to stop this yet.

I'm sorry, Raymond Lennox. You're not the worst of them. But you are one of them.

37

The last thing he intends to do is to take up Gillman's offer and hit the Repair Shop. He circles back to Leonora's flat, again finding it empty, then realises he's right in the neighbourhood for the grim Southside watering hole. It does seem important, though, to be with his Serious Crimes colleagues at this time. And there is a bit of guilt in wishing death on Gillman.

That was extreme. A good kick up the arse would suffice. Those cunts are all you've got. How desperate is that?

So Ray Lennox trudges through the dark, inhospitable city. Tries to imagine what it would be like living somewhere else. Edinburgh is in his DNA, but he thinks of it as a cold, absentee father who's never really loved him. Doesn't put itself out for him. He supposes that all cities must be that way. But Edinburgh appears the truculent Christmas drunk who sits sadly at the bar, painfully professing love for the children it never sees. The two-gram loudmouth in the toilet cubicle with the grandiose plans that will turn into self-loathing as the cruel light floods in. Perhaps the city is disabling anything good in him. Eating him alive from the inside, leaving that hollow shell. And now he is going to a pub he regards as the capital's second worst, just behind his local, run by the mercurial Jake Spiers.

The Repair Shop is practically empty, except one corner where the Serious Crimes boys hang out. They are more tightly packed round the bar than usual. Holding on for dear life like drowning men on a piece of driftwood; Gillman, Harkness,

Notman, Arnott, Harrower, and even the more reconstructed Inglis and McCorkel. They too seem to acknowledge the enormity of the situation. The most furtive is the suspended Tom McCaig, who is almost literally crying into his whisky. — Ah thoat thir wis mair than one tent, he says, sweeping his tangled grey hair back from a lined face.

We are servants of a state that can't even protect us. This should not happen. We feel weak, exposed. This is a new force, perhaps a harbinger of things to come. It has no fear of any consequences. It won't stop.

Lennox looks at the shattered Gillman, thinks about how he's never got on with him, since he first met him as a young officer. Veteran cops often disdain raw recruits. It's the way of the world. Gillman, though, possesses a boorish nastiness, unmitigated by the swaggering bonhomie displayed by the likes of other misanthropes he's worked with, such as Bruce Robertson or Ginger Rogers. Gillman exudes a pure loathing, both sly and overt, for anything he doesn't like. And it was plain from the off he didn't vibe on Ray Lennox.

Now the death of Erskine seems to have unhinged Dougie Gillman further. Vengeful talk spills from his mouth. Not carelessly. It is frighteningly focused. He's nurturing his own hatred, trying to find its depth and range. — I'm gaunny kill some cunt for this. He knocks back his whisky, and stamping his foot, promptly turns and leaves the bar, as though he has just decided who. McCaig visibly shivers, looks relieved as Gillman passes him.

— Dinnae let him go, Ally Notman says to the assembled company, while making no move to restrain his departing colleague.

— I'll go after him, Lennox says, leaving the pub. His exit is too swift for him to register any comment of his fellow officers, but he can hear their thoughts crystallise as an incredulous, communal energy, following him out into the wet streets: *Lennox* is helping *Gillman*. However, Ray Lennox doesn't seek to engage with Douglas Gillman, instead tracks him through the dark coldness of the city.

Trailing into town down Nicolson Street, Lennox can't believe that's he's struggling to keep up with Gillman's unrelenting rolling gait, mysteriously pacy from a man whose fitness levels are so evidently low. Takes it as a sign of his own decline: he needs to get back in the gym.

The night draws further in, with Gillman's venomous swagger the crackling force that propels him from seedy bars to the knocking shops they called saunas. Pursuing him through town is the most unpleasant and lonely of undertakings, even for a seasoned stake-out man like Lennox. Finally Gillman stops outside a tenement block in Marchmont, which he looks up and down. Then he moves across the street to survey it from that vantage point. Lennox knows the flat, not that far from Trudi's; it belongs to Amanda Drummond.

When she emerges, wearing a knee-length coat and jeans with flat shoes, heading off into the night, Gillman ducks into the next stair. He then follows her down the street, and across the Meadows. Lennox's suspicions are confirmed. There is nobody else around this time. No Glover-resembling friend.

You weren't imagining it. It's true. The other woman she was with earlier is irrelevant. It's her he's focused on. Gillman is stalking Drummond.

In the central Meadows walkway, he catches up with Gillman, who has maintained a twenty-metre distance between himself and Drummond. — Dougie, Lennox whispers in harsh urgency.

Gillman stops, turns round to see Lennox, then whiplashes to watch Drummond's back receding. Regards Lennox again. — What you wantin?

302

— You're stalking her? Amanda?

— No. I'm staking her out. Are *you* stalking *me*?

— No, Lennox says, a little wrong-footed by the counter-assertion. — I went after you when you left the bar. You weren't in a great frame of mind.

— So you've followed me since then? Fuck off, Lennox!

— I saw you in pursuit of her the other day. I had to be sure, and now I am. You're stalking Amanda. Why?

— I telt you, I'm staking her oot.

— Why?

— Let's just say ah started tae notice things aboot Drummond and her associates. Gillman's chest expands in pomp.

— What associates?

— Dae yir ain hamework, Lenny.

— Dougie, listen. Amanda's a colleague. A fellow officer. Surely you must see how fucked up this is?

But Gillman seems not to hear him. — Aw these fucking weirdos and they vindictive bitches, he tells Lennox, — they're closing ranks. Those fucking degenerates, who dinnae ken what they are: they're taking ower, Lenny! Watch them!

— Is this aboot the fucking promotion? Lennox snaps.

— It's aboot everything, Gillman spits back as some creature rustles in the tree above them, close enough for both men to briefly look up. — If you're a gadge who feels trapped in a bird's body, have the fucking baws tae get rid ay yir fucking baws. Get them whipped off and have a fanny built. Dinnae prance aboot lassies' lavies and lassies' nicks wi your cock hingin out, tellin every cunt you're a fucking bird. What dae ye think ay that shite? he demands.

Lennox is almost inclined to snigger at Gillman's imagery, but then he thinks of Fraser. — I couldn't give a fuck about the gender of others, Dougie. How the fuck is stalking Drummond working this case?

— And you're working it poncing aboot doon in London? What have you got on Norrie's murderer?

— What the fuck have *you* got?

Gillman pulls out his phone, fiddles around with it. Produces an old newspaper article. It's the Ms X one, that Lennox was sent by Sebastian Taylor.

Lennox reads. Looks up at Gillman. — And? Student bird raped by these snobby cunts in a French ski resort.

— Guess who the fuckers were?

Lennox lets out a long breath. — Well, like you, my money is on Gulliver and Piggot-Wilkins, but we still don't have evidence to connect them to that holiday in the Alps. Piggot-Wilkins won't talk and is being protected by the high-heid yins, and Gulliver can't talk . . .

— Aye. Well?

Lennox stares at Gillman, tries to work out where he's going with this. — You're saying that Amanda is Ms X? That she was raped by them as a student, and subsequently killed Gulliver and castrated Piggot-Wilkins?

— Aye.

— She investigated Gulliver! Questioned him.

— So fuck? That entitled little rapist cunt probably monstered hundreds ay wee student birds. Think he'd recognise one in a ski lift fae fifteen year ago?

— No way.

— Aye way. She was on a school trip tae France back then. It included the Alps.

— You've been secretly investigating her on the basis of that pish?

A couple walk towards them, then sensing the bad energy, veer off towards the edge of the path, quickening their pace as they move past. Gillman looks at Lennox, his teeth bared. — It's fucking Drummond, he declares. — She's involved in this!

— You're nuts. You are totally fucking losing it, Lennox spits. — I know you were close to Erskine, but get a grip.

The chubby finger of Douglas Gillman waves at him. — Because you ride her you're blind to what's gaun on, Lenny!

Lennox's brows fly north. *Has this cunt been stalking you as well? How does he ken aboot –*

— Didnae like that, did ye? Gillman sings in triumph. — No very *professional*, and he mimics the schoolmarm voice Drummond generally deploys using that word.

— You ken fuck all, Dougie.

— Enlighten ays then, Gillman challenges, crowned by the silver crescent of a moon cutting through murky clouds. Then, in face of Lennox's silence, — See, what you dinnae realise, Lenny, Gillman prods his own chest as he looks at him in appeal, — is ah'm fightin for ma life here! What does the likes ay me dae eftir Serious Crimes? he asks. — First thing the new Chief Super does is implement the staffing review. The Night ay the Long Knives and guess whae's the first cunt Chief Super Amanda Drummond recommends for his jotters? *Numero uno* oan her hit list for the Roger Waters is none other than Doogie the Dinosaur, and Gillman takes a peevish stage bow.

— She's no even got the fuckin job yet, ya paranoid cunt!

— See who wins at they interviews the morn, Lenny, Gillman snorts. — It'll no be you or me: tell ye that for nowt.

The morn . . .

Ray Lennox knows the interviews are tomorrow. But this information, lodged somewhere in the back of his mind, hasn't consciously concerned him at all. Considers what is going on in his personal and professional life. Just how irrelevant the promotion is to him. Steps forward, squares up to Dougie Gillman, matches his demented stare. — You're a fucking nut. Seriously, back the fuck off here.

But his old rival isn't standing down. That big square chin slides out like the drawer of a cash register. — Your sexy wee girlfriend ditched ye. So ye started banging that fuckin frigid dyke and couldnae get rid ay her . . . Then, suddenly inspired by something he sees in Lennox's eye, ventures, — Naw, wait, she KB'd you! Buyer's regret!

To Gillman's obvious shock Lennox laughs loudly. — That's pretty much spot on. You should trust your intuition more.

— That's exactly what ah'm daein, Gillman retorts, as Lennox turns and starts to walk away. — Watch her, he shouts back at him, as he himself moves off in departure, vanishing across the Meadows into the mist like a spectre.

In search of a cab, Ray Lennox, just a few minutes down the road, sees something that cuts him to the quick. Turns away before he's spotted by a strolling couple. Pulls into the shadows of the walkway and lets them pass, lost in themselves. Wants to shout out but the words in his throat are drops of water on desert sand. Watches them turn the corner.

Trudi . . . have a good life.

38

...

Sally clears her throat with a sip of water. Crosses her long legs with red-seamed stockings and sable heels. It's enchanting; mesmerising. Her power has been honed by her profession but was crafted for this vengeance. This makes it all the more devastating. — I was eighteen and working in Val d'Isère at an on-mountain restaurant called La Folie Douce. The staff group was fun, quite a few of them British. I bartended there with Chloe, a girl from Ipswich I became friendly with, and Norrie, a constantly joking guy from Glasgow. He hung around with a local man who operated the cable cars for the skiers. The Joker made a clumsy drunken pass at me one night; I told him I wasn't interested. He seemed to get the message. This was Norman Erskine.

— Wigan's Ovation had a cover version of the Northern Soul hit 'Skiing in the Snow'. It was popular among a certain crowd of posh people known as *yahs*. Some of them were actually very pleasant and tipped well. One was particularly nice; he had those blue eyes, and an easy humour. His name was Chris Piggot-Wilkins.

— He kept on at me to go skiing with him and his friends on one of my days off. Eventually I did. In the event, I discovered he had just one friend, a young Perthshire man called Ritchie Gulliver, who was a decent skier. Afterwards we attended an après-ski party on the mountain. It was a fun and exhilarating day; the bars, the cocaine, the alcohol. I was young and naive but I sensed a growing tension in the air as it got near the time to go back. The crowd had thinned out. My own friends had all skied back down the mountain. Gulliver kept saying we were too wrecked to ski back down. It seemed sensible, but the truth was that I was the only one too intoxicated. I later realised that they had spiked my drink.

— So we got into the large gondola cable car we had come up on. It was meant for eight people but we were the only people in it as everyone else had left the slopes.

— On our way down, Gulliver was talking on his phone, while Piggot-Wilkins was looking strangely at me. I'd grow to know that look in men. Then the lift engine cut out. Gulliver put his phone away and smiled. 'Oh dear . . . too bad. Looks like we'll have to amuse ourselves till they sort it all out.'

— That was when it happened.

— When the gondola restarted, they quickly pulled on their clothes. I sat there naked. It stopped at the resort base and they got out, laughing. It was so cold. I was numb in every way as I pulled my clothes on. I saw them joking with the lift operator and his barman friend: Norman Erskine, the underemployed actor. I believe I saw, through my fug, money change hands.

— When I walked past them, Erskine smirked malevolently at me. 'Dozy wee hoors like you need tae learn a lesson.'

— I went to my chalet, locked the door, showered, slept, and left the resort the next day. Sally remains composed, but her eyes are perhaps glassier than normal. — Thank you for letting me talk, Vikram. It is very helpful.

I nod, thinking of Roya. How she could never bring herself to speak out. But now justice will be served on behalf of her, on behalf of all the women we love who cannot speak out.

39

Ray Lennox didn't expect to see Trudi Lowe, his recent fiancée, strolling with her new man. Yet he can no longer even muster the performance of ersatz hate for BMW Dean. Shabby, defeated and useless, all he wants to do is go home, watch porn and snort cocaine. Reasons that these things will find him soon enough: best to stave off the day of execution. Decides to head back down to Leonora's. It's confirmed that this is the right course of action as a message from Jackie pops into his iPhone:

> Have you heard from him yet? What are you doing? Return my calls please, Ray! I'm worried sick that he's in serious trouble!

What the fuck are you doing in your bourgeois life? Nae wonder the poor wee cunt doesn't ken who the fuck he is! Away and munch on your bird's cairpit!

Then a text from Scott McCorkel comes in, telling him that Fraser and Leonora have been messaging Gayle on Twitter. Sends him the screenshot:

> **@killergayle**
> Just tell me where you are. I can help you. I'm worried about you.

@five-one

I'm sure you are.

@killergayle

Come on, what's that supposed to mean?

@five-one

It means: fuck off. I don't want anything to do with you.

@sladest

I don't either. Please leave us alone!

It isn't Fraser you need to find. It's Gayle, that fucking big ridiculous lump. It's always been Gayle! Even at the hospital with Lauren!

Arriving at the flat is a massive anticlimax. It is still dead. Lennox feels deflated. But as he's heading down Nicolson Street, empty at this late hour, Leonora Slade is coming straight towards him, talking into her phone. Her eyes ignite in horror as she sees him. Hangs up and looks around as if to consider running. Decides against it.

Lennox isn't laughing and Leonora's expression becomes rueful. — You're coming with me, he tells her, — either back to your place or to the police station at St Leonard's. You decide.

— My place, she says, so softly he has to strain to hear her.

Back at her flat, Leonora offers him coffee. He declines. — I don't have time to fanny around. You have a voice. You. It's not about being a man or a woman or trans or anything. It's about being a human being and stopping other human beings from getting hurt. Understand?

She nods slowly. — I'd been seeing Gayle . . . Gary. But I stopped because I believed they were planning to hurt Lauren.

— Why?

310

— Lauren was preparing her speech for when Gulliver was doing his talk at Stirling University. She obviously wanted to condemn the transphobes but the speech was also about outing trans hijackers. Gary took it personally . . . She starts to sob. — I believe Gary . . . Gayle . . . was enraged and took this personally. They talked of killing Lauren.

Lennox is about to agree, but something makes him hold back. The build, the clothes and the wig were similar, but the eyes . . . he still isn't sure about the eyes. He thinks back to the person behind the wheel of the van at the Savoy. — What about my nephew? What about Fraser?

— You know she's in hiding, she told you. She was at a friend's flat first.

— Who?

— Linsey, then Dan, I told you.

— This Dan Hopkirk, we've been unable to find him. The university and his family both say he's hiking and they don't know where.

— That's Dan, he just grabs his backpack and goes. I think Fraser admires that in him. I don't know where Fraser is now, she won't say. 'What you don't know they can't beat out of you' was what she said to me yesterday when we spoke.

— Do you think he's with Dan?

— They are good friends, so it's possible.

— What is Fraser running from? Who is he scared of?

— Gayle. Leonora's bottom lip trembles. — She stood up to Gayle. Gayle was going to kill her. They know where Fraser lives. Gayle said they would kill Fraser's family. Burn the house down.

Lennox stares at her. The disparity between this stick-thin elfin figure and the powerful Gary Nicolson is disturbing to him. — Are you still having sex with this fucking psycho . . . this Gary . . . Gayle?

311

Leonora averts her gaze from him. — They phone me. They scare me, and I have to go to them. She starts crying. — I can't stand it. I want to die!

— Look at me, Lennox says firmly, watching her head slowly rise. — At the very least, he's bullying you into a coercive relationship. This can't continue. The next time he calls, here's what you –

He stops as her phone goes. They look at each other as she holds it up to him, the caller ID revealing: GAYLE.

40

She's a fuckin ride is the first reaction of the off-duty cop when he sees the woman standing by the bar. She has long blonde hair with a fringe. There is something both beguiling and unsettling about her. Is she a hooker? It seems too obvious, even for this well-heeled hotel bar. Her accent, as she asks the barman for a Cosmopolitan, is local, but posh. *A woman of this class should be booking herself out as an escort, online, not hooring in hotel bars.* He moves across to her, with the dumb, lazy authority of a servant of the state. — How goes?

— Not bad. She arches a brow. — You?

— Okay. The cop surveys the scene. Drinks in the desperate hope and bilious excitement. He comes here a lot. It's a popular hook-up spot for those who prefer the drama and performance of real life to the tired mechanics of Tinder.

They ease into a light spar around dating and masculinity. She contends that he seems quite the unreconstructed type.

— Unreconstructed, what is that? he asks. Before she can respond, he blusters on, — It's like fitba; every year they talk about reconstruction, as if it's gaunny save the day. Will it fuck save the day. You're stuck wi what ye are.

She looks deeply at him, or at least one of her eyes does. The other, slightly watery, seems to stare at something behind him, or perhaps, beyond him. — Oh, we can all change, she offers, before suggesting, — Back to mine?

— Sound. The off-duty cop is delighted. Yes, he's punching above his weight, but it was always thus. And in spite of his burgeoning waistline and thinning hair, he has an ego. Sometimes that's enough.

The woman tells him her flat is a short walk away, in Bruntsfield. As they wind beyond the looming castle to Tolcross, the moon blinking through the cloud cover, giving her an intermittent magnesium glow, he slyly checks out her contours. She's good-looking, but more than that, she's game: that's the main thing. Romance is rarely on his mind.

Her flat is on the second floor of a Victorian tenement dominated by a big bay-windowed lounge. Inside, it's comfortably furnished, though lacks personality. She heads to a cocktail cabinet and makes them a drink.

He sups at his vodka and tonic as they sit close together on the couch, their knees almost touching. Their conversation continues. It grows more provocative and personal. Then she says something that jars him: — Oh yes you did . . .

. . . but his arrogance fights against the concept that this situation might be spiralling out of his control. Then he realises that he's sweating and his heartbeat is slowing down. Looks at the woman in thuggish, sneering defiance, knowing something's fucked about this and he needs to get away . . . rises and staggers towards the door. His legs are jelly as he tries to turn the handle. It slides through his grasp, then he's on the floor looking up at it.

Suddenly, another voice in the room; it's muffled but deeper and coarser.

— This arsehole is ours.

Then Dougie Gillman can hear no more.

41

The rain's pockmarked dance on asphalt. The streets deserted, save for stragglers trapped in shop doorways. Even though he's parked, Lennox deploys the Alfa Romeo's wipers. Rubs at his eye grit; another sleepless night. His car, all wrappers, cartons and soda cans, a monument to bad living, underscored by the carb-heavy diet bubbling in his guts.

On such grim Edinburgh days, Miami floods his brain. Vivid pastel colours split by black lines delineating sky and lusciously cool art deco buildings. The visualist Britto capitalised on this to be regarded as the defining airport-franchise pop artist. A contrast to Edinburgh's series of gradient shadows, with a menacing sky that seems to have retched out the darkened tenements below it. Yet, in his mind's eye, Lennox envisions them as bordered by electric white lines, like the one that glows magnesium on the top of the dashboard in front of him. Will lacerate his brain, eroding him, yes, but at the same time pumping him with the internal aura of invincibility.

An email from his old journo contact, Sebastian Taylor, pops in:

To: RLennox@policescot.co.uk
From: staylor125@gmail.com
Subject: Ms X

Dear Ray,

Sorry to say I have no information on the identity of Ms X.

Best,

Sebastian

It's Amanda. She's Ms X. Gillman is correct! If only because shit is so fucked up that it just has to be . . .

You always knew we had a connection . . . she's also been hunting them down from inside the force. She was your partner and she listened to your old cases and all your shit about Gillman and Thailand. That's why Gillman was so spooked. Some part of him suspected that she was coming for him!

But this is far-fetched paranoia. Just because she psychologically castrated you, doesnae mean she's in the literal game!

But . . .

. . . she was first on the scene to tell you about Erskine. Where had she been earlier? She was there quickly when Gulliver was found in the warehouse. Where was she before? She was on leave when Piggot-Wilkins was attacked . . .

Then a Toyota Prius pulls up. Tears him from his pounding cocaine thoughts. Leonora emerges from the stair door. Gets inside. Can't make out the driver, but knows who it is. Follows the vehicle to the industrial estate on reclaimed foreshore by the docks at Newhaven.

The invariably cold fishing village, long gobbled up by the city. Its harbour remains intact, looked down on by the towering Chancelot Mill buildings.

The Prius parks outside the Mill and Lennox watches two figures emerge. Leonora and Gayle: the tiny woman in jeans and Doc Martens, and that hulking man in a dress.

Was it Gayle in the hospital with Lauren, who threw your old colleague's urine over you, then smashed you with a formidable right hook? It had to be.

As they vanish inside, he floors the ignition, pulling up close.

Exiting the car, Lennox moves through the entrance, sliding, back to the wall, down the corridor. Hears them step into the lift. Letting the doors close, he moves over, watching an indicator telling him they've stopped on the top floor. Instead of summoning the lift back down, he finds the stairs. It's a long climb as he strides up them two at a time, his thighs and calves and lungs ablaze as he emerges onto the top floor. Assumes Gayle works in security at the Mill, or has a contact who does.

From behind a stair fire door, he can hear voices arguing. He edges closer, gently pushing it ajar, to spy them. A heavy lead weight lies on the floor, and he uses it to partly wedge open the door. Leonora is speaking but is suddenly silenced by Gayle's large hand round her throat. — You're no laying down the law. So get them off. He loosens his grip. As she looks wretchedly at him, he grins. — I want tae fuck ye against that waw, ya fucking wee ride.

— What, I –

— Your daft wee boyfriends dinnae fuck you like I do.

— Fraser and I . . . we trusted you . . . we looked up to you!

— Shut it, ya dopey wee tart, aw ah ever want oot you is a ride. You and your daft wee pals: all you little cunts with your tight pussies and arseholes. To fuck you, and then fuck you up, and he produces a vial of amyl nitrate. — Sniff this. He grabs her hair and pushes the bottle under her nose. — This will open up your arsehole like the Mersey Tunnel!

— Cause this land's the place I love, and here I'll stay, Lennox's voice booms out as the doors swing open. — You're a cunt, Gary.

Gayle looks round. Stares at Lennox, releasing his grip on

317

Leonora. The vial of amyl nitrate smashes to the floor. — What the fuck do you want? Get the fuck oot ay here or I'll –

He falls silent as Lennox moves swiftly over to him. What happens next completely wrong-foots the detective. Gayle's wide eyes suggest compliant surrender. Then Lennox finds out to his cost that he's playing possum, as a volley of punches explode from the big man in the dress, into Ray Lennox's head and body. They have the power and precision of a trained fighter, and stars ignite in the cop's eyes. He swings back but his balance is shot under the onslaught, and he can't generate power in his blows. One hook batters his brain off the back of his skull and Lennox feels his knees going.

Stay on your feet . . .

It's futile, but then, as he looks up at Gayle, his adversary is falling at the same time, and Lennox, as he topples, lunges out, trying to use that tumbling body to hold him up. All that happens is that they crash to the ground together. Fighting a growing nausea, Lennox looks up to see Leonora standing over both of them with the doorstop weight. Gayle's head is burst open with blood streaking down his hair, neck and shoulders, onto his dress. Through muffled ears he hears Leonora's excited squeal: — I never did anything like that before!

— It was a good time to start, Lennox says, hauling breath into his frame as he slowly manoeuvres himself on top of the stunned Gayle, before throwing a vicious right hook into his face. Then: a left. Then: another right. — Where's my fucking nephew! WHERE'S FRASER ROSS!

— I dunno . . . I've been looking . . . I've looked all over for him . . .

— Brilliant, Lennox says, rising. As he does, he kicks Gayle hard across the face, watching his head snap back. Grabbing his cuffs, he threads them round a thick, exposed downpipe, snapping the rolling-eyed Gayle's wrists onto them. — You're a shite bird, but you were a shite guy as well . . . If you're serious about transitioning you'd best focus on personality rather than gender.

— Can we cut their cock off? Leonora screams.

Lennox's eyes glint. — Yes we can.

— No! Gayle begs.

— Then sing, you cunt, Lennox sneers. — Gie me a fucking name!

— I can't!

Then Lennox's phone buzzes: Hollis wants to FaceTime. Getting back on his feet, he thinks it's a good idea to pick up. — Mark, he says, looking at the grizzled visage, — you certainly pick your fucking moments.

— Fuck off, Ray, you narky Jock cunt, Hollis barks smugly. — I've only gone and figured it all out. Lennox is all ears. As Mark Hollis spits out the beats, Lennox looks at the cuffed Gayle. — Vikram Rawat is the name we're looking for.

— I was just getting there, thanks to this fucking ponce. He holds the phone to Gayle's ear. — Can you shout it again, buddy?

— Vik Rawat, Hollis roars. — He was writing Billy Lake's biography, a true-crime wankfest for thug groupies. You know, one of them ego-jerking pieces where the geezer makes out he's as hard as the shit stuck in your old grandma's intestines.

And Confectioner's biographer too! This cunt has been playing us all; cops, gangsters and paedo serial killers. All by pandering to our execrable vanities that we're godlike presences in this world.

— So all this trans stuff we've been following up . . .

— A distraction, mate, a petty diversion from the real farking issues. Hollis's face forms a grin, as Lennox looks at the man in the dress. — Don't look so flaming sad, Ray, I know you lot invented this whole trans thing, poncing around in farking kilts. But if that cahnt Gulliver hadn't liked men in

319

dresses he'd never have lost his tackle, and we'd never have found these cahnts. So where is Vik Rawat?

— I'm going to use the Hollis method on this cunt to find that out, and he shows Hollis and a terrified Gayle each other. — Will brief you later, once I've found Rawat. Lennox hangs up to Hollis's grim nod, and faces Gayle. — Where is he?

— I can't tell you, Gayle whimpers.

— You're scared of him? You're a fucking lump! Why?

— He has this way about him. He gave us belief at first, but ah found out he did Gulliver. Lauren and me were arguing about the movement and ah just blurted it out, telt her who had done Gulliver. I had tae tell him I'd let it slip. He fucked Lauren up. Wanted me to do it. I wouldnae so he did it himself. You saw what he's capable of with Gulliver, him and her. They're killers!

Lennox feels his chest burn: *Ms X.* — The her! Who is the her!

— Sally. Sally Hart.

Fuck.

Lennox feels something heavy fall through him. He looks at Gayle in disbelief. His scared captive starts to ramble. — I was seeing her as a client . . . I'd have done anything for her . . . I gave her all the info our group had on Gulliver . . .

— Then, when Lauren found out and started to get nosy . . .

Gayle's faltering speech seems an acknowledgement of the weight and consequence of his own words. — They . . . they wanted me to fuck her up . . . but I wouldn't! Then they did it themselves . . . or Vikram did, not Sally. But they both . . . they both did Gulliver . . . he begs, his features falling south.

When Sally was listening intently to you, you believed it was your motivation she was interested in. It was the case details, the

320

stuff you disclosed about the violent, manipulative men you came into contact with. From Gulliver to Rab, the Carpenter of Lunacy, to Confectioner to Gillman, you were feeding her; not just the bodies, but the methods.

Not Erskine, though.

Erskine was the third man?

Patience exhausted and with humiliation's rage burning him, Lennox hits Gayle so hard his knuckles sting as he feels the young man's teeth slacken and blood spill from his mouth. — One more time. Where are they?

It is the defining shot, as egged on by Leonora, the one that finally makes the big man in the dress tap out. — There . . . I think . . . He points out the window to the adjoining tower of Chancelot Mill. I got them the keys, the use of the space . . .

Lennox looks over at the structure looming outside. Makes his way to the exit and the connecting passageway between the two towers.

— What can I do? Leonora asks.

— You can go home, he says, — and wait for Fraser.

And Lennox tears off, all the time thinking: *There's nobody waiting for you. You're on your own. You saw her with him. Younger. More her age. It cut you deeply. You pulled into the shadows of the Meadows walkway and saw her; not like she was with you lately, but carefree, despite her father's death. Her and that guy, absorbed in each other, like most lovers. Both unaware that her ex-fiancé was passing by: the man she, until lately, wanted to spend the rest of her life with. How do you lose such love? By absenting yourself from it, either wilfully or subconsciously. And when you lose it, it generally means that you were not worthy of it any more. You don't hate her, or even him now. You don't even have the time to hate yourself. This is who you are.*

Don't lament lost love. Feel lucky you had it.

You'll never love again. It's done. You're finished.

42

I'll never fuck again . . .

. . . is Douglas Gillman's first thought as he wakes up strapped to what he senses is a hospital gurney. Secured at his wrists and neck by the ties, he reflexively tries to kick out, only to learn his ankles are bound to the sides of the trolley. Looks at the cracked Artex ceiling, the neck tie stopping him raising his head. There is what looks like disused plant machinery around him. He's probably in an old factory, perhaps on some abandoned industrial estate. Gillman knows what is happening to him. Knew as soon as he started coming over dizzy in that flat.

Could he go on as a eunuch, solving sex crimes? How strange would that be? Would he be invested in this work? Gillman feels an involuntary laugh ripple subversively through his frame. Then these thoughts deplete his finite pool of resistance and in his mind's eye he sees the remains of Norrie Erskine, naked, blue and cockless, on the Gyle Park. This envisioning accompanied by a despair so crushing he believes he could die on the spot.

A confirming voice from behind him: — Why are men the rapists, paedophiles and killers? Sally Hart asks, stepping past Gillman and turning to face him, her blonde wig discarded, showing collar-length hair of a slightly more magnesium shade.

His brain fizzing, Gillman crackles in sardonic defiance. — Maybe women lack the self-confidence . . . the patriarchy . . . the systemic oppression . . .

— Until now. Sally bends into his line of vision, holding a set of garden shears.

A further crumbling inside Douglas Gillman: again engendered by the sense that this would be worse than death. In the absence of his sex, he would walk through life like a ghost, a permanent poster for the decline of toxic masculinity.

Sally moves to the bottom of the gurney, pulling Gillman's trouser leg up, placing one blade under his garment. Starts cutting upward, towards his groin, looking at his unfailingly defiant sneer as she heads north. — I'm impressed. They usually beg.

Maintaining his outward defiance, Gillman snarls in low contempt, — Fuck off, ya dopey hoor. You think anything's gaunny change jist cause you cut a few cocks off? Probably less likely, so cut the fuck away. No had a ride in ages that ah nivir peyed fir, so dinnae gie a toss, ay no.

— Well, I certainly do, and soon you won't be in a position to give a toss –

— ENOUGH. A loud, booming voice. Ray Lennox stands in a doorway. — It's over, Sally.

Sally freezes, then takes a step towards him, shears in her hand. — Ray . . . you're with us, I can tell.

— You've had shit to deal with. You want revenge. I get all that, Lennox concedes, — you know I do. But he's nothing to do with this.

At least Drummond had nothing to do with this. Gillman blinded himself with all this promotion jealousy.

— Come on, Ray, and she nods to Gillman, — you told me that you hated him, wanted him dead; you're on our side.

Gillman tries to turn his head to them. In open-mouthed incredulity, he struggles to put this together. — What the fuck . . . Lenny, ya cunt . . . Erskine . . . he was a Wall's Feast –

Lennox gives Gillman a guilty glance. — It was a figure of speech when I said that, he unconvincingly contends, twisting back to Sally. — I'm finding castration and genital mutilation a tough bandwagon to jump on. He moves forward, trying to position himself between Gillman and her. — Where's Vikram?

Sally suddenly charges at Gillman with the garden shears, raising them above her head, ready to drive them down into him, but Lennox dives protectively on top of his colleague. The shears gouge the side of his arm through the maroon Hugo Boss, scraping flesh, but it's enough to divert the strike onto the side of Dougie Gillman's breast. As Lennox lies face-to-face with Gillman, both men scream out.

Lennox rolls off the gurney, swings at Sally, knocking the shears out of her hand. She tries to retrieve them, but he stands on them, pinning her hand under them.

Sally squeals and pulls her hand out, running across towards her bag as Gillman shouts, — Get me the fuck untied!

Lennox is in two minds. Watches Sally grab something from the bag. Freezes in dread; believes it must be a gun. But it's a bottle, and Sally opens it, attempts to cram its contents into her mouth, before Lennox rips it out of her hand.

— Let me do this, she begs.

— DINNAE FUCKING STOP HER! Gillman screams from the trolley.

— No, Lennox declares, — you have a story to tell.

— Too late for that, and she runs through the set of doors which lead onto the flat roof.

Lennox follows her, as Gillman shouts out, — LENNY! UNTIE AYS, YA CUNT!!

But he is outside on the roof. On one side, the city winds upwards, the castle half shrouded in clouds. On the other: the flat, oily waters of the Forth. Sees Sally teeter close to the

324

edge. There is no balustrade. The wind swirls around them.
— No, Sally, please! Stand away from there!

Sally Hart half closes her eyes. Her garments billow. She puts out her arms as if she is preparing to fly upwards into the sun, rather than down into the horrendous concrete of the reclaimed land.

— Tell me what to do, Sally, Lennox begs, — you have to try and validate this. Otherwise it means nothing!

— No, Ray . . . it gets too messy, Sally opens her eyes and smiles at him, — you get implicated, and her voice is of the professional therapist. — If you wish to help me, and yourself, you will take the key from my bag, and she holds it up, — and go to my office and destroy the relevant parts of my notes on my laptop . . . the ones that have all your personal stuff in them . . . the other stuff might be interesting to your colleagues. Power will always wriggle off the hook. Terror is all it understands.

— No! I'm a cynical fucker, you know that, Sally! But there has to be another way! Where is he? Where's Rawat?

— No, Ray, the biographer has to finish the story . . . Her voice fades to a dull rasp in the gale. A flash of fear, hesitancy in her eyes.

— It's not your biography, you just stumbled on it through the work you do . . . please, Sally, just tell me where he is . . .

She looks thoughtful, and says, almost to herself, — The very last place you would want to go.

— WHAT DOES THAT MEAN? he cries out in exasperation.

— It means that you have good intentions, but ultimately you're a servant of the state. It's the shame that kills, she smiles, wobbling back.

— I'M RESIGNING! PLEASE!

325

— Too late, and she hurls her bag at him. — Office keys are in there, she says as Lennox inches closer, about to lunge at her. Then Sally Hart launches herself backwards, and as he feels his fingertips brush the material of her dress, she vanishes silently from his sight. Lennox, at the edge, feels himself sway and rock, and is only saved by a change in the direction of the wind, now blasting into his chest, giving him the traction to fall onto the firm terrain, looking up to the clouds, as he gasps for breath, grabbing her bag, fearfully clutching it to his chest like it's a Bible. He turns prone and slides his head over the ledge and can see her, the blonde hair and the red dress, the blood already pooling out slowly from her shattered body on the concrete. Scoots back from the abyss until he feels confident enough to stand up in the buffeting wind.

With shaking hands, he searches through the bag. There is only one set of keys. He pockets them and dusts his prints off the bag before tossing it over the edge.

When he gets back inside, Gillman has thrown himself to the floor, taking the gurney with him. He has injured himself in this act. Still bound securely, blood spills from a mouth that pleads, — LENNY! FUCK SAKES!

Lennox cuts him free and helps him to his feet. Gillman looks at him. — Where is she . . . ? and he darts out the door, looking over the flat roof. — She fucking jump, aye?

— Aye.

— Just as well for that fuckin hoor, he snarls, spitting out some more blood. — Did she say who the other cunt wis?

Lennox decides to use Gillman's rage. — There's a guy in the other tower, cuffed to a pipe, you might want to have a wee word with before you book him and take him in. He heads to the stairs.

— What are you gaunny dae?

— I'll explain later, just make the arrest.

— Thanks for that, Lenny. Gillman pats his groin. — Got attached to this.

Lennox nods, heads out to the empty lift. Jumps inside. With every floor it clears he thinks of Sally.

Oh, Sally, they did a number on you . . . really fucked you up. You threw everything at it but couldn't get past it. Please, please, Sally, be at peace . . .

Why did you tell her that you were resigning?

When he gets outside he heads straight to the Alfa Romeo. Can't look at her smashed body. *You've seen too many bodies distorted by violence. Leave that to the real polis to witness.*

Maybe you are resigning.

Drives through the traffic, passing a shrieking ambulance, probably the one that will take the body of Sally Hart to the morgue. Gillman won't hang around, and he can't afford to. In his left hand as it grips the wheel, the keys to Sally's Albany Street consulting rooms. Driving to the New Town, he pulls in at the parallel Dublin Street Lane, heading back round on foot. The rainfall has cleared the street as he reaches the building doing a double take before he descends the steps and lets himself in. Just as he gets his hands on what he needs, a second set of siren screeches fill the air.

They are coming for this. Your own people are hunting you down.

Instead of going back out the front, he opens the French windows and heads up some steps into the backcourt. Hopes the driving rain and the big stone walls of bourgeois privacy, in one of the most built-up areas in the UK, will do its job. Does not look above to the windows, all that would do is show any onlookers his face. He steals across the backcourt, forcing a rear door in the backing tenements, moving through the building, emerging into the cobbled Dublin Street Lane.

As he rendezvous with the car, paranoia rips through him. The torment about the *very last place* he'd want to go pulses through his brain and he picks the obvious. Heading out to the Colinton Tunnel, he finds it rendered less threatening by new lights and artwork.

Nobody is there.

No ghosts.

He feels crushed. Laughs at his ridiculous flights of fancy. *The last place you want to be? Fettes? Home?*

His iPhone flashes a reminder: INTERVIEW TOMORROW 11 A.M.

43

She's gone. But Sally exits knowing that her work was almost completed; Gulliver and Erskine dead and castrated, Piggot-Wilkins under house arrest, mutilated and terrorised, as he and his ilk sweat about who is next on the list. Not a bad result.

But she's gone. Just like Roya before her. This beautiful angel of vengeance is now no more. Shattered by gravity and concrete after hurtling herself from the roof of that mill.

And Lennox will pay.

But I must now stay concealed until it's time to strike. I got cavalier on the back of our success when Lennox almost got me in that hospital as I went to try and finish off Lauren Fairchild. I now wish I'd been more focused when I tried to run down him and that fat, corrupt Met mess outside the Savoy. That could all be pinned on that freak Gayle. But I was self-indulgent. Set a little test for Sally; to see how she might react to the demise of her favourite cop. I'm glad I missed him back then. Because the worst thing you can do to a man is not to kill him, but instead compel him to live a life of guilt, fear and misery. I don't need to eliminate him. This time, I'll let him do the heavy lifting in his own demise.

Day Seven

Monday

44

In his flat, Ray Lennox unscrews a panel in his bathroom. Exposes a set of lagged pipes, behind which he conceals Sally's laptop. It sits nicely there, the hot pipe away from the casing and unlikely to damage the device. Screwing the panel back, he goes to bed and falls into a troubled slumber. Dreams that the Internal Investigations men are in the flat, looking around.

The light is barely rising as he wakens, paranoia scything him. He unscrews the plasterboard, to check on the stashed article containing secrets that might have – or probably not – made heads roll in a previous era. It's impossible it has been taken or damaged in the night, but he's massively relieved when he secures it in his hands. It contains the dark secrets of so many: including his own.

It may include the story that Vik Rawat, the crazed biographer, was writing in revenge. It will have stuff on Billy Lake. Perhaps even more secrets of Confectioner.

But he can't have the laptop at home. Found in his possession, he would go to prison. Lennox racks his brains: it's over an hour's drive to the only safe haven he can think of.

Reaching his sister's place in Perthshire, to which he still has the keys, he's gratified to see no parked cars outside. Yet his senses are edgy despite the lack of visible signs of occupancy. Lennox tenses himself, as he can't escape the feeling . . .

Somebody has been here . . .

Then a bloodcurdling shriek: — FUCK YOU!! . . . only to

see that the young man standing before him, wielding a knife, is his nephew. Fraser wears a pair of jeans and a Primal Scream T-shirt. — Uncle Ray . . . He drops the knife and starts to sob. — They threatened to kill them . . . said if I went to you . . . Gayle . . . I think they hurt Lauren!

No, that was somebody much worse. Another man, who has darker eyes. You can see them now, between the mask and cap . . .

— You're okay, pal, you did good, tried to protect your family by keeping them away from your shit with Gayle and the group. Fraser could not be expected to know that Gayle, who seemed such an omnipotent bully in his life, was in turn scared of the manipulation of Vikram. Lennox hugs the boy in relief. He cannot believe it. So averse to this place after being here with Trudi, he didn't think it was the obvious place his nephew could hide.

— I came here . . . I've been living off Pot Noodles from the local store, Fraser says quietly, points at some cartons. — Is Mum pissed off?

— Don't worry about that. Let's get some tea. He switches on the kettle, removing the laptop from his bag. — What do you know about computers?

— What? Well, more than an old Gen X dinosaur like you!

Relieved that Fraser has recovered his levity, Lennox takes out the laptop. — I need a password for this.

— Do you know the user account?

— No.

— Do you know the user email?

— Yes . . . Lennox goes into his phone, shows Fraser, who copies it down.

— I'll try.

— Okay . . . you have to come home with me.

— No. Fraser shakes his head emphatically. — Not yet.

I'm fine here just now. Gayle said there were other people they were involved with and they were watching my movements.

— That's bullshit, pal.

— No, Fraser says defiantly, — I'm not going back into town in case I lead them to Mum, Dad and Murdo. Besides, you want me to crack this for you, right?

— Okay, Lennox concedes, thinking about the interview and his future, such as it is. — I have to go now. I'll just be a few hours. You must stay inside at all times.

— Right . . .

— Promise me you'll stay the fuck inside!

Fraser nods tightly.

— But we get a picture, a head-and-shoulder shot, which I send to your mum. She won't be able to determine the locale, but she'll know you're safe. That's the only condition I'm letting you stay.

— Okay, he concedes and Lennox takes a shot.

Lennox gets back in the car. He looks around: there's nobody about. Drives down the winding track onto the village road, then the small main street, through the deserted-looking settlement. It's eerie, but this is good. It's still so early, and not a single car passes him on the way. Sends the photo of a smiling, thumbs-up Fraser to Jackie with accompanying text:

> As you can see, all is good.
> He'll be home soon, and that's
> a promise.

Ignoring the wave of texts coming back from her, Lennox radios in to see if they've picked up Vikram Rawat. McCorkel tells him they're combing the area and that they've been through Sally's office. — What did you find?

— Her laptop's gone. It has all her records on it.

There's a pause and Lennox wonders if the logical McCorkel has gone full cop and is trying to trip him up. — Any way of tracking it?

— We're on it, but it might take some time.

— Right, Scott, thanks. If you hear anything, let me know. I'm just getting in.

As soon as he hangs up, pulling into Fettes car park, a call from Drummond comes in. He knows what it will be about. — Good work, Ray.

Lennox has seldom enjoyed his own deafening silence more.

— I mean, you found Sally . . . that was such a shock . . . Drummond stumbles, then cuts to the chase. — Do you know about her laptop? Now she can't even try to disguise the panic in her voice: her file is on there.

Her anxiety encourages Lennox to step in with his most measured response for some time. — I'm wagering that Vikram Rawat has it. When we get him, we'll find it.

— Doesn't it bother you? Drummond's voice is high, almost screeching in its desperation, as Lennox steps out of the Alfa Romeo and heads to the entrance. — I mean with your files on it?

— Obviously, I'm concerned . . . He stands in a puddle and feels water splash into the arch of his foot. Stifles a curse. Enters the building.

— You should reconsider your attitude, Ray, to the promotion, she contends. — It was you who found Sally. You're the hot favourite!

Lennox can't resist, as he heads down the corridor, — You led me to her, remember? I didn't pick up on anything.

— I didn't suspect, Ray, Drummond mournfully confesses

336

in a low voice. — You do see how potentially embarrassing that could be?

— I didn't either. Not until it was too late for Erskine.

What did you tell Sally? What's on that file? What did Drummond tell her?

He kills the call. Quickly hangs up his jacket in the office. Exits, turning the corner to find Drummond sat outside the boardroom in a long corridor that displays bad artwork. She flushes briefly on seeing him, putting her phone away, not responding to him playfully pointing at her. The calm demeanour is restored, and she looks the part in a bottle-green suit and flat black shoes. Drummond, he considers, plays the organisational game well. Will give the slick and polished interview befitting a high-flyer.

Lennox, painfully aware of his unkempt and unshaven appearance, sits close to her on one of the upholstered chairs, as Drummond informs him, — Dougie's just gone in this minute, and she types some notes on her iPad. Confirmation she doesn't want to talk about anything, let alone *them*. Just as Lennox is about to fiddle with his own phone in solidarity, Gillman storms out. Halts on seeing them, his lip curled up in contempt.

Drummond looks at him in shock. — Dougie, what's wrong? You've only been in there for three minutes!

Lennox fights down a childish smirk, beset with the notion of Gillman on top of a prostitute in one of the saunas he frequents. Opts not to show his nervous humour as Gillman hisses, pointing back at the instantly closed door where the panel deliberate, — Ah telt they cunts they wir fucking scum fir gaun ahead with this shite when a senior detective in this department has just been murdered and mutilated. He glances vindictively back towards the room. — Doubt you'll dae the

same, he shouts at Lennox. Then he points at Drummond.
— Ken you'll no!

Your three minutes is two minutes longer than it'll take me.
Lennox smiles coldly at him. — Your baws, he nods to Gillman's groin, as Drummond looks on aghast, — I should have
let her set them free. Sadly, they're still attached to that mess,
and his finger travels upwards, levelling at Gillman's face.

— Aye, well, thanks again, Lenny, but Norrie's urnae! And
that means fuck all tae they cunts in there!

A beaming Drummond's eyes water, as an equally red-
faced panel member opens the door to call her inside, his head
swivelling in relief as the departing Gillman heads off, like a
storm blowing out. Amanda Drummond rises and moves
towards the boardroom, her flat heels clicking on the polished
floor, composed again, Lennox thinks, already reconfiguring
Gillman's outburst as something that will work to her advantage. Her presentation will be all about equal opportunities,
recruitment of female and mixed-race graduates to detoxify
the poisonous old-white-men environment of Serious Crimes,
as well as better information technology and communication
systems, and counselling for officers with stress, burnout and
alcohol issues.

And she'd be right.
It really is her time.
But she's inexperienced. She needs a hand.

Lennox knows what he has to do. — Amanda, wait a
second, please, he shouts. Drummond looks round at him,
puzzled. Her expression mirrored by the one on the ruddy,
portly man, waiting by the door, who moves towards Lennox. — I'm Rikki Knox, head of Glasgow Serious Crimes.

— I know that, Lennox says. He and Chic Gallagher have
shared moans about Knox and Toal down the years.

— What seems to be the trouble . . . Knox looks at the sheet in his hand, — DI Lennox?

— I'd like to go next. I won't take up much of your time.

— DI Drummond here is next. Knox looks to Amanda Drummond.

Another fucking jobsworth twat. Chic was right about him.

Drummond regards Lennox with a wild-eyed stare of violation. Then calculation fuses in her eyes as she seems to scent opportunity. Shrugs. — It's okay.

— Well, if you've no objections . . . Knox nods to her. Ushering Lennox inside, he suddenly displays bonhomie, whispering in his ear, — Well done on the Gulliver and Erskine murders, and he points to a vacant chair. At a long boardroom table, Knox sits down beside his slightly puzzled colleagues whom he introduces as Chief Constable Jim Niddrie, Cecilia Parish from the Police Committee and Edinburgh council, Bob Toal, and the unfortunately named Archie Mazzlo, from the Police Committee and Scottish government, whose insistence that police resources were prioritised for certain types of youthful delinquent crimes led to the widespread use of the phrase *Mazzlo's hierarchy of neds,* which made it from canteen to tabloids. — DI Drummond has agreed to change the running order with DI Lennox here, Knox explains in studied neutrality.

Lennox sits opposite them, glancing at the stern portraits of Chief Constables past that adorn the walls. All of them old white men. Yes, the force really could do with modernising.

Archie Mazzlo kicks off. — I suppose the most obvious question, DI Lennox, is what makes you want this job?

— Well, says Lennox, and he sees Sally falling into oblivion, a blonde Icarus who flew too close to the sun, to end up smashed on reclaimed land at the bottom of Chancelot Mill.

I'M RESIGNING! PLEASE! He draws in a deep breath. — I've had a good, long, hard think about it and I've decided that I don't want it.

The panel members regard each other. Eventually Mazzlo, gaping at Lennox, asks, — What? Can you explain?

Lennox twists his head slowly around the group. — It just isn't for me.

Celia Parish turns to Toal. — What is going on with the men in your department?

Toal maintains his composure, but his features seem to slacken and fall south as he looks to Lennox in an exhausted compassion. — Can you please give us your reasoning here, Ray?

— I'm sorry I wasted your time. But the force is wasting a lot of people's time. I know that in different ways you've all been able to make your peace with this. Good on you. Unfortunately, I can't any more, and he rises from the chair.

— What are you saying here, Ray? Toal's visible hurt and sorrow strikes Lennox deeply.

— I'm saying . . . that I'm done here. I'm tendering my resignation.

Celia Parish's face is pinched. — Can I ask why? You have an established career –

— I was never really here, Ray Lennox says, turning and walking away.

As the selection committee members look to each other in surprise at his departure, pontificating in whispers about his stress levels, mental health, medication, counselling, they miss a smile as wide as the River Forth estuary on the departing detective.

He strides out past a shocked Amanda Drummond. — It's all yours.

45

A spunky, defiant kid, he put up a spirited resistance. But I know to my cost the futility of being a boy in face of real power. Ultimately, the same goes for being a man and a woman. We had this awareness of being doomed, way before the start of this enterprise. The problem for the likes of Piggot-Wilkins, Gulliver and Erskine was that they were too, but without realising it. Yes, we had a good run, but the state is closing in on us, in its unrelenting, monolithic way. Our terror campaign was successful; I know through my contacts that after the Gulliver and Piggot-Wilkins incidents, the abusive men of power felt fear. Doubled up on their security. Enlisted more servants from the working class to protect them, purchased by the bemused taxpayer, even as they planned to loot our coffers more.

And Lennox, this useful tool for them, simply has to be hurt. Needs to feel the pain of knowing that he dragged his nephew into this. If he's wise enough to realise, or brave enough to come to where we are heading, he will bear witness to his nephew having his hand removed.

Thank you for leading me to what you care about, Lennox.

46

Glover and McCorkel physically cower in their seats as Dougie Gillman storms into the office, grabs his jacket from the back of his chair, causing it to topple, and roars: — AH TELT THE CUNTS TAE STICK THEIR FUCKIN JOB UP THEIR ERSES! His rage instantly turns to shock: the last person he expects to see coming in behind him is Ray Lennox. — What the fuck . . .

— Looks like we were reading from the same script, Lennox says nonchalantly, grabbing his own Hugo Boss jacket from a hook on the wall by his desk. — I'm out of here.

Thus the two men find themselves not so much following each other, as bound by the same energy, which they allow to propel them out of the police headquarters and into the drizzly streets of Stockbridge.

— I smashed that fucking weirdo, Gillman rasps through the silence, perhaps unnerved at Lennox's manic profile. — Big unit, mind, n eh hud a bit ay fight that needed battered out ay him. Nice ay ye to dae the cunt and shackle him up first, he says, a certain amount of both gratitude and admiration in his tone, his gaze asking: *how did you manage that?*

— I got lucky, Lennox swivels to him. — It happens, and he thinks of Thailand. Hopes Gillman does too. — Get anything more oot ay the cunt?

— Probably nowt you dinnae already ken. It wisnae him that did McVittie, or Lauren, or whatever he calls himself now. I think aw this sex-change stuff is for mental cunts, but Jim was one ay us, Gillman concedes as they walk down Raeburn Place.

One ay what?

Lennox elects to keep his counsel. Other people's gender, unless the desire and possibility of sleeping with them exists, remains of little interest. It's only 11.30, and while not united enough to jump a cab up to the Repair Shop, they opt to tap on the door of a local Stockbridge hostelry well known to police officers. The proprietor affords them entry. — One of those days? he enquires, serving up the drinks.

Both men smash down their first Stellas in a series of bonding gulps. Gillman thumps the base of the glass on the bar like it's a gauntlet as two more are ordered. — Thanks, n ah mean it, he mumbles.

Lennox's features remain immobile. — Ah wis waiting ootside, praying that she'd get the fuck oan wi it.

A dry laughter erupts from Gillman, shaking his shoulders. It promptly stops. — You and me never got on, Lenny, and we'll probably still no.

This cunt has a funny way of expressing gratitude.

— Well, they say it takes all sorts, Dougie.

— But ah owe ye big time, and ah never let a debt slide.

— Well, you owe me a fuckin jaikit, he scoffs, looking at the ripped sleeve on his Hugo Boss.

— Aye . . . right . . . I'll get that nicely repaired though. I ken a boy in the Coogate, Gillman says, his head whipping over to the jukebox. — This place is fuckin Lou Reed, he contends. — I'll pit some music on.

Lennox, now strangely a brother-in-arms with his old enemy, nods as Gillman heads over. He wonders where Drummond will be celebrating. Sends her a text:

Congratulations. The best
person got the job. x

343

Bachman–Turner Overdrive's 'You Ain't Seen Nothing Yet' blasts out from the sound system as Gillman returns, making intent inroads into his second pint. Lennox is impressed at how he attacks a glass of alcohol as if it's a nonce. Gulping half of it back and setting the glass down with an intense scowl, he asks for the umpteenth time, — Ye really handed your notice in?

— Aye.

— What will ye dae?

— Fuck knows.

Gillman shakes his head in disbelief. — Cannae fucking believe it. He unleashes more damage on his lager. — No that long oot ay uniform, DI last year, now Chief Super. It's a fucking insult. The job is fucked. Nae wonder yir off, Lenny. But I do owe ye an apology, and he fixes Lennox in a serious stare, signalling up for two more drinks as Whitesnake's 'Here I Go Again' strikes up. — Ah thoat Drummond wis the killer. That Ms X story; ah'd been aw ower that shite. Aye, I let personal shit colour my judgement.

— It happens, Lennox confesses. *You thought she was the killer too.*

Then Gillman moves close, dropping his voice and leering pugnaciously. — I thought you were just defending her because you rode her.

— I thought you were down on her cause you didnae.

Gillman snorts in derision, but his expression turns to stern approval, as Lennox orders two Macallans.

The other male Serious Crimes officers, hearing of the burgeoning session, troop in. Lennox and Gillman learn that Drummond's default victory is only a partial one. She has been appointed as joint head, with Robbie Sives, a veteran senior detective from Tayside. He will work with her for two years, before stepping aside to retire, when she will take over in earnest. Gillman is far from appeased. — If she wis up tae the job, they'd appoint her, end of. Joint Chief Super . . . she gets fucking featherbedded in. Like tae see a male officer get that fucking treatment. Fucking nursery-school shite!

The drinks continue to slide down. There's no doubt that Erskine's demise has fundamentally rocked this coalition of the embittered, inebriated and confused. Lennox experiences an incredible liberation, knowing that he's free from all this.

It's done.

It's over.

They have an all-points bulletin out on Vikram Rawat and they'll find him.

He thinks of Hollis and craves a line of ching. Only the arrival of McCorkel, who enters with Inglis, stops him smashing one back. He's no intention of introducing a fresh young cop to cocaine in the same way a former senior partner did with him.

Now he has to get back to the cottage to bring Fraser home to Jackie. He will fight the power and slip away quietly out the side door, without saying goodbye to his colleagues. He's had too much to drive, but still being a cop has its advantages and he drives better drunk. Idly elated about escaping undetected, he surveys the murky streets, doubling back to Fettes car park for the Alfa Romeo.

The bone-searing cold of autumn cuts through his layers, biting away at his flesh. Fortunately, it's dry and windless, so the purgatory is lessened as he walks with purpose through Stockbridge. Lennox moves on, as dampness starts to roll in from the sea. A clinging, consumptive mist insinuates in the air. The cold seems to have set up home in his back's nerve endings, causing him to hunch his shoulders. When he gets to the car, he calls Drummond. She still isn't picking up. — Congratulations . . .

Drives out the city, back to the cottage. On approach, the whitewashed building seems ominously inert, dark clouds above it. A sinister, overwhelming feeling of despair grips him as he pushes open the unlocked door.

Inside the place is wrecked. There's no sign of Fraser, only evidence that he struggled. No blood. Fraser fought, but he was taken.

Lennox goes back outside and his heart sinks further as he sees tyre marks stretching to the top of the road.

Rawat . . . he tracked you right here . . . he was waiting at Chancelot Mill . . . was watching the flat . . .

You have fucked up monumentally. You need to find him. It's the laptop he was after . . .

Lennox runs back in. Sally's laptop, like Fraser, has gone.

Just as he thinks this, the phone indicates a message from: Fraser. Lennox's blood runs cold. Knows it's not from his nephew. It's a video. It shows Fraser in a dark space, lit by torchlight. His arm is secured to a wooden workbench. There's a rasping buzz, and a power saw is held up to shot. An educated off-camera voice says: — Your nephew is about to lose a hand. You should be here to witness it. You do not have much time, DI Lennox.

He gets back in the car, tearing towards the city at high speed. Drummond calls, and he puts her on speakerphone.

— I should thank you, she gracelessly says, then after a short hesitation, — That was quite a performance from you and Dougie. I'm pleased to be recognised, and I'm looking forward to working with Robbie Sives, but I don't like being handed things on a plate.

Why the fuck did you leave the little bastard? Rawat has been trailing you. He's been one jump ahead all the way . . .

— You're the best person for the job, Amanda, he responds mechanically. — If the department's gaunny modernise, it needs people like you.

— But it needs people like you too, Ray. What were you thinking, walking out like that? What will you do?

You will exhale that breath you've been holding on to for years . . . it's a tunnel . . . it's the Colinton Tunnel . . . but there's nothing there like that now, it's all bright art . . .

— Honestly can't say.

Fraser. We'll go to Tynecastle again, pal.

A silence on the speaker is followed by, — Look, Ray, about the other night, it's best if you don't phone me on matters that have nothing to do with work . . . She stalls, then adds assertively, — You and I . . . that was a mistake.

Mistake? No, Ray Lennox makes mistakes. Big mistakes. Amanda Drummond makes petty errors. She's the best person not just for this job, but for this life.

— Whatever you say. I'll be out with almost immediate effect as I have leave due me.

Rawat . . . where the fuck . . . the darkness . . . the last place you want to be . . .

— Ray . . .

— So not only will we never sleep together again, we'll never work together again, he says with a dramatic pause, making him feel disconcertingly like Stuart. — That should save a ton of social embarrassment.

Jackie . . . you promised her you'd bring him back . . . what the fuck were you thinking? You had him with you. YOU FUCK-ING HAD HIM WITH YOU.

— Oh, please! Don't try to make your resignation out to be about what happened between us. You don't even believe that yourself . . . and she's babbling on but Lennox can't hear her as he's scythed by an invasive thought:

IT'S NOT THE COLINTON TUNNEL!

His run several days back, before Toal called about Gulliver's body being found in the warehouse. How he told

Sally he couldn't go through the long tunnel under Arthur's Seat.

The Innocent Tunnel.

He slams the call off, searching the tunnel on his smartphone. It's been blocked off at both ends for two days. Repairs on some subsidence. What is inside?

47

I look at the young man with a certain degree of pity. His bulging eyes, full of fear above the tight gag I have placed over his mouth. I switch on the camera, which stands on its tripod. Your heart has to be cold to do this. I'm concerned that now, religious zeal aside, there is little to differentiate me from Cousin Bette. But that's the power of the monster: to contaminate. I think back to that ridiculous figure, contemplating the childhood of beatings, humiliation and abuse Bette must have undergone, in order to come out like that.

But this young man will survive, as I did. Who knows what this will do to him? It will certainly give him something to hang every subsequent problem he has in his life on. What a gift I now bestow! For, perhaps strangely, I have no regrets about my own existence. It passed in a sequence of disasters when my parents were murdered and then Roya was raped and took her own life. It may be that he, too, will now lead a more interesting one as a result of this amputation.

It's Lennox who will carry the real pain. He's too sensitive to be efficient at enforcing the silly laws of a disintegrating order. Now his nephew will pay for his inability to understand this.

And as there's nobody else to bear witness, the youth has to listen to my story.

— Sorry about the gag, I explain, — but what you have to say has no relevance. I'm the one with the power, and you are silenced.

The boy's pupils widen. He seems to get it.

— I became a biographer, working exclusively with people I didn't like. Mainly the ones who had the knowledge of others I liked even less. A gangster named Lake told me he outsourced many of his operations, using people who wouldn't ordinarily be traced back to him. But all the idiot was doing was furnishing me with his network of associates, whom I could then manipulate. I learned that a specimen called Toby Wallingham provided rich sex abusers like Christopher Piggot-Wilkins with his victims. So I decided to use Wallingham to engineer a conflict between Piggot-Wilkins and Lake. To stand aside and watch Lake destroy him, then go to prison for this . . . But I'm sorry, I look at the bemused eyes of the young man, — these names mean nothing to you. Nor should they . . . I turn to the blinking red light above the cold camera eye, — But this, as I said, is not for you.

— But Sally Hart . . . and a subverting convulsion bubbles up inside my chest, — she convinced me we had to destroy Piggot-Wilkins ourselves. That my way was too cold-blooded. We had to drink their fear. So while the original plan was superfluous, all its elements remained in place. In one of his many unguarded moments, Lake boasted about the Met source that helped him 'get rid of beasts'. I investigated further, finding out that this was a DI Mark Hollis. I thought it might be amusing to have him unwittingly pulp his partner, through the obnoxious Wallingham. It's easy to divide the confused, the demoralised and those blinded by their own sense of narcissistic entitlement. All just mischief really. It's so strange but what you learn about those men who wield power and randomly destroy our lives is that they're just stupid, bored and unsatisfied. It's the human condition . . .

The boy's eyes seem to bulge further. His face is red. The gag must be choking him. But it will be removed when Lennox enters the tunnel, in order to hear his nephew scream out.

— And you are welcome to it. Minus your hand, unfortunately.

48

He can scarcely feel the shivers now, in the heat of his car. The sense that he is doing this on his own flows through him. It always feels better that way, like in Miami. To be unleashed, unconstrained. The hangover will kick in soon enough. It will be bundled with the dread that he is acting outside of the authority of a state that never responds well to those who fail to recognise its monopoly of violence. But right now, all Ray Lennox is aware of is the metal taste of vengeance in his mouth. His pumping lungs. His heart beating. Just another one in the billions around this planet. Like all of them, his will, at some point, come to its last beat. His body will atrophy and decay. Until then he can think of nothing better to do than this.

The Alfa Romeo carrying him through the city. Oddly like part of him. A force. The engine almost silent.

Fuck the polis.

He stops at the Repair Shop. It's empty. The *boys* – his (former) colleagues – are still in the Stockbridge pub. Orders a double Macallan, knocks it back, asks for another and heads to the toilet where he blasts a line of ching. Pulls a marker pen from his pocket. Writes on the wall:

**ACAB
LENNY
BAR-OX
HMFC**

Laughs manically at his work.

See what the cunts make ay that!

He's had his Dutch courage; he heads to the place of dread. Walks through the mundane development of flats in the gloomy sprinkle. It lies ahead, dark, menacing and incongruous. A chill under his skin; it twists in a spasm down his back. Thinks of how it might seem to a child growing up in such housing, like a portal to a darker, more mysterious world.

Now it's sealed. The bollards and the mesh fencing evident on his last abortive visit have been deployed to cordon the tunnel off. Just on the other side of the barrier, scaffolding pokes into its darkness. He tentatively patrols the sealed mouth, looks at where he might gain access. A door in the mesh fence; padlocked. But in between the edge of the barricade and the wall of the tunnel, a space where the fence post is squeezed into a concrete base. He can slide through the gap; not that easily, but it can be done.

Yet he hesitates.

His heart is booming. The pressure in his ears. The oxygen in his lungs losing its richness. He looks back around the flats. They are completely silent. Only one car parked outside them.

He thinks of Fraser.

Steps inside. As he pushes himself through the gap, he feels his nose and testicles squeezed tight. Thinks of Gulliver and Erskine as he forces them through.

Inside it's dark; the tunnel's overhead lights are switched off. Lennox can do nothing but walk into the black void. After only a few steps the various dark shadows he can discern melt into a formless mass. The air is thin. His heart thumps and his skin creeps. He can see nothing in front of him. Feels he might stumble. Turns his head back, just as his momentum carries him another step forward, compelling him to witness

352

the meagre light behind him fade to pitch-black. Is it possible to witness total blackness?

Lennox senses the tunnel and its darkness have swallowed him up. Part of him wants to run, retreat, call for help, try to gain access from the other end, in the park. But no. He needs to be here. And not just for Fraser.

Carries on into the abyss. Reaches for the phone in his pocket. Operates the torch function. A shaking in his legs.

Fight through it. There are no monsters. You arnae a wee laddie.

Slips off his Hugo Boss jacket, opting for the kickboxer's mobility. As he tosses it sideways into the darkness, a scuttling sound, and a voice suddenly booms out from behind him,
— You don't like tunnels, do you?

Lennox whips round. Nothing but blackness. The voice seems to be coming from his right. He roars at the source,
— WHERE IS HE?!

— Bad things happen to little boys who go into tunnels. You know this, Ray Lennox.

— Where's my fuckin nephew, ya cunt?!

The response is a brief glint of metal in the paltry light from Lennox's phone, before it makes heavy contact with his face, snapping his neck back.

He raises his hand as it again swings his way but he can't deflect it and feels it smash into his jaw as his iPhone flies away. The third strike he does parry, but it's the worst of them all, deadening his arm, which falls helplessly by his side. A sickening pain assails him and Lennox can do nothing, the contents of his stomach exploding from him in the dank air. Ironically this causes his assailant some distress, as his foe lets out a curse, and Ray Lennox senses him taking a backward step, to avoid the splash of vomit. Then he rushes forward and another blow strikes the detective, who feels the ground rising to meet him in the darkness. Then a great force is on him, pinning him down. In the light of his dropped phone, all he can see of the form sitting on him are white teeth and a huge brass hand, poised to strike.

It's all over. He's finished. The pain will end where it all started: in another dark tunnel in this ancient city.

Then, to his surprise the man hesitates. He seems to be jolting and jerking . . . his muscles spasming as he suddenly falls on Lennox and holds him tightly. Two large eyes pop out of the darkness at him, and Ray Lennox flashes back to his ten-year-old self in the tunnel, the one who avoided the fate of Les Brodie, which he now seems set to experience as a man, too weak to fight off this rapist, both men locked together in a bizarre St Vitus's dance. But there's something wrong with the man on top of him, it's like an invasive current is burning through his body, coiling it. His grip on Lennox tightens, that metal hand digging into his back, then it relaxes, as his nerve ends are fried, and his opponent's mass slumps over Ray Lennox.

Lennox feels an arm grabbing his, pulling his panicking frame out from underneath the stricken man. He looks up to see Brian Harkness, lit by his phone torch, yanking him to freedom, before giving the stunned, prone body another blast of the taser gun he operates with his other arm. — Saw you coming out the pub . . . didn't like your body lingo, so follayed ye here . . .

— Brian . . . thanks . . . is as much as Lennox can manage, as he sees the taser threads like spiderwebs glimmer under the light of the phone, which he picks up to retrieve. Harkness, mindful of the brass hand, cuffs the grounded figure alongside him above the elbows.

They find Fraser almost immediately, on what looks and smells like a piss-stained mattress. Bound with plastic ties and almost choking on a ball-gag, his arm is secured to a wooden bench. Lennox traces the torch beam along . . . to a stump.

OH FUCK NAW . . .

The boy's hand has gone.

But no, it's an illusion, and as the beetle-eyed Lennox shines the torch closer, he sees his discarded jacket has landed over the bench, covering Fraser's hand. He pulls it away to find it still intact. The boy has severe bruising on one side of his face. As Lennox removes the gag and Harkness cuts the constraints, Fraser gaspingly intones, — I told him nothing, Uncle Ray . . .

Harkness gets the meaning of Lennox's glance and goes over to the stricken Rawat, leaving Lennox to whisper, — Are you okay?

— Yes. He didn't get it, and Fraser drops his voice out of Brian Harkness's earshot. — You know, what he was after. It's at Condor's place. He turned the cottage upside down, but he never checked Condor's kennel. I told him you had locked it in your desk at police headquarters.

— He didn't see it . . . *ah didnae* see it, Lennox gasps in disbelief.

How did you last so long as a detective . . . and how the fuck did that cunt as a reporter . . . ?

— I heard him coming in through the front door so I ran out the back and put it in the kennel, under the blanket. Then I went back round to confront him, but he has this metal hand and he's a big guy, Fraser says in his Merchant School tones. — I tried to give a decent account of myself, but he was too strong.

— You're a fucking hard-arsed little bastard. He holds Fraser by his shoulders and looks him in the eye. — Whatever you choose to designate yourself, you're a top human being. That's what I'll always think of you, that's who you are, and he embraces his nephew. — I'll bet you lasted longer against him than I did.

Suddenly an all-too-familiar voice roars out of the darkness, — WE FARKING WELL GOT IT FROM HERE!

A flashlight, and Billy Lake's big square head appears.

Lennox feels a crushing dread insinuate, as he steps in front of Fraser. Harkness stands up, pulls out police ID.

Then Hollis appears behind Lake, also carrying a torch. The apology in his eyes seems to Lennox like penitence. Now he's really worried.

Billy Lake seemed to exist in a perma-state of steroid rage. Now it has reached a new high. Lennox wonders how long Lake can live at this intensity, before he takes himself out by popping some vein or artery. Even under the poor lighting, his face is as if a few layers of skin have been torn from it and his eyes shine like demented beacons of Hades. Only his voice is incongruously calm, as he gapes at Rawat. — He's mine.

Lennox looks from him to Hollis, who explains, — Tracked you on the blower, Ray.

Out of his peripheral vision, the cartilage in Brian Harkness's neck bobbles. The Serious Crimes DS flashes the ID. — Police . . .

Ray Lennox knows only one thing: he needs Fraser to be out of here. Whatever happens next, he doesn't want him, or for that matter even Harkness, further embroiled in this. — No, Brian, Lennox says without looking at the cop, — I'll sort this. Take Fraser here back to his family, right now. He turns to face Harkness. — Will you do that for me?

Harkness's Adam's apple seems to have grown to the extent that it might choke its owner to death. — You sure, Ray?

— Yes. Do it.

Harkness hesitates only for a few seconds, looks at the murderous Lake, then Hollis, almost equally deranged, who flashes a Metropolitan Police ID, and says, — Like he says, we got this one, son. Good work.

Lennox forces as benign a smile as he can muster at Brian Harkness, who nods curtly at a grateful-looking Fraser, escorting the boy out the tunnel.

— What's happening then, chaps? Lennox asks Hollis and Lake, a weird composure asserting itself in him.

Lake points a thick finger at the broken biographer on the ground. — This cahnt took the piss. He's gonna pay for that. I ain't having no nonce of a judge pulling favours to keep him out of jail!

As Lennox considers this, Hollis sidles up to him and says urgently, — This is fucked, Ray, but Billy's right; we turn him in and it'll never go to trial. The cahnt can spill the lot on them posh nonces.

— They should have the lot spilled on them.

—⁼ Yes, they should. Vikram Rawat looks up in defiance from the cold, dusty gravel.

— SHUT IT, YOU CAHNT, and Lake silences him with a boot to the face.

Lennox thinks of Sally's laptop. *Your life is in Sally's files. Rawat is one of two fuckers who manipulated you and wanted you dead. But can you leave him with those two other mentalists?* — What happens if I let you two take him?

Lake's face contorts. — Just so we're clear, ain't no farking 'let' involved here, sahn.

— But to enlighten you, Hollis cuts in, — I beat every bit of information outta him, then carry on my war against them cahnts; by fair means or foul, he nods to Vikram Rawat, — makes no odds to me. Then I give him to Bill and he's fish food . . . except for that brass hand.

— We can do this together, Rawat says desperately, rubbernecking to Lennox. — Everything you need is on Sally's files – he has her laptop! He has this information. Tell them!

Hollis and Lake look at him, tumescent stares of incredulity.

— I wish, Lennox says softly. — But I think this one here, he looks at Vikram, — knows where it is. I'm walking out of here and leaving you guys to do what you do, and Ray Lennox turns and exits the tunnel, alone, heading towards the light, leaving one terrified predator in there at the mercy of two others. The screams do not last long, only briefly echoing in the curved structure. They will be taking this dance elsewhere.

As he slips back through the barricade, easier this time, texts, blanked by the tunnel, pop into his phone.

One from Jackie:

When is he coming home, Ray?

It's a relief to text back:

He's on his way with my colleague, Brian. Should be walking through the door any minute now. I'll be there in twenty minutes. Mine is a large Macallan.

A cold wind blows mucky sleet into his face, but Lennox whistles as he heads down the street. Thrusts his hands into his pockets. He needs a drink, hopes Jackie has the fire going in that front room. Only briefly does he think of the biographer, and the last chapter that Hollis and Lake, cop and villain undifferentiated are writing on his behalf. It astonishes him how it holds little interest. Perhaps Toal was right; maybe you get to the point where you're just done thinking about all that shit.

Ray Lennox watches his sister gratefully Venus fly-trapping her son on the couch, until Fraser protests he needs to go upstairs and change his clothing. The gratitude of Jackie, and that of his normally stoical brother-in-law, Angus, is both galling and humbling. Even Condor the Labrador seems to appreciate him, crashing out in front of Lennox before rolling back over his feet, to make contact with his shins. But it's also over-whelming, leaving him no place to go emotionally. Besides, he has something to do. Just one large Macallan and Ray Lennox is compelled to disturb the lazy dog and head off into the night.

He drives back to the cottage through the darkness, to retrieve the laptop. En route, a text from Fraser:

HHGH1902

The device is in the kennel, under the fur-covered dog blanket. He laughs loudly as he slides it out. Once again reflects on how Lennox, the detective, and Rawat, the investi-gative journalist, are both prisoners of the digital age: therefore incapable of detecting or investigating the physical item in front of them.

We are losing ourselves.

Of the many files, Lennox is primarily interested in his own. Then he looks at the file names of Sally's other clients. These include a few local worthies in business and politics, and a couple of police colleagues, most notably Amanda

Drummond. But the set that intrigue him most are the video files of Sally Hart talking to Vikram Rawat about the attacks on Piggot-Wilkins, Gulliver and Erskine, and their plans for people as diverse as Gillman, Lake, Confectioner, MPs, Cabinet ministers and three former PMs.

Lennox doesn't stall at the cottage. On the drive home he pulls into a lay-by and keys in the password: HHGH1902 . . . and starts downloading Sally's files onto a USB stick.

This proves fortuitous, as he has barely gotten settled into his flat when the inevitable compacted knock on the door comes. Slipping the USB into his pocket, he lets in Thickset and Thin Boy, the Internal Investigations men. Offers them coffee.

The chunky internal investigator shakes his bull head in the negative, and in the precise, clipped tones Lennox is already thinking of as *generic polis arsehole* declares, — We need you to hand over the laptop.

On cue Ray Lennox's phone rings, the caller ID indicating Toal.

Thickset nods for him to pick up.

Lennox pushes it hard to his ear. — Cooperate, Ray, Toal warns. — This is as heavy as it gets. Do exactly as they say, then come and see me at my place.

Lennox hangs up, looks at the investigators. — What do I get in return?

— To stay out of prison, Thin Boy says.

— You'll need to do better than that.

The cops remain silent. But they don't reach for the cuffs, which Lennox interprets as a sign that there is still some leeway, albeit limited, for negotiation.

— You can tear this place apart, but you won't find it here. He slowly shakes his head. — As a client of Sally Hart's, I want to erase my own personal files prior to handover. Also, those of Chief Super Designate Amanda Drummond.

— That's acceptable, Thickset says after a long pause. — We're not interested in those, and you are covered by the data protection act –

— Bollocks. Unless I'm a multimillionaire, or went to Eton, I'm covered by jack-fucking-shit, so don't waste my time. And you're internal investigators. You're interested in everything. Just leave now, and come back in twenty minutes.

The internal investigating cops hesitate, looking to each other. Then Thickset dispenses a surly nod and they depart. Lennox takes a holdall, waiting for several minutes before he leaves, heading to his local pub, knowing they'll be tailing him.

The place is empty, save a few seasoned career drinkers. Lennox orders a Guinness.

— Guinness is off, Jake Spiers, the smashed-toothed proprietor, gleefully informs him.

— Murphy's then, Lennox points at the font.

— No got any. Spiers pulls a phantom pint to illustrate. His teeth are like a row of condemned tenements.

— Stella then, Lennox wonders how long he can play this game.

Spiers looks put out, and gauchely pours a pint.

Taking his drink in a leisurely manner, Lennox enjoys the beer slowly sluicing the previous alcohol back through his system. Raises a playful glass at Spiers, who briefly glowers back at him in studied malevolence. Returning home, Lennox removes the device from its original hiding place: back in the toilet wall by the pipes. Placing the laptop on the table, he erases both his own and Amanda Drummond's files.

The two Internal Investigations men return and Lennox hands over the holdall, in which he's placed the computer.

That cunt Jake Spiers will soon be getting investigated in his rat-trap pub. Good.

They take the computer from the bag, putting it in a plastic evidence zipper. Then, with a straight-mouthed but laughing-eyed smile, Thickset says, — I hope you haven't copied any of those files.

— As if, Lennox says, feeling the USB burn in his jeans watch pocket. — I may be all shades of daft, but a copper in prison? Not what I aspire to, thank you.

That response seems to satisfy them. As soon as they take their leave, he is in a taxi to Bob Toal's house in Barnton. His boss welcomes him inside. They settle down in the quiet opulence of the lounge. Lennox is astonished at the postmodernist art gallery decor; white walls showing off high-concept abstract prints, mounted pieces of brass sculpture, tasteful floor-spotted lighting, a large open fire, and floor-to-ceiling windows looking out onto a patio and garden. Lennox would never have placed Toal in such a setting in a thousand years. Oddly congruent with the surroundings, his boss seems much younger, sporting a button-down shirt and straight-legged jeans. His wife Margaret, her greying blonde collar-length hair rendered tasteful platinum by strategic dye, is also a more youthful version than the formal, frumpy-dressed variety present at official functions. Not for the first time, Lennox realises he's miscast in the detective game. Sips at the malt Toal has provided. Not Macallan, but acceptable. — So, they get off scot-free, the establishment nonces, as per usual? Sally's type of vengeance is the only kind that challenges them?

— Who knows, Ray. Toal looks steadily at him. — How many sleepless nights do men who've perpetrated such deeds endure? Sins haunt us as we get older. The blitheness of youth goes as we slow down with nothing to do but dwell on our transgressions. Maybe for such men, that's purgatory. Might

362

even be divine retribution, Toal muses, looking at Lennox, then saying in playful, snidey tones, — And who knows how many other copies of those files are out there?

Lennox smiles, knows it no longer matters. The reality is that opposition has been rendered futile in our power-revering post-democratic paradigm. A Tory prime minister can be caught on camera bollock-deep in a screaming orphan, and the defeated masses would probably cheer him on. Power and privilege are untouchable. We either cow before it, or, worse, defend those who wield it with a truculent snarl. The children of the citizens are, for the one per cent and their underlings, merely the spoils of class war victory. Since winning that battle at Orgreave, they've strengthened their grip, consolidating power. No newspaper or TV channel will cover the content of such files, and when they appear on some quirky radical website they will be ignored or blithely dismissed as a hoax.

So Lennox spends most of the wee small hours drinking malt whisky with Bob Toal, two men who have barely sipped a coffee together, in all the years of working closely.

— The world is changing, Ray, Toal contends. — Spinning away from us all. It's not our time any more. The likes of you, me and Dougie Gillman, for different reasons, can't adapt. Whether it's on the streets or backstage with the power brokers, the politics and the rules have changed and we just don't get it. And you know what, Toal looks at him in sudden smugness, — I think I'm fine with that. It's ultimately not about my career or personal legacy. We're in this game to find the missing bairns that have been snatched by monsters. Then we lock up those beasts. End of. We're police officers, Ray.

— No, boss, I beg to differ, Lennox says passionately, as Toal leans to refill his cut-crystal glass. — The fuckers that mess around with dodgy tail lights and shoplifters are police officers. They are servants of the state. We monkeys in Serious Crimes serve the people. We serve the common good. We serve vengeance, and sees a brief flicker in his boss's eye. The kind of arousal indicating Toal was once like him, a doomed avenging spirit, before he salvaged himself in organisational realpolitik. — We do one of the very few jobs worth doing. Only I can't do it any more, cause the biggest nonces are in the corridors of power, and we can't touch the fuckers. We get the truck drivers from Hull.

— Always crusading, Ray. Toal grins. — I don't know what you'll do without the force!

A wee bit of travelling. Some festivals. Maybe a rave or two. And aye: a bit of shagging.

— What about you? What are you going to do?

— My garden, Ray. Toal's bushy brows, themselves in need of serious pruning, fly north. — God, I used to laugh at the old men who retired to tend them. Now I wish I'd been able to get to that place of tranquillity where I could enjoy it much earlier. But I can't explain that to you, he laughs, — you're still too young to get that sort of thing.

Regarding the youthful Toal, shorn of his working clothes, Lennox looks doubtful.

— One important thing. Toal gazes at a mantelpiece picture of Margaret, long retired to bed. — Find a woman. I know you'll be raw for a while after Trudi, but don't let up on that task. Find a life partner. Somebody who can help you become the best possible version of yourself.

This is the last recalled comment of profundity in a night that dissolves into a much more convivial alcoholic oblivion than Lennox has gotten used to lately. After drunkenly hugging his old boss on the doorstep and quipping, — Better inside the tent pissing out . . . I think, Lennox takes a cab home. Reflects that Toal isn't so bad: a different man away from the job. If his life partner has made him the best version of himself, it's evident that his employment has contrived to do the very reverse. Now, like him, Toal still has some repairs to undertake.

Maybe that's our lot. You're welcome, Amanda.

EPILOGUE

The next day Ray Lennox finds himself outside Saughton Prison, fragile in the weak sun on a cold, squally morning. Jayne Melville took a lot of persuading to get him *one more* last visit. He told her he was off the force officially next month. This would be the very last chance to get more names of missing girls from Confectioner. He didn't need to say *including Rebecca*; that was always implicit. All she says to him in the car park is, — No Gillman-style violence, Ray.

— Of course not, Lennox tells her, — I'm made of different stuff.

Looks at the austere building, wonders when he'll visit this place again. Hopefully never, possibly as an inmate if things go wrong.

When he gets to the cell, Confectioner is reading a copy of *National Geographic*. He lays it down. — Lennox . . .

— I'm going to miss our chats, Ray Lennox says, drinking in Confectioner's puzzled stare, — and I have to say, I do feel rather upset to be usurped by your biographer. Still, it's not really my problem now.

— How so?

— I'm on leave, working my notice, Lennox says cheerfully. — This polis game isn't for me any more. And you might find you need a new biographer. I didn't take kindly to being usurped.

Confectioner looks concerned: something in his old sparring partner's voice and stare. The prisoner is about to speak when Ray Lennox's head crashes into his face. It misses

Confectioner's nose; Lennox feels the front teeth buckle inwards as they scrape his brow and the blood of the two men mingles. Then Lennox is on him, smashing his head off the floor, silent and economical in his brutal assault.

He only stops when he realises that through his panicky, breathless wheezes, Confectioner is naming the names and locations that he knows are essential to save his life. Jolting to his senses, Lennox ceases his battery. Stands up, frigid, pulseless, watching Confectioner slither across the cold floor of the cell, like an eel in a fishmonger's aluminium tray. Pulling out his iPhone, he sets it onto record mode, in order to capture the child murderer's miserable mantra.

When convinced he has everything he needs, Lennox regards the pummelled Confectioner, who has the audacity to look up at him with violation shining through his fear. — Don't lament the loss of your biographer, he tells the short-eyed civil servant. — He ripped the fuckin pish oot ay ye, ya daft cunt. Stick tae picking on bairns, you're just no cut out for the grown-up world, and his boot cracks Confectioner's face with such force that two teeth fly out from another explosion of blood.

Then he leaves the cell, rubbing his skinned hands, nodding at Ronnie McArthur who looks inside and observes, — Looks like the cunt fell.

— Guilt and shame, Ronnie, Lennox says. — They really overwhelm some people. Makes them unsteady on their feet.

He leaves the prison, gets to the car park. Jayne Melville is waiting there. Ronnie has gleefully texted her what occurred in the cell. But she has not received this news with the relish of the retiring prison officer. — You really think you're better than the likes of Gillman?

— Yes, Lennox says emphatically, despite his guilt about the deceit.

Jayne is far from convinced, — Please tell me how you come to that fucking conclusion.

— Because I constantly entertain the notion that I might not be. That's all I have left. Don't take it from me, Lennox begs. Then he sweeps his hand across his skull. — I got more names . . . I'm sorry, Rebecca wasn't one.

Jayne looks at him for a beat. Nods. Then she turns and walks away.

He gets in the Alfa Romeo and drives to the two separate locations to find Confectioner's notebooks. The first is at the cliffs near Coldingham, close to where they found the body of Britney Hamil. He has to paddle up to his shins to the back of a deserted cove, where he finds a yellow book stuffed into a ziplock bag, secreted behind a big rock. The second is in an old cemetery accessed by the disused railway network of north Edinburgh. In a Confectioner touch, the notebook is concealed under a fallen headstone that bears the name:

GREGOR ANDREW LENNOX
1922–1978

As far as Lennox knows, it is no relation. It takes him an age to move the stone and get his hand in the space to yank the bag free.

With his grim bounty, constituting fifteen years of work, Ray Lennox heads to the post office at Canonmills.

He stands in the queue watching old people, *pre-digitals*, as McCorkel calls them, picking up their pensions. The two yellow-page notebooks in his hands. He is letting them go. He mails one to Amanda Drummond and one to Dougie Gillman. Then, on his phone, he sends an email to both parties:

To: ADrummond@policescot.co.uk; DGillman@policescot.co.uk
From: RLennox@policescot.co.uk
Subject: Chocolate

There's a little present winding its way to you both. One for
each of you. Putting them together, a big mystery will unravel.
You each get to make a huge discovery. This will make you stars.
But you'll need to work together and get your story straight.

This could be the start of a beautiful friendship. Play nice,
you two.

Much love,

Raymond

*You've just stopped Drummond from ever being able to sack
Gillman. Of course, that cunt will never thank you.*

Outside, with a sense of accomplishment, he looks in a
shop window, checking out the rough growth on his face. He
has run out of razors, but the last time he went to buy some,
he came back with a six-pack of Stella and a half-bottle of
Smirnoff.

Behind him, the incessant toot of a car horn.

These cunts get on your nerves . . .

Worse, it's somebody in a parked BMW. Lennox doesn't
know what to do: the person seems to be tooting *him*. There's
nobody else in the street. Then the driver puts him out of his
misery by exiting the car.

George Marsden pulls off his light-reactive glasses. — Of
course, you do know that you need to listen to a friend sometimes. Get in the car.

— Where are we going?

— South coast.

Lennox smiles, shields his eyes from the weak autumn sun.

— I'm serious, George says. — Come and check it out. If you like it, work with me. Or alternatively, stay here and drink yourself to death.

— What makes you think I won't drink myself to death down south?

— Oh, you most certainly will, George smirks, opening the front passenger door, — but hopefully you'll just do it a little more slowly!

Ray Lennox throws back his head and laughs. It might be nice to slow down his death wish.

He gets in the car.

The End

ACKNOWLEDGEMENTS

Thanks to:

Graham Bell, Emma Currie, Katherine Fry, Emer Martin, Afshin Partovi and Michal Shavit specifically – immense contributions and inspiration from them. To everyone in Edinburgh, London, Miami, Chicago and Barcelona particularly, but in general all my pals and readers everywhere who kept my chin up and a smile on my face through all the bullshit of the last couple of years.

penguin.co.uk/vintage

penguin.co.uk/vintage